CW00921906

Music Makers

ON RECORD

Music Makers

ON RECORD

by

SUVI RAJ GRUBB

With an introduction by
DANIEL BARENBOIM

HAMISH HAMILTON

LONDON

For C. G.
(to whom I promised
a different book many years ago)

First published in Great Britain 1986
by Hamish Hamilton Ltd
Garden House 57–59 Long Acre London WC2E 9JZ

Copyright © 1986 by Suvi Raj Grubb

British Library Cataloguing in Publication Data

Grubb, Suvi Raj
  Music makers on record.
  1. Musicians – Biography
  I. Title
  780′.92′2   ML385
  ISBN 0-241-11872-7

Typeset by Rowland Phototypesetting Ltd, Bury St Edmunds, Suffolk
Printed in Great Britain by
St Edmundsbury Press, Bury St Edmunds, Suffolk

Contents

Illustrations

The Klemperer *Cosi*. (*G. Macdominic.*)
Otto Klemperer studies the score tensely on his last recording –
   Mozart's Wind Serenade K 375. (*G. Macdominic.*)
Singing to illustrate a point to Ileana Cotrubas and Kiri te Kanawa.
   Mozart: C minor Mass. (*G. Macdominic.*)
With Nicolai Gedda. Mozart Requiem. (*G. Macdominic.*)
With Samuel Sanders. Perlman Encores. (*G. Macdominic.*)
The Barenboim *Don Giovanni* cast – without Zerlina. (*Clive Barda.*)
With André Previn and Itzhak Perlman in Pittsburgh. (*Don Spiegel.*)
With Mstislav Rostropovich. (*Clive Barda.*)
Lady Macbeth playback. (*Clive Barda.*)
Carlo Maria Giulini. Beethoven's C major Mass. (*David Farrell.*)
Vladimir Ashkenazy, Lynn Harrell, Itzhak Perlman: Beethoven Piano
   Trios, second time. (*Don Hunstein.*)
The Brahms Double: Bernard Haitink, Mstislav Rostropovich, Itzhak
   Perlman, Concertgebouw Orchestra. (*Richard Holt.*)

All photographs are reproduced by courtesy of EMI. The author and publishers would like to thank the photographers whose work appears in this book.

Introduction

Recording has, for better or for worse, had an enormous influence on the musical life of our time. As we approach the end of the century, it might be appropriate to ask a few questions, namely: how has recording influenced the practice of music, on the one hand, and what has it done for the appreciation of music, on the other? This book does not pretend to give final answers to these questions, but rather to give the intelligent reader food for thought. Can one really preserve a musical performance? What is the attitude of the performer to recording? The technological advances in our century have made it possible for the human being to exist longer and in greater comfort than was ever thought possible, and it also has given us the tools artificially to reproduce the natural. Many performing artists dream of preserving their 'definitive interpretation', and many listeners allow their knowledge and taste to be guided by recording. In fact, recording might be almost unnecessary if the educational curriculum in our schools would ensure that children learn to read music. Has even the most enthusiastic record collector ever imagined the joys of reading a Beethoven symphony?

The fact, however, remains that music, by its very nature, is meant to be heard, not remain silent. And for those who cannot hear a score by reading it, a performance is essential. A gramophone record, for all its inadequacies, carries a performance to thousands of music lovers who would otherwise never have the opportunity to hear that particular interpretation.

Suvi Grubb tells us of the joys but also of the trepidation that involve making records. His book abounds in charming and humorous anecdotes and provides a penetrating insight into the character of many musicians. That he has been able to cooperate so professionally and intimately with artists as diverse as Klemperer, Boulez, Giulini and others shows his musical competence and gives us yet another proof of the universality of music as a language. After all, maybe we needed an Indian to point out to an Italian the joys and depths of German music. He was able to do this because his love of music, so apparent in this book, is informed by an understanding of the depth and joy of music.

Daniel Barenboim, London,
February 1986

Author's Preface

In the summer of 1933, in the town of Amalapuram which lies in the delta of the river Godaveri in India, I acquired my first gramophone record, a tango, 'Oh Donna Clara'. In June 1979, in the Concertgebouw in Amsterdam, I officiated as the producer in charge of a recording of Brahms's Concerto for violin, cello and orchestra, Op. 102, played by Itzhak Perlman, Mstislav Rostropovich and the Concertgebouw Orchestra, conducted by Bernard Haitink. This is the story of the journey from the one event to the other.

I have not identified by name anyone who is currently or has recently been a colleague. To have named only some would have been invidious – to have introduced anyone without giving a rounded picture of the person would have been unfair – to have done justice to all of them would have made this a different book.

S.R.G.
London,
December 1985

1   Meeting Legge

It all started with an advertisement in November 1956 in the personal columns of *The Times* inviting applications for membership of a chorus which would be associated with the Philharmonia Orchestra and sing under conductors like Otto Klemperer and Carlo Maria Giulini. I had come to England in December 1953 with my wife. We lived in the market town of Aylesbury, this being convenient for my wife, a doctor in the Stoke Mandeville Hospital three miles away, and not too far for me to commute to London; I was a freelance broadcaster for the BBC's overseas programme in English, *London Calling Asia*.

Singing has been a life-long passion with me. I have sung for as long as I can remember. In my childhood it was hymns as part of the congregation in church, where my penetrating treble used to draw, in equal parts, looks of admiration and of disapprobation of this little show-off. In my early teens I went on to popular songs and hits from gramophone records – 'I scream, you scream, we all scream for ice-cream' and the like. By the time my voice broke I had developed an interest in more serious stuff, but still picked up from records; in the privacy of the bathroom I used to indulge in full-throated performances of tenor arias learned from Caruso records, 'La donna è mobile' and 'M'appari tutt' amor', and bass and baritone songs, 'Poor old Joe' and 'Song of the Volga boatmen' from the Paul Robeson and Chaliapin recordings. Later, my voice having settled down to a lowish bass, I sang in choirs, and in the last years before I left for England I myself formed choirs, trained them and conducted them.

One of the first things I did in Aylesbury was to investigate the possibilities there for me to continue to sing. I found the Aylesbury Music Society and was welcomed by them. The standard of the Society's performances was good and I enjoyed myself hugely.

By 1956, however, I had begun to feel that I should like to spread my wings. With the choirs I had trained and conducted in India we too had achieved respectable standards, and for two memorable years in Madras I had sung in a madrigal choir the quality of which I have still not heard equalled. I felt I now needed the stimulus of singing with one of the London choirs. I had been familiar with records of the Bach Choir in India and I was just about to write to them when the advertisement appeared in *The Times*. This chorus seemed to offer exactly what I was

1

looking for; I could not have imagined, even in my wildest flights of fancy, what that application would lead to.

After a few weeks several of us were called up for audition. We had each been asked to prepare a solo piece and I selected the aria 'But who may abide the day of His coming' from Handel's *Messiah*. The man who auditioned us was a short, stocky German who spoke very few words of English, but he was friendly and his easy informality quickly dispelled any nervousness an audition might have induced. The man was Wilhelm Pitz, one of the leading chorusmasters in Europe, especially associated with Bayreuth. His auditioning method was unorthodox. He stopped me after a few bars of the fast-moving, florid middle section of the aria. He then picked out a fairly straightforward melody on the piano and asked me to sing it while he played a weirdly modulating accompaniment which made no sense harmonically with the tune. I managed successfully to blot out the piano and stick to the melody. A few moments later the audition was over; it had taken a little over five minutes, leaving me with a slight feeling of anticlimax. When the results were announced a few days later, I was delighted to learn that I had been successful.

In February 1957 the Philharmonia Chorus assembled. I was in the happy position of being able to provide the chorus with a rehearsal hall. To supplement my fluctuating earnings from broadcasting I had taken up a job as secretary to the Warden of the YMCA Indian Students' Union, where my principal duty was the running of the institution's assembly room, the Mahatma Gandhi Hall. The offer was accepted and the Mahatma Gandhi Hall is still the home of the Philharmonia Chorus.

The chorus was to make its first public appearance at the Royal Festival Hall in November 1957 in two performances of Beethoven's Ninth Symphony, which were to be the climax of a cycle of the composer's symphonies conducted by Otto Klemperer.

During the next six months Pitz drilled us thoroughly, until the day we had been working towards, 12 November, arrived. The first half of the concert consisted of the Eighth Symphony, at the end of which we joined the audience in applauding Klemperer and the orchestra. And then, the Ninth – Klemperer's conception of it was in one long, vaulting line from the mysterious beginning of the first movement to the culmination of the work in the choral finale. When he brought us to our feet on the bass soloist's first phrase some of the audience, who had evidently heard about us, leaned forward in anticipation; when the chorus made its first entry with the triumphant '*Freude*', there was a visible stirring in the hall. At the great double fugue on '*seid umschlungen*' and '*Freude schöner Götterfunken*' I thought the audience was going involuntarily to burst into applause, but they waited till the last chords of the Ninth Symphony arrived, and then they went wild – they stood and they clapped – they stamped their feet and shouted 'bravo'. Pitz came on to the stage to share in the triumph; every time the chorus was asked to rise the applause trebled in volume. As Klemperer beckoned the chorus yet again to rise, I was suddenly transported to Trichinopoly, in South India, where over twenty years earlier, on gramophone records, I had first heard the music we had just performed.

*

The man responsible for the formation in 1945 of the orchestra, and now of the chorus, was Walter Legge, one of the most unusual men in the musical life of Britain. He had had a varied career, as a musical journalist, as assistant to Sir Thomas Beecham at the Royal Opera House, Covent Garden, in the gramophone record industry, in Ensa during the war and as an impresario and concert agent. He was a man of immense enthusiasm and determination, even ruthlessness, and with a driving energy, an extensive knowledge of music and a keen understanding of the problems of music making. He seemed in fact to have all the qualities required to become an interpreter of music, but at some stage had discovered that he lacked the temperament to be a performer and had turned his formidable abilities to promoting it. In 1957 Legge owned and ran the Philharmonia Orchestra; he was also Artistic Director of the Philharmonia Concert Society, which organized its concerts. But it was as Artist Manager of the Columbia label, which with the His Master's Voice label formed the classical record division of the industrial giant EMI, that he was most widely known.

In the world of the gramophone record Legge found the perfect venue for his genius to flourish. He possessed in abundance nearly all the basic qualities required in anyone engaged in the production of records, and had additional gifts – foremost, a wonderful instinct for spotting musical talent; among the musicians he had discovered or whose careers he had furthered immediately after the war were Karajan, Schwarzkopf, Jurinac, Fischer-Dieskau, Ginette Neveu, Lipatti and Cantelli.

Legge was also a man of vision. In the early 30s, in the midst of massive unemployment and a slump, he and others conceived the idea of the Society edition, designed to promote the recording of music not widely popular, by inviting subscriptions to cover the cost of a recording before it was made. The first project was for a set of lieder by Hugo Wolf, which was such a huge success that it was followed by further volumes of Wolf and other music. Again it was Legge who had the imagination and courage in the 50s to champion a conductor whose career many thought had ended long before; thanks largely to him Otto Klemperer became a dominant figure in London's musical life and in the recording studio for the next twenty years.

In two years the Philharmonia Chorus had grown to over two hundred, and inevitably a feeling developed that they wanted a group of their members to represent their points of view to its management – that is, to Walter Legge. In response to this, Legge decided that an election should be held to choose one member from each of the voices to form a committee. He himself supervised the election, and it was on this occasion, he later told me, that he suddenly looked at me with a more than casual interest. We had, of course, met at rehearsals several times before and he had often expressed his appreciation of the services provided by the Mahatma Gandhi Hall.

There was considerable confusion after the votes had been cast; each member of the chorus had four votes and no one was quite sure how they were to be tabulated and counted. I looked on at this with some impatience and after a while offered to do the calculations. Legge agreed and looked on with an astonishment he made no attempt to conceal as I ran my fingers down the rows of figures, entered the totals at the bottom of each column and handed the sheets to him. Since I myself had been proposed as a candidate I suggested that he should get a member of his staff to check my arithmetic; my figures were confirmed and the result was announced. I had been elected as the representative of the basses and I had the largest number of votes of any of the candidates. Legge took this to be a measure of my general popularity but a more probable reason was that everyone knew me as the person who ran the hall we rehearsed in and also, being Indian, I was the most distinctive member of the chorus.

Three meetings of the committee were held before events led to my having to resign from it; one at the Gandhi Hall, a social rather than a business meeting in my flat at which Legge and his wife Elisabeth Schwarzkopf revealed an unsuspected capacity to eat hot, curried, food, and the third, in Legge's house. The day of this last meeting was my last on the staff of the Gandhi Hall. I had resigned, as a recently appointed General Manager had different ideas from mine, and in any case this was not a job I had planned to do for any length of time. After a chorus rehearsal, a little after nine, we adjourned to Legge's house and were entertained to dinner in great style by him and Schwarzkopf. The formal business of the meeting started around eleven and was despatched in a few minutes; we then settled down to what all evenings at Legge's house invariably led to – talk about music and listening to gramophone records. On this occasion we were treated, among other items, to excerpts from the Karajan recording of Mozart's *Così fan tutte* with Schwarzkopf as Fiordiligi, which Legge regarded as one of his most successful recordings. On at least three occasions Legge, Schwarzkopf and I found ourselves catching each other's eyes in shared delight and recognition of very special moments in this, the tenderest of the Mozart operas – at the melting loveliness of the trio 'Soave sia il vento' in which the women, with Don Alfonso, wish their lovers a fair journey, in the exchanges between the two women and the supposedly poisoned men in the first finale when

4

the orchestra seems to chuckle at the absurd carryings-on, and in the great canon in the second finale.

It came as a surprise to all of us when someone suddenly remarked that it was after two in the morning. I said light-heartedly that I was in the fortunate position of not having to go to work on that day, or on any other day in the immediate future. Legge looked at me questioningly and I told him I had resigned from the Gandhi Hall. The effect on him was unexpected – he jumped up from his sofa (for a big man he could move very nimbly) and asked his guests to excuse him for a few minutes as he would like to have a short chat with me.

We went into his study and he first asked me why I had left the Gandhi Hall and when I explained, he replied that he quite understood my not caring to work for an unsympathetic boss. I could not believe my ears when he then said, 'Ever since I first took note of your work at the Gandhi Hall I have said to myself I want that man to work for me. Would you like to work for me?' I was literally speechless. Legge said, 'Well?' and I, still not sure that I had heard aright, said, 'You are not serious, are you, Mr Legge?' He replied that he was, and then asked if I would mind his asking me some questions. He first asked me about my general qualifications and the work I had done in India and since coming to England. I had a university degree and had worked for over thirteen years in All India Radio – my last job there had been that of Assistant Director of the Delhi station. I had given up this permanent, pensionable civil service career to come to England and earn a somewhat precarious living as a freelance broadcaster for the BBC because of a passionate desire to listen to music and experience it at first hand, instead of always from a box. Legge had been listening intently and at this he smiled sympathetically.

He then asked how good my knowledge of music was. I said I played the piano after a fashion, could read piano and vocal scores fluently, and orchestral scores with not quite the facility I would have liked, but that was because of insufficient practice, and I had a fair knowledge of harmony, counterpoint and the general theory and history of music. 'And actual music itself?' he asked. I said that my knowledge of Beethoven was complete and of Bach, Haydn, Mozart, Schubert, Brahms and the German school almost complete – I had an extensive knowledge of the works of the main stream composers of other nationalities and added that there were however considerable gaps in my knowledge in some fields – for example, in that of Italian opera, not of Verdi or Puccini, but of, say, Donizetti and Bellini. Legge exclaimed, 'Who indeed has a complete knowledge of all the byways of Italian opera?' and asked whether he could ask me a few questions to test my knowledge of music. I said, 'Of course.'

Being a man of a very precise use of words he took my claim to a complete knowledge of Beethoven literally and so most of his questions were about that composer. He led off with, 'What are the opus numbers of the

5

piano sonatas?' I started, 'Op. 2 Nos. 1, 2 and 3; Op. 7; Op. 10 Nos. 1, 2 and 3; Op. 13; Op. 14, Nos. 1 and 2. . . .' He cut me off, 'What is Op. 9?' I said, 'String trios'. 'And Op. 1?' 'Piano trios.' 'What is the opening theme of Op. 69?' I sang the cello's opening statement from the Sonata in A Op. 69 for piano and cello. 'How many movements are there in the *Waldstein?*' I thought that this perhaps was a trick question because the slow movement is marked 'Introduction', presumably to the Rondo which follows. I replied, after a slight hesitation, 'Two', but would have been capable of justifying myself if I had said three. Legge smiled, for he guessed what I had been thinking. 'What is the key of the slow movement of the *Pathétique?*' 'A flat.'

There was of course a reason for most of the questions being about the piano sonatas and chamber music. Beethoven's orchestral works are so popular that most casual music lovers would be familiar with them, but only someone with a deeper love of music would be at home in works such as the piano and the cello sonatas. A last question about Beethoven, 'What are the keys of the *Rasoumovsky* quartets?' 'F, E minor and C,' I replied. 'How many minor key piano concertos are there by Mozart?' 'Two,' and I added gratuitously, 'in D minor K 466 and C minor K 491.' Legge smiled again at this piece of showing off and asked only one more question. 'What are the instruments in Schubert's Octet?' 'Clarinet, bassoon, horn' – I paused briefly for I had a sudden inexplicable feeling that an oboe featured in the Octet, but after a moment's recollection added, 'string quartet and double bass.' 'I don't need to ask you any further questions about music. I don't promise anything, but I shall do my best to have you work for me', and he shook my hand. We rejoined the other guests and a few minutes later the guests dispersed.

I was, of course, wildly excited. The prospect of working for Legge and the Philharmonia was dazzling. I knew that he held an important post at EMI but I did not really think that I stood any chance of joining him there. I assumed he wanted me for the organization over which he had complete control – the Philharmonia.

The days went by, then the weeks and then it was months. I still hoped that something would come of it all but with lessening expectation as time passed. We had dined well that evening and sometimes I wondered whether I had built too much hope on what for Legge had been no more than an impulse – and yet he had been serious enough to find out the extent of my knowledge of music. He had not asked me questions about opus numbers and key signatures to find out whether I knew such things by rote. He must have known that only someone familiar with the works themselves could have answered him as I had.

Meanwhile, I had to find another job. A few years earlier, in response to an advertisement, I had sent off an application to a record company for a job in their catalogue section. This had not even been acknowledged, which I now realize merely indicates that the company was badly run and ill-mannered; then, I felt that it proved that I stood no chance of getting a job, however peripherally, connected with music. The occasional broadcast for the BBC was neither a whole time occupation nor a source of regular income. At the suggestion of a friend who one day saw me typing expertly and very fast with three fingers of each hand, I decided to hire myself out to an agency as a 'temp'. I had a fortnight's stint in the appeals office of the Marie Curie Foundation (addressing envelopes) and another in the accounts office of the *Encyclopaedia Britannica* (typing accounts and statements), and ended up in a firm of accountants in the City. The senior partner was curious about someone who did *The Times* crossword and read the *Listener*. After a few days he sent for me for a chat. This interview was naturally very different from the one with Legge. When I mentioned my interest in music, his only response was that there were no top musicians on their books, but several first rank actors and actresses. At the end of our talk he asked me if I would be interested in a career in accountancy. I said I was willing to try it and was duly attached to one of the junior accountants. After a few weeks the senior partner again spoke to me – this time he asked if I would be interested in a job as a trainee accountant. One condition was that I should be willing to sign a contract to work with the firm for five years. He foresaw an excellent future for me and gave me a week to think the offer over – I was to give him my answer on the Monday following.

After long and anxious thought, and discussion with my wife, I had decided by Saturday evening to accept this offer. By now it was June, some five months since that meeting with Legge, and I had quite given up all hope of anything materializing from him. The next morning, at 9 o'clock, my telephone rang. I announced myself – 'Grubb', and the reply was 'Legge' – he hoped he was not disturbing me on a Sunday morning. Then he said, 'You remember I told you I would like you to work for me? I have now found a job for you – as my assistant in EMI. Are you still free and willing to take the job?' I said I was and he replied, 'Good – that's settled. When you are in Edinburgh with the chorus for the Verdi Requiem let us meet after the dress rehearsal and fix up the details. Goodbye, and thank you so much.'

I put down the telephone slightly dazed; then I was appalled at the thought of how close I'd come to being not free to accept the job Legge offered. It took some hours for the full realization of my conversation with him to sink in. I was going to work in the greatest recording company in the world, for one of the most brilliant and accomplished men in the field of gramophone records. If all the jobs in the world had been arrayed before me and I had been invited to choose, this was the job I would have chosen.

2 *Working with Legge*

On 19 September 1960, I reported to Legge at the Abbey Road Studios of EMI in St John's Wood. His office was an oasis of luxury in a rather drab building. The atmosphere was one of comfortable, unostentatious opulence – everything in it belonged to Legge and had been paid for by him.

He welcomed me warmly and introduced me to the other members of his staff. I shared an office with two secretaries and I spent most of that first day getting the feel of the department. Throughout the day visitors dropped in, some with flimsy reasons, others with none at all; I realized that many of the staff of the studios were curious about Legge's new Indian assistant. In the afternoon the senior recording engineer was detailed to show me around and he took me on a tour of the building, beginning with the studios themselves and then going on to the editing rooms, the cutting rooms and the offices. He explained to me in simple terms the technical processes of recording. He meant well and I did not have the heart to tell him that I held a university degree in Mathematics, Physics and Chemistry. Further, because of my work in All India Radio, recording was not an unfamiliar field to me. I had too actually sat in on recordings, as, between our meeting in Edinburgh and my taking up the job, Legge had invited me to attend two of his sessions.

The first was at Watford Town Hall with Callas singing Italian operatic arias. I kept dodging in and out of the control room as Callas did not like strangers on her recording sessions. Half-way through, before I could take any evasive action, she strolled in unannounced and came face to face with me. Legge introduced me. She took my hand and peered short-sightedly at me, slightly puzzled. Legge said, 'You met him, Maria, at the *Lucia* sessions – he is a member of the Philharmonia Chorus and he is soon going to be my assistant.' Callas warmly wished me well and it was only then that I really believed that I was going to work in EMI. The other session was with Hans Richter-Haaser playing Beethoven's Fourth Piano Concerto accompanied by the Hungarian conductor, Istvan Kertesz, whose first record in the West it was. Kertesz knew very little English, so our exchanges were confined to smiling amiably at one another. Richter-Haaser and I took to each other immediately; he was to be my first artist.

Towards the end of that first day Legge walked into my office and announced that for the next five days I was to assist him in the making of three records by Karajan and the Philharmonia Orchestra. These sessions, the first I attended as a member of the recording team, began with Sibelius's Fifth Symphony, which was part of one of the last three records Karajan made with the Philharmonia. The others were 'Ballet Music from the Opera' and 'Philharmonia Promenade Concert'. I could not have had a worthier introduction to the making of gramophone records, for the records produced that week are still superb examples of the art or craft, call it what you will, of recording. The orchestra was at its finest and the principals in charge all masters of their jobs. Karajan, lean and spare, economic of gesture and speech, eyes half closed most of the time, shaped the music with elegant movements of his hands (I wondered, as I have wondered often since, by what mysterious process a great conductor not only sets the stamp of his interpretation on a performance with so little verbal communication, but produces from an orchestra a sound special to him).

Legge used to say that he wanted his orchestra to have style, not 'a style'. They played on these sessions with tight discipline and a brooding intensity in the Sibelius, with wit, elegance and charm for pieces like Chabrier's *España* and the *Skaters' Waltz*, with a swooning sensuousness for the 'Dance of the Persian Slaves' from Mussorgsky's *Khovantschina* and a joyous eroticism in the Venusberg music from *Tannhäuser*. Legge had reason to be proud of them.

The balance engineer was Douglas Larter, who was responsible for the sound on most of the great Legge recordings. Larter had worked in the company for over thirty years. He knew almost by instinct just where to place his microphones, depending on the conductor, the work and also the humidity and temperature of the hall. He listened briefly to Karajan rehearsing, after which he strolled into the hall; he moved three microphones, the two over the strings each a few inches away from them and the one behind the horns fractionally closer to them – and all he did over the next six days was move a few microphones.

These, of course, were the days of two-track stereo recording and it was essential to get the right sound on the sessions; there was no possibility of subsequently fiddling with the balance (even with recent multi-track recording you can never really correct faulty balance of either performance or recording – you can only alter it to make it sound less objectionable). As the session began, hoping that the exhilaration and excitement I felt would not be too obvious to Walter Legge, next to whom I was sitting, I stole a look at him. He too was tense with excitement and when he turned to me and smiled encouragingly I did not feel quite such a greenhorn. His first concern was the sound and he asked for more 'air' – bloom – on the upper strings. During a 'take' (a section or passage recorded at one go and identified by a number announced by the engineer and recorded on the tape) his concentration was absolute; at playbacks, when I dodged into a chair next to Larter, his comments to Karajan concerned the interpretation as well as the performance itself. A point I marked, and stored away in a corner of my mind, was that while he listened courteously to Legge's comments on the performance, Karajan stiffened noticeably when Legge tried to influence the interpretation – in a mixture of German and English he said '*Ja, ja* – of course – *natürlich*', but not paying real attention to what Legge said. All the time Legge kept up a stream of instructions to me – 'Horn crack, 10 bars before letter C.' 'Oboe intonation doubtful 3 after D.' 'Ensemble suspect for three bars after G.' 'I think we'd better repeat F to H – too many things wrong in the section.' 'Take 5 is the master up to letter K – cover the horn crack with take 4.' By the time the session ended the control room was wreathed in smoke, for Legge smoked furiously.

My contribution to this first session was to keep a record of the takes and of Legge's observations; I was pleased with myself that every time something happened and Legge remarked on it, my hand had started to move to the score even before he had started to speak.

For the next four years I served my apprenticeship in EMI, devilling for Walter Legge. I first introduced some order and system into the administration. But office work was not what Legge had employed me for; it was to assist him on all the stages of his recordings, from the sessions to the approval of the test pressings. The aim on sessions is to obtain a body of material from which a satisfactory master, which is a tape of the complete work, can be prepared. This master tape is an assemblage of the best performance of each section of the work – it could consist of a take of a complete performance, or it could be made up of passages, or bars, or even individual chords or notes cut out from different takes – these are literally stuck together with sticky tape to form a continuous performance of the work and the putting together is so skilfully done that the master sounds like a continuous performance. There are no moral or ethical principles involved in 'editing' as is sometimes suggested; the white heat of inspiration cannot, any more in a studio than at a concert, be maintained continuously. At a concert high points of a performance carry more pedestrian sections, but on a record, subject to repeated hearings and a close scrutiny, the level of the music making has to be kept high at all times; and mistakes or lapses of any kind, which would flash past instantaneously at a concert and therefore be of no great importance, cannot be tolerated.

It follows from all this that it is necessary to have an accurate record of all that takes place in a session. I entered in my log book, next to the job number of the recording, the name of the balance engineer, the strength of the orchestra, the serial number of a piano if one was used and the make-up of the chorus if there was one, and I drew a diagram showing any special seating arrangements. When the recording started I kept a list of the takes and the section each covered. I still use the system. The entries are in this form:

	Ist Movement
Take 1.	Start – 3 after G
2.	7 before G – K (abbreviated to 7G – K)
3.	3 before K / F.S. (meaning false start, a breakdown after a few beats)
4.	3 before K – end (or 3K – end)
and so on till possibly:	
8.	Complete (basic Master) 11′ 15″
	IInd Movement
9.	Start – bar 12
10.	Complete (do not use – tempo changed after this take) 8′ 19″
11.	Complete 9′ 13″

The most important job of all was to mark the score so that at every moment one had a clear idea of the progress of the recording – which takes were the best for each passage, whether all sections had been satisfactorily performed and which section still had mistakes. A take number with a minus sign at a certain place meant something wrong in that take at that point; a tick after it denoted a good performance. I introduced double ticks for exceptionally good performances, and a whole vocabulary of abbreviations, all my own, as a kind of shorthand language, which I continue to use. 'NZ' is 'not together', from the German *'nicht zusammen'*; 'NA' is 'not absolutely together'; 'NA poss' – 'not quite together but could be used if nothing better was achieved'; 'NB' is 'not beautiful'; 'NAB' – 'not as beautiful as it could be but still acceptable'; a plain 'N' indicates an extraneous noise; 'N-ign' noise which could be ignored; '56 √ than 58', the tick indicating that the earlier take was better than the later – with a question mark it meant 'check if take 56 is better than 58'. All these are in addition to straightforward 'int x' for bad intonation. 'Hn. ck' for horn crack and such like. Time is so valuable on a session (to have a symphony orchestra in the studio costs approximately £25 a minute) and events move so fast and it is essential to know where you stand at any moment. I took pride in the fact that when Legge asked me something he never had to wait for an answer. After a couple of months, he said to me one evening with an approving grin, 'My dear boy, one of these days you are going to answer a question even before I have framed it!' (He was just ten years older than me but often addressed me, as he did people older than himself, as 'My dear boy'.)

I did all the work which followed the sessions. I marked the score,

11

listened to the edited tape and arranged for further editing to be done if necessary. When there was a technical problem, as for instance an excessive weight of sound on one loudspeaker, or a lack of brilliance or bass or whatever, I took steps to clear it and had a 'corrected' master tape prepared. When the tape had been approved it went into production. Copies of it were made for other territories and one of us listened to those for America, Germany, France and Japan which, with the United Kingdom, were, and still are, the most important markets for our records. In the United Kingdom, a lacquer was cut and sent to our factory for processing.

The culmination of all this work was the arrival from the factory of the test pressing of the record, the white label pressing, or WLP, so called because of its plain white label instead of the label with which it would appear in the shops. This was the form in which our work would be presented to the public and so it was imperative to ensure that the disc reproduced the tape as faithfully as the different media would allow, and that it was free from technical defects such as a centre hole out of alignment or a noisy surface with clicks and plops. All test pressings were subjected to a critical hearing first by me, then Legge. Soon he took to merely sampling pressings I had approved; he knew by then that, if anything, I would apply stricter standards even than he did. He had by this time evaluated my musical judgment too. When we heard the master tape of the Arrau recording of Brahms's Second Piano Concerto, Legge wanted a more legato take for the opening horn phrase. When I presented the reedited master to him, he asked if what I had selected was the best of all the available takes. I said it was, and he asked me to play him the other takes. He asked why I had preferred the take I had chosen to, say, take 'X'. I replied because the intonation in the second bar was better, and he tossed me the paper on which he had made his notes. 'Bad intonation second bar take X,' it read. He started more and more to delegate musical work to me, and in the course of time, to the huge surprise of everyone at the studios, he allowed me on my own to approve pressings of one of his wife's records.

Just how completely Legge trusted me I learnt when the set of pressings of the Klemperer *Fidelio* arrived in our office while he was away in New York.

The recording of *Fidelio* had been attended by unusual goings-on. When I arrived at Kingsway Hall for the first session I found, in addition to our balance engineer, Larter, and his supporting staff, a second balance engineer busily setting up microphones. He was flanked on one side by the Chairman of EMI and on the other by the head of the studios. In a few minutes this second engineer and the studio manager disappeared into the basement where all the tape machines were housed. When Legge, whom I had alerted at his home about the presence of the Chairman and a rival team of engineers, arrived, he showed no surprise. He wished the Chairman a courteous 'good morning' and went on to greet Klemperer and the singers booked for the first session – and the recording began.

There were two recordings of *Fidelio*, though this Legge and I learnt only later. One, of course, was that produced by us; the other was the combined effort of the ad hoc team. Both sets of tapes were edited. Ours was approved by Legge and me; the second version had sound effects superimposed on it. Test pressings were made from both sets of tapes and sent to each of a group of seasoned gramophone record critics. None of them knew what the two sets represented; each was asked to let us know which he preferred. Unanimously, and in no uncertain terms, all selected our version; the other version was discreetly buried.

When the first set of our pressings arrived Legge was in New York. I heard them and after long and careful consideration rejected them – on the transfer to disc, a little of the extreme top and some of the low bass had been lost, as a result of which the sound had become tubby. I was subjected to great pressure by the engineering staff and the head of the studios, all of whom had more than twenty years more experience than I had in the business; I was even told that the Chairman would be greatly displeased if I did not reverse my decision – such was Legge's reputation that no one, not his boss or even the Chairman, had the courage to overrule me. Finally, there was a three-cornered telephone conversation between the head of the studios and me on two extensions in London and Legge. After we had both explained the situation I heard Legge reply, 'I trust Grubb's judgment absolutely; if he has rejected these pressings take it that they are rejected by me,' and he added to me, 'Goodbye and thank you.'

In those years Legge, with me assisting, produced many of the recordings which will ensure that he will be remembered as long as there are gramophone records. The great Klemperer recordings – *Fidelio*, Mahler's Fourth Symphony and his Second (in the choral sessions of which I had perforce to join the chorus, being one of the few basses who could go down to the low B flat), Bruckner's Fourth and Seventh, the *Matthew Passion*, the Brahms Requiem (at the end of which I firmly announced to Legge that I really could not any longer keep up the schizophrenic roles of singing in the chorus during the takes and then dodging back into the control room for the play-backs) – these were some of the recordings on which I began my career. There were also notable recordings by Giulini, Lorin Maazel, Claudio Arrau, a series of Hugo Wolf recitals by Schwarzkopf and Gerald Moore, Lehár's *The Merry Widow* and Mozart's *Così fan tutte*.

They were years of hard, unremitting work. A register I kept at the time lists, for February 1963, 91 pressings and 56 copy tapes listened to mostly by me. These were, of course, in addition to the new recordings we produced. There was really more work than the two of us could comfortably handle and I had to bear the brunt of the routine work – Legge was often abroad. Between 1960 and 1963 I do not think I had more than twenty complete weekends to myself – I would usually work on the Saturday or the Sunday, frequently on both days, to clear up some of the backlog of work. But I thrived on it and all the time was gaining experience and assimilating a great deal of valuable practical knowledge – I was also extending my knowledge of music.

Walter Legge and I took to each other at once. In all the years I worked with him there was seldom a dull moment. There were peaceful evenings of talk and music. He had a large house and after the day's work we would go there and walk around the beautifully laid-out garden. He loved plants and flowers and was very knowledgeable about them. Then we would adjourn to the study; I usually drank whisky, he favoured a very dry Martini made up almost exclusively of gin. He would regale me with stories, sometimes unprintable, of Sibelius, Richard Strauss, McCormack, Chaliapin and Schnabel. Sometimes we would discuss a specific work and try to analyse wherein its power lay. At other times we would talk about India, which he had visited and which fascinated him. He was equally interested when my wife explained the latest developments in her speciality – the pathology of cells.

We got on well together because, while there were vast areas in which we were almost opposites, there were other equally large areas in which we were kindred spirits. Besides music, we shared a great love of and facility with words. We would make outrageous puns. Chateauneuf du Pape was translated as 'the ninth cat of the Pope', Beethoven's overture *The Consecration of the House* was transformed to 'the constipation of the mouse', we would talk disparagingly of 'the piece of cod that passeth all understanding', and the writing on Belshazzar's wall, 'Mene, Mene, Tekel Upharsin' became 'Minnie, Minnie, tickle your parson!'

Sometimes we would discover comical words and use them in ridiculous sentences – as, 'If we recorded *Fidelio* with Giulini and the Verdi Requiem with Klemperer, which of them would be the more discombobulated?' Once Schwarzkopf joined in much to our surprise. We were looking at royalty statements and Legge remarked to her that she had earned the highest sum ever during the previous quarter. She was sitting behind us and calmly replied, 'That's better than a welt across the belly with a wet herring.' Legge and I turned round astonished and Legge was just starting to ask, 'Elisabeth, where on earth . . . ?' when we saw her holding on her lap a dictionary of English sayings which I had just given to Legge as a Christmas present.

I have a great love of Shakespearean verse and a good memory for it, and would regale him with some of the more purple speeches of Iago or

Macbeth. 'Coloquintida – mandragora', 'multitudinous', 'incarnadine' – Legge rolled the words round his tongue, savouring them.

He loved slapstick. I had a permanent brief to bring to his notice the reappearance of any of the great screen comedies of the past; he would drop most things to see one of them. With my wife, the three of us laughed till it hurt at the Marx Brothers classics and *Hellzapoppin*, which we saw for the first time, Legge for about the tenth.

There were moments of shared delight in music. Early one morning my telephone rang. Schwarzkopf was on the line and in the quick, eager, short sentences in which she speaks English she asked, 'Suvi – we're listening to the radio – it must be a symphony – we missed the announcement – the first movement goes like this.' She sang a vigorous theme in what sounded like G major, the first interval of which was a fourth. 'Walter does not know what it is,' she added. In the background I could hear a plaintive melody on the oboe from what was evidently the slow movement. I said, 'Bizet's Symphony in C.' Schwarzkopf repeated the title to Legge and as he took the telephone I heard her say, 'I told you Suvi would know.' 'Where in your misspent years did you hear that symphony?' Legge asked. I explained how over twenty years earlier in India, on short-wave radio, I had heard one of the early performances of the then newly discovered symphony. I too had missed the opening announcement and had racked my mind to work out who it could have been by – it sounded very like Schubert but it could not have been for I knew all his symphonies. When the closing announcement came I was cross, for I should have liked this enchanting work to have been by Schubert.

It was not always fun and laughter; there was a violent streak in him and he could be quite unpleasant. It was never directed at me; fortunately, for if it had been I would have resigned instantly and I think Legge sensed this. He was chatting quite amiably with me one morning when his secretary walked in sporting a spectacular black eye. She said her partner, taking a swipe at a high-lobbed tennis ball, had accidentally hit her. Legge growled, 'I don't blame him', all because on the previous evening the poor girl wasn't there when he asked for her a quarter of an hour after closing time.

There were clashes too – inevitable between the total autocrat that Legge was and the sturdy individualist that I am. We had a set-to one day when he questioned the truth of something I had said to him; I stormed at him that it was not my practice to lie, that one lied through fear, that I was afraid of no man – not even him, for after all the worst he could do to me was to take away the job he had given me and I could survive that. I added, for good measure, that I would never again set foot in his house. He was quite taken aback by my sudden eruption; for about two days there was an atmosphere of glacial politeness. Then, he had to listen to and give the final approval to the test pressings of Richter-Haaser's recording of

15

Beethoven's *Hammerklavier* Sonata, which I had already heard and considered suitable for approval. Normally he would listen to bits at random; this time too he heard selected bits from the first movement and then the second. I put the third movement on and waited for him to ask me to go to the end of the side when I became aware that he was absolutely still. He sat tense, his hands grasping the arms of his chair so tightly that the knuckles were white and his eyes were staring into the distance. I too forgot the business in hand and we both heard the movement through. When the final resolution of the main theme arrived like a benediction we both relaxed and looked at each other even as on that earlier night when we had listened to *Così fan tutte*; I thought to myself that however infuriating he could be at times I could never really be cross with him for long, because of the love of music we shared. He satisfied himself on the second side that at the climax of the fugue there was no distortion or muddying of the sound and that Op. 90, the fill-up, was satisfactory, and having approved the pressings said to me, 'My dear boy, if you had not placed the sign of the plague on my house, we could go home now and have a drink.' I was glad to accept the olive branch.

At his house after dinner I asked Legge why he had selected me to work with him when he could have had the pick of the products of the Academy or the College of Music or the universities. He knew very little about me when he offered me the job and could have made a terrible mistake. Legge replied that an academic training in music meant nothing by itself beyond the fact that it gave one a knowledge of the theory of music. 'For me, the only question is – does music speak to your heart? – does it tear your guts out? – does it delight you and make your spirit dance? I decided you were a man after my heart that night we listened to *Così* – and had I had any doubts, the way you listened to the *Hammerklavier* this afternoon would have dispelled them.'

3   My first recording

In my first twenty months in EMI I did not produce a recording or even manage a complete session by myself, though I had on the odd occasion started off or finished a session when Legge had to be elsewhere. It was a lengthy period of probation but I was not unduly impatient; the belief that 'all things would come to him who waits' had been instilled into me at a very early age. The day did arrive at last when I was required to produce a record on my own – actually, events pitchforked me into it. The recording was of Annie Fischer playing the Schumann and the Liszt E flat Piano Concertos with Klemperer and the Philharmonia. It was a harrowing experience.

I inherited the recording under inauspicious circumstances. Legge and his previous assistant had already had four sessions on the project without anything to show for them. Klemperer had said he was tired of the whole thing but was pressed to have another go. He agreed to only two more sessions, one per concerto. I did not believe it feasible that each of these works could be recorded in one session and expected that Legge would concentrate on one of them and then get Klemperer to agree to another two for the other. Legge was in Italy and was due to return to London two days before the sessions; instead I received a message that he had to go into a nursing home with an unspecified illness – the uncharitable at Abbey Road said the illness was tactical. So, it was I who was faced with the daunting prospect of this recording with a notoriously nervous pianist and a conductor who hated accompanying anybody and usually made no bones about showing it. Legge's advice was to get Fischer and Klemperer to play both works at least twice through and to get as many takes as possible of the difficult passages in each.

When the first session began I was nervous but not apprehensive. I had often met Annie Fischer and as for Klemperer, I had sung many times under him and assisted Legge on several of his sessions. He had always been amiable and on one occasion had mischievously teased me. We were listening to a take of the finale of the *Haffner* symphony when he noticed that I had a book in front of me. 'What is that book Mr Grubb is reading?' he demanded of Legge. 'That's a score of the *Haffner*,' replied Legge. In tones of pretended astonishment Klemperer asked, 'He can read a score?' 'Of course he can, doctor. How could he be my assistant if he couldn't?' Klemperer turned to me and asked, 'What do you think of my performance of the symphony? Is it according to the score?' I mumbled something or other and Klemperer, enjoying himself hugely, asked, 'Is the tempo right?' He did not expect the answer he got. I thought to myself, 'One of these days I shall probably have to make a record with this man – and this is no way to inspire in him confidence in me.' 'Yes, doctor,' I replied firmly, 'a little faster it will be a muddle – a little slower it would be dull.' This time his astonishment was genuine; he said 'So!', and no one who has not heard it can imagine the wealth of meaning with which Klemperer could invest that single syllable.

The day of my recording with Klemperer had now come – why should the sessions not go smoothly? The first went perfectly. Klemperer was geniality itself when he arrived; he shook hands with me and after remarking, 'Why, Mr Legge, how you've changed!' he went into the studio and we began with the Schumann. By the end of the session we had enough material to cover the first and second movements and had the basis for a master of the last movement. Later that day, for over three hours, Fischer and I listened to all the tapes and we agreed that we needed to repeat only the last section of the last movement. The second session too started well. We began with the Liszt, reserving the corrections for the Schumann for later. During the playbacks Klemperer was still agreeable – he asked me why I had bothered to engage a conductor for this concerto as it seemed to have more cadenzas than accompanied passages. He even kept his temper when Fischer's husband, a friend of his from his Budapest days, suggested that a certain section should be taken faster. 'Would Dorati take it faster – or Szell – or Solti – or – ?' He hunted round for other conductors from Hungary. At the interval I knew that we had finished with the Liszt. Fischer seemed to agree with me.

The trouble broke out immediately afterwards. Klemperer's amiability was by now wearing a bit thin; he had had to repeat sections of the Liszt more often than he liked. I was glad that we only had to cover the second half of the finale of the Schumann and congratulated myself on having successfully tackled an extremely difficult job. I showed Klemperer which passages had to be repeated, among them the difficult last section in which it is not easy for the pianist and the orchestra to keep together. Klemperer went back into the studio and Fischer had a brief conversation with him. I was totally unprepared for what followed. There was a roar from Klemperer, 'Mr Grubb, will you come here.' I went into the studio. Klemperer literally bellowed at me, 'You want me to do the last movement of the Schumann, is that right?' I said 'Yes.' 'Miss Fischer wants to repeat passages from the first and second movements of the Schumann also.' I looked questioningly at Annie Fischer but her eyes were fixed on the keyboard. 'And,' Klemperer went on, 'she wants to repeat some sections of the Liszt. What shall I do?' I replied, 'First, the last movement of the Schumann, and then if we have time whatever else Miss Fischer wants.'

'But if you say one thing and Miss Fischer says something else who is right?' I said that the section we most needed to cover was the one I wanted them to repeat. 'Then you are saying that Miss Fischer does not know what mistakes she made?' There was really no answer to this.

The orchestra had gone very still and from the way some of them looked at me I could sense their sympathy. Klemperer could too and that fact seemed to infuriate him further. 'You must exercise your authority. Are you not in charge here? Tell me,' he roared. I now had to fight hard to damp down my rising temper, which then had a very short fuse. I kept reminding myself that my objective was to get the last movement of the Schumann and, whatever the provocation, I must not have a row with one of EMI's major artists. I stuck to my guns and repeated that the finale of the Schumann had serious mistakes in it and had to be done again. Klemperer said, 'Since you will not make a decision, I will decide for you. I will first do the sections Miss Fischer wants and then, if we have time, what you want.' I was willing to stand there till the end of the session if necessary arguing the point with him and once again I said that there were major mistakes in the last three minutes of the Schumann and unless they were corrected the entire record would be unissuable. He glared at me and we seemed to have reached an impasse when suddenly, very surprisingly but ungraciously, he said, 'I will do the Schumann first, but I will also do the Liszt.'

He still made it as difficult as possible. In the middle of a take he grumbled audibly and I rang him. He stopped, asked the orchestra, 'Why has he stopped me?' and then roared, 'Mr Grubb, come here' – he refused to talk to me on the telephone and I could communicate with him only by going into the studio. 'Why did you stop me?' he asked. 'You spoke, Dr Klemperer,' I said. 'I spoke? *I* spoke?' He looked at the orchestra and Hugh Bean, the leader, said, 'Yes, Dr Klemperer, you did say something.' Klemperer glared at him; but he repeated the passage. Soon afterwards I had once again to stop them and then go into the studio to tell him that the orchestra and the soloist were not together. 'It sounded perfectly all right here,' he growled, turning to the orchestra; but he got no encouragement from them. When they reached the end of the Schumann he announced, 'Now the Liszt' and started on that work before I could even reach for the telephone. I knew that nothing would be gained by asking him to repeat the three bars which I was still doubtful about – I knew the rest of the Schumann was all right. Immediately after the session ended, in the presence of the orchestra, Klemperer called his daughter to him and said that he would never again record with me and that Mr Legge should be informed of this . . .

I licked my wounds and thought to myself that that was possibly the end of my career as a recording producer. Many members of the orchestra expressed sympathy – Bernard Walton, the principal clarinet, advised,

'The next time he behaves like that, yell back at him – we'll back you up,' and Annie Fischer came up and said 'You poor man' – she pronounced it 'pure' and I smiled wryly, for my thoughts about Klemperer were far from pure just then. She explained that after the playback the previous evening she had managed to work herself up into a state and had convinced herself that most of what we had already recorded was not very good – just as she had done about the Liszt between the playback and the resumption of the session.

Later in the day I rang Legge to report. As soon as I announced myself he said, 'My dear boy, I know all about it. Six members of the orchestra have rung me to protest at the way Klemperer treated you. But the important thing is, are both works covered?' I said I was not quite sure about the last movement of the Schumann. When the concerto was edited there were indeed a few bars in that movement in which the soloist and the orchestra were not together. We briefly considered not issuing the record but as a great deal of money had been spent on it that was not on. Legge said that when the record came out he and I would probably have to flee the country. Actually, when it was released it was received enthusiastically by everybody; one critic said that since the collaboration had worked so excellently, Legge should arrange for Klemperer and Annie Fischer to make more recordings together. My comment to Legge was, 'Next time, include me out.' Not Klemperer, not Legge, not I could have known then that in less than two years I would become Klemperer's producer and start a close association with him which would continue for the last ten years of his recording career.

The Klemperer and Fischer sessions had a traumatic effect but there was precious little time for me to nurse my wounded self-esteem. Two successful sessions with Annie Fischer a week later, in which she recorded one of Beethoven's Op. 31 sonatas, provided some salve for it, for she was so obviously pleased to work with me again.

There were two major projects immediately ahead – Lehár's *Die lustige Witwe* with Schwarzkopf, and following close on its heels the last major recording on which I assisted Legge – *Così fan tutte*. This had Schwarzkopf and Ludwig as the sisters, Walter Berry as Don Alfonso, Hanny Steffek as Despina, Taddei as Guglielmo and the then comparative newcomer Alfredo Kraus as Ferrando. The orchestra was of course the Philharmonia and the conductor that great Mozartian, Karl Böhm. This was the opera which was to become Legge's swan song in EMI, though none of us knew it would be when the recording was planned. When the tapes had been put together and approved, Legge said, 'And now to *Zauberflöte*.'

In between Lorin Maazel recorded Richard Strauss, Debussy and Mussorgsky. I found him stimulating and we got on so well together that I was delegated the task of getting his approval of the tapes. There was also a recording with Giulini of an electrifying performance of Verdi's *Quattro pezzi sacri*. The special quality of Giulini's performance of this work was an enormous dynamic contrast – sung by a choir of nearly two hundred the pianissimo passages were barely audible in the Festival Hall, while the fortissimo sections nearly raised the roof. Legge wanted this to be faithfully captured on the recording.

There were no special problems on the first two sessions; on the first we recorded the 'Ave Maria' for unaccompanied chorus and on the second the 'Laudi alla Vergine Maria', also unaccompanied, for women only. In the third session we were due to record the 'Te Deum', which too begins softly, with an unaccompanied chorus, for fifteen bars. The faithful Larter was totally unprepared for the volume of sound which was to assail his microphones when the full chorus, accompanied by the full orchestra of some ninety players, thundered out the word 'Sanctus' fortissimo on the sixteenth bar – Legge had deliberately not warned him about what was coming. Larter lunged towards his controls as his indicator needles swung with a convulsive jerk into the red; but it was already too late. He turned to Legge and said, 'That was a lousy trick, Walter,' and added that if on the next morning he took back to the studios a tape with that dynamic range his boss would probably kill him. Legge's reply was terse: 'If you reduce the dynamic range I will kill you tonight. Take your choice.' Larter complied.

The problems of transferring the *Quattro pezzi sacri* from tape to disc seemed almost insoluble. Even with the most sophisticated high fidelity equipment and large, spacious surroundings you cannot reproduce the actual sound of a symphony orchestra in your living room; it has to be scaled down for the sound to be bearable in the confined space of domestic accommodation. But if you scale down soft and loud passages by the same ratio soft passages would be totally inaudible – in every living room there is some background noise and a basic noise (of a needle tracing a track on a disc, of the machinery which rotates the turntable, of the hiss of an amplifier) is inherent in any sound reproducing system and between them they would drown music below a minimum level. In all recordings therefore there is some compression of the actual dynamics into a smaller range. Legge would not agree to the wide range of his recording being controlled. It took much argument, patience, time and money to produce a satisfactory disc of the *Quattro pezzi sacri*. At some stage the matter had been reported to the top management, and shortly after, a fiat was issued by them laying down the maximum dynamic range for all recordings thereafter. The effect of this on Legge seemed out of all proportion. 'This preposterous memo is directed at me,' he complained angrily one evening. He said he was strongly inclined to chuck the whole thing and leave the company, a remark to which, at the time, I attached no great weight.

4   *Legge Resigns; The Klemperer* Zauberflöte

While I was assisting Legge with the Giulini sessions, I was simultaneously engaged in a set of sessions with Richter-Haaser; these gave me
unalloyed pleasure and, even more important, confidence after the
bruising encounter with Klemperer. Richter-Haaser was a large, genial
man of great wit, a delight to work with in the recording studio. He had
already made many records of the highest quality, notable among them
Beethoven's *Hammerklavier*, Op. 110 and Op. 31 No. 2, which opens up
hitherto unexplored regions in music and of which the composer himself
said that in it he was setting out on a new path. My first record with him
was to be the other two sonatas of Op. 31. We finished No. 1 and decided
to do No. 3 in May, but the record was destined to be completed not by me
but by Legge.

In May 1963 I was laid low by a mild heart attack. It was a warning that I
had been overstretching myself; as a result I was out of commission for
three months. I was told by my doctors to keep sensible hours, and avoid
the kind of schedule I had followed, for example, during the Richter-
Haaser sessions – these were at the Abbey Road Studios, from 10 a.m. to
1 p.m. and from 3 p.m. to 6 p.m. – in half an hour I had to get to Kingsway
Hall to assist Legge on the Verdi sessions, which ran from 6.30 p.m. to
9.30 p.m., and I did this three days running. It was not, as many of my
colleagues believed, compulsion or pressure from Legge which drove
me, but an eagerness to take part in all that was going on. I was fortunate
in that the warning had come in time and no serious harm had been
done.

Even before I returned to work news that was to have an important
bearing on my future was announced – Legge had decided to leave the
company he had worked for for over thirty years, and had given a year's
notice due to expire in September 1964. There were many reasons for
this. Foremost was perhaps the feeling, which he never explicitly stated
but was implicit in many of his conversations with me, that after a lifetime
of recording he had reached the peak of his achievement. A further cause
of dissatisfaction was the system, newly introduced, of greater control
over the work of the Artist department. This had been coming for a long
time; no business could continue to give its executives the absolute
freedom that Artist Managers had so far enjoyed. Within the loose

restraint laid on them by a budget which they were supposed not to exceed but which Legge certainly did, they could do pretty well what they liked. Now, every project had to be submitted to a committee, and only if it appeared to be profitable would it get the go-ahead. Legge chafed under these restrictions and he fiercely resented what he took to be a doubting of his judgment when any of his proposals were turned down. He had indeed some cause for resentment since many of his most successful recordings had been rejected at first. It is hardly credible that the Klemperer recordings of the Brahms Requiem, *Fidelio*, Bach's *St Matthew Passion* and the Giulini recording of the Verdi Requiem were all, when initially costed, considered to be unprofitable.

Legge was also a tired man; years of obsessional work had taken their toll of him. The sensible thing would have been to take a year's sabbatical, but having decided to resign he would not reconsider his decision.

In that last year he alternated between concern about my future and maliciously calculating how much disruption it would cause in the company if I resigned with him. I told him that I was capable of looking after myself; he agreed that I probably was – he had been astonished when I had been in hospital how many friends I had made in the short time I had been in EMI. He added bitterly, and perhaps not unfairly, 'If I had been ill, they would have contributed towards a celebration to dance on my grave.'

Amidst all these alarums and excursions we prepared for *Die Zauber-flöte*. Sir Thomas Beecham's recording with the Berlin Philharmonic Orchestra had been one of Legge's greatest pre-war triumphs. I had first come across the name Walter Legge, while still in India, through this recording, for he had written the notes in the accompanying booklet. Immediately after the war he had produced a second great recording of the opera with Karajan and the Vienna Philharmonic Orchestra, this time with a cast including most of the great Mozart singers of the post-war period. This was the first set of long-playing records that I acquired. Both these recordings, over forty years later in one case and nearly thirty years later in the other, are still in the catalogues. In 1964 we were going to record the opera with Klemperer – the Queen of the Night's three ladies were headed by Schwarzkopf, and Agnes Giebel led the three young boys which gives some idea of the strength of the cast. Legge planned to bow out of EMI with this recording; but it was not to be.

On the morning of 11 March 1964, the musical world of London was startled to read in its newspapers that Walter Legge had decided to disband the Philharmonia Orchestra. The news was totally unexpected. The first intimation most of the members of the orchestra had of their imminent dissolution was from the newspaper announcement. Even I, who had spent the previous evening at his house, had no inkling of what was coming, though he had dropped a hint that I should read my

23

newspaper especially carefully the next day. We were in the middle of recording Handel's *Messiah* with Klemperer and at that morning's session all was uncertainty and unhappiness. Legge arrived in the control room and astonishingly asked why no one in the orchestra would speak to him. Officers of the Musicians' Union came and went, and groups of the players clustered together, anxiously discussing the next moves and their future. When Klemperer, with a grim sense of irony, announced the first item to be recorded that morning there was a concerted snort of disbelief from the orchestra. It was the soprano aria, 'Rejoice greatly, O daughter of Zion' – Hugh Bean said to me sadly, 'You could at least have spared us this, Mr Grubb.'

In the days that followed Legge explained the reasons for his decision. The orchestra was no longer as good as it had been in its greatest days. He was finding it increasingly difficult to run it because of soaring costs and, more seriously, there were some players he would have liked to have replaced but Union rules and the orchestra's collective resistance stood in his way. He preferred to see the orchestra die with its name untarnished.

But an orchestra could not just be thrown away; it was a collection of men and women. The Philharmonia had in its ranks some of the most distinguished players of their instruments and collectively it was still a superb body. The general consensus was that it must be saved and strenuous efforts were made towards this end. Finally it was the players themselves who, with promises of help from many of their regular conductors, notably Klemperer and Giulini, solved the problem; they decided to continue in existence as a self-governing body and, since Legge would not give them permission to use their original name, they would become the New Philharmonia Orchestra.

An unexpected result of all this was that Legge fell out with Klemperer and Giulini. He felt that Giulini was a traitor to pledge his support for the new orchestra. The conductor tried to make him see that there was no valid reason for him to break with the orchestra. Had they behaved badly towards Legge he would certainly have severed his connections with them, telling them, 'You have done my friend an injury.' He pleaded with Legge to understand that he could not deny whatever he could do to help the musicians who had given of their best to him and to the world. But Legge would not be placated and to Giulini's distress said he would have nothing more to do with him.

The rift with Klemperer was much more serious and had far-reaching consequences for me. Klemperer was the Principal Conductor for life of the orchestra and so its disbandment was of personal concern to him; he complained that he had not been adequately consulted by Legge. The announcement had been made in the middle of a series of sessions with Klemperer and the conductor could see for himself the devastating effect it had on the players; he also said that he could not detect any falling-off in

24

the quality of the orchestra – indeed they were playing now as if their lives depended on it.

At first the exchanges between Klemperer and Legge had been civil, though a trifle frigid. We had left *Messiah* and had already started on orchestral passages in *Die Zauberflöte*. On the Saturday before Easter, without warning, the disagreement between Klemperer and Legge erupted. As it often happens, what triggered it off was quite trivial. Klemperer was to rehearse three of the singers in his hotel room on Easter Monday. Legge announced that he would be present at the rehearsal. Normally Klemperer would not have objected to this but now he said firmly that there was no need for the producer to be there. Normally Legge would have let it go at that but now insisted that it was his right to be at all rehearsals, to which Klemperer asked where in his contract with the company was Legge's right specified. Legge felt this was the last straw – that someone who, as he put it, 'he had made' should defy him. He gave me a letter for Klemperer to type. I looked at it in dismay – it announced that he was withdrawing from the recording of *Die Zauberflöte* – it was full of bitterness and couched in not very polite language; it was unworthy of Legge and was certainly not the sort of letter to address to a man of Klemperer's eminence. As I handed it to the messenger I again tried to prevent him from sending it, but to no avail. I had just reached home when the telephone rang. It was Lotte Klemperer. Without pre-amble she asked me whether I knew the contents of the letter from Legge to her father. I said I did. 'Do you think it is the sort of letter to write to my father?' she asked. Unhappily, I replied, 'Miss Klemperer, I am, as you know, Walter Legge's assistant.' She said, 'You have answered my question,' and rang off. Half an hour later the telephone rang again – this time it was the head of our division. He had spoken to both Klemperer and Legge, and wanted my version of the matter. But the immediate problem was, who was to produce *Zauberflöte* which was due to start in three days time.

The logical solution was for me to take over the recording. Legge had for some time left the setting up and the mechanics of our recordings to me and I was the only person who knew the details of this one – which singers would be available on which days; who should not be asked to sing anything demanding on such and such a day having sung a strenuous role the previous night several hundred miles away; who liked to arrive at least an hour before a session began to give herself time to warm up, and who would work himself up into a frenzy if he arrived more than two minutes before; I even knew on what days it would be that time of the month for a certain singer who would not then like to be asked to sing anything above top C. I had drawn up the recording schedule and plotted the 'stereo production', which had now become an essential element.

When stereo arrived it was like the invention of electrical recording or the long-playing record, one of the crucial developments in the history of the gramophone record. We now had two channels and two loudspeakers to accommodate much more comfortably all the information which had heretofore had to be crowded through one channel into one loudspeaker – the reproduced sound had a greater spaciousness to it, seeming to emanate not from one small rectangle but spread out between the two loudspeakers. With trial and error and after some initial excesses (of which one of the more extreme was the 'ping-pong' effect, in which the sound came from the extreme left or right and nothing seemed to happen in the middle), imaginative and creative use was made of the new technique. In opera stereo was used to add verisimilitude to the dramatic action. In mono you could reproduce movement towards and away from the front of the stage, giving an impression of depth; now you also had width to represent lateral movement across the stage.

The planning of the production of an operatic recording has become a complicated affair. The recording studio itself is now treated as a stage, the orchestra occupying the foreground as if playing from the pit while the singers stand on a platform behind. A bank of microphones, usually five, stands along the edge of the platform – as a singer moves from the microphone on the extreme left to that on the extreme right his voice, having been successively picked up by microphones one to five, travels from the left-hand to the right-hand loudspeaker, giving the impression that he is moving. You have, of course, to follow certain basic rules – too fast a movement makes it appear as if he were performing a series of kangaroo hops; if he moves, say, from microphone one to three while not actually singing, he would appear to have taken a flying long jump. The production schedule consists therefore of instructions detailing the exact spot at which any singer should be at any moment. A carpet ruled off into a grid in which squares are numbered and each row given a letter is laid out on the singers' platform and Papageno, for example, on first sighting Papagena might be required to move from G2 (mike 1, rear) to A8 (centre, mike 3, front). Entries and exits have to be consistent; if some pattern were not observed the impression created would be one of a confused, purposeless wandering around. If you spread an extended piece, such as the finales of the Mozart operas, over more than one day, each time you picked up the piece again you had to place your singers in exactly the same spots – otherwise you would get a jerk in the sound, similar to that visually produced in a badly spliced film. The production script of *Die Zauberflöte* ran to twenty-six pages of foolscap, even though with the experienced operatic singers of our cast one could afford to give generalized directions, 'Papageno sighting Papagena at the words "Nun Papageno" moves rear mike 1, laterally to front mike 3'. Walter Berry, our Papageno, would have translated this into the movement required. Even if Legge had produced the recording, it was I who would, before each scene, have explained their movements to the singers and asked one of them to produce any sound effects which were required.

I should rightly have taken over *Die Zauberflöte*, but I had a shrewd idea what the head of our department had at the back of his mind when we talked about it. I had, up till then, assisted in the production of over a hundred records, but on my own produced only one record with an orchestra. This was a major operatic recording involving some of the leading singers in the world; it was going to cost not less than £50,000 and it must have appeared hazardous to entrust the project to someone as untried as I was. The overriding factor in my mind though was that the conductor was Klemperer. He had already said that he would not work with me again, and remembering the details of that last session with him, when there was only one soloist, I shuddered at the thought of what he might be capable of with fourteen singers around. Had the conductor been anyone else I would have felt confident of handling the recording and would have said so, but in the circumstances, when the head of the department said he realized it was essential for me to be on these sessions and possibly run them, but hoped I would not mind if a more experienced colleague from the His Master's Voice stable was put in formal charge, I did not hesitate – I agreed at once.

All this happened on the Saturday and presumably the decision was conveyed to Klemperer on Easter morning – I would think, at about ten in the morning. At five minutes past ten his daughter was on the telephone to me; her father wanted to discuss one or two points in connection with the recording of *Die Zauberflöte*. Throughout the day and on the Bank Holiday Monday following I had a stream of telephone calls from Klemperer – when was the scene of Pamina's and Tamino's ordeal through fire to be recorded and would Mr Morris (the orchestra's principal flute) be there on the day? It was unlikely that Morris would have been absent on any Klemperer session and I would have had to be a half wit to schedule a scene in which the flute has as important a role as the two singers on a day when he was not there. I did not however go into all this but merely said, 'Yes, Mr Morris will be there.' Half an hour later – was the second finale to be recorded in one stretch or broken up? I said that it would be in one stretch spread over two days. Some while after, when was Miss Popp arriving and how long would she be staying? 'We must have a second chance to do the Queen of the Night's arias, if we feel it is necessary. They are very difficult.' Again I refrained from telling Klemperer that I knew just how difficult those arias were; I merely reassured him that Miss Popp would be available for not less than five sessions. And so it went on until, in sheer self-defence, my wife and I went to the cinema on the Monday afternoon. Seconds after we came back the telephone rang and an accusing Lotte Klemperer asked where I had been as they had been trying to get me for hours. Klemperer's nervousness was understandable; for the first time ever he was going into a major recording without Walter Legge and to replace him was someone comparatively unknown and someone he knew to be comparatively inexperienced. I wondered whether those telephone calls were genuinely prompted by his wanting to be sure I had everything under control or by his wanting to test my attitude to him. Had my chief rung me on Monday evening my confidence would have been sufficiently boosted by Klemperer's nervousness to insist on doing the recording on my own.

The next evening, the first session with the singers, took place with a triumvirate of producers – my HMV counterpart, his boss, whom he had brought along for moral support, and me. Klemperer knew that without my wholehearted involvement in the project it would be in jeopardy and in the early sessions he watched me intently. I was faintly amused by this; he was afraid that out of loyalty to Legge I would perhaps either wreck the recording or at least make it difficult for it to be successful. It was only on the third session that he relaxed. Before it began, the tension was at its greatest. It was Schwarzkopf's first appearance on the recording and everyone was apprehensive; that is, everyone but I, for I alone of all those present knew what sort of person she was. She arrived, graciously greeted everyone, courteously suggested to my colleague when he started to speak to her in German that in the interest of everyone present he should confine himself to English, asked me where she should stand for the first item and took her place on the stage with the utmost composure.

We started on that day with the opening scene in which Tamino comes on the stage pursued by a serpent. I had asked Nicolai Gedda, who was singing the part, to stand at first on the extreme left and smoothly, but fairly swiftly, move to the centre, while the Queen of the Night's ladies approached the front of the stage on either side of him. Klemperer seemed a little puzzled that Gedda was not standing directly in front of him but to one side. As he started the number and Gedda, singing 'Zu Hilfe! Zu Hilfe!' started to move to the right, Klemperer stopped beating time and asked in bewilderment, 'Where is Mr Gedda going?' Gedda muttered something about 'production, doctor' but the doctor, who had no knowledge at all of the technical aspects of recording said to him accusingly, 'But you were walking away.' Gedda doubled up with laughter; I took the steps leading to the hall three at a time and went up to Klemperer and explained why I had asked Gedda to move from one side of the stage to the centre. At last he understood that we were trying to reproduce what happens on a stage, and he said, 'So! good,' and for the first time on these sessions he smiled.

Some of the tension *I* was operating under had also been dissipated earlier on that session. A group of the singers were on the stage – as I walked through the orchestra to talk to one of them, the principal horn, Alan Civil, called me. 'Mr Grubb, do you think this screen behind us could be moved a foot back?' he asked. I knew that a horn player hated to have the sound of his instrument ricocheting back to him from a hard surface behind him and so I asked, 'Is the reflected sound bothering you?' 'No, no. We cannot, because of the screen, see the beautiful Lucia Popp.' The incident brought a sense of proportion into the situation. I had the screen moved back.

At the end of the final session Klemperer called me to his room and, having sent everyone except his daughter out, he thanked me for all I had done. I replied that I had only done my job. He said he knew it had been a difficult situation for me and that I had acquitted myself with great credit; he was personally much indebted to me. This was the first step towards the wonderful years ahead of my association with Klemperer.

5 The Alter Ego in the Control Room

The row over *Die Zauberflöte* did not seem to affect the relationship between Legge and me. We still spent evenings together, and except when I was on the Klemperer sessions I continued to work as his assistant. He was in a curious kind of no man's land; having to put in another few months before his notice expired, he went through the motions of being Artist Manager of the Columbia label but was unable to plan anything ahead. He was moody and ferociously bitter about the company. Quite unprovoked, he sometimes erupted into violent rudeness – on one occasion a colleague entered his room and as he talked to Legge placed a friendly hand on my shoulder. 'Don't paw my assistant – he is not a queer,' snapped Legge, and the visitor pulled his hand away as if it had been scorched.

On his very last day with the company we listened together to test pressings of *Così fan tutte* at the studios. Only one fellow employee came to the listening room to wish him goodbye. When the playback was over, he turned and looked up at the window of the manager's room, turned back to me and said, 'Let's go.'

Opinion was divided as to what effect Legge's departure would have on the record division. There were some who felt that the loss of such an outstanding figure should be made good by finding another such person, but Artist Managers of quality are not as easily found as all that. There were others who believed that Legge's departure would make no difference at all; we had the artists, the technical know-how and were, in size, the greatest recording company in the world – the loss of one man, however talented, was not going to make a scrap of difference. No one would voice the real fear at the back of most people's minds, that Legge would join another company. For the moment I looked after the Legge empire.

I had already acquired my first artist before Legge left. It was never specifically stated but, after the first sessions I had done with him, it was taken for granted that I would look after Richter-Haaser. The second record I made with him was of one of the great masterpieces of the piano literature, Beethoven's *Diabelli Variations*. He briskly polished off the theme and then played the variations in groups of three or four. As he went on, we both savoured and relished, in addition to the music,

30

Beethoven's characteristic and revealing directions, which, if properly understood, are the key to the interpretation of this work. It is almost like having the composer sit next to you on the piano stool and tell you how to play each section. The first variation bears the superscription '*maestoso*', majestically, as if Beethoven were announcing himself imperiously with 'enough of Diabelli and his silly little tune with its sequences – this is I, Ludwig van Beethoven.' '*Serioso*', '*dolce e teneramente*', '*pesante e risoluto*', '*scherzando*', '*piacevole*' and, a direction he uses for very special moments only, '*molto espressivo*', with the utmost expressiveness. At the end of the last playback, as the magical coda in which the theme, now transformed from bucolic waltz into elegant minuet, seems to dissolve and float towards the heavens, died away, Richter-Haaser and I looked with satisfaction at each other.

That had been in November of the previous year. He now recorded four more of Beethoven's sonatas and two of Schubert's. Recording with Richter-Haaser was admirable training and gave me experience in handling an artist though, admittedly, a very easy, even-tempered one. I could tell him anything and argue with him over points of interpretation and sometimes these arguments got very heated. On one such occasion we were both very surprised when the balance engineer asked, 'Are you still on speaking terms?' It had not been personal. When we heard the first take of the minuet of Schubert's C minor sonata I asked for the tape to be stopped half way through and said, 'You know, those accents in bars two and three and again in thirteen and fifteen and so on – this is a gentle Schubert minuet – I would interpret the accents as a slight leaning on the notes – don't you think you are going at them too brutally?' Richter-Haaser heard the take again and said, 'You are absolutely right – but you know, being German, when I see an accent my inclination is to go – wham! wham!' and he waved his hand as if violently slapping somebody. These sessions too developed in me that special concentration required for piano recording; wrong notes, smudges, notes which do not speak are all much more difficult to pick up than mistakes in an orchestra with its wider range of colours.

And Richter-Haaser was the first of the friends I was to make in the musical world. After one session he dined at my flat and spent the evening with us. The talk came round to historic recordings and I mentioned the Toscanini *Otello*. Richter-Haaser complained that he had been hearing about this recording for years but had never been able to get hold of a set. I told him I had the original HMV set, still the best version; would he like to hear a bit of it. 'Just a sample,' he replied, 'it's late.' It was after eleven and he had a plane to catch early the next morning. I put on side one and we experienced the fury of the storm and the frenetic gaiety of the drinking scene as realized by Toscanini. We could not possibly stop at the end of side one leaving us up in the air after the tender introduction by the cellos to the Otello–Desdemona duet. Two hours later, all three of us with tears in our eyes, we heard Ramon Vinay start Otello's farewell 'Niun mi tema'. It was a very special evening. Late the next day Richter-Haaser rang to tell me that he did manage to catch his plane.

When Legge left there was a rearrangement of the division; HMV and Columbia were merged into one. Legge's opposite number in the other camp retired in due course and the head of the department took direct charge of the producers – now four, as two additions had been made to our group. Six months after Legge's departure, the head of the department had asked to see me. Everyone knew how devoted I was to Legge, he said, and if, out of loyalty to him, I felt I wanted to leave the company he would not stand in my way. This sounded to me suspiciously like an invitation to leave, but I decided not to make it easy for him – to force him, if that was his intention, to put it in plain words. I did him an injustice; he had meant just what he had said. By the end of our meeting he had raised my salary and given me permission to get myself complimentary copies of all those records I had worked on.

With the reorganization a new look was taken at our list of artists and there was a certain amount of pruning. Alas one of the earliest casualties was Richter-Haaser. Even before the Schubert record had been released a committee had decided that his records were not selling well enough for us to continue with him. It wasn't just Richter-Haaser; it seemed that no piano records were profitable. 'Why can't we get a new Schnabel or Horowitz or Rubinstein,' desperately asked the sales manager of our American company at one of our international conferences.

At this particular conference, as sometimes happens with committees, we started with the intention of reducing the number of pianists and ended up with a brief to recruit more. I fought vehemently for Richter-Haaser but to no avail. And so, very reluctantly, I had to wish my first artist goodbye as far as the recording studio was concerned. It is something I have been called upon to do often over the years and it is still as distasteful as it was then.

Other recordings which offered greater technical challenge and enlarged the range of my experience followed. I was called upon to take over one session of Elaine Shaffer playing Bach flute sonatas from a colleague who had to attend a meeting; Shaffer and I got on so well that she asked that I should complete the recording. She was a delightful, gentle person with a quiet humour and steely artistic determination. At the end of our first session she said to me, 'You make me feel so secure in the studio – it is almost as if my alter ego is in the control room.' I knew that this was a precept that I would carry with me throughout my working life, that a producer should aim to make an artist entrusted to his care feel secure – and he should function as the artist's alter ego, not exercise his own ego.

Of all the forms of music, chamber music is that closest to my heart – it has been ever since I discovered Beethoven's C sharp minor Quartet in India over forty years ago. I was especially pleased when asked to produce a record of the Melos Ensemble playing the two great quintets for piano and wind of Mozart and Beethoven. Each player of the Melos was a virtuoso performer and through playing together over the years they had been welded into an integrated ensemble. The only problems that arose on these sessions were those of balancing instruments of different timbres, registers and power, discussing the occasional point of interpretation and arbitrating between the players when they had differences of opinion – these were not as infrequent as I had thought they would be; I had to intervene often to decide between rival claims to importance of parts assigned to players.

The quintets are for oboe, clarinet, horn, bassoon and piano, as incompatible a group of instruments as you could expect to find, but the main problem is the piano. Mozart and Beethoven had written the works for the fortepiano, an instrument which produced a clear, bell-like sound of considerable carrying capacity but no great sustaining power, not for an instrument of the massive sonority of the modern concert grand. The piano today can too easily swamp instruments it is teamed with unless the pianist respects at all times the registers in which his fellow players are placed. I had no fears on that score in our sessions, for we had that paragon of pianists in chamber music, Lamar Crowson; besides, in a recording studio we could help with skilful microphone placings. Even so, it took some time on the first session to ensure that every instrument would be heard with equal presence and clarity and that the tone colour of each was faithfully reproduced.

We began with the Mozart. The composer himself played the piano at the first performance and wrote his father soon afterwards that he considered it his finest work up to then. It is also the first real chamber music with piano. After the Mozart I asked the players for a few minutes to rebalance the piano and the other instruments in relation to it – they were surprised and didn't see why this was necessary, as both works are for the same group of instruments. I explained, in the Beethoven, the piano is the dominant partner; all the thematic material is first stated by the piano and even when one of the other instruments takes up a theme the piano keeps breaking in, as if it cannot bear to be left out. When we had reset the microphones I said, 'Let it rip for this one, Lamar.' After the sessions we celebrated in my flat and I was gratified when Crowson turned to me and asked, 'Where have you sprung from? What have you been doing all these years and why haven't we met you before? I hope we make more records together.'

6 'Where have you sprung from?'

Artists and friends who ask me at which conservatory I studied are surprised to hear that I have had no formal training in music. I am self-taught. I have always loved music and it has always been western music; my knowledge and experience of Indian music is very slight and I derive only a limited pleasure from some forms of it. To an Indian ear, the biggest obstacle to an enjoyment of western music is harmony, for in Indian music there is none, either explicit or implicit. I was born in a Christian family and so, from my very early years, had been familiar with hymns. Harmonic music had therefore never been strange for me. I learnt and sang 'Abide with me', 'Rock of ages' and, thanks at one time to several uncles, aunts or cousins getting married in quick succession, 'The voice that breathed o'er Eden', even as I learnt to speak. As I grew a little older I found more interesting hymns with independently moving harmonic lines, like the Bach 'Passion' chorale, which made bearable part of that tedious stretch of devotion I was forced to attend, the three-hour Good Friday service. I went on to light music – dances, popular ballads and songs – in my early teens. We had always had a gramophone and records in the house. The gramophone was a clockwork model in which the sound travelled from the soundbox through an arm which started with a 'U' and straightened to lead to a large horn. After placing the needle on the record you had to rise very cautiously to avoid knocking the horn over. I never discovered exactly where the records had come from; they were probably a legacy from one of my father's English colleagues. They were a motley bunch. One, with a Regal-Zonophone label, bore the intriguing title 'John, John, put your trousers on', with 'In the land where the women wear the trousers' on the other side. Then there were the two titles which featured in every household which owned a gramophone, 'The whistler and his dog' and 'The laughing song'. We also had 'Departure of a troopship', and I seem to remember 'Sinking of a troopship'. To these were added the latest dance tunes as they appeared – 'Ice Cream', 'Yes, we have no bananas' and I contributed to this lot my first gramophone record, 'Oh Donna Clara', a haunting tango the memory of which even today transports me to my teens and the pangs of youthful love, for I had at the time a crush on a young neighbour, appropriately named Darling.

Along with the dance records we also bought records of less ephemeral music – Robeson singing 'Old man river', Galli-Curci singing what sounded like 'Ome, sweet ome' and 'Lo! here the gentle la-ha-ha-ha-hark' and Caruso's ever popular 'O sole mio'. The first record of serious music we acquired was of two excerpts from Handel's *Messiah* – 'For unto us a child is born' and 'Glory to God', sung by the Philharmonic Choir under Charles Kennedy Scott with Elsie Suddaby singing the soprano recitatives preceding 'Glory to God'. My father selected this record at random from the catalogue as suitable for waking us in the small hours of Christmas morning for the service at four o'clock. You could hear it at other times, but only if he was not around. On the sleeve of this record was a picture of a lady and a gentleman, elegantly and decorously poised for the dance, advertising HMV D1285, a record of Stokowski and the Philadelphia Orchestra playing Weber's *Invitation to the Waltz*. It was impossible to resist this record and everyone in the family loved it. I was emboldened to launch out on other records of the Philadelphia Orchestra. From the 'Passion' chorale I knew the name Bach hyphenated with an arranger, so, I felt I could not go wrong with Bach-Stokowski. I hazarded a month's pocket money on two records of 'Toccata and Fugue in D minor' and the little 'Fugue in G minor' with the choral prelude 'Christ lag in Todesbanden' as its coupling. Even at the first hearing the two fugues and the choral prelude sounded agreeable but the toccata required determined grappling with for over a month to yield any pleasure.

Over the next two years we acquired more records – waltzes by Strauss, *Blue Danube* with Lehár's *Gold and Silver* on the other side and *Tales from the Vienna Woods*, all played by Marek Weber and his orchestra – marches by Sousa played by the Black Dykes Mills Band and, again, one of my contributions, the Scherzo and Nocturne from Mendelssohn's music to *A Midsummer Night's Dream*. I found the nocturne ravishing and I often wondered what magical instrument it was which played the theme at the beginning. I did not try to find out what it was, which I now find inexplicable, for I have always had an enquiring mind. Such then was the extent and range of my musical experience and knowledge when I reached college.

We never had a piano at home but we did have a portable harmonium which folded down to the size of a small suitcase. (When we had it lacquered it looked exactly like a child's coffin!) This was practical in our family circumstances, for my father was a civil servant liable to be transferred every few years to places as much as eight hundred miles apart. The bottom of the box divided into two halves. They dropped on hinges one to either side to form the supports on which the instrument stood. A pair of pedals released from a hook operated the bellows. The top of the box opened to reveal a keyboard of five octaves from F to F. The instrument produced a slightly reedy, mellow sound.

My father believed that music was not a suitable recreation for a boy, certainly not for me, as he had ambitions of high government office for his first born. My sister though had piano lessons at school. I do not remember what provided the initial impetus, but when I was fourteen, using my sister's tutor as a guide, I started painfully and laboriously to teach myself to play the harmonium. There was no question of developing a delicate touch, for the instrument uttered the same sound whether you banged the keys or stroked them gently. The action of the keys was sluggish, making fast passage work difficult. You could only increase or decrease the volume. This was by operating with the sides of the knees two levers which varied the amount of air reaching the reeds.

An hour's informed coaching would have saved me a great deal of struggle and prevented my developing wrong habits, but there was no one to teach me the simple fact that the numbers and the cross on top of the notes were aids to the most economical and convenient use of one's fingers. Not knowing this, I had to invent weird and ingenious move- ments to overcome awkward situations. If the little finger of my right hand found itself, say, on G and the next treble note was the C above, my palm would swivel round for the index finger to vault over the other fingers and reach the note – I could not have executed this manoeuvre more expertly if I had had piano lessons from Chico Marx. Fairly soon, I could play hymns, which were easy because the chords mostly moved in blocks. After some hard work, I was able to cope with simple pieces like Schumann's *Träumerei*, Rubinstein's Melody in F and Handel's Largo.

During my early years in college I met a few other students who liked music but no one with much greater knowledge than myself. It was during the long summer vacation of my third year in college that the event took place which dramatically opened my ears to great music. We were at the time in Trichinopoly, one of the bigger towns in South India. One of the colleges in it was run by English missionaries and I had casually met one of them, the Reverend E. R. Richardson. He called at our house one morning to see my father. He heard me playing one of my records and asked my father if I was musical. My father appears to have said that I spent far more time on music than was good for my studies. Later that day, a box of records arrived with a note from the Reverend Richardson saying he thought I might like to listen to them and that I could keep them till the end of the holidays. They were Beethoven's Ninth Symphony on nine twelve-inch discs and Schubert's 'Unfinished' on three, both played by the familiar Stokowski and the Philadelphia Orchestra; the Reverend Richardson certainly believed in tipping one into the deep end. All I knew at this time about Beethoven was that he had written a Minuet in G, which was easy to play having only one sharp, and about Schubert, that he was the composer of a 'Moment Musical' which had four flats and was therefore so very awkward that I had never even attempted to play it.

I have ever been a believer in tackling the more difficult jobs first and so decided to get to grips at once with the Ninth, the longer work. I had not heard a symphony before, neither did I know what the word or the form signified; it was no surprise that the work as a whole made very little sense. But I persevered, since some of the music was mildly agreeable – the passage in the middle of the first movement in which bits of the main theme were tossed around from instrument to instrument and the second main theme of the third movement. Only one section had an instant impact – the surging melody on the cellos in the second movement, which I felt was the most beautiful tune I had ever heard. It seemed an awful lot of music to get through for about two minutes of this tune and yet I never cheated – every time I wanted to hear it I played the whole symphony through. And then, one day about a week later, I found myself humming something I could not at first place, and then realized that it was from the Ninth Symphony. Gradually over the next few times more and more bits started to fall into place – the bare opening fifths which so mysteriously prepare the way for the tremendous unison theme, the awesome downward slide in the coda before the final defiant return of the opening theme, the driving energy of the scherzo and its brilliant orchestration, the alternation of two distinct tunes in the third movement and that they appeared to recur somewhat disguised. The last movement remained a slightly unsatisfactory affair (and was to remain so until, four years later, I heard it on the radio conducted by Toscanini). I now actually liked listening to the Ninth.

Having come to terms with the Ninth I turned to the 'Unfinished' and instantly fell headlong in love with it. From the first playing it captivated me – the sombre opening on the lower strings, the restless, tossing figure over the throbbing pizzicato which followed, the lovely second theme on the cellos so tenderly ushered in by the horns, the long-breathed lines of melody of the second movement, the syncopated accompaniment to the second theme, and the final descending pizzicati with which the work ends – all this was magical and if this was a symphony, I wanted to know what a symphony was – I wanted to know the name of the instrument which so comically leads off the second half of the Ninth's scherzo – I wanted to know more about music and the men who had created it, and above all I wanted to hear more symphonies.

At the end of the holidays, I reluctantly returned the records to the Reverend Richardson and went back to my college in Madras. There was an excellent bookshop in the city and I asked one of the haughty young Englishmen, exquisitely and correctly dressed in dark suits and white shirts with stiff collars who served in the shop, for a book which would tell me something about symphonies. He thought for a moment and produced the American critic Olin Downes's *Symphonic Masterpieces*; it was exactly what I wanted and was to prove an invaluable guide in the years to come. As for listening to more music, the problem solved itself in 1936. Just after the abdication, to keep in touch with the latest news my father bought a powerful short-wave radio set. A whole world of music became accessible to me – London, Moscow, Rome, Hilversum, Berlin, New York, Montevideo, Rio de Janeiro and, somewhat improbably, Teheran, Ankara, Batavia, Manila, Singapore which broadcast records of western music.

My sister's piano primers listed books on music on their back covers, and from these I made up a list on the theory of music, on instruments of the orchestra, on harmony and counterpoint (not knowing quite what that was) and on musical form and sent for the books from London. Armed with these, I set out to teach myself music. For the next two years I wrestled impartially with logarithms and right ascensions and declinations for my university degree in Mathematics, Physics and Chemistry and with fugues, canons, inversions, diminished seventh chords and so on for my own pleasure – this reached new heights when on paper I was able to harmonize a given melody and, playing it over on the harmonium, found it agreeable and adventurous. As my knowledge increased I took up more ambitious subjects – score-reading, orchestration, and I even got myself a text book on chamber music composition, though that really led to nothing.

All the while, on the radio, I heard vast quantities of music of all kinds. Orchestral music predominated but there was also instrumental and chamber music. My knowledge of the repertoire, of standard and out-of-the-way works, increased by the day – there were symphonies by the great classical masters and also by J. C. Bach, d'Indy, Borodin, Saint-Saëns – and overtures, symphonic poems, suites, ballet music, concertos, sonatas, trios, quartets. My appetite for music was insatiable and anything that I could pick up on the radio, I listened to. It was like cramming a lifetime's concert going into five years of radio broadcasts. There was one form of music I avoided – vocal. The delights of vocal music were yet to be revealed.

I made some wonderful discoveries and heard unforgettable performances in those years: I caught one item just after the opening announcement and feverishly thumbed through Downes, for I remembered his mentioning a symphony which began with a glorious theme for the solo horn (I knew by now what a horn sounded like) – that was my introduction to Schubert's great C major. In 1939 I used to sit up night after night till well after two in the morning for the concerts of the London Music Festival and heard Bruno Walter conducting Mozart's 39th, all nine symphonies of Beethoven and the Missa Solemnis conducted by Toscanini, his violin and piano concertos in concerts conducted by Boult. I kept a log book of all the broadcasts I listened to and I see from it that in 1940 I heard altogether 190 symphonies, with Beethoven's fourth symphony, unexpectedly, leading, with fourteen performances – I heard too, in that year, the Bizet symphony four times.

My harmonium playing developed too, and I became skilful enough to attempt fairly difficult pieces. By this time I had worked out for myself a more efficient and less awkward method of fingering and had rid myself of some of my more outrageously bad habits. The first volume of music which I bought and still have is an arrangement of the incidental music to *A Midsummer Night's Dream* and the date on it is October 1936. The reason for getting this was that, somehow, I had got myself appointed as organist of a local church and the Wedding March was, of course, a must for a church organist. *Beethoven Sonatas*, Volume 1, followed in December 1937. By the time of my twenty-first birthday my father had apparently accepted that music was an essential part of me – my two volumes of piano arrangements of *Beethoven's Symphonies* bear the inscription 'To dear Suvi, with love and birthday greetings from papa and mamma, 7 October 1938'. I got arrangements of other orchestral and chamber music which helped me to a greater understanding of the forms of music and also an insight into their design.

Soon after I graduated I started to work for All India Radio. An unexpected bonus of this was that I obtained access to libraries of gramophone records – from three to four thousand discs at each of the major stations. When I began, as a lowly children's scriptwriter, it was specified that part of my duties would be to assist in programmes of western music and, oh joy, look after the record library. As a first step towards bringing system and order into the broadcast of records I set out, in spare moments, to time every single disc, noting also the number of vacant grooves before the music began – the announcer could twirl the turntable round that number of times and spare the listener a long stretch of irritating surface noise before the music began (one side of the Toscanini *Semiramide* overture began with 17½ blank grooves). Of course, I heard a great deal of new music and new interpretations of familiar music. Soon, I was put in sole charge of music programmes and now could actually order records myself. Each station's budget allowed for about three hundred a year and I was not confined to the local issues, a pitifully small list, but was able to order from the parent companies in England. I gradually filled up the gaps in the libraries, and in my own knowledge of music. Long after I had been promoted to senior positions and it was no longer part of my duties, I continued to look after and time records – even in my last job as Assistant Director of the Delhi station.

It was while timing records that I stumbled on Beethoven's last quartets. I had heard the occasional broadcast of the Op. 18s and the Rasoumovskys but do not remember hearing any of the last works. The Busch Quartet's recording of the Quartet in C sharp minor Op. 131 had newly arrived at the Calcutta station and came up, in due course, for timing. The music began and I was overwhelmed; halfway through the opening fugue I abandoned the timing of it and listened, enraptured by the music. The work came to an end and I leaned back and wondered whether I would ever, however long I lived, understand and fully experience all that this quartet held – in twelve years I had come a long way from considering the *Gold and Silver* waltz of Lehár to be the greatest piece of music ever written.

My introduction to the delights of vocal music was through my first chief at AIR, Victor Paranjoti, like me a South Indian Christian; he was the organist of the local Scots Kirk and a very respectable pianist. He ran the Madras Madrigal Choir made up of a group of amateurs. The choir sang only unaccompanied music – there was no orchestra or group of instrumentalists in Madras anywhere near the standard of the choir. My voice was untrained but quite powerful and Paranjoti invited me to join his choir. On my first rehearsal he took us through Orlando Gibbons' 'The silver swan', Morley's 'Shoot, false love, I care not', Wilbye's 'Adieu, sweet Amaryllis', Weelkes' 'O care thou wilt despatch me' and Tomkins' 'When David heard that Absalom was slain' – a fine selection from some of the greatest madrigal composers and I was hooked on a new branch of music. To enlarge my knowledge of vocal music was simple – the Madras station had records of the choral repertoire, all the Mozart Opera and Schubert Lieder Society recordings. When, eight years later, I returned to the Madras station, now as Assistant Director, I myself formed a choir from members of the local YWCA, their friends and a group of enthusiasts from consulates and conducted the first nearly complete performance of Bach's *St Matthew Passion* given in India. It took me six months to train the choir to the standard I wanted – at the end of that period I knew by heart every part of every chorus in the work.

This had been my training in music before I came to London. I had not heard a professional symphony orchestra in the flesh. I had, however, heard three of the world's great instrumentalists – Menuhin, Solomon and Stern, all of whom had visited India on concert tours. My most cherished memory is of Solomon, who in response to a casual remark from me that I was sorry his programme did not include Beethoven's last sonata, sat at the piano and played Op. 111 to a mere handful of us who settled down on the floor around him.

When I arrived in London I went to concerts with the avidity with which I had listened to music on the radio, principally to the Royal Festival Hall, where you could then get standing tickets close to the stage for just two shillings – I could now not only hear, but see at close quarters, the legendary figures I knew from records. My knowledge of music was further enlarged and there was a new love, opera, with a new discovery each week – there could not have been a happier introduction to it than through my first opera, *Le Nozze di Figaro*, at Covent Garden, and the second, Smetana's *The Bartered Bride*, at the Sadler's Wells Theatre.

7   Berlin: Singers. London: Pianists

My first trip abroad on EMI business was to Berlin in 1965 to be in overall charge of three recordings by Schwarzkopf – a lieder recital, the Brahms *Deutsche Volkslieder* with Fischer–Dieskau singing the men's songs, both accompanied by Gerald Moore, and Strauss' *Vier letzte Lieder* and some of his other songs with Georg Szell and the Berlin Radio Orchestra. It was my first visit to a city, which even after a dozen trips, induces in me a curious mixture of exhilaration and claustrophobia. Legge was to produce the recordings – it would have been awkward for anyone else to have done so, for, as Schwarzkopf's husband, he would in any case have been present and I cannot imagine any producer fancying having Walter Legge breathe down his neck. That apart, Schwarzkopf might not have agreed to work with someone else. I was ostensibly there to make things as easy as possible for everyone, but had been told, unequivocally, that, as the company's representative, the final responsibility for the project rested with me. It was not an enviable position and Legge's attitude made it even more difficult. Some of his resentment against EMI spilled over onto me; this worsened over the next few years, so that during the last four years of his life Legge and I, sadly, were not on speaking terms.

I had met Gerald Moore several times in London when I assisted on sessions with Schwarzkopf or Christa Ludwig, but I had mostly kept in the background; Moore probably thought that I was a dull stick.

When the lieder record had been finished Fischer-Dieskau arrived for the Brahms folk songs; I had, so far, seen him in action in the recording studio as Jesus in Bach's *St Matthew Passion* and as the baritone soloist in the Brahms Requiem – I now saw him as a lieder singer and marvelled at the effortless ease with which he sang. When he dropped his voice to a pianissimo it seemed unbelievable that so clear, limpid and smooth a line of melody should come from a human throat; when he opened out into a fortissimo it was almost like a physical assault. The two singers spurred each other on to greater heights, both of them wonderfully supported by Moore – and there is just the right amount of acting with the voice legitimate for lieder.

Superb examples of all this are the infectious, teasing gaiety of 'Jungfräulein soll ich mit euch geh'n' with Moore's piano dancing in delight at the antics of the young maid and her amorous swain, and the unspecified, chilling tragedy of the girl in 'Schwesterlien'. At first, the brother wants to go home; she is reluctant. And then, on their way home the boy anxiously asks why she is so pale. Fischer-Dieskau's voice drops into a sudden pianissimo and he broadens and slows down the tempo – the colour of Moore's piano is veiled. The sister – and how magnificently Schwarzkopf takes over the new tempo and slows it down even further – replies, 'That is the morning light on my cheeks, wet with dew.' And the last verse, 'Why are you tottering?' and the girl, 'Lead me to my bed – it will be fine to be under the turf.' The accompaniment points up and intensifies the tragedy. In a third song the consternation of a timorous lover as he realizes that nothing is going to stop the girl from getting him into her room and her increasing impatience with him are beautifully conveyed. 'How shall I get in at the door?' 'Draw the latch.' 'How get past the dog?' 'Give him a kind word.' 'What about the fire?' 'Put some water on it, and mother will think the rain is beating in.' Schwarzkopf, in the phrase 'Schütt ein bisschen Wasser . . .' beautifully uses the sibilants to imitate the hiss of water on a fire. Her last 'Komm du mein Liebchen komm' is wonderfully made up of a combination of amorous yearning and exasperation. This is interpretation of lieder at its very best.

During a playback of one of these folk-songs, 'Ich weiss mir'n Maidlein' I noticed that while the German text said 'Sie hat zwei Brüstlein die sind wiess' the English translation was 'She has a breast as white as snow', and was so amused by this piece of bowdlerization that involuntarily I exclaimed, 'Whoops, she's lost one tit in English!' Schwarzkopf uttered a slightly scandalized 'Suvi!' but accompanied by a delighted gurgle. Gerald Moore looked at his score and then up at me and smiled as if he was seeing me for the first time. Our friendship grew apace in Berlin and continues to be a close and affectionate one.

After leaving the company Legge had moved to Switzerland and I had not seen much of him. In Berlin we had the opportunity to talk. After two days in one hotel my wife and I had moved to another and had persuaded the Moores to follow us; Schwarzkopf and Legge moved in too after another couple of days. (My hotel-hopping has always been a source of great amusement to my secretaries – the record so far has been three different hotels in three days in Paris.) Late one evening I asked Legge why he had left EMI. I could understand him disbanding the orchestra, but there had been no need to give up the work which had been, and obviously still was, close to his heart. He replied bitterly that he had not really expected to give up recording. 'I thought every gramophone company in the world would be at my doorstep, but there has been nothing – nothing at all,' he said.

I had been charged to take especial care of Szell, making his first record for EMI for some years. In actual fact, the efficient, well organized

Georg Szell took care of me in Berlin, but our meeting was the foundation of a warm friendship which lasted during the few years left of his life. Szell's hotel was next door to mine and I used to pick him up and drive him to rehearsals and sessions. He knew Berlin well and would point out places of interest. As we drove up Kurfürstendamm, he snorted at the Gedächtniskirche and said, 'That was always an eyesore and an abomination. When during the war it was damaged, any sensible people would have thankfully torn it down; instead of which, what do the Berliners do? – they build a new church even more hideous than the old one, patch up the old one and elevate it into a shrine. Bah!'

At a roundabout or when I was just going to turn left or right, without changing his tone of voice he would say, 'I think you are just about to forget that you are in a right-hand drive country' – and then would continue with his story. The car had two keys, one for the doors and the other for the ignition. After he had seen me twice fumble for the right one he gently took the ring from me, looked carefully at the two keys, and returned them remarking, 'One of them has a double flange. If you work out whether it is the ignition or the door key, you would save yourself time and trouble.' His wife, who was with us at the time, said to me, 'Take no notice of him, Mr Grubb – he is infuriating.' But I didn't find Szell infuriating – he had an orderly mind and hated to see time or effort wasted when they could so easily be saved by application of method.

I asked him whether he wanted a vocal score for his piano rehearsal with Schwarzkopf; I knew he would play the piano himself. 'You are joking, of course,' he replied and, a little abashed, I remembered that this was the man who had astonished Strauss by his playing on the piano one of his operas. He played for Schwarzkopf with the full orchestral scores on the stand but not bothering to look at them. At the end of the rehearsal he enquired of her what else she had recorded and she said she had just finished a recital of popular lieder with things like Schumann's 'Widmung'. Szell replied, 'Ah! it has a wonderful piano part' – and played it faultlessly. We all looked at him in wonder and Schwarzkopf remarked that he must have played the piece recently. 'I don't think I've seen the music of "Widmung" for forty years,' Szell replied. With anyone else it would have sounded like showing off but with him it was just a statement of fact.

The Berlin Radio Orchestra were going through a lean patch and the orchestral writing in the Strauss songs is quite taxing. When Szell started to rehearse Legge and I looked at each other in dismay; the unspoken thought in both our minds was that this record was not going to be good enough. We had reckoned without Szell. What followed was an object lesson in how to cram the maximum amount of work into a given period of time. Not a moment was wasted – nothing not immediately relevant was said and there were no high-faluting exhortations or perorations. Szell's instructions were precise as he coaxed and cajoled the orchestra into playing the notes, first, exactly as written, and then to imbue them with feeling.

'Three before letter B – clarinets, a little more – just a little less oboes – one, two – No, no, don't get quite so lost, oboes – we must hear you too. Once again – one, two. Good – good . . . Violas, there seems to be a mistake in your part – the second note seven after B is A – second violins, bravo – sing like that – yes – don't lose intensity – and no diminuendo.' Endlessly patient, never raising his voice, he took them through the *Vier letzte Lieder*, and the orchestra, which I knew had looked forward to their encounter with Szell with some trepidation, responded by giving of their best. I listened in some astonishment. Was this the martinet orchestras all over the world feared? Was this the tyrant Szell who could cow the most arrogant orchestral player? An hour later he came up into the control room and sat down mopping his brow. 'When I began I wasn't quite sure whether we would get a satisfactory record', he said, 'but now I think we shall, because they are anxious to do well and working very hard.' Later, when Legge asked Szell, 'Georg, what about a little more' – and described a long, expressive arc with his arm, Szell replied, 'Give me three more sessions and I'll get all the' – and he imitated Legge's expansive gesture – 'you want. With the sessions we have, let us be satisfied with the right notes at the right time.' 'And together,' said Legge. 'Being together is having the right notes at the right time,' said Szell severely as he walked back into the hall. Szell, Schwarzkopf and the orchestra did much more than produce the right notes at the right time. After the recording Szell guided us to a beer cellar with sawdust on the floor and hard wooden benches, and we ate a rich glutinous *Eisbein*, the Berlin speciality of pigs' trotters, preceded by schnapps and washed down with a dark brown beer.

Sometime later my wife and I met the Szells again when he was in London, for the last time, to conduct the New Philharmonia in Beethoven's Ninth Symphony. He had said they liked Chinese food and we invited them to a restaurant in Limehouse which we proudly announced was the best in London. Szell asked us first to have a drink with them in their hotel. He mixed four Manhattans and passed them round. By the time the rest of us had had two sips Szell had finished his and started to pace up and down the room. He had had a drink and was now impatient to get to the restaurant. His wife said, 'Georg, sit down – you're making us all uncomfortable,' and reluctantly he did. On the way to the restaurant he noticed some wine in the car. 'A light Burgundy,' I explained. 'French wine with Chinese food! Impossible!' he cried. I did not argue the point but in the restaurant I persuaded him to try it and rather gingerly he took his first few sips. Three-quarters of the way through the meal he said to me, 'I must thank you for having taught me something new. I love Chinese food. All my life I have had beer or China tea with it. Today I've learnt that

44

a gentle Burgundy, such as this, is an admirable accompaniment to it. I must have more of these prawns.' When his wife said, 'Georg, aren't you eating too much,' he replied, 'I probably am but I cannot resist these prawns.'

When I started to get interested in music it took some time for me to come to terms with the piano. But by the time I joined EMI I loved piano music and was very knowledgeable about it, so whenever a new pianist appeared I was first choice as producer. By 1966 I had made a clutch of piano records, one of the best of which never saw the light of day. When Marta Argerich walked into the studio it was her dark, smouldering looks which first struck me. As soon as she arrived she asked for coffee; when I offered her a cup she gulped it down in one go and asked for more. I sat her in the studio with a large pot of coffee and went into the control room. At first, her hands moved casually over the keyboard as she tested the piano. Then she launched into Chopin's Polonaise Op. 53. I sat up in my chair with a long drawn out 'Jee-sus' – the balance engineer said 'Wow!' If this was a sample of her playing, Argerich was quite the most formidable player we had ever come across. The big chords sounded huge, the runs between them clean; in the trio, a great showpiece, the difficult left hand runs were even and the crescendo controlled. I peeped into the studio to make sure that this wash of sound was really originating from the slip of a girl seated at the piano. It was quite unbelievable. I smiled as I recollected Clara Schumann's remark to Brahms about his *Paganini Variations*, regretting that it was beyond a woman pianist's capability. Nothing would have been beyond this woman. She came into the control room, looked at me and beamed, for she knew she had had a shattering impact on me. Over the next few days, fortified by gallons of strong, black coffee, she finished a Chopin recital which included the third Sonata, the third Scherzo and, fashioned like miniature jewels, a group of Mazurkas and Nocturnes. The last movement of the sonata is in one flawless take. She said she had enjoyed the sessions; she liked the sound of the piano on the record, and looked forward to working with me again. To my bitter disappointment, we learnt a few weeks later that her commitment to another company would not permit us to publish the record, and, not for the first time nor the last, I wished that there were no such things as exclusivity clauses. In due course a record with the same repertoire was released by our rivals – when I heard it I knew that our Argerich was the better of the two.

The next piano record was of the Brahms Variations on a theme of Paganini and its companion piece, the Variations and Fugue on a theme of Handel. The pianist was a young American of Spanish and Mexican parentage, Agustin Anievas; it was his first record for us. Anievas was a little tense when we started – but I soon got him to relax. I was pleased when at the end of the session he said that recording did not seem to be such a hair-raising a business as he had expected; my aim has always been to make an artist feel at ease in the studio and enjoy his music making.

I first asked Anievas to try out the two studio pianos. One had a brilliant, even, clean tone, the other was warm and mellow, with an exceptionally rich sonority in the lower half. Anievas said rather wistfully, 'If only I could play the Paganini on the first piano and the Handel on the second.' 'That's exactly what I hoped you'd say,' I replied. The first piano was ideally suited to the Brahms–Paganini, a virtuoso piece. Characteristically, he chose to begin with the more difficult work. At the first playback of each part we discussed points of interpretation – one of the big problems in a set of variations in which each half of each variation is repeated was how to remain faithful to the score and yet introduce a fresh element into each repeat. Anievas had two intriguing solutions to this – one was to play either the first statement or the repeat more freely, with great rubato. The other was much more unusual – in the repeat he subordinated the principal melody, which had been emphasized the first time round, to an inner melody, or line, or even rhythm. The effect was sometimes quite startling, as if a fresh theme had intruded into the proceedings. Having finished with the Paganini we moved to the other piano for the Handel. Finally he played the first of the Chopin Etudes as a foretaste of the next record.

In the course of these sessions I made suggestions about pedalling and other aspects of piano-playing. Anievas suddenly said to me, 'You must, of course, be a brilliant pianist.' I said I most certainly was not – I played just well enough to derive some enjoyment out of it but not well enough to give pleasure to anyone else. Had I known him then as well as I do now I would have given him my definition of a producer, 'A producer is a eunuch who knows how it should be done but cannot do it himself!'

Anievas went on in the years ahead to make a number of first-class records for us – Chopin's Etudes and Waltzes and third Sonata, Liszt's Sonata which tests a pianist's stamina and sense of musical design, a set of the four Rachmaninov Piano Concertos and the Paganini Rhapsody and Schubert's Impromptus. I play his records over and over again with pleasure.

The next pianist was Emil Gilels. Friends ask me how artists react to the fact of my being an Indian – they seem disappointed when I reply, no differently from the way they might have had I been English or German or whatever. I think immediately of Gilels. When we first met in Studio No. 1 he did not seem surprised that the 'Mr Grubb' he had been told would produce his record was a very brown, compactly built Indian instead of, as he later confessed he expected, a large, red-faced Englishman. He was to record Schumann's *Nachtstücke* Op. 23 and Schubert's *Moments Musicaux*. We first recorded the Schumann. The four pieces which make up the work are seldom played – I, who had a fairly extensive knowledge of the piano music of that period, had never heard them. I wondered at this

46

neglect, for the pieces are hauntingly beautiful and show Schumann at the height of his powers, and I was delighted to discover a new work. He then went on to the Schubert, which, of course, was a familiar, well-loved work. These miniature pieces were written in the year before Schubert's death; he was thirty and in this, as in all his late work, he takes us into areas of feeling and poetry uncharted till then. It is poignant to speculate on what companion pieces to the C major string quintet, the *Winterreise* song cycle and the Heine songs and the three sonatas of 1828 have been denied to us by Schubert's early death.

Gilels played Nos. 1 and 2 and jumped to No. 4, which starts like a Bach toccata but with a trio which is Schubert at his heart-breaking loveliest. He then went on to the best known one of the set, No. 3 in F minor. He played it four or five times and each time was plainly dissatisfied with the result. I could sense what he was aiming at – a simplicity, an artlessness that seemed for the moment to elude him. He said he would play No. 5 and return later to No. 3. He attacked it, playing it faster than I had ever heard it; he had obviously been put out of joint by No. 3. No. 5 was not very satisfactory either. We had heard less than half the take when Gilels said 'no' decisively and went back into the studio looking angry and frustrated.

We had five more goes at it, without getting it right. And then, he jumped up from the piano and disappeared out of sight. When I looked in through the window he was angrily pacing up and down in the far corner. I knew it was only a temporary hiatus in the proceedings but I was concerned. I went into the studio, not quite sure how he would receive me; he wheeled round, stomped up to me and, pointing a stubby finger at me, said 'You – my friend' and the next moment, to my surprise, I found myself enveloped in a bear hug. Some of the tenseness went out of him. 'Now,' he said, 'I play No. 5.' It was a much more disciplined perform-ance. 'Once more,' he said, and at the end of that take I told him I couldn't imagine it better played. With that smile which so changes his counte-nance he said, 'Now, I show you' – and proceeded to play it even better. He then returned to No. 3; in a few takes that was recorded, and finally No. 6. We had a difference of opinion about No. 3 – I felt that the penultimate take was the best but Gilels preferred the last take and I accepted his decision. Some weeks later, when we heard the edited tape, Gilels said he was not quite happy with No. 3 and asked to hear the tape I had liked. He now agreed with me that it was indeed more spontaneous, and it was inserted into the master tape. About No. 5 he said, 'When I heard the test lacquer I asked myself "Have you ever played it better?" and I had to say "No" – and "Will you ever play it better?" and again I had to say "No". Bravo Suvi!' I was somewhat taken aback and asked him why bravo to me. 'I think you know,' he replied, and I think I did. Gilels still considers this one of the best records he has ever made.

Later that day, in my flat, before we went out to dinner, he told my wife when I was out of the room, 'Your husband is *molto simpatico*.' He could not have said anything that would have given me more pleasure.

8   Enter Barenboim

On 19 September 1966, the day after the last Gilels session, a young pianist walked into Abbey Road's Studio No. 1 to make one record of piano sonatas by Beethoven. There were no fanfares to announce what a momentous occasion this was for the pianist himself, for EMI and for me. Daniel Barenboim was to make over one hundred records for the company in a little over ten years. He introduced many new, young, exciting musicians such as Itzhak Perlman and Pinchas Zukerman to our catalogue of artists and formed musical and other alliances with artists long established with us, such as Klemperer, Jacqueline du Pré, Janet Baker and Fischer-Dieskau. His recordings included piano music, chamber music, orchestral and choral music and operas. I produced all but five of them and he is now part of my family, as I am of his.

Barenboim was 23 in 1966 and looked even younger. He had made a few records for other companies but I had not heard them, nor had I heard him in person. I did know of his reputation as an immensely talented young man who even at this young age was celebrating the tenth anniversary of his first appearance on the London stage with a symphony orchestra. EMI had entered into a contract with him for the next few years and this was his first record.

In the studio Barenboim first tried out the piano – he played softly, he played loudly, some delicate lines of part-writing and some full-blooded, thunderous chords, he tried out trills at various registers and declared that though it was not a perfect instrument it would do. He then said that he would like to begin with the 'Pathétique'. While he rehearsed the engineer adjusted his microphones. We announced we were ready. I remember thinking as he started the recording that I wished that at least one unfamiliar work had been included; the other sonatas were to be the 'Moonlight' and the 'Appassionata'. By the time he had played four bars of the slow introduction to the first movement I had been jolted out of my slightly patronizing attitude towards the 'Pathétique'; Barenboim was playing it as if he had just discovered it, and I found myself hearing unexpectedly fresh things in it. I looked closer at my score. He was meticulously following Beethoven's markings, which even in this early work are as precise as in the *Diabelli* twenty-five years later; but there was much more to it than that. The first three bars each begin with a *fortepiano*

49

and the weight of sound for each was different – the third beat of the third bar is marked *sforzando* and the fourth bar begins with the same direction, and the degree of accenting was different for these too. I was struck also by his total command of tone colour – the *decrescendo* and *crescendo* in the fourth bar were completely controlled and the sound brightened as the music moved to the brighter key of E flat. As the movement unfolded I realized that Barenboim was something quite out of the ordinary.

The movement came to an end and he started on the slow movement. I had by now almost forgotten the score. The third movement followed. We listened to the take; there were a couple of passages in the outer movements which he wanted to tidy up. I suggested that he should play the second movement right through once again. He looked at me questioningly and I said that it sounded a little static at times, to which he replied, 'I think you mean self-indulgent.' We grinned at each other; the rapport between us was immediate and complete.

In another half an hour we had finished with the 'Pathétique' and he played the 'Moonlight', again the complete sonata. The range of tone colour in this work was even more noticeable – a hypnotic haze in the first movement, a crisp, delicate staccato in the middle movement and turbulent, surging power in the last. There was only that one take of the first two movements – some bits of the third required a second take, and then we adjourned for lunch. In two later sessions we recorded the 'Appassionata'. When the record had been completed, as he left the studio, he asked me, casually, 'Any reason why you should not do all my records?' I replied, 'None at all, Danny.' 'Well, that's fixed then,' and it was.

When I heard the edited tape of that first record I wondered how he would play some of the other sonatas – Op. 2 No. 2, the 'Waldstein', Op. 79, Op. 110, and as the opus numbers raced through my mind, the brainwave hit me – I would like to hear him play all the remaining twenty-nine and I believed that the record-buying public would too. A few days later in a hotel room in London, I asked him what he thought of the idea. He didn't hesitate. 'Nothing would give me greater pleasure.' At twenty-three Barenboim had lived with the Beethoven sonatas for at least fifteen years and, remembering his performance of the three we had already recorded, I glowed at the prospect before me. I still had to get approval for the scheme but there would be time enough to work out the best way of doing that. A woman journalist from a record magazine was due in a few moments to interview Barenboim, and he asked me to stay on. In the course of the interview the girl said that she knew he had made a record of Beethoven sonatas for EMI – might he make any more? Barenboim replied, 'Shouldn't you ask Mr Grubb that question?' She turned to me. I said, 'Yes, we hope to record the whole set.' I thought no more of the exchange until, a month later, the interview was published including a statement that, according to Mr Grubb, EMI planned to record Barenboim playing all thirty-two sonatas of Beethoven. All hell broke loose. What did I think I was playing at? my irate boss asked me. The last time we had actually recorded the complete set was with Schnabel, a mature artist in his middle fifties; another set from Gieseking had been left unfinished as he had died in the middle of the series – and here was I committing the company to do them with a youngster of twenty-three. The sales people were equally discouraging. It was all very well to sell the 'Moonlight', the 'Pathétique' and the 'Appassionata', but what about the less well-known sonatas such as those opus tens and opus fourteens. To all of them I kept repeating, patiently at first and then with increasing exasperation, 'Listen to the recording we've already made and then we can discuss it further.' When my boss finally did he was so impressed that he gave me the go-ahead for one more record. The rest is history.

The second record was of Op. 111 and 'Les Adieux', a 'name' sonata to counteract the supposed sales-killing effect of the last sonata, with Op. 49 No. 1 as a lightweight fill-up. (The title on the spine of the record sleeve reads: 'Sonata No. 26 "Les Adieux" etc'; there is no mention of Op. 111, one of the great masterpieces of piano literature!) Barenboim's recording of Op. 111 was even more economical than of the earlier sonatas; he played the first movement twice and then did three corrections; the second movement he played only once and did two short passages to be inserted into the complete take. I was amazed at the insight of one so young into this profound music; his concentration was so absolute that at the end of that slow movement he sat still at the piano for a few moments as if in a trance, and then seemed to shake himself out of it before jumping up and striding briskly into the control room. The second record was released soon after the first. There was no more resistance from anyone, for in a few months the sales of the two records was reckoned in tens of thousands; normally that happened only to records of popular orchestral pieces.

In the next two years Barenboim made four more records of the sonatas; we were specially pleased that the record which contained Op. 10 Nos. 1, 2 and 3, about which the salesmen had been so dismissive, sold over nine thousand in the year of its release. We decided to record the rest in 1969 so that the set would be ready for the bicentenary of Beethoven's birth in 1970. For this, Barenboim set apart seven days in July and it is a measure of the speed at which he works that in those seven days we recorded sixteen sonatas on six long-playing records. (He has since bettered this by recording five long-playing records of Mozart's sonatas in four days.) Every morning he worked on the sonatas he was due to record that day; the sessions started at half-past two and went on for as long as he felt like playing. Throughout the recording of the series Barenboim was full of joy at the pleasure of playing such great music. Sometimes on playbacks he would indulge in the pretence that we were listening to orchestral music – in the scherzo of Op. 2 No. 3, for example, as the main theme chased its tail in canon, with twiddles of his index finger he kept bringing in the strings, one after the other at each entry – big chords for the full orchestra were brought in by outstretched arms and in the trio the triplets were assigned to the woodwind while the supporting bass was played by the trombones and bassoons. In the last movement of Op. 2 No. 2, every time the arpeggio flourish which heralds the main theme recurred, he nudged me and said with mock severity, 'As I was saying when I was interrupted . . .' Musically the sessions were pure magic.

He seemed always to get to the heart of the music. For instance, in Op. 28, the Sonata in D, popularly known as the 'Pastoral', the drugged feeling of a hot summer afternoon in the first movement, stillness in the second, joyous abandon in the scherzo and, par excellence, the bucolic character of the last movement, which has, woven into it, the humour, the skittishness, the tenderness and above all the strength of Beethoven. In Op. 78 in F sharp – that short, enigmatic work which occupies a unique place in the canon – he played the seventh and eighth bars of the second movement, marked *piano*, so softly that I did not believe that the *pianissimo* of bar nine could be softer. It not only was, but the tone colour was different. I asked, 'How on earth did you manage to do that, Danny?' With a wave of his hand and a mischievous smile, he replied, 'That was a Barenboim de luxe'. It is a phrase which has gone into the private language that we share.

I had agreed when we began the set that Barenboim would be allowed to rerecord any work if he was later dissatisfied with its performance. In the event it was not necessary. As the last A major chord of Op. 101, the last sonata to be recorded, died away we both felt exhilarated, but also a little sad that there were no more Beethoven sonatas to record. Barenboim said he was pleased with the set – there were some minor things which he wished he had done a little differently, but on the whole he was satisfied to let it stand as his current reading of the Beethoven sonatas. In the years to come he is bound to record them again, but this set will be unique, for there is a vernal freshness about these performances which it would be difficult to reproduce. Beethoven himself, in the white heat of creation, might have played them like this – testing out a point here, drawing out a phrase there, delighting in the sudden flooding of a singing theme at another point, discovering an unexpected modulation to a new key, or lingering at a moment of exquisite tenderness and perhaps stopping to mark the score *molto cantabile e teneramente*.

While recording the Beethoven sonatas I continued to record Barenboim in other works and other artists and ensembles. My first orchestral record since the Schumann and Liszt concertos was also with Annie Fischer, this time playing Mozart's C minor and his last piano concertos,

With Walter Legge on a session. Gerald Moore, Elisabeth Schwarzkopf.

'It's a Schubert *minuet* – a gentler accent?' To Hans Richter-Haaser.

'Let it rip for this one, Lamar.' Gervase de Peyer, Lamar Crowson (centre). Beethoven Quintet for Piano and Wind.

'Is it easier to record this cello?' Jacqueline du Pré.

Holding forth to Otto Klemperer on Haydn's 95.

'Next, the sextet.' To the singers on stage. The Klemperer *Cosi*.

'Less clarinet – the violin sho[uld]
take over.' Schubert Octet: Me[los]
Ensemble. Standing: the bala[nce]
engineer; Ivor McMahon (viol[a];
Adrian Beers (double bass); Emman[uel]
Hurwitz (violin). Seated: Willi[am]
Waterhouse (bassoon); Terence W[eil]
(cello); Gervase de Peyer (clarin[et];
the producer; Cecil Aronowitz (vio[la];
Neill Sanders (hor[n).

Bartok Piano Concertos: Pierre Boulez,
Daniel Barenboim.

The Menuhin items for Gerald Moore's seventieth birthday record.

The only recordings I made of Indian music: Bismillah Khan and Vilayat Khan (seated), Shantaprasad (leaning over).

André Previn and the Yale Quartet: Brahms's Piano Quintet.

Beethoven Piano Trios, first time. Daniel Barenboim,
Pinchas Zukerman, Jacqueline du Pré.

'Only you get *that* sound from the strings.' To John Barbirolli.
Appalachia session.

'Look who's talking.' With John and Evelyn Barbirolli.

No. 1 Studio, Abbey Road: Jacqueline du Pré, London Symphony
Orchestra, John Barbirolli.

with the New Philharmonia Orchestra under Efrem Kurtz. Easy sessions these.

A couple of chamber music records with Yehudi Menuhin followed. The first was of the two Mozart piano quartets with Fou Ts'ong at the piano, Walter Gerhardt, viola and Gaspar Cassadó, cello. Menuhin was the first major musician I had ever met – in India in 1950. The concert he gave at the Museum Theatre in Madras was broadcast and I was the announcer. After the concert he autographed the first record of Bach's D minor Partita, a disc I still possess. Now, sixteen years later, I was to produce a record by him – I felt like pinching myself to be sure that it was not all an extended dream.

The G minor has always been for me one of the most disturbing of Mozart's works. I have never found a satisfactory explanation as to why certain melodies and themes, which after all are only juxtapositions of notes rising or falling in pitch and varied in rhythm, can touch one's inmost being – why the opening theme of this G minor quartet seems to tear at one's heart. To analyse its structure doesn't take one very far – a drop of a fourth from the key note of G, a rise of a semitone and then a fall back, why should all this, in a particular rhythm, mean so much? Is it purely subjective? If so, why do some themes and works have an almost universal appeal? Why is everyone who knows it so moved by the Schubert string quintet? Why is the second theme of the first movement, in which the two cellos twine almost amorously together amidst changing harmonies, so heart-breaking? Perhaps there are no general answers to these questions, though I shall presently state mine.

We started with the G minor, having first to solve the usual problem of balancing the piano against a body of strings. The piano, even by itself, is probably the most difficult instrument to balance over a microphone. The basic problem arises from the fact that the energy content of a note when it is struck is enormous at the moment of impact – an instant later, even if the note is sustained, with the key held down and the dampers raised by the pedal, its energy content is a minute fraction of that at the time of impact. You have to ensure that the initial impact is not too violent for microphones to accept, and the subsequent die-away not too feeble – it is the proportion between the two which is the vital element in producing an acceptable piano sound.

Fairly early in the history of recording, the pioneers of the business arrived at a solution which is still valid today – it was to give the piano on records the presence and immediacy it would have in the sitting room of one's house. We are all so accustomed to this that we forget how artificial it is, for the sound of a piano reproduced on a gramophone can completely fill a sitting room in a way in which no piano, or pianist, can fill any full-size concert hall. Conversely, no one would accept, on a record, the sound of a piano as heard anywhere beyond the tenth row of the stalls.

The difficulties of balance are greatly magnified when the piano is joined by other instruments. Chamber music players like to work in close proximity, first so as to keep together, but more importantly, to be able to play to and respond to each other's nuances of phrasing. If you seat them in an intimate grouping around the piano, inevitably the piano's sound will spill over into the microphones of all the other instruments – if you try to give greater weight to any of the other instruments by increasing the output of its microphone the piano's spill-over also is increased, and that is usually not a clean sound. In concert halls there is an increasing tendency to open the lid of the piano only partially – to use the short stick, or a coat hanger (I have seen this done) or, as in one extreme case, a matchbox stood on end. I have always been opposed to this in the recording studio, for though it does decrease the amount of sound from the piano it also makes it wooden and muffled. (More of this anon!) It has to be left ultimately to the skill of the pianist not to swamp his colleagues; we assist him by angling microphones so that the spill-over is minimized.

When on this session we had obtained a reasonable sound, I asked the group to play two passages – first a bit of the development section of the last movement in which the piano and the strings play antiphonally, to see that both had equal weight, and then the coda of the first movement to test the balance between the two groups. In any work, there are key passages which provide the touchstone by which you can determine whether you have a good recorded sound.

The second record was of Brahms trios with Menuhin, his sister Hephzibah at the piano and Maurice Gendron on the cello. Our last sessions, of the Trio in C minor Op. 87, were scheduled for the morning and afternoon of Saturday, 30 July 1966. Things went so well that it began to look as if we might not need the afternoon session. Menuhin did not know why, when this possibility arose, Gendron and I started pressing to get the work done in the morning. Halfway through a playback Gendron said, 'Come on, Yehudi, let's do it again – we know what the rest of it is like,' and rushed him back into the studio. When Menuhin asked me at one point whether they should not listen to what they had just recorded, I said no – I would tell them exactly which passages needed to be repeated.

Finally, at half past one, we finished. Gendron and I heaved a sigh of relief for, at three o'clock, England was due to meet West Germany in the World Cup Final at Wembley and we hoped to watch it together in my flat, on television. Menuhin had gone out of the studio and we congratulated ourselves on having manoeuvred things so well. At this point Menuhin returned and brightly announced to me, 'Since Op. 87 is finished, I've asked for your colleague to come along this afternoon so that we can start the next record.' The look of anguish on Gendron's face was indescribable. When Menuhin had gone out of the room I suggested that he tell him that he wanted the afternoon off, and why. 'No, no,' he wailed. 'How can you ask Yehudi to give up a Schubert trio for a football match?' I said I thought he did Menuhin less than justice and that I was sure he would understand, but Gendron did not even try. I left him looking dejectedly at me through the glass window of the studio.

9   The Ideal Listener

I have at times asked myself about my job: what was my aim in making a record? Was it to be literally a record of a performance including some warts, or so refined, with all the imperfections weeded out, that it bore no relation to any performance? Which should I choose of two takes, a more musical one but with the odd smudge or not-togetherness, or another technically immaculate but lacking fire and spirit? And what anyway is 'musical' in this context? I could not define it, but I never have any doubt when an artist asks me to listen to other takes of a passage and use the most musical of them. What should be the sound to aim for on a record – that which one would hear in an ideal concert hall? Apart from the fact that there is no such hall, all recording involves some degree of reduction of the original sound to make it suitable for reproduction in domestic surroundings, and once you embark on that process there cannot be any fidelity to the original – the amount of reduction has to be selective. If, say, in the climaxes of the first movement of Walton's First Symphony you took down all the instruments equally you would hear nothing but brass chords and timpani, for the strings and the woodwind would be blanketed.

Once this premise is accepted, the question following immediately is, how much detail to balance for; on a record you can hear more of the inner parts than in a concert and you can make an important line ride effortlessly over accompaniment which would normally drown it. Furthermore, the producer, in consultation with the conductor, has also to decide how much detail the composer might have wanted you to hear. For example, in Dorabella's aria 'E amore un ladroncello' in *Così fan tutte*, while the first clarinet sedately follows the vocal line the second clarinet is given a deliciously agitated, comic 'oodle-oodle' part – Mozart must have meant this to be heard but not too prominently. However, when a second clarinet can play it with precision and panache, there is a temptation, which I myself have not always avoided, to overemphasize the subordinate role.

On the other hand there are some details which must be heard. In the first movement of Beethoven's Eighth Symphony the recapitulation begins with the main theme being carried by cellos and bassoons in their lower register while all the other instruments play fortissimo above them – the theme must come through but cannot unless the conductor fiddles with Beethoven's orchestration or, in a recording, the cellos and bassoons are specially miked and helped at this point. (At a Klemperer concert I could hardly credit it when this theme cut cleanly through the accompaniment; and then I saw that he had made the horns play with the cellos. When I went back stage after the concert and asked him, 'What is all this, doctor, Beethoven arr. Klemperer?' he laughed and replied, 'I am glad to note you were awake during the concert.')

Over the years I had evolved a kind of working philosophy about my job. I had, though, never consciously, tried to define the relationship between an artist and his producer. I had once to pronounce on this at short notice. It was another session with Menuhin, his sister and Gendron. When the morning session ended, Menuhin asked me if he could bring two visitors to the afternoon session, and I said of course he could. I was in the control room getting ready for the session when Menuhin escorted in two ladies. I took one look at the leading one and cast about in my mind to find the right form of address for a Royal Duchess – it was Princess Marina with her lady-in-waiting. Menuhin introduced us to Her Royal Highness. 'It is very kind of you to let us come to your recording, Mr Grubb,' she said. For the first part of the session she sat in the studio and then asked if she could sit with us in the control room. I said certainly, and she sat unobtrusively on one side intently watching everything that was happening.

During the break, halfway through a cup of tea (chipped saucer, I noted, and decided to wring somebody's neck when the Duchess had gone) she turned to me and said, 'Mr Grubb, I am glad to have been able to watch a recording. I would like to ask you something. What Mr Menuhin, Miss Menuhin and Mr Gendron are doing in the studio is obvious. I think I understand what functions these other gentlemen in this room perform. I can see that you are in charge of the entire operation. I also observed that the musicians seem to depend heavily on you. Why? What is this special relationship you seem to have with them?' I had to think fast. There were the obvious factors of sympathy, a fellow-feeling each for the difficulties of the other's job and a joint love of the music. The artist has to have complete faith in the musical sensibility of the producer and in his judgment – and the producer must have confidence in the artist. What Princess Marina wanted to know was about the factor which lay beyond. I had no time to think, but I knew the answer. 'When Yehudi Menuhin plays in the studio he is not playing to the inanimate microphone in front of him. His playing is addressed to an ideal listener capable of responding musically and emotionally to his performance – on this occasion I am that ideal, and perhaps idealized, listener.' It is a statement that I have not found necessary to alter or adapt even after I have thought it over in depth. The Duchess found it reasonable, and when she had left, Menuhin said he did too.

All this while, as a legacy from *Zauberflöte*, I had been producing records

57

of Klemperer in tandem with the colleague who had been in formal charge of that production. The major Klemperer recordings done under this system were Beethoven's Missa Solemnis, Mozart's *Don Giovanni* and Mahler's *Das Lied von der Erde*.

Klemperer was in the middle of recording Haydn's 'Oxford' symphony when I presented him with the schedule for the recording of the Beethoven mass. One would expect, once the artists, the conductor and the orchestra are available to record during a certain period, a studio found, an engineer engaged and a producer allocated, that the drawing up of a recording schedule would be a formality. Not a bit of it – this is where your problems begin. All manner of improbable circumstances have to be taken into account and when you have finally drawn up what looks like a reasonable schedule, you come up against Klemperer. He took the Missa schedule back to his hotel. On the next day's session I wished him good morning when he arrived. He replied 'Good morning' and, holding up the schedule, said in tragic tones 'I have great sorrow.' I tried to recollect the details of the schedule and wondered what I had done wrong. I could not have left out a chunk of the 'Gloria', or not included the repeat of the 'Osanna' for my system of drawing up a schedule for a major work is, as Legge used to say, 'damn-fool proof'. I asked Klemperer what was wrong. He said, 'You have put down the recording of "et resurrexit" before the recording of "et sepultus est". this cannot be – you cannot "resurrexit" before you "sepultus est". I have great sorrow.'

There was an excellent reason for my scheduling the passage relating to the resurrection before that dealing with the passion and the death. For a long stretch up to 'et sepultus est' Beethoven employs both soloists and chorus. From 'et resurrexit' there are 250 bars in which only the chorus sings. I had drawn up the schedule to allow most of the choral sections to be recorded before the soloists arrived. Soloists like to have their recording periods kept as short as possible – besides, soloists cost money, in the form of hotel and subsistence allowances, while hanging around to sing just a few bars in a session. I tried to explain all this to Klemperer but he was adamant. He would, though reluctantly, agree, in the 'Gloria', to start at the beginning, jump from 'gratias agimus', where the soloists first enter, to 'Quoniam', which again is just choral, and go on to the great final fugue, 'In gloria Dei patris'. But 'You cannot "resurrexit" before you "sepultus est". I have great sorrow.' I sympathized with Klemperer. The basis of his music making was the building of a long architectural structure and it was unreasonable to ask him to start at one of the climactic points of the 'Credo' without the impetus of what had gone before. I had to rearrange the schedule.

Since he had got his way with the Missa Solemnis, I knew there would be trouble when I sent him, to his home in Zürich, the schedule for *Don Giovanni*. Two days later I had a telephone call from his daughter, 'About that recording schedule for *Don Giovanni*, my father. . .' she began, and I cut in, 'Yes – I know, he has great sorrow.' She burst out laughing and I could hear an angry roar in the background, 'It is no laughing matter – give me the telephone'. He simply said, 'Come to Zürich – we shall talk about it.' I went and we had a fearful three hours on the schedule. 'What is the problem?' he asked. 'We start with the overture – go to number one and then number two and so, till we come to the finale of Act II. All the singers should be there from the beginning to the end.' I said, 'Doctor, while we are recording the scenes between Leporello, Anna, the Don, the Commendatore and Elvira, what is Zerlina going to do?' He said, 'Go for a walk in Hyde Park.' Our Zerlina was Mirella Freni, and knowing what the weather in London is usually like, if I'd made the suggestion she would probably have instantly pulled out of the recording. In the end we each made concessions.

Over a sherry Klemperer learnt that my wife, whose birthday it would be the next day, was in Zürich with me. He invited us both to lunch and took us to a splendid restaurant which not only served excellent food but was a miniature art gallery – there were original Renoirs, Manets, Monets and the other Impressionists hung on the walls. Klemperer was a charming and entertaining host. While he confined himself to a modest hamburger, he recommended to us a saddle of venison which was all that he said it would be. At the end of the afternoon, swaying alarmingly, he insisted on helping my wife on with her coat, while his daughter and I hovered anxiously on either side of him. It was the first of many experiences I was to have of unexpected aspects of Klemperer. As he got into the taxi, he asked casually what we were doing that night to celebrate. 'We are going to Zürich Opera,' I said. He stopped dead in his tracks, looked at us with great concern and said earnestly, 'Don't. Have you seen *Mary Poppins*? No? Go and see it instead – it's much better.' On his next visit to London, he saw me waiting to welcome him as he came through the customs at Heathrow and waved; when he came within earshot, without any preliminaries, he asked 'Have you seen *Mary Poppins* yet?'

In between Klemperer sessions, we produced an electric *Carmina Burana* with Frühbeck de Burgos and the enchanting Lucia Popp and the third of the great Boult recordings of Holst's *Planets*. The work easily lends itself to spectacular recording, for it uses instruments and sounds imaginatively, but, above all, the scoring is clean-textured. There are composers who are masters of orchestration and who have an instinctive feel for the right combination of instruments to produce the effects they want – everything is in proportion in their scores, so that even when they use all instruments of a large orchestra the sound is clear, weighty but never congested. Mahler, for example – it would take a team of real duffers to make him sound turgid. On the other hand, for performers and recording staff, composers like Tchaikovsky and Dvořák are extremely difficult to balance – they allot a melody or a line to four or five separate groups of instruments at three or more octaves apart, frequently with a fast tremolo accompaniment in the strings, all of which makes for denseness. Only the very skilful conductors, and Boult was one of the most expert of them all, solve the problems posed by such scores.

On one of these sessions, during the break, we were all having tea or coffee, some eating biscuits and one of the junior engineers a large bun. Boult had refused everything I had offered him. A few minutes later, still feeling uncomfortable, I repeated my offer. He said, 'It seems to be bothering you that I am not drinking anything – to please you, may I please have a cup of hot water?' Concealing my surprise I sent for the hot water and Boult sat contentedly sipping it. He must have caught me surreptitiously eyeing him, for after a few minutes he said, 'Something is still worrying you. Well, I'll have a few drops of milk in my hot water if that will make you happier.' This was done, and for the rest of the break I carefully averted my eyes from the extraordinary-looking liquid in his cup.

At the end of the last movement, 'Uranus', Holst asks for the women's chorus to gradually die away to nothingness, as if the music were moving off into the interstellar spaces. Three times we tried it but each time one soprano voice kept coming through all too clearly when all the others had died away – I knew whose it was, having noticed this unusually penetrating voice at the rehearsal before the session. As everyone got more and more irritated I said to Boult, 'Let me deal with it, Sir Adrian.' 'My dear chap, I had better come up with you' (the chorus was in the gallery) 'in case there are ructions.' We went up together and I said to the chorus that their dying away at the end didn't sound right. 'I think there are too many of you – at bar so-and-so, you, you, you and you' – and I pointed to four of the sopranos among whom was the one with the offending voice – 'stop singing, hum for the next two bars and then stop altogether.' We tried it that way and of course it worked perfectly. Boult's parting comment to me was, 'You would have a wonderful career in the diplomatic service – if ever you decide to apply, let me know – I shall give you a splendid reference.'

10   The Recording Studio

The major body of work originally envisaged for Barenboim was a complete set of the Mozart piano concertos, with him playing the dual role of soloist and conductor. The art of accompanying a soloist in a concerto requires special skills; above all, it demands the capacity to subordinate one's own ideas of a work to that of another person. The perfect solution, of course, is for the soloist himself to conduct and play, but this requires that the soloist has to be a fully trained conductor. Barenboim maintains that only when one has the capacity to conduct a Mozart symphony does one have the right to accompany oneself in a Mozart concerto. He himself had studied conducting nearly as long as he had studied the piano and had many years' experience of playing and conducting Mozart.

The orchestra was to be the English Chamber Orchestra, one of the best of its kind in the world. It had individuality and character. Several were soloists of distinction and some of them were members of chamber music groups such as the Melos Ensemble. Barenboim had worked extensively with the ECO and there was a special bond between them. Everything looked set fair for a notable set of records.

The first record of Mozart concertos was scheduled to begin at 2.30 on New Year's Day, 1967; the works were two of the best known in the canon, in D minor K466 and in A major K488. The previous evening we were all at a party at Fou Ts'ong's to see the new year in – the 'we' included Jacqueline du Pré. Barenboim and she had met a few weeks earlier; each had suffered a bout of glandular fever and when friends mentioned du Pré's illness to Barenboim he was intrigued enough to ring her and arrange for them to meet. They were instantly taken with each other and by December 1966 were constant companions.

Whenever Barenboim is around there is, sooner or later, bound to be music making. On this night he asked du Pré what she would like to play and she said, the Beethoven A major sonata. They settled down and du Pré played the soaring opening theme with superb control and the delicious slide from the first to the second note of it, very special to her, and turned to Barenboim as if to say, 'Match that if you can.' Barenboim responded to the challenge and we had wonderful music making for the next three hours.

This was the first time I had heard du Pré in person, though I knew from her records what an exceptional player she was. As she played that first phrase I turned to a colleague sitting next to me and said, 'That sound has not yet been fully captured on records – bags I her next recording.' When my wife and I left the party at about three in the morning, Barenboim was still going great guns. He was so obviously enjoying himself that I didn't have the heart to remind him that in less than twelve hours' time he was due to start a new and very important series of records.

I can hardly sit still for excitement at the beginning of any session: it would not, in any case, be possible to sit still in the midst of all the bustle and the constant to-ing and fro-ing of the engineers in the control room. There are two sets of them involved in a recording – and all of them, from about half an hour before a session is due to begin, will seem to be dashing madly around, but actually, methodically preparing for the session.

The balance engineer is the person responsible for the sound in association with the producer. Some of our balance engineers are themselves trained musicians, and those who are not have long experience of music, and so consultation between them and the producer consists usually of two or three brief phrases such as 'A lush, treacly sound, I think' for, say, Rachmaninov's Second Symphony or 'Clear and brilliant and not too mushy?' perhaps for Stravinsky's *Petrushka*. The microphones would have been set up earlier; now the balance engineer makes the final adjustments to their heights and the angles at which they incline towards sections of the orchestra. He then checks how much sound is coming over each channel and adjusts his controls till he has plenty of reserves of volume from each – as he moves his levers up and down, one moment you hear the horn blaring in unnatural close-up, the next you might, as I did on one occasion, hear one of the violinists telling her neighbour, 'In our house we do it with onions.'

Meanwhile the second engineer, who operates the tape machines and keeps a log of the takes, puts a reel of tape on each of the two machines; all recordings are done in duplicate for it would be ruinously expensive to have to reassemble an orchestra, and perhaps a cast of singers, because a tape machine had developed a stutter. In addition to his other duties the second engineer is a general dogsbody and cheerful purveyor of tea, coffee, cigarettes to artists who have forgotten to bring their own, and the latest gossip.

The electrical engineers enter trailing yards of cable and armed with screw drivers with peculiarly shaped heads. They are responsible for maintaining all the recording equipment in the studios and ensuring that everything is functioning to its peak capacity. They introduce a new set of sounds into the control room, the pure tones at various frequencies with which they check tapes and tape machines, muttering the while, 'One kilocycle, left hand is a little high – come down a wee bit – just a gnat's whisker' (a favourite phrase of theirs) 'five kc's looks okay. Bass – well, that's as near as possible right. Phase, beautiful, couldn't be better. There you are, it's all yours.' Gradually the tempo of activity increases, and just as you start to wonder how any organized operation could possibly commence in two minutes' time, everything dies down. The balance engineer sits at his desk and fades in the microphones and the sound which ever sets my pulse racing comes over – that of an orchestra tuning up.

As the orchestra rehearses, the balance engineer alters the relative proportions of the sounds from his various microphones; as he experiments with various combinations he and the producer have a running dialogue: 'Is that hard sound of the violins you or them?' 'Have a heart, how can you expect them to play like Heifetzes at ten o'clock in the morning – give them time.' 'I'm hearing too much of the front desks. Can you get more of the main body of them? Ah! that's much better. Why are the basses galumphing around like a herd of hippopotamuses – or is it hippopotami? Will somebody please go into the studio and strangle that – hello, he seems to have died a natural death.' 'I've faded him out.' 'Good – lovely, lovely, keep that basic balance. Perhaps a whiff more of violas and cellos? Yes – yes – breathe on the horns' (a bit of EMI jargon coined by me to ask the balance engineer for a fraction more of something). 'Right – there you are – I think that's it. Are *you* pleased?' 'Yes – and now having done my bit I propose catching up on my sleep over the next two days. Over to you.' To the studio: 'We are ready to do a little test,' and to the balance engineer, 'Otherwise known as a testicle.'

On this session, in addition to the tension engendered by the beginning of a new project, we were all conscious that this was an extremely important series for Barenboim and for the company. Mozart piano concertos are not exactly an under-recorded body of work, and we faced formidable competition, but I had heard Barenboim play many of them and knew we had the beating of any rival recordings. The works had always been favourites and I looked forward to the delights the series would bring.

Barenboim arrived for the session a quarter of an hour early, looking bright and fresh. I said it had been a marvellous evening and he replied, 'Isn't she incredible?', referring to du Pré. We decided to begin with the D minor. It is one of the most unexpected of Mozart's works, an angry, violent explosion which threatens to burst the form of the concerto. Mozart seems almost to catapult himself into the middle of the next century and the heart of the romantic movement. From the opening figure all is turmoil and unrest – the calm of the placid Romanze (the title is significant) is suddenly shattered by a wild outburst in G minor, and the last movement too is full of agitation – only in the coda of this last movement does Mozart suddenly appear to remember that this is a piano concerto and, modulating abruptly into D major, he ends the work with a cheerful exchange of pleasantries between the piano and the orchestra. The miracle of the work is that, despite its turbulence and violence, the music itself is euphonious; Mozart's good taste does not allow him to produce harshness or ugly sonorities.

For this concerto I had asked for a sombre, slightly distanced sound to match the music; my specific requirement was that the surging opening theme on the cellos and basses under the restless syncopated figure on the other strings should not be heard as separate notes but as a menacing growl – with, in a phrase coined by me, 'no daylight between the notes'. We recorded a section of the opening *tutti* and one quiet and one loud passage for the piano and orchestra; Barenboim said he was satisfied, the balance engineer announced 'take one' and the series was under way. Each movement was recorded complete – the first, three times, the second twice and the third twice – there were two corrections each in the first and last movements. To the great surprise of the orchestra, this, one of the most difficult of the Mozart concertos, was completed by the half-way mark on the second session. Martin Gatt, the first bassoon's, reaction was, 'I feel a fraud, accepting money for doing something which gives me such great pleasure. I have never before found recording such fun and appear to be so ridiculously easy.'

When he had heard the last take of the D minor, Barenboim said 'The A major now'. I asked for a few moments to alter the balance slightly. He raised his eyebrows; we had a good sound, why was it necessary to change? I explained that K488, being a very different kind of work from K466, required a different sound. It is a sunny, cheerfully orchestrated work, needing a clear, bright sound, as against the distant effect we had obtained for the D minor. Barenboim said, 'There's obviously more to recording than I thought.'

That was the first record – the last record, of the early four, K37, 39, 40 and 41, was done in June 1974, seven and a half years later. The range of these works, the variety and wealth of musical invention in them, is astonishing. Nearly always we finished each concerto well within the time allotted, for in this period Barenboim and the orchestra were regularly playing these works in concerts; for instance, the C minor, K491, a work of which Beethoven said to one of his pupils. 'Ah, Ries, we shall never equal *that*', was recorded the day after they returned from a week's tour of Europe during which they played it five times – they gave a concerted groan when, as a joke, I welcomed them back from a week's holiday on the continent!

On these sessions we always had standby music to record (this is now forbidden, the only result of which has been the loss to orchestras of extra sessions to complete works already begun). In time filched from Mozart piano concertos we recorded such varied pieces as Dvořák's *Serenade for Strings* (Barenboim announcing joyously to the orchestra as they replaced

Mozart with Dvořák, 'We can now slide around like hell'), Schönberg's *Verklärte Nacht*, Wagner's *Siegfried Idyll* and a record of popular Mozart pieces including *Eine Kleine Nachtmusik*. This record still needed a substantial item to complete it when we finished a concerto, K175, early on 12 March -- we had another session booked for it on the 14th, and on the evening of the 13th Barenboim and I each leafed through a volume of Mozart divertimentos. I handed him my volume open at K205 -- he glanced quickly through it and said, 'Right, we'll do it tomorrow.' The next day he knew it nearly by heart -- the parts were all meticulously and exactly marked and he had made up his mind about one or two difficult phrasings and had corrected a few wrong notes. Amazingly, this twenty-minute piece too was completed ahead of time, and Barenboim whispered to the orchestra, 'We all deserve half an hour off. Go quickly away, before Suvi produces a march or something else to record' -- as he had unsuspectingly leaned forward towards the string microphone, the remark came through loud and clear into the control room.

The only works by Mozart for keyboard and orchestra we could not record were those for more than one piano. Barenboim had always insisted that Ashkenazy should be the other pianist for the two-piano concerto and one of the others for the concerto for three pianos. We came up against the old problem -- Ashkenazy was under contract to another company. We tried strenuously to get him released, but no -- short-sightedly, for they earned a great deal of ill-will from all concerned -- the company would not release him. Then a concert was arranged at which, with Fou Ts'ong as the third pianist, Barenboim and Ashkenazy were to play the two concertos, and now Barenboim pleaded with us to release him to record them for the other company. After some consideration, at my insistence our company agreed, for to use Barenboim's exclusivity clause to prevent him from making this record would have been sheer dog in the manger.

Less than four months after that New Year's Eve party a day I had been eagerly anticipating arrived; Jacqueline du Pré walked into Studio 1 to record Haydn's C major and Boccherini's B minor cello concertos. Her accompanist was Barenboim, with the English Chamber Orchestra.

We set about getting the right sound for the cello. We sat her in front of the orchestra as she would have at a concert. That did not work. We then turned her around to face the orchestra, then sideways, facing the conductor, and finally set her plumb in the centre with the orchestra in a loose horseshoe around her. A special difficulty in balancing the cello is that alone among solo instruments (apart, of course, from the piano) it is played sitting down -- it is on a level with the orchestra and there are instruments in the orchestra with much greater power, not to mention the groups of orchestral strings each of which outnumbers the soloist by at least five to one. To counteract this we placed her on a rostrum about nine inches high. When we had finally moved her to the correct position, wondering whether her proximity would cramp the conductor's movements I asked him whether she was too close. Barenboim's reply was a crisp 'She can't ever be too close for me.' We worked fast, for du Pré was in good form and the pieces lay at her finger tips.

When we reassembled after lunch I noticed that the cello sounded different. I asked the engineer whether he had changed anything – he had not. When the first take began I knew something was wrong – the vibrant sound of the cello had gone; what came over was uncharacteristic of du Pré. I stopped the players and asked the engineer to check his solo mike. There was nothing wrong with it. I asked them to start again, but it was no use. Barenboim wanted to know what the problem was. I went into the studio and asked du Pré whether she had moved her chair. No. Or changed her cello. Again no. Even whether she had changed any item of her clothing. We changed her microphone anyway – that didn't work either. For about half an hour we tried everything; nothing worked. We were all sitting despondently in the control room and Barenboim asked, 'What next?' I turned once again to du Pré and asked her was she sure that nothing had changed. She started to say no, and then her face went pink. Looking abashed, she replied, 'Oh, I'm using a different bow this afternoon.' As relief flooded through me I said reproachfully to her, 'Jacquie, don't ever frighten me like that again.' Barenboim burst out, 'How can anyone be . . .' and then, looking at her face, relented and said, 'Come on, let's start again – with the old bow.'

There were two more du Pré records in 1967 – the first was of the Brahms cello sonatas with Barenboim (they were now married). They are marvellous works but the two instruments are incompatible. The cello's entire register lies within the compass of the weightiest and most sonorous section of the modern piano – when both instruments are required to play forte the cello cannot be heard unless the pianist allows it to come through. I have heard the Brahms sonatas often and usually for long passages have not heard the cello, though I could see the player sawing away desperately. The exception was when these two were playing. Barenboim never allows the cello to get submerged. It is an extraordinary feat when you consider the gyrations of the cello in, for example, the fugue of the E minor sonata. There is an eager spontaneity about these performances, for du Pré and Barenboim were still in the process of discovering each other and it is reflected in their playing.

In between session with du Pré, Barenboim recorded the two Brahms clarinet sonatas with Gervase de Peyer. When they arrived at the studio for the first session, I asked them whether they had rehearsed the works, which are full of musical and technical difficulties. They both replied airily, 'Oh, we've talked about them on the telephone.' I looked reproachfully at them and settled down to a long, tough grind. We began with the E flat – at the end of the first take of the first movement I asked in disbelief, had they really not rehearsed the piece – they played it as if they had spent half their lives performing it together.

When they went back into the studio, over the loudspeakers we heard de Peyer say 'Danny', Barenboim reply 'Yes, Gervase', and then what sounded like a long drawn out, wet kiss. I said to them on the talk-back, 'If I didn't know that you were both happily married I would begin to suspect all sorts of things'. De Peyer had moistened the clarinet's reed and sucked in air through it to make it more pliant, and that had produced the extraordinary sound we had heard.

Barenboim's output in that year was prodigious – he made altogether eighteen records. They encompassed piano sonatas by Beethoven and Mozart, piano concertos by Mozart, Beethoven, Brahms and Bartók, wind and string concertos by Haydn, Mozart and Boccherini, the Brahms cello and clarinet sonatas, symphonies by Mozart and orchestral works by Wagner and Schönberg. It was a year of intense activity. Record making was only a small part of it; the major part was taken up by concerts. It was in this year that he made his debut as a major orchestral conductor at the Royal Festival Hall. He took over, at short notice, a concert by the New Philharmonia Orchestra which included Mozart's 'Prague' symphony and his Requiem Mass. At the break, during the first rehearsal, Hugh Bean asked me, 'Where on earth did you get this young man?' I said that he had made some piano records for us and that he had embarked on a series of the Mozart concertos as soloist and conductor. Bean was forthright. 'He's wasting his time playing the piano – he is a born conductor with the gift of communication that only the great ones have.' That concert was one of the most memorable that I have ever attended.

There were two records of piano concertos with the New Philharmonia Orchestra. The first was of Bartók's Nos. 1 and 3, the conductor Pierre Boulez. It was very rewarding to work with Boulez, a major composer and a front-rank conductor. I called on him at his hotel to discuss the recording and saw a score of *Tristan* on the table. I turned over the pages while I was waiting for him; oddly there was not a single mark on them, no blue pencils marking horn entries or red pencils picking out dynamics. I knew that Boulez was shortly going to conduct the work at Bayreuth and so when he came in I asked was this his study score. He replied it was; pointing to his head, he said, 'The markings are all here, and they are also in the score. There is no need to underline what Wagner has already put there.'

Boulez spent the first part of each session rehearsing the orchestra while Barenboim waited; and then he took great pains over the tuning of the various sections of the orchestra – first the groups of strings, then each section of the woodwinds and the horns and then the brass and the timpani. An orchestra would normally have not taken kindly to this, but they accepted that Boulez was someone special. I confessed to him at one point that I found very modern music a tough proposition. He replied, 'Don't forget that "modern" music has been that all through the ages. Remember the voice heard shouting at the first performance of the *Eroica*, "I'll give another kreutzer if this would only stop!" '

The other record was of Brahms's first piano concerto with Sir John Barbirolli conducting. Barbirolli was an exuberant person – enthusiasm came bubbling out of him. It was infectious – you could not help being carried along by the swell of his excitement. I found him irresistible and he responded with a friendship which continued to deepen in the three years left of his life. The work itself, a monumental, fierce, dramatic piece, suited both soloist and conductor down to the ground and we made short work of it. I have often regretted that Brahms abandoned the path he treads in this concerto.

While we were wrestling with the concerto, England were playing Pakistan at the Oval in the final Test, and I discovered Barbirolli shared my fanatical interest in cricket. Every spare moment, he closeted himself in the green room, a transistor radio clutched to his ear. At the end of the interval between sessions I had to almost drag him away from the television set in my flat, where he would have happily spent the whole afternoon watching the cricket. Barbirolli had been for years a name on a record label, as accompanist to Kreisler and Rubinstein; I relished the fact that, on meeting him for the first time, we were enthusing, not about Beethoven or Tchaikovsky but about a thrilling innings by a new Pakistan batsman called Asif Iqbal.

On the concert platform and in the recording studio Barbirolli very often got carried away and would audibly encourage his players to greater efforts; at other times he would join in in a beautiful passage, singing or humming, sotto voce and slightly out of tune. In the Brahms D minor Concerto, after the initial drum roll, you can hear a growl from him, urging the strings on just before their menacing tremolo figure. A few months later he accompanied du Pré in the Haydn D major and Monn concertos. He had a special affection for du Pré, having been himself a cellist. He also could not resist joining her, and kept happily humming and singing under his breath. On one playback I leaned over and said to him, 'You are in good voice this afternoon, Sir John'. He looked at me blankly and I don't think he knew what I was talking about. Later Lady Barbirolli, who had dropped in, suddenly said to him, 'Darling, you are singing quite audibly with Jacquie.' Barbirolli looked at his score and snorted, 'Nonsense, darling, Jacquie's playing high on the A string – and that's not within my range.' Indeed it was not – he was singing two octaves lower. At a later playback, it suddenly registered with him that someone was singing and he asked brusquely, 'Who is that?' We started to laugh, and only then did it dawn on him that it was himself. He looked at me, slightly shamefaced, and asked, 'Does that bother you?' I said, 'Sir John, I'll start bothering when you stop singing at a beautiful moment,' a reply which pleased him greatly.

11   Gerald Moore Farewell Concert

The idea of the Gerald Moore farewell concert was born out of a casual conversation in Berlin in April 1966. Schwarzkopf and Moore were recording the women's songs from Hugo Wolf's *Italienisches Liederbuch*. Legge was the producer and again I sat in on the sessions. During a playback, Schwarzkopf asked Moore what dates he had free during the 1967–8 season, and whether he could do a concert tour of America with her. Moore said that he would probably have retired by then, adding that he wanted to go while in full possession of his powers. Schwarzkopf intervened with 'Gerald, please can your last concert be with me?' Moore said, 'Elisabeth, both Victoria and Dieter too have asked the same thing – I really don't know what to say.' Schwarzkopf looked disconsolate. Legge suddenly sat up. 'I know the solution – let it be a joint farewell concert with all three of you.' It was an excellent idea, but I do not think that anyone really believed that such a concert would take place.

When the Royal Festival Hall's programme for February 1967 came out, on the 20th was announced a concert in homage to Gerald Moore. It was to mark the occasion of his last public concert appearance in England, and the singers – Victoria de los Angeles, Elisabeth Schwarzkopf and Dietrich Fischer-Dieskau. It would be a memorable event and we decided to record it, and I suspect largely because I was the only person then in EMI with whom Legge was on speaking terms, the job was assigned to me. There were various suggestions made about an extra session in the hall for corrections but I was firmly opposed to them. The recording was to be unique and no artist, however experienced, was going to match in an empty hall the intensity of a performance before a packed and emotional audience; besides, the idea of an *ersatz* farewell concert touched my professional pride.

There was a brief rehearsal on the morning of the concert. Moore arrived first and the three singers came one after the other. I was unhappy to see that the piano lid was to be open only slightly, on a very short stick, and no amount of argument would persuade Legge or the singers to agree to open it fully. I wanted to capture the full range of Moore's playing and I knew that a less than half open lid would make the task that much more difficult.

Legge would not agree to any microphone being placed where it might stand between any member of the audience and any of the artists. We were forced to depend solely on the three microphones suspended from the ceiling and even those, Legge insisted, should not obstruct any view from the Grand Tier. It was an extraordinary stand by someone who had once been concerned with making records.

In theory, the Festival Hall's acoustics are supposed to be unaffected by the presence or absence of an audience, but that is simply not true. We had therefore to guess at the effect the audience would have on the sound of the piano and of the singers, each of whom sang a couple of verses of one of their solo items.

The programme was brilliantly devised to show off the special qualities of the pianist and each of the three singers. For Gerald Moore it would be a marathon evening; he alone would be on the stage for every item. Trios by Mozart and Haydn were to begin and end the concert – Fischer-Dieskau was to sing Schubert, de los Angeles Brahms and Schwarzkopf Hugo Wolf. There were three sets of duos – Rossini with the two women and Fischer-Dieskau down to sing Schumann with Schwarzkopf and Mendelssohn with de los Angeles. The handsome programme carried eloquent tributes to Moore from many of the great artists he had worked with. For me, the most poignant reminder that we were marking the end of a great career was provided by the only two advertisements – they were for recitals by de los Angeles and Schwarzkopf and in neither would Gerald Moore be the accompanist.

As the audience assembled that evening, the customary excitement I feel before the start of any recording was overlaid by more than a tinge of anxiety. This was an historic occasion and we had to capture it faithfully on record. If anything went wrong there would be no repeat take to correct it.

As the four artists walked on to the stage for the first group of items we in the control room were tense. Barenboim was presently due to meet du Pré at Heathrow and so as not to have to walk out of the hall in mid-concert he had come into our control room to hear part of it; he placed an encouraging hand on my shoulder. The prolonged and affectionate applause died down and the first item began. At first I looked incredulously at the engineer – then I wondered if something had gone wrong with the loudspeakers, only to dismiss the thought. It was like a nightmare. Barenboim voiced what was in all our minds, 'It sounds as if Gerald Moore has already said farewell and gone.' The presence of the audience appeared to have no effect on the singers; their voices came through in full splendour, but the piano seemed to have disappeared. The reason for this, I suspected, was that, as the singers had come singly for the rehearsal in the morning, we had not been able to try out any of the duets or the trios and the effect of three fairly ample bottoms in front of a slightly

71

opened lid was to kill the piano's sound. It looked as if the whole thing was going to be a fiasco.

For a few seconds the engineer frantically juggled with his controls, and then, miraculously, even before the first item was half-way through, the piano was not only audible but had something of the sound we had heard in the morning. I slumped back in my chair, letting out a long breath of relief, and looked questioningly at the engineer. He laughed, 'I wasn't going to let Legge prevent our getting a good recording.' After everyone else had left in the morning, still worried over the problem of the piano lid, he had managed to sneak a microphone behind the piano and fairly close to it, so that it was out of sight from the hall. As an added precaution he had lowered two of the microphones from the ceiling. It was these three which he had fully faded in to pick up the piano. 'That's more like it,' said Barenboim approvingly as he left.

The rest of the concert was pure delight. My attention was focused on how perfectly Gerald Moore captured the character of every item – the playfulness of the Rossini duets, the varying moods of the lieder and the duos; above all, in the Wolf songs, the passionate intensity of Goethe's 'Kennst du das Land' and the bleak despair of Byron's 'Sonne der Schlummerlosen'. I would have loved to go into the hall, at least for part of the concert, but felt compelled to stay in the control room in case an unexpected emergency arose.

The next day, we all realized that we had not only a record of a special concert, but of great performances. I am sometimes asked what I feel about recording 'live' concerts instead of studio performances. There are practical difficulties in the case of music using a large body of performers – you cannot festoon a concert stage with the number of microphones nearly always necessary to obtain a fair and accurate balance of even such an uncomplicated score as a Beethoven symphony. If things go wrong you would not get a second chance. When there is only a small number of players the odds are favourable, and the rewards could be performances which simply cannot be equalled in the studio. Fischer-Dieskau has recorded Schubert's song 'Im Abendroth' at least four times in the studio – his performance of the song in the farewell concert has a special intensity not quite equalled in any of the studio performances. You can sense he has a rapt audience in front of him, and he dares a pianissimo more extreme and finely drawn than in the studio.

On the subject of 'live' recordings, three years later one such venture was hit by a hazard so unexpected that it could not have been foreseen. We were recording a concert of Beethoven's music at the South Bank Festival which included the Grosse Fuge originally for string quartet and arranged by the composer himself as a duet for four hands on one piano; the pianists were Barenboim and Alfred Brendel. Part of the writing is very close for the two pianists, with all four hands bunched together in the middle of the

72

instrument. At the rehearsal in the morning, the artists wore short sleeved shirts. That night, during the concert, I was meditating on whether the piano version was an improvement on the original when I was jerked upright by a most extraordinary jangle of the keys; it sounded as if Barenboim and Brendel had fallen over on to the keyboard. I looked at the television monitoring screen and doubled up with helpless laughter. The cuff links on Barenboim's left sleeve and on Brendel's right sleeve had got entangled and in their struggle to free themselves their arms were hitting the keyboard; in a few seconds they were free but on such occasions seconds seem hours. After the audience had left we had to rerecord the section that had gone wrong.

From 1966, when he first entered it, till 1977 when he made his last record for us before deserting us, I hope only temporarily, for other pastures, my working life was dominated by Barenboim. I made about ten records a year with him. I made another dozen or more distributed between a wide range of artists and repertoire. In 1967 I made thirty-six records; the number was boosted by unexpected projects and new recordings by familiar artists. Anievas did a recording of Rachmaninov's second piano concerto and Paganini Rhapsody which was to become a best seller. These sessions were held in Abbey Road between 10 a.m. and 1 p.m. and 7 p.m. and 10 p.m. – on two of these days I had to rush to Kingsway Hall, some four miles away, for sessions from 2.30 p.m. to 5.30 p.m. with Frühbeck de Burgos conducting the Mozart Requiem. The memory of my spell in hospital in 1963 was beginning to grow dim, and the lesson it taught me to fade, but the fact is that no one should be doing three three-hour sessions in one day.

A big challenge came at the end of the year – the Schubert Octet with my old friends the Melos Ensemble. It is after the 'Trout' Quintet probably the most popular of chamber music and has been recorded many times – the competition was therefore fierce. I was determined before we started that our recording was going to be the best version of the work and said as much to a sales colleague.

One of the principal problems of balance in this work is the double bass, an awkward instrument which does not really belong in chamber music. In the event, this did not raise any difficulties. I asked Adrian Beers, our double bass player, for a smooth, rounded sound which would provide a firm bass line and a singing cantabile when the double bass had a tune. 'Leave it to me, Suvi,' he said, and that was that.

The record was acclaimed as the finest recording as yet of the work. The sales colleague to whom I had made what could have been a rash promise raised his eyes skywards. 'He says he's going to make the best recording of the Octet and what does he do? He does just that! Tell me, have you any good tips for the Grand National?'

I continued to be first choice for pianists. By 1967, John Ogdon was an old friend; I had already made a couple of records with him of Liszt. He is a large, powerfully built man and has a shattering effect on piano stools – after one session even a new, extra-sturdily built stool would begin to squeak, impossible for the recording. He is a gentle person, most amenable to suggestion. I had once or twice commented on points of interpretation. 'John, are you perhaps pedalling a bit too much between bars 15 and 20?' I would ask, and his reply would be, 'You think so? I'll pedal less then.' The first time this happened, being accustomed normally to bellicose artists who would defend their interpretation and then, back in the studio, possibly pedal just a little less, I was agreeably surprised. The third time it happened I was worried and then became cautious about making further suggestions. When I had got to know him better I once said to him, 'John, why don't you, once in a while when I make a suggestion, ask me to go to hell?' and he replied with a twinkle in his eye, 'You think I should? All right – go to hell.'

Musically, of course, Ogdon is a considerable personality. When I was asked to produce a record of the Busoni piano concerto with him and the Royal Philharmonic Orchestra conducted by Daniell Revenaugh, an enthusiast for the composer. I was not overly enthusiastic. I had sung in a performance of it in 1963, but remembered very little of the work. I was due in less than ten days to go to King's College, Cambridge, and did not want to be distracted by any early twentieth-century behemoth. My reluctance vanished when I saw the score; this was a large-scale work, not merely a long one, and to record it successfully would be an achievement. The piano part is fiendishly difficult, but this presented no problem to Ogdon. And his stamina was amazing. I know of no one else who could have played the Busoni concerto through twice in one day with no sign of fatigue or loss of concentration.

After the warm, languorous waters of the Busoni it was like dipping into a cool, clear, invigorating stream to turn to the 'Messe de Minuit', the mass for midnight on Christmas Eve by Charpentier and Purcell's 'Te Deum', with David Willcocks and the King's College Choir accompanied by the English Chamber Orchestra. I had briefly visited Cambridge in 1963 for the day, to see Frank Worrell's West Indians play the University team, and welcomed the opportunity of living in the town for a few days. The atmosphere was most congenial and I spent much of my spare time in the many second-hand shops there. An additional thrill was to see an elderly gentleman trundling across the green in front of the chapel and to recognize him, as he drew near, as E. M. Forster.

Recording teams have over the years got to terms with the famous echo of King's College chapel, and it is now possible to obtain a reasonably clear texture in even the most intricately woven music. The sessions were easy – the choir had been fully rehearsed and my principal concern was to remember various Acts of Parliament such as the one which forbade the 'employment' of juveniles after 7 p.m.

The scholarly David Willcocks is a wonderful choral conductor and a very agreeable person, which added to the joy of working in Cambridge. The scheduled works ended ahead of time and so, as a bonus, we recorded Bach's unaccompanied motet 'Jesu, meine Freude' and a group of chorales. I was greatly impressed by the young organ scholar who played the interludes in the mass and was sure he would go on to make a notable career. His name is Andrew Davis, and it gives me great satisfaction to note his success, even though he records for another company.

12   Klemperer, Barenboim, Pollini

The first set of records I produced on my own with Klemperer since the disastrous Schumann-Liszt sessions was of the five Beethoven piano concertos and the Choral Fantasia. We had been trying for many years to find a suitable soloist to do these works with Klemperer. Of the composer's major orchestral works only those with the piano remained. Early in 1967 Klemperer met Barenboim, when together they performed Mozart's C major piano concerto K503, and the conductor immediately took to the younger man.

At the very first run-through of the work Klemperer kept, every few moments, twisting round at some considerable discomfort to observe Barenboim at the piano; when the latter went up to him and asked if anything was wrong, Klemperer replied, 'I am making sure you are not conducting behind my back.'

We recorded K503 and Klemperer said to my delight that he had now found the pianist with whom he would like to record the Beethoven concertos. In the early part of the 1967–8 season nine sessions were possible. We planned to record the concertos in reverse order and I hoped in this period to get Nos. 5, 4 and 3. In actual fact things went so well that by the middle of the fourth session I knew that we would be able to record the lot, and so I had to book a choir for the Choral Fantasia.

On these sessions too the eighty-two year old Klemperer and the twenty-four year old Barenboim continued to enjoy themselves. When recording No. 3 they tried to imagine what Mozart's concerto in the same key would have sounded like had it too been composed in common time. During a play-back of the third movement of No. 5 Klemperer said, '*Poco ritard*, Barenboim, *poco ritard*' with a heavy accent on the *poco*, and beat time with his foot to indicate what he thought the tempo should be. Barenboim replied, 'Yes, doctor, *poco ritard*' with a heavy emphasis on the *ritard* and he too tapped out with his foot what he felt to be the right tempo, which was nearly half that of Klemperer's. When Barenboim began No. 4 with a hushed statement of the first theme, Klemperer was moved and involuntarily murmured, 'So,' and when Barenboim stopped, asked, in genuine surprise, 'Why have you stopped?' A few moments later, after the orchestral *tutti* had begun, Barenboim went up to Klemperer and whis-

76

pered something. 'All right,' said Klemperer and then wheeled round again and asked, 'You want it *slower*?'

Jacqueline du Pré had come to visit us on one of the sessions and during the interval Klemperer, who had heard of her phenomenal sense of pitch, played a weird combination of notes and challenged du Pré to identify them. Without even a moment's hesitation she replied, 'A, B, C sharp, D sharp, F' – Klemperer had to look down at the keyboard to confirm that du Pré was right. He then started to play a Schubert march, on which Barenboim drew up a second piano stool, plonked himself next to Klemperer and made it a duet; when he tried to help out Klemperer's less mobile right hand he got a smart rap on his knuckles for poaching. In the middle of this, Klemperer suddenly said, 'Hold up your hand.' Barenboim held up the palm of his right hand. Klemperer placed his own left hand against Barenboim's; it was nearly half as big again and Klemperer shook his head, wondering at the miracle of Barenboim's virtuosity with such small fingers. For me, the sessions were a delight for my two special artists were involved.

The one storm which broke out did not develop into a major one, but it had an important bearing on the relationship between Klemperer and me. He intensely disliked to be asked to do bits of movements over and over again. In fact, for a man who spoke English very well, surprisingly he did not know the meaning of the word 'bit' till I explained it to him while we were recording the last movement of Mozart's symphony No. 29 – or perhaps he merely pretended not to know. He had rehearsed the piece and done one take of it, listened to it and discussed it with me and then had done another take. When he came into the control room I said to him, 'That movement is all right, doctor, except for two bits.' He said, 'Bits – what means bits?' I explained. 'A little piece – a small section' and in German, 'ein Stück'. He repeated the word 'bit' two or three times with increasing distaste and then settled down to hear the take. At the end of it he said, 'I will now do three bits – two bits for you and one bit for me.' He went back into the studio and, having spoken to the orchestra about the three sections, announced, as I knew he would, 'The whole movement once again – from the beginning – with repeats.' At the end of the take he rang me and asked, 'Are all the bits all right now?'

Back to the Beethoven piano concertos – Klemperer had rehearsed the Choral Fantasia and they had done a complete take of it. We had listened to the take, discussed various points which required attention, and they ran through it again; then there was silence in the studio. I knew that this meant that Klemperer felt that as far as he was concerned we had finished with the Choral Fantasia. There were actually some sections which were not right and rather than try to explain this on the telephone I went into the studio with my score. The orchestra was fidgetting. Klemperer turned to me and rather belligerently said, 'Well?' The score of the Choral Fantasia on his desk was closed. I said there were passages which had to be done again. Angrily he opened the score and slammed it down in front of me, 'Tell me what is not right.' I said at a certain place the oboe and the bassoon were not together. Klemperer looked at the woodwind and said, 'Oboe and bassoon, he says you were not together at so-and-so.' 'And what else?' he asked me. I said at another place the clarinet was late. 'Clarinet, he says you were late – were you?' The clarinet player mumbled something. Klemperer turned to me. 'He says he was not late. Anything else?' I said the intonation of the string quartet had not been very good. He replied, 'Then I must be going deaf because it sounded perfectly all right to me.' At this, the leader of the violas said, 'Doctor, we were out of tune in that passage.' Klemperer looked angrily at him for a moment and turned to me: 'Is that all or is there more?' I mentioned another passage, in which the strings and woodwind were together instead of being in syncopation. He shouted at me, 'But it was perfectly all right in here.'

Remembering the Schumann-Liszt session, I knew that this particular crisis had to be resolved right then. If I submitted to his bullying Klemperer would never respect me again; nor would he attach any weight to anything I said to him in the recording studio. Very quietly, but firmly, and the orchestra and chorus and Barenboim, who had sensibly kept out of the dispute, could hear me, I replied, 'Doctor, it gives me no pleasure to ask you to repeat passages, but these and others are not right. When I ask you to repeat them it is to protect your name – for it is your name, not mine, that will be on the record.' Klemperer muttered something about not caring about his name on records and then said, 'I shall do it once again and that's all.' Even before I had gone out of the studio he had begun, but naturally the tape machine had not been started and the red light which indicated that we were recording had not been switched on. The leader of the orchestra pointed this out to Klemperer. 'Am I playing this again for *my* pleasure?' he roared, but the storm had spent itself; he stopped and started again. At the end of the piece, as the last chord died away, he announced loudly, 'Second concerto.' Some passages of the fantasy were still not quite right but I knew that it was not the time to press Klemperer further. When he left the studio that evening I had no idea in what kind of mood he would arrive for the next session. He was however his usual self and before the session started asked if I wanted any sections of the fantasy repeated. I gave him a list and he said he would do them first and then continue with the second concerto.

Klemperer and I never again had that kind of disagreement. Some years later, when he recorded the Bruckner Ninth, I pointed out a high G on the violins and remarked that it was not very beautiful. He said that he did not think that there was anything the matter with it. We heard it again and I said that the note was slightly sour. Klemperer asked the leader of the orchestra whether he thought the note was sour, but in a tone of voice which dared him to say 'yes'. The leader replied hesitantly that it seemed all right (later, I warned him that if ever again he let me down like that, I would stamp heavily on his toes). I insisted that the note was not perfectly in tune, to which Klemperer said, 'But I cannot do it any better.' 'Perhaps the orchestra can play it better,' I replied. After the playback Klemperer told me which sections he was going to repeat – the violin passage was not included. 'And the bars which go up to the high G,' I added. He wagged his finger at me and said, 'You are a very stubborn man' and went back into the studio. I still did not know whether he was going to repeat the passage. After he had done the other corrections he addressed the orchestra, 'Now, the high G for the violins in bar – whatever. Mr Grubb says it does not sound beautiful. I did not myself hear anything wrong, but let's play it again – better, this time.'

*

The Mozart piano concertos with Barenboim had been so successful that we started a set of recordings of the composer's late symphonies. On 18 January we had two sessions in which we recorded the Fortieth Symphony. At 5.30, after the second session, we were exuberant; we knew we had a good record, and with du Pré we went to my flat for coffee. I do not remember feeling ill that evening, only unaccountably tired; the sessions had not been especially strenuous. The next morning I woke up at half past six, and I knew instantly what was happening. Less than ten minutes later I was speeding to the Royal Free Hospital in a wailing ambulance. This time the warning was not mild; it was extremely painful and frightening. I spent the next three days with an oxygen mask over my face and in a drugged haze through which I surfaced occasionally to recognize Barenboim, who seemed to be always at my bedside with my wife when I woke, and once Jacqueline du Pré in tears.

A week later I had recovered enough to have repeated the seven-year-old Macaulay's reply when asked how he felt some time after he had spilt hot tea on himself, 'The agony is much abated'. Three days later, I was moved out of the intensive care ward into a private room. Barenboim was a constant visitor. On one visit I said to him I was bored. 'He is his usual self, now that he's started to complain of being bored,' he declared, and left soon after. About half an hour later he returned carrying a large cardboard box. He dumped it on my bed, and unpacked it to reveal a portable record player. 'There,' he said, 'you won't be bored any more. Sorry though, it's made by one of your rivals.' He brushed aside my attempts to thank him and wished me goodbye as he was leaving the next morning for the United States. 'You listen to what the doctors say' was his parting admonition.

The record player was a life saver. From America Barenboim kept in touch with me, ringing me daily. Late one evening the ward sister came into my room wheeling a commode. I looked at her in surprise; I had not

79

asked for one. 'Who is Daniel Barenboim?' she asked. I said he was a friend of mine. 'He's on the telephone from Chicago – the call has been put through to my room and we can't switch it through here.' With the aid of another nurse I was helped on to the commode and wheeled to the telephone. 'There, I knew they could do it' were Barenboim's first words to me. 'Danny, you organized the whole thing'. He chuckled. 'Are you quite comfortable on the commode? They said they couldn't switch the call to your room. I asked them to get a wheelchair, and that they said would take time. So I suggested they get hold of a commode, put you on it, and use it as a wheelchair. How are you?' When we had finished talking, I explained to sister who Barenboim was. She shook her head, bemused. 'I still don't know how he persuaded me from four thousand miles away to get you out of bed so late at night. That is a very determined young man and a very persuasive one. I would hate to have to say no to him, face to face.'

After I came out of hospital, I needed an extended convalescence at home. By 28 February I was allowed to get out of bed and sit in a chair for up to four hours a day. I was still very wobbly on my legs. That morning a German woman who helped out in our house was cleaning in the sitting room when the telephone rang and from the bedroom I could hear, 'Ja-ja-ja, Herr Doctor – ein Moment bitte.' She came into my room and announced, somewhat superfluously, 'That is Dr Klemperer – he wants to visit you now.' While I was in the hospital Klemperer had sent me a cable expressing his concern and had made frequent enquiries about the progress I was making. He had now arrived in London to record *Der fliegende Holländer*; this was the first time for nearly eight years that I would not be on one of his recordings.

The problem about his visiting me was that my flat, though on the ground floor, is reached by a flight of twelve steps. How was Klemperer going to negotiate those steps? He now moved around in a wheelchair; with help he could walk some distance on the straight, but steps were difficult. I didn't attempt to get our German friend to explain all this to him – merely to tell him that my wife would ring him back in a few minutes. Klemperer apparently couldn't understand the fuss; he wanted to visit me and so why should he not get into a car and come straight away. However, my wife explained the situation to him. She arranged for two stalwarts of the New Philharmonia to meet Klemperer that evening at our house and carry the wheelchair up the steps.

At 5.30 that evening he arrived; I was propped up on the sofa. 'Why have you deserted me?' he said as we shook hands. He settled down comfortably, asked about my health and remarked with satisfaction that I looked well. He stayed with me for over an hour. We spoke about India, what sort of person Jawaharlal Nehru was and whether I had ever met Mahatma Gandhi. I said I had seen Gandhi only when he had been laid out on his bier after his assassination, and Klemperer remarked how strange it was that a man who practised non-violence should have died so violently. We talked about Richard Strauss, whom he had known. For Klemperer, Strauss's highest achievement was *Der Rosenkavalier* and he maintained that the operas after it were repetitive. I made a strong plea for *Capriccio*. Klemperer granted that it was a fine work but that it did not disprove his contention. We both marvelled at Strauss's capacity to detach himself so completely from his surroundings as to be able to write such a tender work as *Capriccio* in the middle of a war. He accepted some of his favourite chocolate biscuits – 'cookies' he called them, and a cup of coffee and went on to give me a fascinating account of his work and of musical life in Berlin in the twenties. We spoke of the musicians he had known and worked with – including Schnabel, Erich Kleiber and the Busch brothers.

He asked me how the Beethoven sonatas with Barenboim were going. I said that just before my illness we had recorded two of the early ones. 'Which?' he asked. I said Op. 10 No. 2 and Op. 14 No. 2. To my astonishment he knew both sonatas and could recall special moments in them; I was even more astonished when he started to sing the melting D major theme, one of Beethoven's most affecting melodies, from the last seventeen bars of the exposition of Op. 14's first movement. He suddenly stopped and asked, 'Do you remember the bass line?' 'Yes,' I replied. 'Well sing it.' He started the tune again – and I sang with him the chromatic bass which so movingly supports the melody.

It was a surprise to all of us when we realized that it was a quarter to seven and he was due at the studios in fifteen minutes for a session. I said I hoped to be able to go to the concert performance of the opera in ten days. He wagged a finger at me. 'If you are not allowed to sit up for longer than four hours today you should not try to go to a concert in ten days. You listen to the performance from the records.' He left me refreshed; he knew I would be chafing at not being able to be on the sessions which I had planned and discussed in detail with him, and he had come to cheer me up and reassure me that he had not forgotten me.

*

My first recording when I got back to work was Bach's 'Magnificat', with Lucia Popp, Ann Pashley, Janet Baker, Robert Tear and Thomas Hemsley and the New Philharmonia Chorus and Orchestra conducted by Barenboim. It was my first big choral recording; it was pleasing to work with Popp and Baker again and, of course, Pitz, and to make friends with the new singers. The venue was All Saints' Church, Tooting.

For some time we had been searching for a recording site additional to Studio 1 and Kingsway Hall. There were times when we had to mount more than two recordings simultaneously and there were works which needed more space than was available at either of our regular sites. One of our engineers had made a preliminary survey and had produced a short list of six, including All Saints. I decided it was *the* one as soon as I saw it.

The church was not much to look at from the outside; inside, it had very fine, carved choir stalls and iron screens transported to London from an Italian monastery in the early years of this century, when the church was built. The great advantage of the place was that it was spacious and seemed to have just the right amount of reverberation; it appeared to be ideal for church music, and perhaps for other large-scale works. The control room was in the robing room, a long corridor away from the church, but it was now common practice to have television cameras relay to the control room information about what was taking place in the recording hall. The fact that this was a church certainly did not inhibit me. We had brought in a portable organ as being more suitable for Bach than the heavy, Victorian church organ. When one of the engineers said to me, 'Even though it looks small it is a powerful organ.' I could not resist, 'As the actress said to the bishop.' In the next five years I was to record in this church, four masses, a 'Te Deum', one act of a Wagner opera, Dvořák's Violin Concerto and even Brahms's Piano Quintet.

There were two major drawbacks to Tooting. One was that it took anything up to an hour to get there from central London. The other was more serious. After some trial and error we were able to obtain on tape a clean bright sound with the right amount of warmth. Inside the church itself, the sound swirled and eddied around messily. Conductors hated it – singers and other soloists loved it, for it made them sound rounder and richer. Orchestral players had to be wary and watch the conductor's beat carefully – if they listened to other players to pick up their cues, they were hopelessly late. A last problem. The heating was not adequate and we had to supplement it with portable gas fires which were not noiseless. On at least one Tooting recording, in very soft passages, you can hear a background hissing as of an infuriated cobra.

There were ructions even on this first session, when Barenboim found it very difficult to judge the balance between the vocal soloists and the instrumental solos accompanying them in the arias. This blew up into a full-scale storm when he came to do the coupling, Bruckner's 'Te Deum'. He had to rely entirely on comments from the control room to balance his choral, solo and orchestral forces. Understandably he objected to being, as he said, 'reduced to a metronome, just beating time', and vowed he would never again set foot in Tooting. But when he heard the final record, he relented and returned there for Mozart's Requiem Mass and Bruckner's Third Mass.

Following the 'Magnificat' I went to Paris. Maurizio Pollini had in 1960 made a brilliant recording for us of Chopin's First Piano Concerto; this had been sensational and even today it is accepted as one of the best ever of that work. Soon after that he had gone into seclusion and had almost been forgotten. He was now emerging to take up the threads of his career again and to make another record for us. He had had one go at it in London which produced nothing more than large quantitites of fluff, which his piano tuner had scraped off the dampers of our studio piano, rendering it practically useless thereafter; there were reports of a temperamental, moody person, difficult to manage. Pollini had gone back to Milan and there had run into Barenboim. He now wrote to my boss asking that '. . . un indiano che si chiama Grab, il quale ha lavorato per i dischi di Daniel Barenboim' ('An Indian called Grab [sic] who has worked on Daniel Barenboim's recordings') should produce his record. So off I went to do my first record in Paris at the Salle Wagram, a ramshackle old dance hall a short distance away from the Arc de Triomphe.

Pollini is a perfectionist. It took three days to get exactly the sound he wanted, during which he ran through three balance engineers, one of them French and the other two English, and exasperated everyone, including his wife – but not me. I knew that he was aiming at that little extra which lifts the good to the excellent – I also knew that if, in the Salle Wagram, we achieved it, it would be by sheer chance, for the hall is not really suitable for recordings of the piano. But we toiled on, experimenting with microphones, screens placed around the piano and curtains drawn to absorb some of the excessive reverberation. Finally, we did have the luck we needed and I said to Pollini that I thought we had captured the sound of his playing exactly. He was still doubtful and turned to his wife for support. He got very little encouragement from her. 'I think it sounds beautiful – Mr Suvi thinks it's beautiful – why don't you accept what we all say?' Without a word Pollini went down into the studio, and the next thing I heard was the slamming of the heavy doors of the hall. After a few moments I called down. 'Mr Pollini?' There was no answer. I waited a few more moments and then asked his wife where he might have gone. 'Back to Milan, I think,' she replied cheerfully. I sincerely hoped not, but there was nothing to do but wait, and after what seemed a very long time, but was only ten minutes, we heard the Wagram's doors open and shut; a few seconds later we heard the opening theme of Chopin's first Ballade. I congratulated the engineer on his foresight; he had looked at me questioningly when we heard the doors open and as I nodded he had started his tape machines. Now that he had accepted the sound, Pollini worked fast, playing each work through, complete and without any mistakes. It was a Chopin recital, the other pieces being the Polonaises Op. 44 and Op. 53 and three Op. 15 Nocturnes. There was immense power, poetry and imagination and a feeling for design in his playing. This was a pianist after my heart. In two days I had enough material to have made up three separate masters, each perfect. I then had to return to London; Pollini, still in search of something elusive, asked me if after I left he could have one more session with one of our French producers. I said he could.

A month later I received an agitated call from him from Milan. 'It is terreeble,' he said. I asked what was. The French producer had assumed that Pollini had been dissatisfied with what he had done with me. So he had sent him a master using only those takes done on the last day. Pollini wailed, 'It is no good at all.' I pacified him, saying that I would look into it. I got all the tapes from Paris and in two weeks Pollini had a new master. He came on the telephone again, this time with relief and joy. He approved the tape with one exception; he asked me to remove Op. 15 No. 3 from the record, though to me that Nocturne was no less perfect than the other two.

It almost passes belief that, even before the record was issued, a committee decided that Pollini should be dropped; one of our sales representatives said that his career would never take off again; he was a 'has been' and the public had forgotten him. I pleaded, I raved and ranted; at one meeting the sales people were incensed by my saying loudly, and looking directly at them, that against stupidity the gods themselves battle in vain. I asked, at least, that the decision be postponed till after the record had been released. No, the fiat went out; it was done. We actually paid Pollini not to do the second record which was due under his contract. The Chopin recital record went on to win various awards and prizes (not that that means much), and it is one of the few piano records still in the catalogue after fifteen years; and Pollini has gone on, not only to achieve the notable career I foresaw for him, but to become one of the most successful of money spinners in the classical record business.

13   'Lotte, ein Schwindel!'

The idea of the record, 'Tribute to Gerald Moore', to celebrate his seventieth birthday, was also born of a casual conversation, this time over luncheon with him on 28 September 1968; a touch of piquancy was added to the occasion by the fact that Brigitte Bardot was sitting at the next table. I do not remember what specifically we were talking about when Moore said, 'My dear Suvi, when you come to my years . . .' I cut in with, 'Come off it, Gerald – you're only a few years older than me.' I found his reply difficult to believe, 'I shall be seventy on 30 July 1969'; like most of his friends, I thought him at least ten years younger. The incident remained in my mind; clearly we had to do something to mark the occasion.

It is now accepted as a matter of course that in music with the piano the accompanist is as important as the soloist; it has not always been so. Of course in the more organized forms of music such as the sonata or the piano trio, the piano has never been considered as just an accompaniment; Beethoven, for example, calls his violin and cello sonatas 'Sonatas for *piano* and violin or cello'. But in lieder or in occasional or slighter pieces, say, Schumann's *Drei Fantasiestücke*, the pianist has not been accorded quite the same importance. Gerald Moore was one of the pioneers who elevated the art of the accompanist to the place it occupies today.

One has only to glance casually at the score of any lieder by Schubert to realize that the concept of the accompaniment being merely a subsidiary part is absurd. Take the song 'Die liebe Farbe' in *Die schöne Müllerin*; it starts with four bars of solo piano in which an F sharp (in the original key of B minor) tolls like a knell as harmonies shift and dissolve around it, and it rings remorselessly through the lied. Or 'Letzte Hoffnung' from *Die Winterreise*, which is almost a tone-poem for piano with a vocal obbligato. It depicts a winter landscape in which the few leaves still on the trees are haphazardly blown about – the song starts with four bars on the piano of inconsequential, random-sounding notes and chords, the rhythm going across the bar lines – the piano has the last word too with a postlude of four similar bars after the singer's last 'Hoffnung' with that heart-breaking diminished fifth. The piano part in music such as this could not possibly be considered 'subsidiary' – but it took a Gerald Moore to underline the fact.

I had first come across the name Gerald Moore in India, naturally through gramophone records. A young violinist by the name of Josef Hassid had made a great stir and I had ordered a set of his records for All India Radio. When the records arrived I discovered that the accompanist was a 'Gerald Moore'. I was impressed by the pianist. I had a 1943–4 HMV catalogue and looked under Moore to see what other records he featured in – there was no 'Moore, Gerald'; 'Moore, Grace' was preceded by 'Moonlight Sonata' and followed by 'More Chestnut Corner'. Mind you, he was not an obscure pianist then – already featuring as an accompanist in Volumes 5 and 6 of the Hugo Wolf Society, and it was not a grudge against him in particular which kept his name out – Marcel Gazelle, who was the pianist in ten records by Menuhin, and Coenraad V. Bos, who appeared in five of the Wolf volumes, had no entries either. By perseverance, and by showing what can be done with an 'accompaniment', Moore, and a handful of others, has made our experience of lieder deeper and richer.

But how to show our appreciation? He had retired from the concert hall, and in any case it would have been impossible to match the farewell concert. Since he did continue to record it came instantly to me that we would make a record with Moore. And a special one, accompanying all the principal EMI artists; each item would be brand new, it would not be a cannibalized affair made up of dismembered segments of records already issued.

The list practically wrote itself: the singers, de los Angeles, Schwarz-kopf, Baker, Fischer-Dieskau and Gedda; two string players: Yehudi Menuhin and Jacqueline du Pré; add de Peyer and Goossens to represent the woodwind, and for the tenth item Moore himself should play a solo item. I knew that all the artists would be delighted to be on such a record, and, more importantly, would go out of their way to make it possible to record their contributions – this was vital, as I had but seven months in which to record.

I rang Moore at his home and put the project to him. He said yes, he was interested, but sounded hesitant. I rang off, slightly dashed. In five minutes my telephone rang – Gerald Moore, this time excited. He said he had not really taken in what I was proposing; it was only when he had talked it over with his wife, Enid, that the possibilities had become clear. He would love to do such a record but would it be possible to arrange in the time available. 'Leave it to me, Gerald,' I said brightly.

The first thing I had to do was to get permission from the management. My boss, by now, knew me well enough not to turn down out of hand any proposal I made, however far-fetched, but he was highly dubious about the project. He too thought it couldn't be done. But I had already done my homework, having obtained from their agents a list of the artists' engage-ments for the next six months and confidently, I could reply that I would make the record entirely in London. He was still doubtful but gave me the go ahead, warning me that expensive foreign trips were out.

The first items we recorded were Victoria de los Angeles's contribution. She was due in London for a concert early in December, and had agreed with enthusiasm to stay on an extra day. There was, however, one snag – on that day Studio No. 1 was booked for two sessions of the London Symphony Orchestra conducted by Antal Dorati, from 2.30 p.m. to 5.30 p.m. and from 7 p.m. to 10 p.m. I was not going to let a trifle like that stand in my way and booked our session from 5.45 p.m. to 6.45 p.m., admittedly cutting it very fine, but I felt that if I could not record seven or eight minutes of voice and piano in one hour, I was not the producer I believed I was.

As I arrived I heard over the loudspeaker Dorati asking the orchestra whether the second session should not start at 6.30 so that they could all go home earlier. I dashed in and told them that I had a session booked to go up to 6.45, and would they please all get the hell out of Studio 1 as quickly as possible as my session was due to begin in ten minutes. De los Angeles arrived, we spent a few minutes on balancing her voice and in less than three-quarters of an hour I had the first two items of the record – a Galician folk song, 'Panxolina', sung in Gallego dialect, and a traditional song arranged by Nin, 'Malagueña'.

The next three artists were all resident in London or thereabouts and presented no special problems. In the event all three of them recorded their contributions on one day, late in December. The first was Menuhin; we had all tried to find an original piece or pieces for violin and piano with a duration of about five to six minutes but had to settle in the end for two arrangements – Ravel's 'Pièce en forme de Habañera' and Debussy's 'La fille aux cheveux de lin', favourite Menuhin items, and he played them with feeling. As he went out of the studio Janet Baker walked in; I had caught her on the day before she was due to leave on an extended tour of America. She sang two songs by Mahler – 'Frühlingsmorgen' and 'Scheiden und Meiden' – with characteristic warmth, and not a trace of the cold from which she was just recovering; normally she would not have sung that day, but this was a special record to commemorate a milestone in a special artist's life.

Exit Baker, enter de Peyer, whom I greeted with, 'Next customer please – short back and sides, sir?' The item for the clarinet was Weber's Theme and Variations Op. 33 – there was no recording of it in the catalogues and it is a considerable work, lasting for about fifteen minutes, with a very difficult piano part.

I now came up against what appeared to be an insurmountable obstacle; no matter how we tried to juggle dates, or to alter concert dates, or shift dates of journeys, there seemed no way in which we could record Moore with Schwarzkopf or Fischer-Dieskau in London, or indeed anywhere else in the world. Everyone tried hard, everyone was cooperative but it was a physical impossibility. It was unthinkable that a record to celebrate Gerald Moore's seventieth birthday should not include items from two of the artists with whom he had been most closely associated over the years, both in the concert hall and on gramophone records, and I was determined not to use old material. For a while I felt very dejected; it seemed cruel to fall at the last hurdle. The solution, when it finally came to me, was so simple that I could have kicked myself for not having thought of it before; the items were ready-made. Fischer-Dieskau had made two records of Strauss lieder which would be released only when the complete set of seven had been made. I asked him if we could use two of the songs, 'Hochzeitlich Lied' Op. 37 and 'Weisser Jasmin' Op. 31 No. 3, and he gladly gave permission. As for Schwarzkopf, I remembered that in February 1961, eight years earlier, she had recorded two of Wagner's 'Wesendonck Lieder'. They were superb performances, but they had not been issued as they did not seem to fit into any of the records she had since made. She agreed that one of them, 'Träume', should be her contribution. What looked like being the collapse of the whole idea had been overcome; there now remained four more items, three of which were recorded in one triumphant spell of two days.

On 1 April Jacqueline du Pré recorded the Fauré 'Elégie', and even before she had finished Barenboim arrived in tearing high spirits, showing no trace of having rehearsed with the English Chamber Orchestra for six hours. Fairly soon after the idea of this record had been born, Moore had said to me that he did not really want to play a solo item. He did not want people to say that perhaps he had been a frustrated soloist all his life and for his seventieth birthday was being allowed to record a solo as a special treat. What he would love to do instead would be to play a duet with Barenboim, whom he admired greatly. The only condition Barenboim made was that he should play *secondo* to Moore's *primo*. So here he was, ready to play the 'accompaniment' in Dvořák's 'Slavonic Dance in G minor', in its original version for four hands. They both played with great panache and brio. At the playback, when we heard the trio played by Moore with a beautiful cantabile line and tone, Barenboim involuntarily exlaimed, 'Lovely'; Moore was affected by this tribute, though he merely said, 'Steinways always produce that sound.' At the end of the playback Barenboim shook his head as if worried by something and said to Moore, 'Gerald, something is bothering me.' Moore asked what it was. With a straight, innocent-looking face Barenboim asked, 'Am I too loud?' – the title of one of Moore's most famous books. Moore, with a delighted chuckle, replied, 'Danny, you insisted on playing *secondo* just to make that crack!'

Gedda was in London to sing the title role in Berlioz's *Benvenuto Cellini*. When I looked at his schedule, only one day was free – 2 April, and he had performances at the opera on the 1st and 3rd. When, rather hesitantly, I said that the 2nd seemed the only suitable day, he consulted his diary and said, 'Great – let it be the 2nd.' He sang two songs by Tchaikovsky in the original Russian, 'Don Juan's Serenade' and 'At the ball', with that melting, liquid voice that seems to get more and more beautiful as the years go by. At the end of this session, even though we still had one item to record, we all adjourned to the restaurant where the idea of this record had first come to me. The contribution by Goossens, the Siciliano from Bach's Cantata No. 29, was recorded three weeks later. She and Moore are old friends and delighted in teasing each other. At one playback, when there was a slight smudge on the piano, Goossens leaned over to me and asked, 'Did you say *eightieth* birthday, Mr Grubb?'

The record was presented to the public at a reception held in Moore's honour, two days after his birthday; when it was over Gerald and Enid Moore and my wife and I had a private celebration. By then I had already experienced something I had long hoped for – the recording of a song recital with Moore as pianist – the artist was Janet Baker.

The first record of Baker's that I had produced was with Raymond Leppard and the English Chamber Orchestra. She sang three arias by Monteverdi allotted to two tragic heroines of the kind she portrays with such dramatic intensity on records and on the stage. The part of Ottavia in *L'Incoronazione di Poppea* is one of her great roles and the arias are popularly known as 'Ottavia's Lament' and 'Ottavia's Farewell'. The other aria is from *Arianna*, in which Ariadne, deserted by Theseus, sings of her sorrow. These three dramatic arias are framed between a gentle 'Salve Regina' by Domenico Scarlatti and a lovely 'Cantata Pastorale' by Alessandro Scarlatti.

Baker is a tough artist with a sturdy spirit. On recording sessions she wants the highest standards to be applied to her work and not to be coddled. I pointed out to her early on in a session that one of her vowel sounds had a tendency to broaden. She replied, 'That's the Yorkshire lass in me coming out – watch it, Suvi, and stamp on it whenever it rears its head.' I did this. After a while Leppard started to get worried; he took me aside and said, 'Hey, go easy. Aren't you being very hard on her? She might take offence.' I thought I knew Janet Baker well enough to be sure that she'd never take offence at an honest opinion. All the same I went up to her and said, 'Janet, Ray thinks I am getting at you – am I?' In genuine surprise Baker replied, 'Of course not. How's the "Regina" sounding now?'

The friendship with Baker had started when she was one of the soloists in the Klemperer Bach B minor Mass, and had grown since then. I had worked with her on other projects and on occasion, laying aside my EMI mantle, I had given her impartial advice about her recording career. Our friendship had been given a fillip when my wife and I discovered that Baker shared our passionate fondness for westerns – she was glad to find someone with whom to see them, for her husband, Keith Shelley, was not all that keen on them. So, particularly at weekends, we used to pop a roast into the automatic oven and go to the cinema. I discovered that she had not seen two of the great films of the genre, and knowing that they kept reappearing in London kept a close watch on the cinema columns of the evening papers. Our enjoyment of *Shane* was in no way lessened by the fact that we saw it in the local flea pit – Janet agreed that it was one of the all-time greats. *The Magnificent Seven* we saw in luxury in the West End of London. Baker kept exclaiming in delight as she recognized variously Steve McQueen, Charles Bronson, James Coburn and Horst Buchholz, all of whom went on to fame and stardom through *The Magnificent Seven*.

The record with Baker was made a fortnight before Moore's seventieth birthday. It was a recital of French songs by Debussy, Fauré and Duparc. I had a special interest in one of the Fauré songs, for Baker had committed it to memory in my presence. Two years earlier, we had returned together from Zürich, where she had sung in a performance of Mahler's Second Symphony conducted by Klemperer. As we settled ourselves in the plane Baker said would I please give her fifteen minutes to study a new Fauré song, after which she would be free to chat. At the end of ten minutes she gave me the score and said, 'I'll sing it by heart to you – make sure the notes are correct'; she did this *mezza voce*, and was note perfect. I asked how long she had been studying the song, and she replied, 'Ten minutes!'

On sessions, whenever the producer suggested a break for refreshments Moore would ask quizzically, 'Strawberries and cream?' Everyone took it for granted that he was joking. On the second of these sessions, when I announced the tea-time break, Moore asked, 'Strawberries and cream?' The door of the control room opened and my secretary walked in carrying a bowl containing some ten pounds of strawberries; behind her came another secretary with a large jugful of cream and plates and spoons. Moore stared at them speechless. Keith Shelley declared, 'Tear up all the offers from other companies – from now on it's EMI all the way.'

The Beethoven piano concerto sessions with Klemperer had been so much more satisfying for me than those done as half of a two man team that I firmly declared my intention thereafter to record Klemperer by myself or not at all. I was convinced too that this would be greatly to the advantage of the records, for when Klemperer did not feel like repeating a passage he was not above trying to play one producer off against the other. And so I took over as Klemperer's sole producer while my colleague went on to other fields. The first group of records we did under the new dispensation included the Bach Suites, Schumann, and Beethoven's Seventh.

During the recording of Schumann's First Symphony, an incident occurred which brought sharply home to me just how close, almost telepathic, is the relationship between artist and producer. Klemperer had done a first run through of the last movement – we discussed various points of balance. At one point I felt the clarinet did not seem to be coming through enough and asked the engineer whether we should not move the microphone a shade closer to him. Klemperer peered at his score, turned sharply to us and said, 'No – leave that to me – I need to ask him to play more.' He made recording so much more natural because of his feelings for balance. At another point when everything sounded thick and congested I asked him if anything could be done about it. He looked closely at the score and replied, 'That's Schumann, not me – and you cannot do anything about it.'

At the end of the playback he said to me, 'You don't seem to be very happy, why?' I was not aware that it showed in my face but I was concerned about the tempo, because of which the steady pulse, the backbone of Klemperer's music making, seemed to be lacking. For a moment I hesitated, remembering the well-known story of Klemperer's retort to Legge when the latter suggested to him that the tempo of the 'Peasants' merrymaking' movement of Beethoven's 'Pastoral' Symphony was too slow. 'You think so? You will get used to it.' Bracing myself, I said, 'Doctor, I think it's too slow.' Klemperer bristled. 'Why?' he asked. 'It is marked *allegro animato*.' 'And what does that mean?' 'I know it doesn't mean anything precise, but the metronome marking is 100,' I replied. 'All right, you beat that and we shall see whether I am slow.' I started my stop-watch and counted the beats. 'Almost exactly my tempo,' Klemperer announced triumphantly. 'Doctor,' I said reproachfully, 'the marking is minim equals 100 with two in a bar.' He started magisterially, 'Are you suggesting that I cannot beat two in a bar –' took one look at my face, which had a large grin on it, and went off on a new tack. He said, 'That is the way I feel the music – and I must play it as I feel it.' I replied, 'Then there's nothing more to be said, doctor.' He went back into the studio, made various comments to the orchestra, and said, 'We do the whole movement again.' This time the tempo was faster and the pulse strong. When he came in again for the playback, he looked pointedly at me before settling down, defying me to say that the tempo was now faster. When he had heard the movement he smiled and said, 'That is good.' I was pleased that I could now talk to him about any aspect of his music making without his taking offence.

I have been asked often enough whether I did not find Klemperer's tempo slow at times. I have always replied that there was no such thing as a Klemperer tempo – his tempo was at all times suited to the conditions prevailing at the time. While we were recording *Don Giovanni* Ghiaurov, who was singing the title role, asked me to request Klemperer to take 'Finch'han dal vino' faster. Klemperer's reply was instant. 'I can conduct it faster, but can he sing it faster?' The correct tempo for that aria was that at which the singer and orchestra could clearly articulate all the notes.

The most illuminating example of Klemperer's tempo changing to suit acoustic conditions was provided by the first chorus of the *St Matthew Passion*. We were not quite decided where this work should be done. A trial session was held in St Augustine's Church, Kilburn, with a very resonant acoustic – the opening chorus, 'Kommt ihr Töchter', took 13¼ minutes. For the second trial we moved to Studio 1 – the same chorus took just under 11 minutes. The recording was actually done in Kingsway Hall, more reverberant than Studio 1 and much less so than the church. The first movement here took 11¾ minutes. I timed the performance at the Royal Festival Hall, the driest of all the venues we had been in – the first chorus there took just 10¼ minutes. There was a three minutes' difference between the fastest and the slowest performance. At each place he had had one overriding consideration – that there should be no blurring or muddying of the intricate polyphonic lines of the music, and he had adjusted his tempo to that end.

Balance and propriety – these were two of the fundamental aspects of Klemperer's music making. Just because a symphony was labelled 'Fantastique' he did not whip it up into an orgy of grotesquery, nor did he indulge in exaggerated lugubriousness because it was named 'Pathétique'; he let the music speak for itself, and the fantastic or pathetic elements, if they were in the music, came through of themselves. Propriety, but not tameness – because of his restraint in the first three movements of the 'Fantastique', the last two make a shattering impact; the snarling brass and the violent timpani have a frightening intensity in the 'March to the scaffold' and in the 'Witches' Sabbath' the debased 'beloved' theme sounds really obscene. In *Fidelio*, in the quartet 'Er sterbe', when Pizarro arrives in the dungeon to kill the helpless Florestan, Klemperer lets the horns blare right through the rest of the orchestra to underline the menace of the enraged governor of the prison – he follows Beethoven's markings exactly – fortepiano, crescendo to forte – there is no holding back there. In another context he might have remarked mildly, as he once did to the horns, 'Not so much' – his usual remark when some section of the orchestra let their enthusiasm run away with them.

On the Beethoven sessions I once again delighted in the antiphonal dancing of Klemperer's first and second violins on either side of him. In the seating customary at present the strings run clockwise from the left in the order first violins, second violins, violas and cellos – sometimes cellos and violas – with the basses behind the cellos. Klemperer's arrangement was firsts, cellos with the basses behind, violas and second violins. In almost all classical writing there is a great deal of interplay between the first and second violins. They hardly ever have parts in unison; instead, they support each other harmonically, or they play counter themes to each other; they answer each other, they take themes over from each other and sometimes play in canon with each other – in other words, each enriches the other's part. In this kind of writing the advantages of having the first and second violins on opposite sides are obvious. I wonder that Klemperer's seating of the orchestra is not common practice.

I was reminded again, while recording the Beethoven, of Klemperer's total ignorance of the technical processes of making gramophone records. On the recording of Mozart's 33rd symphony, he played each movement of the piece, in full, three times – no correction required – as one or other of the three takes covered slips in another. In the last take of the fourth movement there was a glaring horn crack and Klemperer, when he heard it, looked at his score and noted the place; I knew that in the previous take the passage was all right. After the playback Klemperer said, 'We must do the movement again.' I told him that it was not necessary; there was no horn crack in the previous performance. He replied that there were other mistakes in that performance. I tried to explain to him, with the score, what editing was. 'From the beginning to this point, we will use this performance – then we will cut the tape of the second performance and stick that in – we stay in it till here – after the horn crack in the third performance – we come back then to the third take. I think the ending is best of all in the first performance – so we will probably go back to that.' Klemperer had been listening to me with growing consternation – he now looked aghast. 'Then the performance is not by me,' he said. I replied that it was, for all the three performances were by him. 'No, no,' he repeated, 'it is not a performance by me but by you. It is not my performance.' He turned to his daughter and said in tragic tones, 'Lotte, ein Schwindel', and would not be comforted. At the end of the recording of the Beethoven, again at a horn crack, he looked at me and asked 'Ein Schwindel?' and I replied, 'Ein Schwindel.'

During the recording of the fourth movement of Schumann's Third Symphony a very touching but funny incident took place; it also shows how Klemperer was never at a loss for the right reply. Towards the end of the movement, chords for the brass and horns are interspersed with long-drawn phrases for the strings. It had been a fairly tiring session, and after bringing in the brass for one of their perorations, Klemperer's chin, which had been falling lower and lower, finally sank on to his breast, and he fell fast asleep. The orchestra somehow managed to get through the remaining bars and, slightly raggedly, the movement ground to a halt. The librarian of the orchestra went up to the rostrum and, gently shaking Klemperer, said, 'Wake up, doctor, it's all over,' to which Klemperer replied, 'Was it good?' There were still forty minutes of the session to go, but he rang me: 'Mr Grubb, would you please come in here for a moment.' He was tired and wanted the session to end. Of course I agreed. His daughter said to me, 'You know, you get more out of my father than anyone ever has in a recording studio; you know when to press him and, more important, when not to press.'

14   Barbirolli's Last Recording

1970 was my tenth year of working in EMI and it brought me several firsts: a full opera, lieder with Fischer-Dieskau, recordings with Maazel, Giulini, Richter and Zukerman, and, sadly, the last recording of an old friend.

The first recording of the year was, however, none of these but a set of Beethoven's piano trios which overflowed into 1970 from the previous year. The phenomenal success of the sonata series had led to demands for more records of Barenboim playing Beethoven, either alone or with others. The cello sonatas were due to be recorded with du Pré after the 1970 Edinburgh Festival; for the violin sonatas and the piano trios we were able to get Pinchas Zukerman. Barenboim had spoken to us earlier of this new young Israeli violinist who, he said, would be one of the leading players in the world. We had perhaps moved fractionally late, and the fact that his mentor worked for another company might have played a part, but Zukerman had been snapped up by somebody else.

He had, however, made sure that his contract would permit him to make records of chamber music with whomever he wished. Barenboim, du Pré and he had played often together as a trio, and they now announced that they were ready to record the Beethoven trios. In five days of concentrated work, astride New Year's Day, we recorded, on ten long-playing sides, all the trios, the variations and all the WoO's. These WoO's included the delightful B flat trio of 1812, in one movement. It is mature Beethoven, but has a comparatively easy piano part, for it was written for the twelve-year-old daughter of a friend 'to encourage her in her piano-playing' – it shows an endearing side of Beethoven. Du Pré was destined to make only two more records; the illness which has laid her physically low but has not subdued her spirit had already touched her with its chill hand.

I had earlier produced one act of an opera conducted by Klemperer. In his latter years in London he was known primarily for his concert appearances. Before the war, in Germany, he had worked in an opera house, and again after it, in Budapest. The three operas he had done had been very successful and it seemed appropriate to set up another operatic project. Wagner came to mind at once. He was nearly eighty-five, and it would have been difficult for him to cope with a complete opera of Wagner's in one go; I knew it would have to be done in acts. The first act of

Die Walküre was the obvious first choice, being a complete entity. Klemperer said he would be delighted, but insisted, as a postscript, that it should be followed by *Le Nozze di Figaro*.

The two lovers practically cast themselves – Helga Dernesch was an obvious Sieglinde and William Cochran the ideal Siegmund. For Hunding I went to Zürich to audition, with Klemperer, a bass about whom there was a lot of talk.

The bass, Hans Sotin, arrived with an accompanist at three o'clock. He said he had never sung Hunding – his latest Wagnerian role had been King Marke in *Tristan und Isolde* – nor had he had time to study the part. He started with 'Des Dach dich deckt'. By the time he had sung ten bars Klemperer and I were satisfied; it was a magnificent voice, ideal for Hunding. Sotin looked nonplussed. Didn't we want to hear the rest of the section? Klemperer said, 'No, Mr Grubb and I are happy to engage you for the part. And now,' he went on, 'sing me King Marke from "Halte, Rasender!" in the third act.' Sotin began and, without any music in front of him, Klemperer filled Kurwenal's and Brangäne's parts and brought in various instruments at the necessary places.

The opera was recorded in Tooting. Klemperer arrived for the first session after a longer journey than usual – it was the rush hour – took one comprehensive look at the church and said to me, 'Have you brought me all this way to see *this* architectural masterpiece?' He accepted the swirling acoustic without demur and started happily to rehearse. In the middle of a heavily scored passage, he suddenly stopped and, peering at the woodwind, he said, 'I do not hear the third bassoon. I must hear him – third bassoon, will you please stand up.' In danger of stumbling over the cables and breaking my neck, I raced from the control room into the church, for the personnel manager had informed me that the third bassoon had not arrived. I had hoped Klemperer would not notice, but no, an incomplete chord had instantly caught his ear. I explained that the third bassoon had not yet come and we did not know why, to which he cheerfully replied, 'Perhaps he is dead.' The remark did not go down very well with the orchestra, one of whose members had died the day before in tragic circumstances; to spare Klemperer's feelings we had kept this fact from him.

When the break came, he was helped off the rostrum and his chair was wheeled to the top of the nave. He took out his pipe and started to fill it. I leaned over to him and said, 'Dr Klemperer, this is a church.' Quite unmoved, he went on stuffing tobacco into his pipe, took out a box of matches, lit one, turned back and looked at the altar, said 'Blasphemy, isn't it?' and calmly lit his pipe. As he sat puffing, I prayed that the vicar was not anywhere within a mile of the church and turned to see him walking up the aisle; Klemperer, enveloped in a cloud of smoke, was directly in front of him. As the scene registered on him, calmly, without haste, the vicar turned on his heel and walked straight out. Five minutes later he came into the control room, chatted amiably with me and made no reference at all to the incident. Thereafter, at every break, I made sure that Klemperer was wheeled out of the church and into the control room.

He enjoyed conducting *Die Walküre*, shaping the long contrapuntal lines of Wagner's music with his customary feeling for design and structure. I shall for ever carry the memory of a moment we shared at one of the playbacks. Just after Hunding angrily orders Sieglinde out of the room, against a menacing figure on the lower strings, a tender motif is stated by the clarinet and then taken up by the cor anglais, as Siegmund and Sieglinde exchange glances. Klemperer was staring straight ahead, oblivious of his surroundings; as the phrase ended he turned and for a second or two looked through me. Then his eyes focused on me and we smiled at each other.

That had been in 1969; in January 1970 it was *Figaro*. The cast was headed by Gabriel Bacquier as the Count, Elisabeth Söderström as the Countess, Geraint Evans as Figaro, Reri Grist as Susanna and Teresa Berganza as Cherubino. We also had three promising young singers in the cast: Margaret Price as Barbarina, and Kiri te Kanawa and Teresa Cahill as the two bridesmaids. There had been no ructions this time over the schedule, for Klemperer now accepted, as one of the unavoidable inconveniences of recording, that he could not start at the beginning of an opera and work his way through to its end.

One of Klemperer's most engaging characteristics was his delight in music. When we were recording the Bach Suites he kept exclaiming, 'And to think that this music was written over two hundred years ago!' On the *Figaro* sessions his reactions to every felicity of the opera was that of one who was discovering the work for the first time. In the second Figaro-Susanna duet, even as we heard Figaro's opening phrase in B flat, his long finger was ahead, tracing the bar in which B flat modulates with a side step to the ambiguity of G minor as Susanna sings 'Così se il mattino il caro contino', informing Figaro for the first time of the Count's designs on her. In the finale to the second act, as the C major section began with the Count's 'Conoscete, signor Figaro', he hushed all those in the control room with his hand held up and listened with a look of pure delight to Mozart juggling with his three main themes.

He now trusted me so completely that he seldom objected when I asked for a passage to be repeated – not that he liked doing it, but he had learnt to accept this as another of the nuisances connected with recording. When I would say to him, 'Doctor, can I ask you please to do something for me.' He would go very still and wait suspiciously for what he was going to be asked to do. There were various ingenious ways in which he would try to put off the inevitable. In *Figaro*, he rehearsed the first duet, 'Cinque, dieci', and did a take of it. We heard it and discussed several points relating to it, and Klemperer and the singers went back into the studio. They did another take, at the end of which there was silence; on the television screen I could see Klemperer sitting with his hands crossed on his lap, and recognized the signs.

I rang the telephone and saw him pick it up. (First hurdle crossed, I thought, for on an earlier occasion he had ignored increasingly frantic rings of his telephone by a colleague, and when the leader of the orchestra had picked it up and held it out to him saying, 'Mr so-and-so to speak to you', Klemperer had replied loudly, 'Tell him I am not at home.') I said, 'Doctor, that was a good take, but there are still a few things not quite right. At bars 9 and 10 the oboe's intonation is not perfect. On the first "sembro fatto in ver" Figaro and Susanna are slightly apart. At bar 71 the upper strings are not absolutely together and I am sure the horns would like to have the opportunity to repeat their last triplets. It is only about four minutes or so; instead of doing bits and pieces I think the best thing would be to do one more complete performance.' All this time he was holding the telephone to his ear, but he did not say a word. Still without a word to me he replaced the receiver and looked at the stage. 'Miss Grist,' he said, 'did you like that performance?' 'Yes, doctor, I thought it was good.' 'Evans, did you like it?' 'Yes, doctor, very much,' said Evans. 'Orchestra, did you like the performance?' Various voices replied, 'Yes, doctor, we liked it.' Klemperer said, 'I also liked it and Mr Grubb likes it so much that he wants to hear it again. Once more, from the very beginning.'

I went to Zürich later in the year to discuss further operatic projects. The first act of *Walküre* was on three sides and I suggested that we should now go on to Act II, which I promised to lay out in such a way that it would not be a strain for him. Normally a project like this would have brought a sparkle to his eyes, but he looked uninterested. I commented on this. He said the first act of *Walküre* was complete in itself and a wonderfully constructed piece of music. As for the rest of it, he could not muster enough enthusiasm to commit himself to the hard work that would be involved. 'All those Walküre and their Ho-jo-to-hos can be very tiresome at times. If it had been *Die Meistersinger*, well . . .' and his eyes lit up.

I had dreamt for years of Klemperer conducting *Meistersinger* and was delighted that he himself had brought the topic up. I said we would cast it together. I would divide the opera into convenient segments so that it would not be a burden to him. He would have as much time as he wanted for rehearsals and we could spread it out over, say, two years. He was looking at me intently all this while and I was congratulating myself that I captured his interest. Suddenly, in a plaintive voice, Klemperer called out 'Lotte' to his daughter, who was in the next room. She popped her head in at the door and Klemperer, pointing accusingly at me, said, 'He's trying to kill me.' She looked startled, and I, realizing that he had been leading me on, started to laugh. He explained that he now had to accept that there were limitations to what he could undertake. 'If it had been some years ago . . .' He shrugged. He agreed to record the last scene of *Walküre* to fill the fourth side and we planned another Mozart opera, *Così fan tutte*.

When in June 1962, six weeks after my first disastrous sessions with Klemperer, I assisted Legge in the production of two records conducted by Maazel, it did not seem very likely that I might one day myself produce a record with that conductor – it seemed even less likely that I would discover and make friends with the warm, friendly person behind that somewhat aloof exterior of cool efficiency. Eight years later, almost to the day, that is exactly what happened.

My first record with him had an unexpected angle to it – Maazel not only conducted the orchestra but also played the violin in two of Mozart's concertos, the G major and the A major. The orchestra was the English Chamber Orchestra. I briefed Maazel about the orchestra and his eyes gleamed with anticipatory pleasure. 'I think we will enjoy ourselves,' he remarked. Nevertheless, when the first session began, I could sense an uncharacteristic tenseness in him. The orchestra too was slightly wary, a little suspicious of a conductor assuming an unfamiliar role. But very soon they all settled down. I was intrigued to see how Maazel's Mozart was based on the sinewy strength underlying the music – he did not wallow in a sensuous phrase or a melting change of harmony. The two violin concertos certainly gained in strength as a result.

In the middle of one session Pinchas Zukerman, who had come to discuss his own concerts with the orchestra, sauntered into the control room. Maazel's reaction was to throw up his hands in mock horror and say, 'Pinky, I have enough problems without having to play to you in the control room. Please go away.'

Maazel's next record was Prokofiev's Fifth Piano concerto with Sviatoslav Richter. I had been warned that Richter had to be handled with great tact, and that he was very sensitive to any deviation of the keyboard from the horizontal. I had taken considerable pains, with the aid of a spirit level, to ensure that the keyboard was absolutely straight. Richter arrived, gravely accepted my greetings, walked up to the piano, stood in front of the keyboard and played one upward scale. He turned to me and with palms upwards lowered the left hand and raised the right, to indicate that the piano tilted to the left. I placed the spirit level on the keyboard and, sure enough, the bubble was no longer dead centre; it was however only a couple of millimetres out of position. We inserted a thin piece of cardboard under the front left leg; the bubble moved five millimetres the other way. After a great deal of trial and error we finally found what was required to bring the bubble to the exact centre – two thicknesses of cigarette paper! Once more Richter played a scale, this time descending. He declared he was satisfied and the recording began.

On these sessions there was no evidence of Richter being highly strung

98

and temperamental. He worked hard with an almost grim concentration and no expression on his face. When he listened to what he had recorded he was equally impassive – except on two occasions. Once he grimaced. I looked surprised for I could see no reason for his dissatisfaction. He pointed to the piano line; it was a descending series of broken chords and his playing of it had the utmost clarity and polish. When he played it a second time it had, in addition to these qualities, poetry, which converted an apparently ordinary phrase into one which touched the heart. Another time I uttered an involuntary murmur of appreciation and the dour face relaxed with a fleeting smile. The recording itself presented no problems. In less than a month I would be working again with him – that recording was not going to be quite so uneventful.

I do not remember the exact circumstances which led to my being asked in July 1970 to produce a record of Sir John Barbirolli conducting Delius's *Appalachia* and *Brigg Fair* with the Hallé Orchestra. I had so far done only records of him accompanying my own artists. Through the years we had had lively exchanges about cricket and generally kept in touch. He expressed himself delighted to be working with me. We would start with *Appalachia*, which is the longer and more complicated work. There was one session on the first day, two, from 2.30 p.m. onward on the second day and on the last day one session from 10 a.m. The choir and soloist had been called for the last two sessions. Barbirolli asked that there should be a chorus rehearsal on the second day between 11 a.m. and 1 p.m.; I was very concerned at the prospect of his having to work from 11 in the morning to 9.30 at night. I knew he had not been well for some time and had had the occasional black-outs when he had pressed himself too hard. I tried to dissuade him from having that rehearsal. The chorus was the Ambrosian, its director the seasoned John McCarthy; could he not discuss the score with McCarthy, who would make sure the choir was rehearsed in accordance with his view of the work? But no, Barbirolli insisted that he should conduct the rehearsal himself.

He arrived at Kingsway Hall for the recording in high spirits. He was a superb interpreter of Delius and it was his own orchestra, the Hallé. 'They are my children. Aren't they marvellous?' He discussed with them various points of interpretation. 'Cellos, watch your intonation' – this about a high passage for them. When discussing a difficult entry one of the players said, 'Sir John, here, I think . . .' Barbirolli interrupted, 'Don't think – it's fatal in these circumstances – just come in when I give you the signal.' He walked over to the percussion player, pointed to the score and with a mischievous twinkle in his eye said, 'At this point you must bash away like a drummer in the Boys' Brigade'; as he walked away he winked at me and said, 'I've never seen anyone in the Boys' Brigade shaped quite like that, have you?' The percussionist was an attractive, generously proportioned girl.

The next morning he rehearsed the chorus. It took all of the allotted two hours to get across to them the special points of phrasing, dynamics and colour he wanted. 'You see how right I was to insist on having this rehearsal, but it will make it that much easier for us this evening.' I asked if he would like to lunch in a restaurant round the corner; he said 'No' and suggested a pub next door. It was a rare and precious hour.

We spoke of many things. I said I had first heard him on 78s accompanying Kreisler in the Beethoven Violin Concerto. His eyes lit up and he sang the major and the minor versions of the first movement's second theme in that gruff, slightly tuneless, but very expressive voice. 'That, my dear fellow, is genius.' He was due in three weeks to conduct Beethoven's Ninth Symphony at the opening concert of that year's Edinburgh Festival. 'You know, after a lifetime of studying the Ninth, I am only now beginning to understand it fully.' He compared the opening – 'all misterioso – the theme appearing in fragments and gradually taking shape' – to the recapitulation. 'There, all hell must break loose. There can be no holding back. You must give everything you've got.'

He was a collector of rare glass and he described the joy of spotting, in an obscure shop, a splendid piece covered in dust, of cleaning a corner of it with a wetted finger and recognizing it to be a genuine old piece. And we talked about the game we both loved; of the Test series between England and West Indies the previous year. I said Garfield Sobers was the most exciting left-handed batsman I had ever seen and added that I wished I'd seen Frank Woolley in his heyday. He of course had seen the Kent left-hander in his prime and was a passionate admirer of him. Using a tankard as the batsman's wicket and a salt cellar as the bowler's he described to me 'the exquisite poetry' of a cover drive by Woolley. 'And as for his late cut,' Barbirolli kissed his fingers in homage, 'it was so late that he played the ball almost out of the wicket-keeper's gloves. They don't make 'em like that any more.' A group of people had gathered round us; one of the older men said, 'I saw Woolley too. I quite agree with you, sir.' Barbirolli replied genially, 'Of course you do. Any reasonable chap would.'

The afternoon session went as well as the first one and, before the evening session, he and I again went to the pub. I persuaded him to have an extra sandwich, for he looked tired. I said, 'Sir John, you really must avoid a working schedule like today's.' He replied that the only way he could live was wholeheartedly, giving everything of himself. 'I can't live cribbed, cabined and confined. I want my last moment to come while I am still alert and doing what I love doing – making music and being with my friends. I am sure Evelyn and you and all who know me will remember that even as you sorrow when I am gone.'

At the end of the break we walked back to Kingsway Hall. As we entered the hall he took my arm and I felt him leaning more and more

100

heavily on me. Once, he stumbled and I managed to steady him. Then suddenly, without any further warning, he keeled over. I was just able to prevent him from falling. For an instant, as I gently lowered him to the ground, I thought the moment he had spoken of had indeed arrived. Events happened in a blur in the next few minutes. Clive Smart, the orchestral manager, rushed up and while I slid a cushion under Barbirolli's head he gently eased a small pill into his mouth. Barbirolli's face was white; he did not seem to be breathing.

Still on my knees I beckoned one of the orchestral staff towards me and said, 'Ring 999 and ask for an ambulance – say emergency heart condition – Go.' I called one of the others over, 'Someone is on the other telephone – get him off it – locate Lady Barbirolli – don't alarm her – just tell her that Sir John has fainted and that we are doing everything possible – I want her to come here at once – ask her who his doctor is and try to get him over.' I looked down at Barbirolli and noticed that a little colour was creeping back into his face. I could also see the chest moving slightly as he took short, shallow breaths. I told Clive Smart, 'Keep an eye on him.'

I could see members of the orchestra beginning to stir. Some were craning their heads to see what was happening. I walked on to the rostrum and said, 'Everybody sit down please. Don't move. Sir John has been taken ill and we are doing everything possible. Is there a doctor here? If so will he please come to me.' There was a sprinkling of visitors at the back of the hall; one of them approached me. I led him to Barbirolli. He took his pulse and said it was feeble but not unduly irregular.

As we stood waiting two things happened simultaneously. Barbirolli stirred and opened his eyes, trying to focus on us, and two ambulance men carrying a stretcher walked in through the swing doors. By the time they had reached him, Barbirolli with the support of Smart had managed to sit up. I told him that I felt that he should go to hospital, at least for the night. The voice was feeble, but it was the Barbirolli will behind it. 'No,' he said, 'I shall be all right soon, sorry to cause such an upheaval.' I saw that we would not succeed in persuading him to go to hospital and apologized to the ambulance men for having brought them out unnecessarily. We helped Barbirolli to walk unsteadily into the green room. I went back into the hall and once again asked that everyone should remain seated. Sir John was much better, as they could see, and a further announcement would be made shortly.

In the green room Barbirolli was sipping a glass of water. I told him that I was going to cancel the session. He exclaimed in dismay. 'Oh no, think of the enormous amount of wasted money. We may not be able to finish this record, and what about all those musicians waiting in the hall? Besides, I am quite well now.' I replied, 'Sir John, I want us to go on making records with you for many years to come, and if we do not complete this record now, we can do so later. But now, you should rest. I promise you that if

101

your doctor and your wife agree, tomorrow's session will go ahead as planned and I'll arrange an extra one in the afternoon to finish the record.' He saw that nothing would persuade me to let him do the session; he smiled and said, 'Let me go and speak to them in the hall.' He said that he had been taken ill but as they could see was now quite all right. However Mr Grubb insisted that he should not work that night. He was sorry to disappoint them all, but would see them in the morning.

Barbirolli's doctor had arrived. I told him I would only agree to the two sessions the next day if he would examine Barbirolli before they started and provided Lady Barbirolli was with us throughout the day. This was agreed and we sent Barbirolli home in a car with one of the orchestral staff.

Just before I left, Clive Smart said to me, 'I am very impressed at the way you handled this evening's events – you remained so calm and you knew exactly what to do at every stage.' 'Remember, my principal artist is an octogenarian', I replied. 'It would have been irresponsible of me not to have worked out in my mind what steps to take if anything untoward happened.' But if Smart had been in the taxi on the way home, he would not have thought me quite so cool, for suddenly, without warning, my hands started to shake and I felt cold. It was, as I remembered from a car accident I had been involved in years earlier, shock.

The next day the doctor pronounced Barbirolli fit and, with his wife joining us, we had two happy, satisfying sessions – not altogether carefree. Occasionally Lady Barbirolli and I each caught each other looking with concern at Barbirolli. Characteristically, on the first playback, Barbirolli, who knew of my heart condition, asked me, 'Grubb, are you looking after yourself?' The camera caught us as I pointed to him and said to Evelyn Barbirolli, 'Look who's talking!' Twelve days later, on 29 July, I was telephoned in Salzburg and told that Barbirolli had died early that morning.

15   Fischer-Dieskau, Giulini

Earlier in the year, I had recorded 'live' from the Festival Hall a recital of duets by Janet Baker and Fischer-Dieskau. On that visit Fischer-Dieskau somewhat bitterly remarked to me that he wished that the International Classical Department would at times show some interest in his recordings: 'Gerald and I keep turning out reel after reel of songs in Berlin and we do not know whether anyone here in London is interested or even knows about what we are doing.' I was concerned; Fischer-Dieskau was under contract to us. It was only because he lived in Berlin and spent part of each year in Munich that we left records made by him in those two places to the local German company. I asked him when his next lot of sessions was scheduled for and said I would visit him then.

So, in May, I went to Berlin and sat in on sessions with Gerald Moore for lieder by Strauss. I was only an observer but Fischer-Dieskau was pleased that I had responded so quickly to the conversation we had had. When I promised him, before I left, that I myself would thereafter produce as many of his records as I could manage, he was delighted.

The first record I produced under the new arrangement was Brahms's *Die schöne Magelone*, a setting of a collection of poems based on a fourteenth-century prose story telling of the 'wondrous love of the fair Magelone for Count Peter of Provence'. It is not a song-cycle like the Schubert cycles, but it tells a connected narrative. The pianist was Richter. The venue for the recording was the Burgerbräukeller in Munich, which had been a meeting place for Hitler and his cohorts. Five days after the recording, singer and pianist were due to give a recital of the work at the Salzburg Festival.

When I arrived at the hall I noted with satisfaction that the piano lid was on the long stick. When Richter arrived shortly after and saw the piano, he recoiled in horror; he shook his head and, lest there be any misunderstanding, he exclaimed in as many languages as he could muster, 'No! Nein! Non! Nyet!' If he had known Hindustani he would probably have added 'Nahin.' I suggested he try it out; if it did not work we could half close the lid. He shook his head vigorously. I pleaded, begged, entreated – all in English. He did not understand half of what I said but he caught the general drift. There was no problem about my understanding his 'no'. A few minutes later Fischer-Dieskau arrived. He, being accustomed to

103

recording with the lid fully open, was not surprised to see the piano. Richter fell upon him with a torrent of German, accompanied by some very Russian gesticulations and clasped parts of his anatomy which variously suggested despair, a broken heart, lumbago, an agonizing toothache or an acute attack of indigestion. I asked Fischer-Dieskau to get him at least to try out the arrangement. After a further prolonged exchange between them Richter bowed his head in resignation; he came up to me, took my right hand, placed his left hand on my shoulder, heaved a deep sigh and, shaking his head tragically, as if he were bidding me farewell before embarking for the steppes of Central Asia, turned to the piano. He sat down on the stool and waved a weary hand to indicate that the proceedings could begin.

They ran through the first few songs; when I invited them to listen to a test recording there was a certain amount of muttering and argument in the hall and then Fischer-Dieskau came in alone. Richter did not want to hear any of it; he was convinced that the singer would be drowned by the piano. We had to rig up a single speaker in the hall to play back to them, monoaurally. The last day of the recording was enlivened by the arrival of Barenboim and Jacqueline du Pré; Barenboim too was due to give a recital in Salzburg.

The news about Barbirolli arrived in Salzburg the day after the Barenboim recital. It was not totally unexpected to me but I knew that it would be a great shock to Barenboim and du Pré, and so my first thought was to get hold of them and break it gently; but they had left for the airport some ten minutes earlier. The news saddened me, but the legacy of records Barbirolli had made would ensure he would always be remembered and the memory of a warm, rich human being would live in the hearts of everyone who knew him.

That evening I walked into the Mozarteum in Salzburg for the *Die schöne Magelone* recital by Fischer-Dieskau and Richter. At first sight the lid of the piano on the stage seemed to be closed; a second and closer look revealed that it was open but only by about five inches. As my wife and I settled down I found that Richter's wife, whom I had met briefly in Munich, was seated on my other side, and the three of us exchanged pleasantries. Presently Fischer-Dieskau and Richter walked on to the stage, acknowledged the applause and the first song began. In this there are four introductory *forte* bars before the singer enters. Even in the solo bars the piano sounded dry and distant, when Fischer-Dieskau entered on the fifth bar it was swamped and seemed to disappear altogether.

Mrs Richter and I looked at each other in dismay, but there was nothing to be done, or at least so I thought. Mrs Richter had other ideas. In a loud stage whisper she said to me, 'Go on the stage and open the piano lid.' I did not believe that she could be serious; it was some kind of Russian joke. 'Go on,' she repeated. I looked at her and realized that it was no joke. She really wanted me, in the middle of a recital, to shuffle past ten other members of the audience to get to the aisle, walk through it, climb up on the stage, open the piano lid and prop it up on its long stick. There was, of course, the possibility, in fact the probability, that Richter, objecting to what I was doing, would respond by taking the lid off its long stick and restoring it to its original position. I was still more amused than alarmed at the thought of wrestling with Richter, in full view of a Salzburg audience, for possession of the piano lid.

'This can't go on,' said Mrs Richter. 'You must open the piano lid.' 'I can't. It's not possible. I can't go on the stage in the middle of a concert.' I tried to keep my voice down but several people could hear us and disapproving glances were directed at us. 'But you must. We can't hear the piano. God, this is terrible.' And then, spacing out the words slowly as if she were addressing someone of subnormal intelligence, she said, 'Go – to – the – stage – and – open – the piano – lid.' I shook my head and whispered, 'It can't be done; it would look ridiculous.' The angry glances were now aimed at me and several voices hissed 'Sh!' I dreaded to think what they imagined; the most charitable interpretation was, 'This ignorant Indian obviously doesn't know that you should not talk at a concert.' And then Mrs Richter said 'You *must.*' I replied, 'I can't' – again, 'You must', 'I can't' – there was clearly no future in this conversation but it went on for the first four songs – by the time the fifth song began, the section of the audience nearest us looked ready to lynch me. By the natural perverseness of things they always seemed to turn towards us when I was talking.

Mrs Richter finally accepted that I was not going to budge and gave up, though periodically there were angry rumblings from her. The interval arrived and she turned to me. 'Now you can go on to the stage and open the lid.' 'No,' I said, 'if you want the lid opened, go backstage and ask your husband to do it.' I managed to get away and stayed in the bar, strategically close to the gentlemen's toilet, into which I proposed to dive if I saw Mrs Richter bearing down on me, though I was not fully convinced she would not follow me there.

When I went back to my seat one look at the stage showed that the lid was still on the small wooden block. The second half of the concert went off peacefully. I went backstage after the concert and as I was talking to Fischer-Dieskau I could see Mrs Richter volubly haranguing Richter; he now looked as if he wished he actually were in the steppes of Central Asia.

My next assignment with Fischer-Dieskau was in Berlin; along the way I had to fight off a determined attempt to take over the recording by the local company, who quite wrongly thought my going to Berlin was a reflection on their capacity to handle the singer. The project was of songs by Mendelssohn, with Wolfgang Sawallisch playing the piano.

The first session of a Fischer-Dieskau recording is strenuous. His voice is difficult to balance because of its enormous dynamic range, much greater than that of any other singer I have recorded. No microphone can comfortably accommodate this range of dynamics; at close quarters even the ear cannot do so. We have had to compress it; in the best Fischer-Dieskau recordings this compression has been kept down to the minimum, and has been successfully camouflaged by the engineer's anticipating extremes of dynamics and compensating for them in advance. But once these initial hurdles have been negotiated the recording proceeds fast, as Fischer-Dieskau works very fast. He comes to recordings well rehearsed. He sings a song through once, and repeats any section he feels needs to be improved; it is very rarely that he thinks it necessary to sing a song through a second time in full. On these sessions he came into the control room two or three times at the beginning of the first session; once a good sound had been obtained he was happy to listen to playbacks on a single loudspeaker in the studio itself. By the end of the first session he had dispensed even with playbacks except for a few songs he felt posed special problems.

The fifth item he recorded was the 'Frühlingslied' Op. 47, by Lenau. After the first take he said he wanted to repeat the first verse and the second half of the second verse; I added, 'And the last line of the song, "Frühlingsmachtig eingedrungen" – I am sure you would like to do that once again.' Fischer-Dieskau said in a surprised tone, 'We here thought that last line rather good.' He added, 'I didn't know you knew German so well' – to which I replied that I didn't, even though I could read fluently the most difficult German text. When he heard the take he agreed that the last line should be done again. The next time we had an apparent difference of opinion I asked would he like to hear the take, to which he replied hastily, 'No, no – down here we believe you absolutely.'

There was something special about these sessions. Fischer-Dieskau was pleased that I had cared enough to go to Berlin myself for them despite the considerable expenditure of time, energy and money. For me, this was our first major project together. Altogether, there was generated that *frisson* which is always attendant on the first encounter between an artist and a producer.

We recorded one long-playing side in each session. The understanding between singer and accompanist was absolute. I knew that Sawallisch would be a sympathetic accompanist – he was a great operatic conductor – but frankly I had not expected such incredible virtuosity on the keyboard. Some of the writing is as difficult as in Mendelssohn's most glitteringly effective solo pieces. They held no terrors for Sawallisch, who despatched the most complex passages with ease. During the recording, he probably played no more than half a dozen wrong notes, and a casual look at any of the songs would indicate what a considerable feat that was.

I could not be in the studio when Fischer-Dieskau sang, but I could imagine him standing tense, almost as if coiled for a sudden leap, the eyes only occasionally looking down at the score, singing effortlessly, the only unusual gesture, now and again he would cup open palms behind his ears, so as to give him, from the reflected sound off them, a closer idea of what his voice sounded like to somebody else. Later that year, when we saw in our garden the shrub *Dicentra spectabilis* in bloom, each flower having two petals curved back, my wife and I with one voice said 'Dieter!'

One of the delights of Fischer-Dieskau's singing of lieder is his enunciation of the text, not only of the more obviously expressive and beautiful sounding words such as *Narzissen, Hyacinthen, Lavendel* and *Basilien* (from the 'Altes Kirchenlied') but also in *silbernen* and *goldenen* (you can almost see the gleam of the precious metals). The word *Tanze* itself dances in the 'Hexenlied', and *seligen Traum* from 'Auf Flügeln des Gesanges' (more familiarly, 'On Wings of Song') has the drugged, half-sleepy colour of a 'blissful dream'.

The attention he pays to the consonants is notable; even more significant is his shaping of the vowels. They are elongated and drawn out, shortened to the point of being clipped, or shaped naturally, depending on the demands of the musical line. For example, the 'iss' of *Narzissen* is clipped, while the same sound in *Wiessen* is pulled out to the fullest possible within the rhythm.

And what wonderful songs they are. The four days of these sessions passed in a flash. I had to leave the final songs in the hands of a local colleague; I was required in London for a recording with Giulini. Leaning into my taxi as it was pulling away, Fischer-Dieskau asked how I would feel about lieder by Brahms? My reply was, 'If you want to read the Berlin telephone directory we'll record it.' So was launched the next major Fischer-Dieskau project.

*

My first recording with Giulini was Beethoven's C major Mass, written in the middle of one of the most prolific periods of creative activity enjoyed by any composer. It belongs to his middle period, though with Beethoven it is misleading to call any work early, middle or late period.

I had never heard the C major Mass or seen a score of it. I knew the Missa Solemnis very well, had sung in it several times under Klemperer and studied the score and Beethoven's masterly and very individual setting of the text. I had read that the earlier mass was a trial run for Op. 123 and had not felt stirred to get to know it. It was with delight that I discovered the many beauties of the work. The setting of the text is no less authoritative here than in Op. 123 – there is the same sense of awe, of the unworthiness of man before the might and the majesty of God, the creator, or the all-powerful or 'Brahm', the god of Hindu mythology referred to in the document known as 'Beethoven's creed' – for Beethoven's god is not merely a Christian god but the *fons et origo* of all mankind. As in the later work, key phrases of the mass are pinpointed and highlighted: 'Christe eleison', 'Et in terra pax', 'Et incarnatus est', 'Et expecto resurrectionem', 'Benedictus', 'Dona nobis pacem' and so on. Less significant sections of the text such as those relating to the holy Catholic church, the saints and the apostles are summarily despatched. In the Missa Solemnis, the immensely powerful outer voices, the sopranos and basses, intone the word 'Credo' with increasing fervour and rising pitch so that the actual text of the mass, given to the inner voices, is swamped. In the C major, he employs a different method – the music modulates through meltingly beautiful harmonies and strange keys so that, as the various lines intertwine to magical effect, the ear is seduced away from the text. In both works, the text once again clearly emerges at 'Et exspecto resurrectionem'. Beethoven himself claimed in a letter to his publishers, 'I have treated the text in a manner in which it has not been treated.'

The venue for our recording was All Saints' Church in Tooting. Giulini uncomplainingly accepted the acoustic of the place – it was only after the record had been issued that he voiced his reservations. When I asked, 'Did you like the Tooting church?' he replied, 'That should be two questions. – "Did I like conducting in Tooting?", the answer "Absolutely no". "Do I like the record made in Tooting?" "Yes." ' To illustrate the problem, the soloists were stationed on a dais in front of the orchestra and slightly behind Giulini's left hand and almost within the reach of an extended baton, yet we had trouble with ensemble. We had to repeat the 'Qui tollis' section of the 'Gloria' several times before we got a take with all of them together. After the third attempt I could see Giulini turn to the soloists and vigorously conduct them from two feet away, leaving the orchestra to fend for itself – and yet I had to ring the hall and tell him that they were not together. Giulini said, 'I can see their lips moving, but I cannot make out clearly what each person is singing.'

We did get it right at last but at the cost of untold distress to Giulini. No conductor, when he is in the full flood of a phrase such as 'Glorificamus te', likes to be rudely interrupted by the discordant jangle of a telephone bell; they react in different ways. Some yell in anger – 'But why have you stopped me?' – some express dismay – 'Oh, no!!' and you can hear the double exclamation marks – others become icily polite – 'And please may we know what was wrong with that?' – and I once heard a conductor utter a very brief Anglo-Saxon word and then attempt to cover it up by nonchalantly humming the phrase which had been cut off in its prime. Giulini did none of these things; he said nothing at all, but every time the telephone interrupted him, I could see him start convulsively as if a bradawl had been jammed sharply into the small of his back. On his face as he reached for the telephone was the look of the martyred Saint Sebastian. Having seen this once, I had asked, on the first session, for a wad of cotton wool to be stuffed into the telephone bell to damp down its strident ring; Giulini thanked me profusely.

During the first take of the last section of the 'Credo' I noticed that Marius Rintzler, the bass soloist, left out one of the two 'Amens' printed in my score, and on the playback I said to him, 'Marius, don't forget the first "Amen" in bar so-and-so.' He looked puzzled, but waited till the end of the playback and then asked, 'What is that "Amen" you were talking about?' I reached for his score to show him the place and found that in it the first 'Amen' was missing. I looked at Giulini's score; it was not in that either, and at the appropriate moment I showed Giulini my score, saying I thought the bass part should have two 'Amens'. Giulini, preoccupied with some other problem, peered absentmindedly at my score and said vaguely 'I suppose so'. They all went back into the church and we had a perfect take of this not so easy section. I was so glad not to have to stab Giulini several more times with the telephone bell that I quite forgot about the 'Amen'.

The next day I went to the Royal Festival Hall for the concert in which the mass was to be sung. As soon as each of them saw me, in succession, the librarian of the orchestra, its personnel manager and Wilhelm Pitz said, 'Giulini wants to see you urgently in the conductor's room.' I found him pacing up and down looking acutely unhappy. He said, 'At the dress rehearsal this morning I realized what it was you were saying to me about that "Amen" for the bass in the "Credo". Of course you are right; I asked Rintzler whether he ever sang the first "Amen" and he says he didn't. What shall we do? We cannot let the record go out without it.' I asked him for a few minutes to sort out the problem, and left him looking incredulous.

I went to the male soloists' room and cutting short Rintzler's 'Giulini wants to see you urgently' asked at what time he was due to leave London the next day. He said at about two o'clock. I said, 'Wait here – don't move', went to a telephone next door and rang the studios. Was Studio 1 free the next morning? It was not, but number two, the smaller one, was. I asked about the engineer who had balanced the mass; he had a day off. I said, 'Hold Studio 2 and book any engineer who will be around tomorrow morning for Beethoven's Mass in C.' 'But you can't get a symphony orchestra and a chorus into No. 2.' 'I don't want to,' I replied, 'only one bass singer.' I went back to Rintzler and said to him, 'Be ready for a car to pick you up at your hotel at eleven in the morning – and practise your first "Amen"'. 'Can I get to the airport in time from Tooting?' he asked. 'Not Tooting,' was my reply, 'Abbey Road.' Rintzler looked puzzled. 'Leave it all to me,' I said.

And then to Giulini. 'It's all fixed,' I said. The next morning I would take Rintzler to the Abbey Road Studios – Giulini interrupted, 'The Tooting church?' I said, 'No – Abbey Road – I'll stand him in front of a microphone and get him to sing the first "Amen" till the sound matches that of the second "Amen"; and then I'll record it on top of what we've already recorded.' Would not the sound be different? asked Giulini, still incredulous. Again I said, 'Leave it all to me.' And that is exactly what happened – except that we almost, but did not quite, match in No. 2 the spacious sound of the Tooting church. As I said goodbye to Rintzler he remarked that I must have noticed the slight change of quality between the two 'Amens'. I laughed. 'Marius, I bet you it will be said by someone what a consummate artist you are to colour the two "Amens" differently!' Again, that is exactly what happened.

1971 began splendidly, with *Così fan tutte*, conducted by Klemperer. Margaret Price and Yvonne Minton were the sisters, Popp was their maid, the lovers were Luigi Alva and Geraint Evans and Hans Sotin was Don Alfonso. Four of them had worked with Klemperer before and the singers new to him, Minton and Alva, adjusted to his ways without difficulty. I had hoped, through my production, to make explicit a point of view I firmly hold about this opera – that Don Alfonso did not set out merely out of devilry to show that 'all women are like that', that is, inconstant, but with the more specific and practical objective of demonstrating to the lovers that they are wrongly paired. He is really a wise old philosopher (the libretto is explicit on this) and tries to show that they should change partners. It would be ridiculous for Fiordiligi, after her surrender to Ferrando in the duet 'Fra gli amplessi', to go back to Guglielmo.

In the concerted piece which brings the opera to an end I placed Alfonso and Despina as the organizers of the plot on the centre microphone. Fiordiligi and Ferrando were to the left and Dorabella and Guglielmo to the right. On the first take, these four singers went wildly astray. There was much whispering among them before the second take. This was better but, 'Why are you all belting out this whole section at the tops of your voices?' I asked. 'The dynamics are from *sotto voce* to *forte*.' Evans put the score in front of me and explained: 'You see how the parts of the two men and of the two women intertwine – and it's very fast music. The only way that Luigi and I can be together is to be able to hear each other and that goes for Margaret and Yvonne; and the only way we can hear is to shout at each other across the stage. Have a heart, Suvi, the old man's beat is not always easy to follow. You've got to get us all closer to each other.' I have never allowed a beautiful theory or a fancy conception to override a practical consideration and so, after having tried various other groupings, had to place the women together and the men together, wryly remarking, 'I do hope no one thinks, hearing this recording, that any of us believes the resolution of the opera is a homosexual and incestuous one!' But I did not want to give up.

After experimenting, I thought we had found the solution – to pair them electronically by coupling the outputs of the relative microphones. Alas

– somehow the lines got crossed and to my chagrin the two pairs ended up as at the beginning of the opera. I wonder whether it was Mozart himself who did the switch.

We were all very sad at the end of this recording; it had been a friendly, cohesive company of singers and producer united in our affection and respect for Klemperer and determination to do all in our power to help him realize his interpretation of the work, and we all had a feeling that this could be our last recording with him.

16   Refurbishing

For some six years past, in addition to my normal work, I had been engaged in another activity which gave me as much satisfaction as producing new records. This was the refurbishing of old recordings from the archives of EMI, which contain a rich treasury of great performances by legendary musicians. I had taken this on almost casually. For the four years from the time I joined the company till Legge left, an item had figured regularly on the weekly progress sheet. I had watched the entry, 'Furtwängler: *Tristan und Isolde* – reissue' accompanied by remarks indicating its lack of progress; the projected date of release travelled from January 1961 to September 1964. Occasionally Legge wrote rude memos on the subject, but nothing actually happened. Normally the entry 'Pending with Mr Legge's office' would have irked me, but this was one of Legge's most notable recordings and if he was not concerned about it, it would have been presumptuous of me to get involved. When Legge left I took stock of the department and when the next report arrived I rang a colleague at headquarters to ask what it was all about. He laughed, 'Why? Are you going to tackle the problem?' I replied that I might if I knew what the problem was. He explained that the recording dated back to 1953. Since then cutting machines and techniques had greatly improved; the idea was that we should get a better sounding set for reissue. Of course it sounded simpler than it actually was; my colleague was concerned that I shouldn't burn my fingers. 'Suvi,' he said, 'leave it alone; it has dragged on because, given its great reputation as a performance, people are afraid to touch it. If the reissue is a disappointment the responsibility would fall on them.' Well, if to everyone else the Furtwängler *Tristan* was a sacred cow, to me it was just another recording. 'I bet you I shall have cleared this thing up in two months' time,' I ventured. 'Ha, ha, ha,' he replied. 'I'll give you six months and you won't have sorted it out even then.' The recording was actually ready for reissue in just a month.

Two of the original twelve sides were very short and so I managed to get the set on to ten sides. That got rid of a risible turn-over point in Scene II of Act III, which heralds the final sublime moments of the opera. Side twelve began with Isolde singing, 'Ich bin's, ich bin's', while side eleven ended with the single syllable 'Ha'; this was abruptly cut off and sounded on the record like 'Hup' – exactly as if Flagstad had made a valiant but unsuccessful attempt to suppress a belch.

Having done that I ran the discs and the master tapes in synchronization and switched from one to the other. The tape, naturally, was better than the disc. I made notes as I concentrated on the sound. The main problem was the balance between the voices and the orchestra. At the time the recording was made it was believed that in opera people wanted to hear the singers. Nobody cared much about the orchestral part. The conductor was there merely to produce an accompaniment to the singers, whether it was just an 'oom, pa, pa' in Donizetti or Bellini or even early Verdi, or the lines of counterpoint and leitmotivs of Wagner. So the singers were placed prominently forward and the devil take the orchestra. I felt that the balance had to be tilted away from the voices so that they and the orchestra were equally prominent. Since the original recording was basically an excellent one, with my training in science, I found the answer easily. The range of the human voice, from basso profondo to high soprano, mostly lies in the region between the second C below middle C and a little above the second C above middle C on the piano – roughly four octaves and a bit; in terms of physics, between 65 and 1046 vibrations a second. All I had to do to give the orchestra greater prominence was, judiciously, to emphasize electronically the frequencies above and below the range of the voices – and considering that a tuba starts from about 43 cycles per second and a piccolo can play notes of up to 4000 cycles per second, taking only the fundamentals into account, a wide field was available. I experimented with various combinations of settings till I found that which seemed to produce a satisfactory balance without affecting the kind of sound special to the conductor – and I had a set of lacquers cut to demonstrate the new sound I proposed for the reissue. My chief heard selected bits and said, 'Splendid – let the reissue go ahead.' I rang my colleague, 'John, *Tristan* is ready and it's only one month since I took it up.' And so the item went off our progress report. The reissue was a success. At that time the policy of EMI was that its producers should be anonymous and so the press reported that the EMI engineers seemed to have done an excellent retransfer.

I had found the job immensely rewarding – and now requests started to come in from colleagues and sales people for me to tackle other old recordings. *Tristan* was followed by the Kempe *Die Meistersinger*, another great performance, and this had an even greater impact, for this time the difference between the original sound and that on the reissue was startling; the Berlin Philharmonic, from providing a rather cloudy backing to firm voiced singers, had now leapt forward to the plane of the singers as an equal partner.

The Wagner operas were succeeded by several other recordings – of lieder, orchestral works and other operas. Perhaps the most spectacular

113

successes I have had in this field, and the most enjoyable, are of three great Karajan recordings. When in 1970 I heard that a rival company was proposing to mount a new recording of Strauss's *Der Rosenkavalier*, my first thought was that this was an unnecessary exercise; I felt *the* recording of this opera was that by Karajan with Schwarzkopf, Ludwig, Edelmann and Stich-Randall in the leading roles. It had been made in 1957, when the cast was the best available, the Philharmonia Orchestra in its prime and Karajan at the height of his powers. Recording too was in its primal stage of innocence – with a straightforward two-track stereo set up, and before engineers and producers had started to become self-conscious and to theorize about their work – fatal in any branch of artistic activity. All in all, I did not believe that the quality of *Der Rosenkavalier* was going to be matched, leave alone excelled. And then it struck me that this recording should be refurbished.

I started with the usual exercise of comparing the tape of side 1 against the disc – as was to be expected, the tape sounded better. So, even if we transferred the tape to disc without any tinkering with it, the result would be superior to any other set currently available. Having disposed of that, I turned to the tape. At one point I heard what appeared to be an audible edit. However, when the tape was run back, there was no telltale sticking tape to indicate an edit. I asked the engineer to check the tape and tell me how many edits there were in side 1. There was just one. I knew at once that the tape I had was a copy and not the original master tape; wonderful artists though they all were, I refused to believe that they could have produced this near-flawless performance of nearly thirty minutes, with just one edit. I asked for the original tapes to be produced and after much running around they were found.

I ran this tape and knew that it was indeed the original master, for it had the number of edit points I would have thought usual. When I ran this master in parallel with the master used for the transfer, the difference was startling. There was a bloom, a sparkle, a warmth and a natural resonance and air about the original in comparison with which the copy was, in Legge's favourite phrase, 'a travesty'.

It took me quite some time and a great deal of delving into old files to discover the reason. In the first scene the curtain goes up on the Marschallin and Octavian lying on a bed having just made love. On the recording, for this scene, Schwarzkopf and Ludwig were placed half left and half right of centre, which was an eminently sensible and well balanced arrangement. Someone had apparently been disturbed by this positioning and had raised the point that half left to half right of centre on a stage would measure anything up to thirty feet and therefore the placement of the singers would suggest a bed thirty feet broad or long. There was an agitated, and, to my 1970 eyes, extremely foolish and ill-argued, exchange of correspondence on the subject, at the end of which it was decided that the entire side would be copied with the stereo spread narrowed.

By 1970 we had grown up to accept stereo as an aid to better recorded sound and did not take positions of singers to relate directly to the stage. I decided to go back to the original tapes for the reissue. After having ironed out some clumsy edits I gave orders for the transfer – this consisted simply of my telling the cutter: 'We both agree on what is a good sound; this set needs the usual slight fattening of the low bass and a little titivation of the top. That is all. If you think it necessary let me have a test lacquer.' When I had heard the lacquer I issued a further, even briefer instruction. 'The top needs to be added higher up – not at 5000 cycles.'

The reissue was a stunning success. Purely by accident, though our rivals would not believe this, our recording and theirs were released in successive months and the verdict was unanimous that the new set was a good one but the thirteen-year-old recording was a great one – in every respect better. At a party a few months later the producer of the new recording arrived. Our host said, 'You know each other, don't you? – John Culshaw, Suvi Grubb.' Culshaw shook my hand with a friendly smile and said, 'You are a dirty swine.' I put on my most innocent-looking face. 'What have I done?' He replied, 'You know perfectly well what you've done.' Our host was taken aback, but I reassured him. 'Don't worry. We are still friends' – and later, he saw us engaged in an amicable conversation.

The competition for the refurbished *Falstaff* has been of an altogether different calibre – it is from Karajan himself. The stereo recording of the opera had been issued in 1961. For fifteen years, it had been the best recorded version in the catalogue. In 1976, when all Columbia recordings had been transferred to the HMV label, I had taken the opportunity to refurbish *Falstaff*. Two years later, I saw Karajan in a Berlin restaurant and went over to pay my respects. In the course of our conversation I said I hoped he had no plans to rerecord either *Der Rosenkavalier* or *Falstaff*. He replied that I was quite right. He considered them as near perfection as we could hope to reach in an imperfect world. Some years later I learnt that he *was* going to rerecord *Falstaff*. I decided to have another go at our recording with the even more sophisticated equipment we now had. To make our reissue even more competitive, I managed to get the opera on to four instead of the previous six sides.

Again, fortuitously, our set and the new Karajan recording came out almost at the same time. But this time it was difficult to arrive at a clear decision as to which was the better. The wizard had done the nearly impossible – he had achieved near perfection a second time, and even I would be hard put to it to decide, on purely musical grounds, which one to keep if I was permitted to have only one of them. As a postscript, I was told that the maestro was not amused.

The third set of Karajan recordings was that of the Beethoven symphonies recorded by him in the fifties with the Philharmonia. These, for me, are the best performances by Karajan of these works. There is a concentrated intensity, passionate feeling and a sure shaping of the architectural design of the symphonies in these performances. As recordings they are first class and capable of standing up to any later versions – in the exposition of the *Eroica*, for example, the first subsidiary theme is given in succession to the oboe, the clarinet, the flute and the first violins, while the cellos and basses play a fragment of the main theme *staccato* – every detail is clear in this recording and what is more every instrument has the same degree of intensity, presence, colour and bloom. I know of no other recording in which the sense of perspective of these instruments is so vivid and natural.

They were, however, monoaural recordings, and the sales departments insisted that a refurbished mono set of Beethoven's symphonies stood no chance in the market of the late seventies. I was equally unyielding about not allowing the tapes to undergo the usual process of conversion into 'mock stereo', for that would have destroyed the diamond-sharp clarity and sparkle of the sound; a demonstration tape prepared of the *Eroica* in mock stereo showed this. So I had to experiment to find a new method of producing a stereo tape from mono tapes. I was immensely gratified, and a little amused, when one German reviewer of this reissue made special mention of the stereo spread; our method, which is confidential, seemed to have worked.

*

Current projects included two more recordings with Fischer-Dieskau. Over the years Fischer-Dieskau had made records with many other pianists in addition to his principal accompanist, Gerald Moore. Ever since I had actively taken over as his producer, it had been one of my ambitions to set up a record of him with Barenboim. They had performed together in the concert hall with great success, and there was an exceptionally close understanding between them. The opportunity arose in 1971. I had hoped that the lieder would be by Schubert but that could not be. We selected Mozart – in some ways a better choice, for Fischer-Dieskau had never recorded Mozart lieder before.

The first session of this record was quite terrible – we did not record a single note in two and a half hours. We tried everything, moved the piano to every conceivable corner, some of the positions being quite ridiculous; we tried the singer facing the piano, standing in line with the keyboard and all the other combinations which had been tried in Studio I and had been known to work and some which had never before been tried. Colleagues of the engineer, the head of the studio and others turned up with helpful suggestions. Nothing worked. The piano posed no problem at all – within the first few minutes Barenboim declared he was happy. But wherever we placed Fischer-Dieskau we could not get him to sound natural at the two extremes of his dynamic range. It was lovely when he sang softly and up to *mezzo-forte*; louder than that the voice sounded ugly and forced – or rich and rounded in fortissimos only to disappear when the voice fined down to even *mezzo-piano*. He and Barenboim patiently saw out that session; there was no outburst. But we of the recording team were agonized. Towards the end of the session I asked Fischer-Dieskau if he would give us one more hour that afternoon; I promised that, if we were not succcessful, we would abandon the session. Fischer-Dieskau agreed and we broke up to meet again at 4 p.m.

I had a session in the afternoon, also for voice with cello and harpsi-chord continuo. Elly Ameling had to sing an aria from Bach's Cantata No. 147. The rest of the work had been recorded at King's College, Cambridge, and owing to a shortage of time this aria had been left out; I now had to match in No. 1 Abbey Road the completely different sound of King's. At any other time this might have appeared to be a formidable undertaking but after the experience of the morning it seemed a mere bagatelle. Curiously enough, when we started with the last set-up we had tried for Fischer-Dieskau it worked perfectly for Elly Ameling and the session finished ahead of time, giving us a little breathing space.

We began the second Fischer-Dieskau session, using the same positioning of the piano and the singer, and, oddly, the sound now was perfect – singer and piano were matched exactly, Fischer-Dieskau's voice was captured with all its richness and expressiveness and Barenboim's colouring of piano tone came through with fidelity. After having frowned on us in the morning the gods had suddenly relented.

The anxieties and tribulations of the first session were more than compensated for by what followed. I shall always carry with me the memory of these sessions as particularly rewarding. The first steps were taken which were to lead to a close friendship between Fischer-Dieskau and me. Up till then our relationship had been formal, but towards the end of the second session, after the first take of 'Abendempfindung', I made various suggestions and Fischer-Dieskau asked, 'And what about the last stanza, Suvi?' From now on we were on first name terms.

If anyone feels impelled to rush out and buy a copy of the record about which I have just written, they are in for a disappointment; it has long since been deleted from the catalogue. And before someone else begins to talk about philistine gramophone record companies interested only in money and caring nothing for artistic values, let me briefly relate the history of this record. When I first proposed a recording of Mozart lieder with these two artists I was left in no doubt that we would be lucky to break even on the project. The English and the German companies put in modest estimates, the French said they might have put in a small estimate for

French songs, but for Mozart said 'no, thanks', and the Americans, the fourth of the big markets, said that they would be lucky to sell a couple of thousand records. Nevertheless, in the full knowledge that we would lose some money on it, it was decided to make the record. Why? For reasons of prestige – we wanted it to be our company to record Fischer-Dieskau singing lieder he had never before recorded; we wanted to be the first to record him and Barenboim together in lieder.

And so the record was made, received excellent notices, made a stir and went on the market. The public was quite indifferent – they did not buy it even in the small numbers which would have made it worthwhile to retain it in the catalogue – for it costs money just to have a record stay there. After twenty-four months, it had to be taken out and is unlikely to be available ever again. The next time anyone feels like criticizing a record company it would be as well to remember this cautionary tale.

We next went to the Tooting church and were joined by Sheila Armstrong, Janet Baker, Nicolai Gedda, the John Alldiss Choir and the English Chamber Orchestra for the Mozart Requiem. Since Barenboim's performance of the work in 1967, I had wanted to record it with him, and here, at last, it was. There was no concert performance of it before the recording, but Barenboim was able in one rehearsal to communicate his vision of the work. This is a dramatic and highly charged view – almost fiercely so at times – the 'Dies Irae', for example, is furiously driven, but it lies within the context of the interpretation as a whole, and does no violence to Mozart's directions.

17 Perlman Arrives

For some time Barenboim had been telling us of another young Israeli violinist who, he said, was in the Zukerman class and whom we should try and get. It did not seem possible that there could be in one generation two violinists of world class appearing from a country the size of Israel, but from the Zukerman experience we knew the danger of ignoring Barenboim's advice in these matters. By late 1970, I myself had heard enough of Perlman and his records to know what an exceptional player he was. Aided by Barenboim, who advised Perlman that both musically and in the interests of his career it was to his advantage at that time to throw in his lot with us, we managed to get Perlman to sign a contract with us for the next three years. It laid the foundation for another of those richly rewarding experiences of my working life.

Three days after the Mozart Requiem, with a lively anticipation of musical delights to come, I welcomed Itzhak Perlman to Studio 1 for his first record. As it was his first visit, I would have taken special steps to ensure that he felt at home, but they were largely unnecessary, for with me were two of his closest friends, Zukerman and Barenboim. We were to record three violin concertos by Bach – the E major played by Perlman, the two violin concertos by Perlman and Zukerman and a G minor concerto played by Zukerman, all with Barenboim conducting the English Chamber Orchestra.

We started with the last concerto, so that Perlman was not required till the second session. When he came in we had only to seat him and Zukerman on either side of the conductor and ensure that they balanced each other and were balanced with the orchestra. This took just a few minutes. After they had all listened to the test the two violinists expressed satisfaction each with the sound of his instrument. However, as they went back into the studio, they both privately told me that they thought the other had slightly more presence than he himself '. . . nothing to really get worried about, but I thought I would mention it to you . . .' Their comments were couched in almost identical words. I waited till they were both seated and went up to them and said, 'Each of you feels the other has more presence, I think that is the surest indication that the balance is fair and I am quite content to leave it at that. The moment one of you stops complaining I shall start worrying.'

119

There were three complete takes of the first movement – there was no need for any corrections, for the last performance was flawless. There were three takes again of the second movement, and one correction to cover a slight fluff. There were two complete takes of the last movement and we repeated two sections to cover mishaps. It was wonderful to hear such soloists; when they took over from each other, the join was seamless – it was as if one single musical mind and pair of hands was in command. On the sessions, without the help of the score or the stereo positioning, I could not decide who was playing at any time. When the record was released, I was told, even their parents could not make out which one was *primo* and which *secondo*. Barenboim presided over the music making genially, as the elder statesman he already was in the hierarchy of EMI artists.

Three weeks later, in Kingsway Hall, came the first big test of my association with Perlman, as a soloist on his own. He was to record Paganini's First Violin Concerto and a dazzling fantasia on *Carmen* by Sarasate with the Royal Philharmonic Orchestra conducted by Lawrence Foster. Perlman produces a pure, clear and sweet tone on his violin, a Stradivarius that has one idiosyncrasy – the G string has about twice the power and richness of the other strings. To capture this sound faithfully requires the placement of microphones at a critically exact distance from the sounding board and the angle of tilt has to be even more exact. On every session, these have to be worked out afresh – even on an afternoon session when the sound in the morning has been perfect; a little extra humidity, a slightly warmer or colder air temperature, a minute change of position by Perlman on his chair – any one of these is likely to change the quality of the sound sufficiently for it to be less than ideal.

On this first session, he and I had first to find a common terminology with which to communicate. This is not as easy as one might expect, for sound quality is incredibly difficult to describe in words. Take for instance the word 'resonance'; the dictionary definition is 'sonority; sympathetic vibration'. In recording terms we use the word to describe the 'sympathetic vibrations' which are set up in a studio, hall or whatever. Resonance can be insufficient, or too much; in the former the sound is hard and brutally clinical, and in the latter it is ill-defined and swimmy. It can be top-heavy or bass-heavy, in each case making the upper or lower frequencies muffled or unclear.

'Presence', on the other hand, is the quality by which you feel that an artist is in your presence even though you hear him through a pair of loudspeakers. Presence is actually obtained from the direct sound from the sound source. On that first session there was a great exchange of explanations between Perlman and me. This was only the first, somewhat hesitant, step towards the total understanding which now exists between us.

Even on that first solo record of his I marvelled at Perlman's virtuosity and his ability to infuse poetry into pieces of no great profundity – with a turn of phrase, a suggestion of a slide between notes, a sudden pianissimo, a leap of two octaves or more dead in tune, harmonics, again dead in tune, sounding like angels on the flute, he can produce a catch in one's heart.

This was to be Perlman's first recording on our label. However, unexpectedly, and at a rather late stage in the proceedings, the sales people said that in their opinion the Paganini concerto was not, on its own, a strong enough title to launch a major artist. They had a point but, I felt, should have thought of it earlier. And so I persuaded Perlman to fly from his home in New York to London for three days to record Paganini's caprices for unaccompanied violin as a companion piece for the concerto. No studio was available for all three days. On the first day we recorded caprices numbers one to six, and had two trial runs of number twelve, in our Studio No. 1; on the following two days we recorded the other eighteen in Brent Town Hall, which could comfortably have accommo-dated two No. 1 Studios in it. I defy anyone to identify the three bars from Studio No. 1 inserted in number twelve, the rest of which was recorded in Brent!

This was my first experience of Perlman's extraordinary stamina. He arrived in London late in the evening on 9 January; on the 10th he recorded from 6 p.m. to midnight; on the 11th from 2.30 p.m. to 10 p.m., and on the 12th from 10 a.m. to 5 p.m. And in every session he had to play without let-up – there were no orchestral or piano interludes to give him any breathing space – it was an unaccompanied violin all the time. The caprices are not comfortable pieces; they are diabolically difficult. He did not flag until he reached the last caprice, the eternally popular No. 24. After he had played it through for the first time there was silence in the hall. I called out, 'Itzhak!' There was a weary sigh. 'Yes? I suppose you want me to hear that.' The recording was edited in two days and the cassette I sent to New York nearly overtook Perlman on his journey back.

That night, having listened to unaccompanied violin music for five days without rest during my waking hours, the fiddle invaded my sleep. I woke up at about two in the morning with a start and what the Count in *Capriccio* calls a tickling of my ears by a fiddle. I lay awake for a while and could not rid myself of the feeling that two inches away from my head a violin was playing trills, arpeggios, spiccato runs, runs in consecutive thirds and fifths and glissandos. I ducked my head under the pillow to kill this feeling. I lay with my eyes open. I recalled all the notable woodwind solos in the Mozart piano concertos and the brass themes in Bruckner. I even tried to conjure up some of the juicier 'X' films I had seen. All to no avail. In sheer desperation, I got out of bed, went into the sitting room, switched on the record-player, and at its lowest possible volume, with my head practically in one loudspeaker, so as not to disturb my wife, I listened to music for unaccompanied voices till I had finally exorcised the ghostly violin.

Two days later I was back on the unaccompanied violin. Perlman had heard the cassette and for sixty-seven minutes, on the transatlantic telephone, he listed the sections he wanted improved; since there were no bar numbers in his score, quite frequently we had to sing bits of the music to each other. Perlman's capacity to make something magical out of ordinary material is brilliantly demonstrated on this record. These caprices can sometimes sound like exercises; listen to Perlman in No. 5 – the long scales at the beginning and at the end are dead in tune and even in duration with perfectly shaped crescendos and decrescendos, and the middle section is terrifyingly fast but beautifully shaped; it is difficult to believe that fingers could move so fast and accurately.

I had an additional reason for satisfaction when these records were released. EMI had always insisted on anonymity for its producers. The argument ran that a recording was not the production of one man but the result of a team to which the manager, the accountants, lawyers, secretaries and everyone else belonged. But it was plainly absurd to claim that a producer's contribution was no more important than that of the supporting staff. From the time a recording began – till its release, one man and only one, the producer, carried the sole responsibility for it, holding in his hands the reputation of the artist and the fortunes of the company.

The real reason for this anonymity, one suspects, was the fear in record companies that if producers received publicity they might start to develop ideas above their station and perhaps claim the benefits and perquisites enjoyed by the administrators. This attitude led to some quite ridiculous situations; the recording of *Die lustige Witwe* carried a credit to an 'assistant producer' who was not on the staff of EMI, but no credit to the producer, Walter Legge. The first Perlman recordings were among the earliest on which EMI finally agreed to accept the inevitable and print the names of the producers on record sleeves.

Actually, much earlier, I had seen just how well-informed some record collectors were about producers; at the time, it was an acutely embarrassing experience. I was in Edinburgh for a concert in the Usher Hall of Barenboim and Zubin Mehta with the Israel Philharmonic Orchestra. Before it started Mehta, Barenboim, du Pré and my wife and I were standing outside the conductor's room, at the foot of the stairs leading to the gallery. A young man dashed in, looked cursorily at us, and rushed up the stairs taking them two at a time. He pulled up with a jerk on the landing, turned round, looked at us again and came down the stairs three at a time. Having reached us he opened his programme, thrust it into my hands and said, 'Please sign.' I was completely flummoxed. Why should he want *my* signature? Perhaps he was under the impression I was the

Indian conductor Zubin Mehta – he could not possibly have believed I was Daniel Barenboim – although Mehta was in tails and I in a lounge suit. Feeling extremely foolish I pointed to the musicians and said, 'Surely you want one of them to autograph your programme?' He was positive about what he wanted. 'No, I want you to sign. You are Suvi Raj Grubb, aren't you – the person who produced his (pointing to Barenboim) Beethoven concertos with Klemperer? Please sign here.' He pointed to the relevant item in the EMI advertisement about Barenboim. Du Pré, Barenboim and Mehta were all trying not to laugh – my embarrassment was, I am sure, comic. Feeling silly and something of an impostor, I signed the programme. 'They are very good records,' he said. 'Thank you,' and once more dashed up the stairs. Mehta provided the postscript to this incident. 'Grubb sahib,' he said, 'to work behind the scenes and still be recognized – that's real fame.'

18   The Last Records of Two Great Artists

There were two recordings in 1971 which, in retrospect, assumed a special significance.

Klemperer had earlier recorded Mozart's Serenade for eight wind instruments in C minor. I felt that its companion piece, the E flat Serenade for the same combination, would make an excellent coupling for it and so a recording of this work was set up in September. He had never conducted the work, and there was no concert performance of it. There was an extraordinarily single-minded concentration by Klemperer on these sessions; there was no raillery or gossiping – all his energies were focused on the music.

Neither of these serenades is easy to bring off. They pose problems of balance arising from the usual reason that modern wind instruments are different from those of Mozart's time. It was especially evident in the third movement of this one, the wonderful adagio. We did a runthrough of the movement towards the end of one session. Klemperer was plainly dissatisfied with the balance, not on the recording but in the studio. He held up the score, peered at it and shook his head. I suggested that by a slight rearrangement of the microphones the recording team should assist him to obtain the sort of balance he wanted; he rejected the offer. When he left for his hotel he said he would look again at the score that evening. The next morning, at the crack of dawn, my telephone rang; there were no polite formalities, Klemperer came straight to the point. 'I think I have found the answer to the Serenade – we have much work to do today,' and rang off. When my wife asked in a sleepy voice, 'Who was that?', equally sleepily, I replied, 'Nobody. I've just dreamt that Klemperer spoke to me.'

When he arrived at the studio, he showed me his alterations of dynamics – the main object was to make the instrument carrying the melodic line come through clearly at all times – the horns from bars eight to fifteen, the first oboe from sixteen to eighteen and again for two bars from forty, the first clarinet from forty-eight to fifty-four, and so on. He explained the reason behind each alteration, and said, 'I shall play these passages – you hear them and let me know if they are as I would desire.' I had worked with Klemperer so long that I did not feel unduly weighed down by the responsibility he was placing on me. He went through the first four sections; after each one he reached for the telephone and asked me was it as he desired; I said yes four times. On the fifth passage the theme still did not stand out enough for me, and I told him I was not quite sure of this one. He replied, 'I will come and listen to it myself.' He heard only two bars and said, 'No, that is not enough. I shall mark the other parts *piano* instead of *mezzo forte piano*. Listen again.' This time, when the telephone rang, 'Is it now what I wish?' I replied, 'Yes, doctor.'

At the end of the sessions we made plans for the recording of Mozart's *Die Entführung* in January 1973. But this was Klemperer's last record.

*

He had had a long, fulfilled life and had made a vast library of gramophone records representing the various stages of his artistic development. Jacqueline du Pré was only at the threshold of her maturity when, in December 1971, she made *her* last record.

She herself cannot pinpoint the exact time when she started to experience mysterious and inexplicable symptoms of a vague nature, a general malaise. Occasionally these became more specific – a slight tingling at the tips of her fingers, a curious feeling, as she put it, of her arms and legs appearing to be made of lead, the apparent unwillingness of her hands to obey the commands of her mind, and often a lassitude which seemed to drain her of all energy. None of these was severe or incapacitating enough to cause her alarm but were nonetheless irritating. It is hard to believe, when you look at photographs of her in the album of Beethoven Trios with Barenboim and Zukerman, and in Gerald Moore's Seventieth Birthday record, that she was already labouring under the handicaps of the earliest stages of a serious illness. By early 1971 the symptoms had become sufficiently acute for her to be unable, on occasions, to play up to her normal standards and she had to cancel some concerts and tours abroad. One of these was a long-cherished project for which all the preliminary arrangements had been made and of which I had high hopes – Schubert's 'Trout' Quintet with Perlman, Zukerman, Barenboim and a suitable double-bass player. It was at first thought that her complaint was psychosomatic. Whatever Jacqueline du Pré herself might have thought she kept to herself, dutifully going for psychoanalysis and following other doctors' orders.

It was a period when she grew even closer to my wife and me. She lived around the corner from us and at least once a week she visited us, pottering around the kitchen while my wife cooked, sipping a glass of dry sherry, taking pot luck with us, talking about music and literature. She discovered in herself as natural a capacity to respond to the beauty of words as to music. Once we listened to Schubert's String Quintet and I asked her which of the two cello parts she would choose to play. She replied in mock despair, 'Can't I play both parts?' All the while, Barenboim watched over her solicitously, only occasionally allowing close friends, such as ourselves, to catch a glimpse of the immense strain he was under.

Between the Beethoven Trios around New Year's Day 1970 and the end of 1971 she had made one record – the Dvořák Cello Concerto with Barenboim and the Chicago Symphony Orchestra. By rights I should have gone to Chicago to produce this record, but it was taken over by a colleague. The reason advanced for this was that recording in America was fraught with tension and worry and the company did not wish to risk serious damage to my health – and that it would be unsafe to send a brown-skinned person to Chicago. It sounded quite unconvincing to me and I was bitterly disappointed not to be with two of the artists closest to me in one of their major recordings.

For nearly two years du Pré made no records at all in London. Looking back with the benefit of hindsight it seems such a tragic waste of time. We could have made another ten to fifteen records, for she worked very fast. Her intonation was almost faultless (and for string players that is the most time-consuming factor in recording) and she hardly ever produced an ugly sound. With the right people working with her she could complete one side of an LP in one session. If only I had known; but I had no reason to think that anything would come in the way of a long career.

During those years the staff of Abbey Road missed 'Jacquie', as she was to everyone. Those who worked with her adored her, for she was the ideal recording artist, undemanding, understanding and sympathetic to other people's problems. The engineers in particular loved her. She never complained, however long it took to get the right sound on the tape, and the range of her dynamics and the subtleties of tone colour she could produce made her difficult to balance. For me, the all too brief six years which was the span of our working partnership are a golden memory of unaffected, joyous music making. It is very rare in the musical world for anyone to be universally loved. Jacqueline du Pré is one of possibly three artists I know of whom I have never heard anyone say anything unkind.

On 8 December 1971, Barenboim rang me to ask was Studio 1 free on the 10th and the 11th. He asked would I please book it for a test recording for two days, and then explained that Jacqueline du Pré had two days earlier suddenly taken her cello out of its case and started to play. 'It's incredible,' he said. 'You wouldn't believe she hasn't touched the cello for over five months; it's as if she last played only a few days ago.' Barenboim did not want to raise my hopes, nor did he want to put du Pré under any stress. They would play in the studio, and if all went well we would have a record. They had been studying the Chopin Sonata and the arrangement for cello of the Franck Violin Sonata. I arranged for two sessions on each of the two days and waited impatiently for the 10th.

Du Pré and Barenboim duly arrived, and settled down in the studio to warm up. She played with all her usual spirit and complete technical mastery. Truly, this girl – she was only twenty-five then – deserved what Klemperer once said of her to Barenboim: 'She is a genius.'

She made light work of the two sonatas. We needed only one take of the Chopin third movement and by lunch time on the 11th the record had been completed. She was in exuberant spirits and suggested that on the afternoon session we start on the long awaited Beethoven cello sonatas. Barenboim and I exchanged glances; she looked tired, but we decided to play it by ear. They played through the first movement of Op. 5 No. 1. Du Pré placed the cello back into the case, snapped it shut and said, 'That's all, I am afraid, for today.' We did not know it at the time but that was her last appearance with a cello in a recording studio. To paraphrase the epitaph on Schubert, her records 'entomb a rich treasure but still fairer hopes.'

In 1973 her illness was at last given its dreadful name, and in me, as I am sure in the hearts of all who knew and loved her, there was an anguished cry of, 'Oh, no!' What was it that made Jacqueline du Pré so special an artist and that makes her loss to music so unbearable? First of all her total mastery of the instrument. The cello is a difficult instrument to play. Its very size makes it difficult to control and it requires strong muscles and fingers to handle it and coax a beguiling sound from it. With du Pré, however, one's immediate impression was that the cello was an extension of herself. She carried it and handled it easily and comfortably. She is tall and well-built and this contributed to the effortlessness with which she played.

She had the capacity to produce amazing gradations of colour and shade, and had an instinctive feeling for the emotional content of the music. She was an unselfish player and so was an ideal partner in chamber music. She has often said to me that she hated practising and I have never arrived at her house to find her practising – playing music, yes, but not scales or arpeggios or exercises. (Sometimes I have seen her engaged in more improbable occupations such as hammering in a nail, steadying it with her fingers while I watched horrified!) I cannot explain how the notes came so easily to her, but then you cannot explain genius. This last du Pré record brought to the forefront a problem which had exercised me for some time.

The use of tape for recording was one of the most notable advances made in the development of recording. The range of recorded sound was greatly expanded. You could cut the recorded tape and splice together bits from several different performances to obtain a recording free of all blemishes or imperfections. When stereo arrived it was possible to achieve an even greater degree of fidelity. For stereo, as for mono, the tape is a quarter-inch ribbon of plastic or other material one side of which is coated with a chemical compound which reacts to magnetism.

In course of time a more sophisticated use of tape was developed; this was multi-track recording. Its name describes it exactly. The quarter-inch tape with two tracks was replaced by a half inch, or one inch, or two inch tape carrying more tracks – four, six, eight, or as many as you liked.

Why more than two tracks? For flexibility and economy. Session time costs money. Multi-track recording was, and still is, considered to be a means of getting a satisfactory sound quickly – you record the various components of the sound on different sets of tracks. The violins, violas and cellos on two; the woodwind on two; the brass on two; horns and basses, two difficult groups of instruments to balance, on one each; timpani and percussion, if any, on two; singers or soloists, if any, on another two; and the ambience or reverberation of the sound in the studio on two. You still had two tracks of a sixteen-track system free. In peace and the leisure of an extended period later, you could put all these various tracks together and reduce them or 'mix' them down to the quarter-inch two-track stereo tape from which the disc would be cut. It was therefore welcomed as a flexible method of recording.

Perfect in theory – in practice, there were shoals of snags. First the leeway you wanted to increase or decrease the volume of sound from any set of tracks was severely restricted. This was simply because no track had on it only the sound you wanted it to carry – it had on it a clear, close, well-focused image of the sound it was intended to pick up but also carried a confused, ill-defined mixture of all the other sources of sound in the studio. The string tracks, for example, would carry a clean string sound, not necessarily beautiful but in clear focus; and if the sound was somewhat dry the ambience of the strings picked up on the other tracks would modify that. But the string tracks also carried a muddy, swimming sound of the other sections of the orchestra – the woodwind, the brass, the timpani, the percussion and whatever else was around. So, if you wanted more strings at a certain point and raised the string tracks, you also raised the 'mush' of the other sections of the orchestra – and at a certain point, these other instruments would go spectacularly out of focus; and, of course, it worked the other way round. So, all in all, multi-track recording is not an easy way of balancing. It is full of pitfalls and any producer or balance engineer who settles for a basically unbalanced sound on a session hoping to correct it later by juggling with his controls is asking for trouble, and usually gets it in abundant measure; the words 'we shall fix it on the re-mix' are the most dangerous that could be uttered on a recording session.

This is not to say that multi-track recording has not got advantages in certain circumstances. As will be seen presently, it once saved one of my opera recordings from utter disaster.

A more disturbing aspect of multi-track recording is that the laziness in the control room tends to infect the artists in the studio. Instead of a conductor balancing his forces, he learns to rely, hesitantly and for genuinely difficult passages at first, and then for anything he does not feel able to or cannot be bothered to balance correctly, on the recording staff juggling with their controls; and if you have learnt to depend on outside agents to balance your performance in a studio you cannot change your spots instantly when facing the public and do your balancing yourself.

Any little belief I had in multi-track being an aid to overcoming problems of balance was finally destroyed when we started to mix down to two-track the du Pré Franck and Chopin cello sonatas. We had recorded them on four tracks. At certain points we all felt that there should be more cello, but every time we opened out the cello tracks the piano went out of focus. It was not merely that Barenboim's clear, articulate and athletic playing sounded flabby and as if he were over-pedalling to conceal defects in technique; that was bad enough but you also got the impression that he was playing in a totally different acoustic from that of the cellist. Finally, I asked the engineer to set the four tracks as they had been on the recording session and not to control them at all – the result was completely natural, the cello occasionally less prominent than one would have wished and the piano, oddly enough, occasionally blanketed by the cello; there is nothing in the sound which is either objectionable or even ill-balanced. I have over the years fought a rearguard action against multi-track recording, not perhaps always as forcefully as I might have done.

To return to 1971. Late December took me to Berlin for the start of the complete recording with Zukerman and Barenboim of Beethoven's violin sonatas. Or, 'Sonatas for piano and violin', as they were called by the composer and Zukerman reproachfully said they sounded like. There was the usual fraught first session when the engineer and I struggled to obtain satisfactory balance. As usual, the piano posed no problem – in about ten minutes after we began Barenboim pronounced that he was happy, and we then set out to balance Zukerman's violin with the piano. This was beset by unexpected difficulties, not the least of which was my discovery after an hour of struggle that what Zukerman meant by presence and resonance was different to what the engineer and I understood these terms to mean. Barenboim stuck around, manfully trying to assist, then he went into a room leading off from the control room for a glass of water; a loud cry of joy announced his discovery of a camp bed in the room. He popped his head out and said, 'The piano is fine, as soon as you have sorted out the violin wake me up.' Incredibly, just five minutes later, when I peeped into the room, I found him fast asleep.

Much of the argument centred round the usual complaint of a violinist when hearing a recording of himself: 'But my violin doesn't sound like that to me.' Of course it doesn't, for he has his instrument less than two inches from his ear. Zukerman voiced this complaint, 'On your tape my violin has a k-k-k-k sound which it doesn't have in the studio.' 'Yes it has,' said the balance engineer and then asked, 'Mr Zukerman, could I please have your violin for a minute.' Understandably Zukerman looked very reluctant to part with his Guarneri, but the engineer reached over, took the instrument from him and drawing the bow across the strings played three or four spread chords with an aplomb Zukerman himself might have envied, and then the passage just recorded; I'd forgotten that he was a fully trained violinist. 'Hey! how about that!' a delighted Zukerman said. 'Do it again!' Just then a yawning Barenboim walked into the studio and, seeing the violin in the engineer's hands, said to Zukerman, 'I thought it wasn't your sound.'

In time, of course, he was satisfied and we started on the recording. The artists had played together a great deal and we made rapid progress, despatching five sonatas in three days. The recording had been set up in Berlin as Barenboim was conducting the Berlin Philharmonic in six concerts with Zukerman as soloist. Our daily schedule was 11 a.m. to 4 p.m. recording; 4–7.30 p.m., rest; 8–10 p.m., the concert, and from 10.30 p.m. into the small hours, dinner and unwinding from the day's activities.

This business of unwinding is essential for artists whether after a concert or a recording; no one can switch off, get into bed and fall asleep. An artist brings to bear an enormous amount of concentration during a performance and all his emotions are engaged. One cannot give a committed performance of the slow movement of the C minor Violin Sonata, for example, and switch back instantly to normal life. As a producer, even I need time to discharge the nervous and physical tension which is engendered by a session.

I returned to Berlin, again with Barenboim, to record this time with Fischer-Dieskau. Since the Mozart record I had wanted more from the two of them. Fischer-Dieskau made the suggestion of some of the Brahms lieder. During this recording I learnt a great deal about Brahms lieder; the setting of Heine's 'Der Tod, das ist die kühle Nacht' and of Rückert's 'Mit vierzig Jahren' were a delight. 'Feldeinsamkeit' was a revelation, beginning with relaxed, somnolent contentment, suggested effectively by the suave harmonies supporting the voice, and then suddenly breaking into the stark statement, 'mir ist, als ob ich längst gestorben bin' – accompanied by bare octaves on the piano. With their phenomenal speed of working, the two records were completed in three days. Next – Paris.

I had worked with Seiji Ozawa in 1971, when he accompanied Perlman in the two Wieniawski violin concertos, and had liked him. He is another of the modern breed of recording artist, quick and economical of time and, with me, his trust was absolute. He knew his score intimately and how to get the best out of it and out of an orchestra. The orchestral part of the

Wieniawski concertos are no great challenge to a conductor. In Paris, I recorded him conducting one of the great scores of twentieth-century music, Stravinsky's *Firebird* – the full 1910 version – with the Orchestre de Paris.

Over lunch after the last session Ozawa said that he would like to continue our association. Alas exclusivity once more raised its ugly head. This time it was tied up with Ozawa's appointment as principal conductor of the Boston Symphony Orchestra, which had an exclusive contract with another firm. But these things are only temporary, of course, which makes it all the more inexplicable why record companies feel they have made a major coup when they succeed in signing up another company's artist. I quite often suspect that managers of record companies are scoring off each other rather than obtaining any great advantage for their companies.

I went straight from lunch to the airport for my return journey to London. Two hours after my arrival I was back again in the Royal Free Hospital. Again I had only myself to blame. During the previous week I had been asking for trouble. On Friday I had two sessions in London from 2.30 to 5.30 p.m. and 6.30 to 9.30 p.m. with Barenboim and the English Chamber Orchestra, in which we recorded Mozart piano concertos. Early the next morning – it had taken me up to midnight to unwind and go to bed – back to Paris for a *Firebird* session from 3 to 6 p.m. The next three days were free and I hired a car and with my wife went off to the peace of a marvellous hotel in the woods of the Barbizon. Back to Paris for a session on the 28th and a concert that night with Ozawa and Oistrakh playing the Brahms – how could one pass that up? – and the next day, the last session.

I was not in any pain. For the first week I found it extremely difficult to keep my eyes open, then, having rested enough, I began vociferously to demand my discharge from the hospital; but with my previous history, I had to go through the dreary routine of three weeks in hospital and then gradually acclimatize myself to getting up and returning to normal life. Altogether, it was not as bad as it might have been; it was only an interruption of my work, which was a nuisance.

I was back at work in four months to complete the Beethoven violin sonatas. Zukerman and Barenboim were both a little dissatisfied with the exposition of the first movement of Op. 30 No. 3, recorded in Berlin, but neither said anything to me. They thought that they would have to put up with the performance as it stood, for they knew that it would be ridiculous to go back to Berlin to record some four minutes of music. It was when we assembled for the first session in London that I got an inkling of what they felt. I told them there was no problem; they could, if they wanted to, record three bars only to be inserted into the Berlin tapes. But would the sound match? I said, as usual, 'Leave it all to me.' It took some time though to get an exact match. We had to match the relative balance between the two instruments, the quality of sound of each, the degree and kind of resonance surrounding each and the two of them together, and, above all, we had to ensure that their positions in the stereo spectrum were exactly the same.

At last we could begin Op. 96. It was at a morning session. As they went into the studio I heard Zukerman say, 'About the beginning – I've been thinking, Danny . . .' Barenboim broke in, 'Pinky, don't think about it – just play it.' He rushed Zukerman into the studio saying to me, 'Suvi, light. We are ready.' The red light went on and Zukerman played, with exactly the right feeling of artlessness, that marvellous trill which begins Op. 96, making it sound as if music which had been going on elsewhere for some time had suddenly become audible to human ears. The whole sonata was done in one complete take; some corrections were done at a later session. The recording of this work has the special quality of music making that results when a sudden spark seems to set a performance going.

19   A Piano Tuning Session

The system prevailing in EMI of an artist being assigned to a producer, who thereafter looks after all his affairs, is convenient and by and large good. Its main shortcoming is that artist and producer could get so accustomed to each other that there is no longer the excitement or the rapture of a first coming together. The system, naturally, does not work rigidly – if a soloist belonging to a producer A is accompanied by a conductor who is looked after by producer B, usually A does the recording, but it could also be B or even C, an outsider. Or if a producer is not available for some reason or other, another will take over his artist.

In twelve years in the company I had worked with almost all of EMI's principal artists and most of those who recorded for us only occasionally. There were some gaps which I hoped would be filled in due course. I wanted to work with some of the great European orchestras. I would have liked to experience recording in America. I had had extensive experience of recording orchestral and choral music, piano music and chamber music. I had sadly never recorded a string quartet. To capture the rapture of that form of music was a delight I hoped would come one day.

One of the EMI artists with whom I had not yet made a record, though I knew him well and we had the usual amiable exchanges whenever we met, was André Previn – and I was somewhat envious of the producer who worked with him. I was introduced to him at a dinner given by Barenboim, at which we sat next to each other. My first impression of him was of a thoughtful, well-informed, stimulating conversationalist with a rather shy personality very different from the outgoing, extrovert figure he subsequently appeared to be on the television screen. He was newly arrived in England and had been appointed Principal Conductor of the London Symphony Orchestra. Some time later I learnt that Previn had entered into a contract with us.

The opportunity of producing a record with Previn came out of the blue. I was telephoned at home one evening and asked was I free three days later. I said I was and was told that the recording was of Brahms's Quintet for Piano and Strings with Previn and the Yale Quartet. 'Whacko,' I said, and then 'Previn?' I asked, convinced that my caller had made a slip of the tongue. The firm reply was 'Previn'. My surprise was caused, not by the fact that Previn played the piano – I had heard a superb

133

performance by him at the Royal Festival Hall of Mozart's C minor Piano Concerto, as soloist and conductor – but the Brahms Quintet was pure chamber music and would only be within the purview of a serious pianist. I wondered how Previn found time in the midst of a very busy life to keep up his piano playing.

Previn and the Yale had played the work at one of the concerts of the South Bank Festival. It had been such a success that Previn wanted it recorded; his producer was away and so the job had landed in my lap. My delight was considerably tempered by the fact that all the regular recording halls were tied up. The only place not occupied was All Saints' Church, Tooting, excellent for choral works but hardly ideal for a piano quintet. But it was either Tooting or no recording and we set about planning how to get the best results from the church. We aimed to seat them in one half of the transept, hoping that the sound of the piano would not swirl around uncontrollably.

When Previn walked into the church with the Yale Quartet he was startled by the sound eddying around the church when he said, 'Good morning, Suvi.' He turned to the quartet and said, 'Being together is not going to be a problem here – if we are within one bar of each other we'll sound together.' When we had balanced them to our satisfaction, the sound was only a little more reverberant than we would have obtained in a normal studio. Before the recording began, I asked all five players to check their scores with mine, which was a new revised edition based on the manuscript and Brahms's corrections in the first printed edition. Previn was very surprised. 'You mean you go through various editions to check for authenticity?' he asked. I explained that was not necessary, but one should always consult an authoritative edition. We compared scores and found a number of differences not only in phrasing and marking of slurs but also in notes. There was, particularly, an inexplicable and incorrect G sharp in the bass of the piano part in an otherwise straightforward G major chord.

Once that had been got out of the way, we completed the recording in one day, stretching from ten in the morning to about six in the evening. I was amazed at how effortlessly Previn played the formidable piano part, and delighted at the range and depth of his musical sensitivity and feeling. This again was no conductor dabbling in piano playing, but someone who would have had an equally exalted career had he concentrated on the piano.

On my next recording with him, Previn went back to his customary baton to accompany Perlman in the Mendelssohn and the Bruch Concerto Number One – Perlman insisted on my calling the latter by its appropriate number, the full significance of which did not become apparent till three years later. It was the first of a series of notable recordings made together by Perlman and Previn. Previn is one of the most accomplished accompanists. He is also a sympathetic one, which is sometimes even more important than mere skill.

Two old friends, Gilels and Lorin Maazel, came together for a recording of the three Tchaikovsky piano recordings. Like most music lovers, I knew only number one. When I got down to studying numbers two and three there was no discovery of any neglected masterpiece but of much agreeable music. Up to two days before the sessions were due to start, I was not quite sure whether Gilels would be able to come, and since the orchestra had been booked there was a feverish search for orchestral repertoire which we might perforce have to record instead of the concertos – there was, of course, no shortage of possibilities as Maazel's musical sympathies were extensive. On the last but one day, and not really expecting to get through, I rang Gilels in Moscow. On the first ring it was picked up. 'Hello!' I recognised his voice. I said, 'Emil, it's Suvi'. He said, 'Hello, Suvi. You must be quick I have to leave soon for the airport.' I breathed a sigh and said 'Good. 'Bye for now. See you soon.'

Knowing how particular Gilels was about touch and the action of the piano I had had a second piano brought in as a stand-by to our studio piano. He arrived about fifteen minutes before the session was due to start, tried out both pianos, selected the new one and then dropped his bombshell. 'This piano is tuned to 440; it must be tuned up to 444.'

I did not think he could be serious. If you have ever watched a piano being tuned so that slightly out-of-tune strings are adjusted you know how long a process even that can be; the mind reeled at the thought of pushing up the tuning of all the strings, and there are three each for most of the notes. At the end of it all, I was quite certain that the piano itself would take a hand in the proceedings. The pins holding the strings taut would have been accustomed to a tightening or loosening within a very small arc. They would now be tightened to a considerably greater extent than usual, and I was convinced they would not like it; nor would they settle down to their new positions, and so, resisting this forced raising of its pitch, the piano would gradually, through slackening pins, start to go flat, not evenly but at random.

If I had been of a nervous disposition, and my skin had been some shades lighter my face would probably at this point have gone white. Many of the orchestra had already arrived, as had Maazel, and conductor and I tried to argue with Gilels about the impracticability of what he was asking for. But no, he would not be moved, and so I asked the piano tuner to get to work. When he finally realized what it was I wanted him to do, and in the shortest possible time – in, say, fifteen minutes – he did turn a not so delicate shade of pink, but manfully he sat himself down and began. The orchestra had by now assembled in full and I had to ask them to keep absolutely silent so as not to distract the tuner and, most importantly, not to utter any musical sound which might disturb his sense of pitch.

135

In the control room, completely oblivious to the surreptitious glances Maazel and I had at our watches every few minutes, a benign Gilels chatted gaily as if sitting around gossiping while a symphony orchestra cooled its heels in an adjoining room and a frantic piano tuner was gradually going puce were everyday occurrences. After a long forty-five minutes the tuner came in, perspiring freely, and announced that he had raised the pitch as high as he dared and would Mr Gilels care to try it out.

We went into the studio and Gilels played a few runs and said that it was still not quite 444 and would the tuner push the pitch up further. I knew that I had now to intervene, for the piano tuner was shaking his head. As I turned to Gilels to expostulate, Alan Civil, the principal horn player of the New Philharmonia, settled the matter. He rose and said firmly, 'If that piano is tuned further up, the horns will probably be flat throughout this recording. We cannot guarantee to keep in tune at any higher pitch.' Gilels looked hard at Civil, who he knew to be one of the great horn players in the world, and then with a serene smile said, 'All right, let us start recording.' One hour adrift, the massive opening chords of Tchaikovsky's Second Piano Concerto launched the project. I had to keep my ears keenly alive to the piano's intonation, but the modern grand piano is a magnificent instrument, and though there were a few notes that sagged in the course of the recording, as a whole it caused no problems.

My problems with pitch and the piano were not yet over. We completed the Second Concerto and then went on to the Third. We had an hour of the session left when we had completed the Third. Gilels said there was not enough time to really tackle the first movement of Number One, but he felt that we could get the shortest movement, about seven minutes long, out of the way. And so we started on the lyrical second movement. It was obvious at the first playback that he was not happy. He was not really listening to the music for he did not look at the score; with a heavy frown he was thinking of something else. We did a second take which he did not even want to listen to; Maazel and I wondered what was bothering him. After a few moments he said, 'Let's try again.' We did the third complete take and this time he did listen, but only for two minutes, at the end of which he said, 'I don't like the sound of the piano.' I was surprised. This was the fifth session and till then he'd been happy with it. Now he was saying that the piano did not sound right.

This was a genuine problem, for Gilels is not the sort of person to complain on frivolous grounds. I felt that perhaps he was tired after a hard slog at Number Three and so suggested dismissing the orchestra, which we did. Then we tried to tackle the problem of the piano. We went into the studio and Gilels played a section of the movement. I said to him that the sound on the tape matched, almost exactly, the sound of the piano in the studio. Maazel agreed, but Gilels was still unhappy. I knew now what was

136

worrying him; it was the piano itself. He could not on this piano produce the limpid kind of sound he wanted for this slow movement.

Without calculating what might result, I asked him to play the same passage on the other piano. He did, and a pleased smile spread over his face. 'That's it. I shall play the second movement only on this piano.' I thought to myself, 'This is what cuts years off the life of a record producer', but aloud just said, 'But, Emil, this piano is tuned to 440, and being an older instrument will certainly not stand up to having its pitch raised.' Gilels was unmoved. 'In Russia,' he said with a quiet smile, 'we have machines that can alter the pitch of a recording. Does the West not have such machines?' Over his shoulder I could see Maazel's eyebrows knotted in disbelief. I said, 'Of course we do,' and the crisis was over.

After Gilels had left Maazel asked me whether we could really alter the pitch. I said we could and explained that, by altering the frequency of the current operating the tape machine, we could make the tape run fractionally faster or slower, thus changing the pitch of the recording. Maazel looked dubiously at me and asked whether he would have to slow down the tempo to compensate for the increased speed of the tape. I replied that the tempo would only be altered to a negligible extent. At the end of all this I thought to myself, there are times when it is all *ein Schwindel*.

20 A Singer Turned Conductor

Klemperer made no records in 1972. His concert appearances during the year were considerably reduced; he conducted works he had already recorded and resolutely refused to make new recordings of them. The plans to record Mozart's *Seraglio* in February 1973 still stood, and I was as eager about this project as he himself was. The cast was excellent, including Sotin as Osmin and Lucia Popp as Constanze. So that there should be no pressure on the eighty-seven year old conductor I had allowed twelve sessions for the recording.

Some weeks earlier Klemperer was due in London to do two concerts. Two days before the first of them I was called to the telephone by his daughter. Klemperer came on and said very quietly and simply to me, 'I do not feel I can go ahead with my concerts,' and even as I hoped he was going to say that he would continue to do recordings, he said, 'Or the recording planned.' There was silence for a few seconds, for we both knew that we had arrived at the end of Klemperer's career, and then briskly he asked, 'Now tell me what you have been doing since we last met?'

The effect of his announcement really hit me only after I had put down the telephone. I looked back on my long association with him stretching over nearly twenty years. I had first seen him in 1954, walking firmly on to the stage of the Royal Festival Hall, and through the years had been one of the most faithful followers of his concerts. Then followed the three years I had sung under him in the Philharmonia Chorus. In my years in EMI I had been associated with all his records. It was all over now and some of the joy and the eagerness which has always been an essential part of my attitude to my work went out of me. I would never again wheedle him into repeating a passage, or argue with him about tempo or try to persuade him to record a work which I wanted to hear him conduct, or hear that quizzical 'So!' But it had to come. He was eighty-seven, and even that active mind had at last to accept the limitations of an increasingly frail body. Before I rang off I had promised to visit him in Zürich; it was the last time I spoke to Klemperer.

I now had to fill the twelve sessions left vacant by the cancellation of *Seraglio*. It required imagination, hard thought and a brainwave for me to be able to arrange for three different kinds of records. Each of them was an interesting project and none of them consisted of the usual, un-

138

imaginative stand-by of record companies when a session has to be filled at short notice – Rossini overtures.

The first was easy enough. Anievas had already recorded the Rachmaninov Piano Concertos Nos. 1, 2 and 4 and the Paganini Rhapsody. To complete the set I set up a recording of No. 3 with a conductor new to me, Aldo Ceccato. By some curious chance, my extensive listening to radio had not included this work. After the recording I felt I much preferred it to No. 2.

The second record was more adventurous and took a great deal of organizing and telephoning around to set up. The idea was initiated by my accidentally pulling out of my library a copy of the score which was next to that of the Mozart Requiem. The Requiem has always been a favourite but Mozart's other unfinished mass, the C minor, which mercifully no one has attempted to complete, has been an even greater favourite. It represents one of the very highest peaks of Mozart's creative life. Even with the greater part of the 'Credo' and the 'Agnus Dei' missing, the work takes about an hour; if it had been complete it would be at least as long as Beethoven's Missa Solemnis.

In practical terms, the work requires two sopranos of musical sensitivity and what Mozart himself once described as 'agile gullets'; each has a taxing aria and a gruelling duet with the other and sings in a trio and a quartet. The tenor and the bass sing only in the ensemble numbers. Lucia Popp would take on one of the soprano roles. Werner Krenn, due to sing Pedrillo, and Hans Sotin would be the tenor and bass. All we needed was a second soprano, a suitable chorus and, of course, a conductor. There was never any doubt in my mind who this should be. Raymond Leppard, who had a fine feeling for Mozart, was the only conductor I knew who could at this short notice deal with the many problems raised by an incomplete score. I knew he was a very busy man but felt sure that if I found him I would be able to persuade him to undertake the recording unless it clashed directly with any other commitment he had undertaken.

But first, to find him. This was not made easy by his agent, who said that he was not free, that there was no point in telling me where he was as I could not possibly persuade him to give up his other engagements – all this to my secretary. I got the information in two seconds flat by simply threatening to insert an ad in the next day's *Times*, 'Will anyone knowing the whereabouts of Raymond Leppard, last seen conducting the BBC Northern Orchestra, please ask him to get in touch with Suvi Raj Grubb to discuss a matter to the advantage of both.' When I finally got Leppard he told me he had rehearsals on the days in question. I said, 'It's a pity, Ray. You would have loved to do the Mozart C minor and I cannot think of anyone who could do it better.' Though he must have known the answer he asked, 'Piano concerto or mass?' I replied reproachfully, 'Would I try to lure you away from the fleshpots of Copenhagen to

139

accompany a piano concerto?' Instantly the reply came back, 'Suvi, you're on. I'll arrange to be free.'

The singer I wanted for the second soprano was finally traced to one of the lesser known Greek islands and she replied would I please send her a score to see what the part looked like, as she had never sung it. She got the score in two days through someone who knew someone who knew someone on the national airline. In a surprisingly short time her answer came back: Kiri te Kanawa would love to take part in the recording. The day before she was due to arrive in London, Lucia Popp went down with a virus, but we were able to grab Ileana Cotrubas who had appeared at Covent Garden the previous evening.

There were four sessions left, and at first no bright idea seemed to come to mind. I began to feel it might after all have to be what has been inelegantly, though aptly, described as 'titty-bum, titty-bum, titty-bum-bum-bum' music, and was running through the Rossini specialists when the brainwave arrived.

Some eight months previously, when we recorded the Brahms lieder in Berlin, I had seen in Fischer-Dieskau's study books on orchestration, on the horn and other instruments, on the history of the orchestra and the gradual evolution of the modern conductor. Barenboim and I had teased him, asking him was he considering a new career as a horn player or a bassoonist, or perhaps as both! Fischer-Dieskau took this in good part, explaining that his voice was still in fine shape, but the time would surely come when he would have to give up singing. It was unthinkable that he should give up music making altogether. He was too old to seriously take up the piano, the only completely self-sufficient instrument. The field which seemed to offer the widest possibilities was conducting. He had a vast knowledge of the orchestral repertoire, and he had always been in love with the orchestra. He was now working hard to equip himself with the other skills which a conductor must possess; the one snag, he said, was that there was no way in which he could practise the art of conducting, as it was not really practicable to hire the Berlin Philharmonic Orchestra for daily rehearsals. Not even half-seriously, but wholly in jest, I said to him, 'Dieter, I hope I shall be the producer of your first record as a conductor.' We all laughed, and Fischer-Dieskau said, 'That, if ever it happens, is a long way off.'

It actually was not, for here, six months later, the thought had suddenly come to me to examine the possibility of an orchestral record with Fischer-Dieskau as conductor. Without stopping to weigh the pros and cons, I rang him in Berlin and asked what he felt about the possibility of making his debut on record as a conductor in two months' time. There was a slight pause, and he asked what works might I have in mind. I had not given the matter any thought – in fact between the arrival of the idea and my talking to him less than ten minutes had passed – but replied instantly, 'Schubert – five and eight.' There was a longer pause this time before he said, 'Eight? Suvi, all the great conductors have recorded the work, and everyone else as well. Do you really think . . . ?' I cut in, 'Dieter, some day you are going to have to conduct a popular work such as the "Unfinished". I believe in jumping in at the deep end. Think about it and ring me back in a day or two.' Then I explained to him how this situation had arisen and gave him details of the dates and times of the sessions.

I then set about trying to get approval for the project. We had the inevitable meeting at which opinions were divided between the two extremes of those who thought it a great idea and those who felt it would be a catastrophe. I was never in doubt about the outcome, for basically EMI is an adventurous company even though we are not financially cushioned as some of our rivals are. I was asked to speak immediately to Fischer-Dieskau and get his reaction to the idea. At this point, on cue, my secretary put her head into the room to announce that Fischer-Dieskau agreed and would I please ring him that evening to discuss details. It looked for a moment as if my chief would blow up, but he decided to accept the situation peaceably.

I have seldom felt more anxious about a recording than on the morning of Fischer-Dieskau's first session. I was not worried about whether he would acquit himself creditably; he would never have accepted an assignment which he did not believe he could carry out. I wanted him not merely to go through the sessions and make a record, but to get memorable performances of the two works. Very few people had lived so closely, for so long, with the composer's lieder; I wanted Fischer-Dieskau's Schubert symphonies to be as characteristic of him as his Schubert lieder.

I am positive that none of the anxiety I felt showed obviously when he arrived at the studio and I met him at the front door, but that queer telepathic communication must have been working again, for after a few moments Fischer-Dieskau looked at me, suddenly smiled and said, 'Don't worry about the recording, Suvi – if the first session is a disaster, I shall fly back to Berlin this evening.' I stoutly maintained that I was not worried, and now that the actual moment had arrived, I really was not. When I presented Fischer-Dieskau to the New Philharmonia they greeted him with the prolonged and enthusiastic applause orchestras reserve for musicians they respect.

Within a quarter of an hour I realized just what it meant to have an orchestra on the side of a conductor. Fischer-Dieskau's conducting technique was just about adequate. How could it have been otherwise, for until the beginning of the session he had not stood in front of an orchestra and conducted it; any rehearsing he might have done could only have been in private, and perhaps in front of a mirror. His gestures were sometimes ambiguous and his instructions to this or that section of the orchestra were

141

not always precise. But none of this mattered – the orchestra sensed that he had a clear conception of the 'Unfinished' Symphony and he was able to transmit it to every member of the orchestra. The leader, Desmond Bradley, was a tower of strength, acting, when required, as an interpreter between Fischer-Dieskau and the orchestra, and everyone responded. By the time the break came I knew that this was going to be a very special Schubert B minor. As the leader of the cellos put it: 'He's made me play the second theme exactly as he might have sung it.' This judgement was echoed in my flat that evening.

I had had a test disc cut of a take of the first movement, primarily, as my wife and I call it in a family joke, to 'try it on the dog'. Though she has no technical knowledge of music, her emotional response to it is as full-hearted as mine and very often I get valuable help from her reactions to performances and recordings. While we were listening to it there was a ring at the front door and Barenboim dropped in unexpectedly. He knew at once what I was listening to, for he is very well-informed about what goes on in musical circles. After a few moments, he said, wonderingly, 'The son of a gun, he makes them play exactly as he sings.' Having tackled the powerful, dramatic 'Unfinished' Fischer-Dieskau turned confidently to No. 5, which is lighter and sunnier but actually more difficult to perform, for its problems of balance, of getting fast-moving passages together and of intonation. These too were finally overcome.

But the record did not sell as well as I'd hoped. The public is very conservative. Fischer-Dieskau was known as one of the greatest singers of Schubert's songs – but Schubert's symphonies? – record buyers did not seem to be interested. And this despite excellent reviews. One reviewer considered that, compared with recordings of the 'Unfinished' by Karajan, Cantelli, Böhm, Giulini, Toscanini and Klemperer, Fischer-Dieskau's was, by and large, the most satisfying. But that too did nothing to boost the sales of the record – the public seem to disregard reviews of records as they do blurbs of record company advertisements.

Do critics affect artists and the people engaged in the making of records? Not to any significant extent. We all read reviews of our work and are sometimes elated or dejected by them, but only temporarily. Everyone concerned in the creation of a record, musician, producer and engineer, has a clear idea of the quality of the work he has done and no outside evaluation of it will affect what he knows to be its worth. We all know when something has gone wrong, or has not been absolutely right. When inspiration has perhaps been lacking, when a lack of insight has made a performance perfunctory, when the sound has not been right. In a perfect world, in which money was not a consideration, we would all in such cases like to scrap the record and start afresh. But equally we also know when our work has resulted in something of quality – and then no review can affect us.

In any case, reviewers can sometimes be ludicrously off target. For instance, of one record I produced, it was said, 'The repertoire is first-class' (which it wasn't), 'the performance excellent' (again it wasn't) and 'the recording is superb' (which it wasn't either). In fact it was probably the worst record I have produced and I hope I never have the misfortune to be involved in another such. Of the Monteverdi/Scarlatti record of Baker and Leppard it was said, more or less, 'Dear, oh dear, oh dear – what can one say about this record. It is superb music, superbly performed, and recorded, but is it Monteverdi or Scarlatti?' The answer to that was 'Yes, as realized by Leppard' and not as the reviewer thought it should have been done. All too often a critic falls into the trap of not listening to what the artist has done and upbraiding him for not doing something the critic felt he should have done. One can only smile wryly when one sees in a review the phrase 'We, who know Handel' or, as the final summing-up of a recording of the *Eroica* by Toscanini, 'Tut-tut, this will not do.'

The conservatism of record buyers was also responsible for the comparatively poor sales of two of the records I made about this time with Barenboim. Till then, there had been no record of his that had not sold in vastly greater numbers than anticipated. In the last months of 1972 Barenboim recorded the Bizet symphony with the Orchestre de Paris. He was getting increasingly associated with them and had great success with them in concerts. He now wished to record the *Carmen* and *L'Arlésienne* suites and *Jeux d'Enfants*. Artistically the record was a success, for Barenboim brought to them the right kind of flair and abandon that these works require. An excellent stimulus to us was provided by our listening, on the eve of our recording, to a record of Beecham conducting this music, after which Barenboim turned to me and said simply, 'Suvi Raj – perhaps we should pack up and go back to London'.

Since his recording of the Chopin Cello Sonata with Jacqueline du Pré I had wanted to hear Barenboim play Chopin. He had done so in recitals and in time announced he would like to make a record. '*Formidable,*' I said appropriately. The repertoire consisted of popular pieces: Barcarolle, Berceuse, Fantaisie in F minor, Polonaise-Fantaisie Op. 61 and Variations Brillantes Op. 12, and one little lollipop, 'Souvenir de Paganini'. At the beginning of the first session it took longer than he was used to for me to say 'Danny, let's go', and he asked was there a problem. I said I thought that the bass sounded lighter than I was accustomed to from him. He came into the control room, listened intently to a passage we had recorded and declared that the sound was exactly what he was producing in the studio. I said, 'That's not the bass you normally produce.' He replied, 'Not what I produce in Beethoven, but for Chopin that's all the bass required to support the middle and the top. If, in Chopin, you pile on the bass you could make him sound like a second-rate Brahms.' As the recording went on I realized how right he was. Chopin was a great harmonic innovator and with no more than the right amount of bass the texture of the music seemed to become translucent. It was a Chopin sound I had never heard before and the music acquired a luminance. It was a pity more lovers of the composer's music did not invest in this record; they might have had an unexpected insight into Chopin. But no. Barenboim? Mozart, Beethoven, Schubert – yes. Chopin? – not really.

21   *Don Giovanni* in Three Acts

I suppose ever since he had cancelled his last scheduled concerts and, in effect, had announced his retirement, I had known that, sooner or later, it would happen; but when it did reach me, on the morning of Saturday, 30 June 1973, the news of Klemperer's death was a shattering blow. I had accepted that the days of music making with him were over, but now I had to come to terms with the fact that I would never see him again. I reviewed, sadly at first, and then with increasing delight, some of my memories of him. All the same, ten days later, when I was conducted to the ante-chamber in the synagogue to pay my respects, the sight of the coffin almost undid me. It was very large – he was a big man – and the thought that in it was all that remained of Otto Klemperer was unbearable. There were resplendent wreaths from the German President, the Berlin Phil-harmonic, the Vienna Philharmonic, Philharmonia, EMI. There was only one musician in the gathering, Rafael Kubelik, as, after a simple ceremony, Klemperer was laid to rest in the next vacant grave in a row of other graves.

Back in London I had no time to brood. I was plunged into plans for recording Barenboim's first essay into the opera house. When it was announced that he was to conduct Mozart's *Don Giovanni* at the Edin-burgh Festival of 1973 many people were surprised, but it was merely an inevitable extension of his wide ranging activities. He had conducted orchestral music from Bach to Webern and so many religious works that he once ruefully said to Pitz, 'One more mass and I shall probably automatically turn completely into a Catholic.' Opera was the field still untried; it was fitting that his first venture should be of an opera by Mozart.

Barenboim wanted his performance of *Don Giovanni* to be recorded. There were some in the company who said he should not be conducting the work – irrelevant since that was what he was going to do; others that we should not record it. This left the problem in the air, for Barenboim said he wanted it recorded and if we were not interested would we please allow him to offer it to another company. There were others, and they had a legitimate point, who agreed to the recording but wanted it made in the second year of its run. Finally, taking everything into account, it was decided that Barenboim's debut as an operatic conductor should be on the label he had graced for over six years. Agreement was reached in my flat between my chief and me, with my wife as a non-participating but silently influential spectator.

I had met and worked with some of the cast, while others were totally unknown to me. Roger Soyer was the Don; Geraint Evans, Leporello; Alva, Don Ottavio; Alberto Rinaldi, Masetto; Peter Lagger, the Commendatore. The women were Antigone Sgourdas, Donna Anna; Heather Harper, Donna Elvira; and Helen Donath, Zerlina. The orchestra was the English Chamber Orchestra. We planned to record the opera in Edinburgh in ten sessions, packed into one week, between two sets of performances. The duration of the opera was about 185 minutes and so we would average 18½ minutes per session, well above par for most operatic sessions but well below for Barenboim and me. I foresaw an easy run, for singers and orchestra would come to the sessions well rehearsed and with three complete performances to tune them to their peak. When I drew up the recording schedule and the production plan I had no idea what fate had in store for me; this was to be technically the most complicated recording I had ever undertaken.

I studied the score lying flat on my back in a bed at the familiar Royal Free – nothing serious this time but a prudent measure intended to keep me under observation immediately after the very painful extraction of three wisdom teeth. I made notes and marked the sections which would require special attention during the recording. For instance, between bars 129 and 140 in the overture, the woodwind and the violins should come through with equal presence. I circled the contrasting *sf* for the first violins and the *sfp* for the seconds and violas at the start of the duet 'Fuggi, crudele'. 'Must come through as clearly as the solo voice' was the superscription for the twenty bars of seconds playing quaver runs in the same number. And so on to the duet 'O statua gentilissima', where I pencilled, 'Watch violins throughout' to indicate the very important part they play in this number; and at Leporello's 'Ah Padron mio, mirate' in bar 23 I wrote, 'Must indicate terror with voice', for it is that phrase which jerks a comic scene into a world of menace. I also underlined the *p* on Don Giovanni's 'Bizzarra e in ver', which if ignored would result in Leporello, an octave lower, being drowned.

The recording plan presented no problems – all the singers were going to be anchored to Edinburgh and available for all sessions. Oh joy! All I had to ensure was, say, if Donna Elvira was down to sing 'Mi tradì' in the afternoon, she should not be asked to sing anything taxing in the evening. I was extremely pleased with the schedule; little did I know that it would be rendered totally irrelevant half way through the second session.

It was with a keen sense of anticipation that I arrived at the theatre. I was not disappointed; the performance was all that I had expected it to be. The brooding menace of the andante of the overture, with its unsettling syncopations and sforzandos, set the mood of this production. It was well rehearsed and even on that first night there was a feeling of an integrated company. Once we had obtained a satisfactory sound the recording would proceed apace.

Two days later, I went again, determined this time to give myself up wholly to enjoying the music. All went well in the first act, though at the back of my mind there was a nagging feeling that the Don was somewhat off form. Almost as soon as the curtain went up on the second act I was shaken out of my state of contentment; there was now an edge on the upper part of Soyer's voice which I knew was not natural to it. It was very slight, but it was there, and was first noticeable on the high Ds in 'Eh via buffone'. I now realized that Soyer was more than merely off form, there was something wrong with his voice. Being an experienced professional, he got through the second act successfully, disguising what began to sound to me like a sore throat. Backstage in his dressing room after the performance I found him gargling and enquired after his throat; he cleared it a couple of times and said he thought it would pass by the morning. He did not seem unduly worried and I was reassured; singers know their capabilities.

The first session began at half-past two the next day. The venue of the recording was the Assembly Hall of the George Watson College: I had heard large scale recordings there in the past and foresaw no difficulty in balancing a Mozart opera. What no one had warned me about was that the hall was being redecorated and had an intricate network of scaffolding over half its area. The effect of this random pattern of ironmongery was that the sound whirled around unpredictably; one moment the woodwind blotted out the horns and trumpets, the next you couldn't hear them. On the first session I had called only the chorus, Zerlina and Masetto. I wanted to obtain what I felt should be the ideal balance for this opera, which was for the singers and the orchestra to have equal presence and clarity. There is no 'oom-pa-pa' accompaniment in Mozart; the orchestra always takes an active part in the dramatic action. Take the opening scene; you don't need a dimly lit stage to tell you that something mysterious is afoot, the stealthy *piano* unison figure on the strings conveys that quite effectively on its own. Then when Donna Anna and Don Giovanni erupt onto the scene the stabbing fortes followed immediately by pianos for the violins on the first and third beats of each bar underline the violence of what is seen on the stage. Or the passage in the first finale, when the Don sights Zerlina; even before he says anything the orchestra launches into a seductive, wooing theme and poor Zerlina is quite justified in trying to hide among the bushes to get away from this assault on her senses.

On that afternoon we tried everything and we got everything but what I wanted. It was hopeless trying to balance the singers, and I didn't bother during the first half. They had been exceptionally patient, as had been

Barenboim: suddenly, in the middle of the second half, he and I found ourselves engaged in a furious argument about the horns, whom he wanted on the right of the orchestra and I wanted on the left; I felt that from the right their sound would cut across the woodwind microphones and, more dangerously, the battery of five microphones for the singers. The discussion waxed fast and was very heated. After five minutes we found we were the sole occupants of the control room; everyone had vanished. 'Well, what next?' asked Barenboim. Just then the junior engineer timidly popped his head in and said, 'Mr Barenboim, Miss du Pré wants you' and to me, 'Mrs Grubb wants you.' We came out to see our wives sitting together and when we went up to them both said, 'Everybody thought you two were fighting', and when we expressed surprise that anybody should have thought this, they both pleaded that the next time we had a friendly discussion, we should please have it in private.

By the end of the first session we had managed to secure a respectable sound and I said to myself, 'It's just as well to get the bad luck out of the way on the first session.' The full cast arrived for the second session and we set about balancing Leporello, Anna, the Don and the Commendatore for the first scene. There was no need to rehearse the number, for the full opera had been run through three times in the previous four days. Just before we started to record I told Barenboim on the telephone that Soyer seemed to be singing *sotto voce* and he replied that on the take he would sing out, and we began. By the time the Don had sung 'Donna folle . . .', his first two words in the opera, I knew that his voice was badly affected. A few seconds later Barenboim realized this too and stopped, and he and I met on the stage as the other singers hovered anxiously around Soyer.

He had a very bad attack of laryngitis and even he knew only just then how bad it was. There was no possibility of recording anything with him that evening – and, I felt, not for the next week, though this I kept to myself. We decided to rest him and try something else. We did the Masetto and Zerlina arias and the chorus and then Soyer, who was feeling wretched at having upset the schedule, said he would like to try again – this time, the section from the second act finale just after Leporello sights the Commendatore's statue. Barenboim decided to continue even if Soyer stopped singing; after the first few bars he sang only *mezza voce* and we stumbled through to the Don's final exit.

As soon as the take was over we persuaded Soyer to go back to his hotel and arranged with the Festival people for a doctor to see him at once. We had another go at Zerlina's and Masetto's arias and the chorus and decided to call it a day; it had been a gruelling one for me. As we drove back to the hotel Evans, who shared my car, expressed great surprise at how calm I had been throughout the two sessions. 'How could you possibly remain so unperturbed when everything possible was going wrong? Or are you one of those people who really are seething inside while

The piano, at last, at the right pitch. Tchaikovsky concertos:
Emil Gilels, Lorin Maazel.

'Woodwind fractionally late.' Prokofiev's fifth concerto. Lorin
Maazel and Svlatoslav Richter.

'After another six years.' Daniel Barenboim to Janet Baker, in reply
to: 'When are you two going to record together again?'

'Nooo?' Itzhak Perlman and Pinchas Zukerman. Bartok Duos.

Dietrich Fischer-Dieskau as conductor, with Desmond Bradley, the Leader of the New Philharmonia Orchestra.

'Why are you all so loud?' The Klemperer *Cosi*: Yvonne Minton, Margaret Price, Luigi Alva, Lucia Popp, Geraint Evans. (Absent, Hans Sotin.)

Otto Klemperer studies the score tensely on his last recording – Mozart's Wind Serenade K 375.

I am singing to illustrate a point to Ileana Cotrubas and Kiri te Kanawa. Mozart: C minor Mass.

A pleasant reunion with Nicolai Gedda.

'Sam, bar 110 is OK.' To Samuel Sanders.

'At "Ecco il birbo" the Don moves centre rear to mike 3, forward.'
The Barenboim *Don Giovanni* cast – without Zerlina.

With André Previn and Itzhak Perlman in Pittsburgh.

'Singers, behind me – over there?' *Lady Macbeth:* Mstislav Rostropovich, London Philharmonic Orchestra.

Carlo Maria Giulini. I am asking him for far more of the dancing violins and violas in the Credo of Beethoven's C major Mass.

Lady Macbeth: Galina Vishnevskaya, Dimiter Petkov, Nicolai Gedda (leaning over).

'Does that worry you?' Beethoven Piano Trios, second time:
Vladimir Ashkenazy, Lynn Harrell, Itzhak Perlman.

The Brahms Double Concerto for violin and cello in Amsterdam:
Bernard Haitink, Mstislav Rostropovich, Itzhak Perlman, the
Concertgebouw Orchestra.

presenting an untroubled exterior?' I replied that when very young I had learnt two complementary lessons: first, that when things started to go wrong, it was essential for the person in charge to stay cool and collected; and then, that there was no point in fighting against something which could not be changed. 'The basic fact today,' I said, 'was that Roger could not sing. There was nothing I could do to alter that. Had I run around wringing my hands and calling on the gods to come to my aid, I would have looked ridiculous and achieved nothing. Besides, I have actually seen a chicken running around with its head cut off; gruesome, but extremely undignified, and I have no desire to emulate it! Tomorrow, if we still don't have a Don, I'll just have to work out how to make the best of the situation – and I hope I shall continue to remain calm.'

The doctor's verdict was that Soyer was under no circumstances to sing for another week. When I met Barenboim before the afternoon session, I already had a plan of action. There was no possibility of completing the recording in Edinburgh on this trip – no one could stay on after the Festival. I had worked out that, for about half the duration of the opera, the Don does not sing – in terms of time, for about eighty-nine minutes. We could therefore record eighty-nine minutes of music. As for the rest, we would have to reassemble the cast later on and complete the job.

We began the third session with straightforward items, such as Leporello's 'Madamina' from 'Guardate questo non picciol libro' of the preceding recitative, Donna Elvira's recitative 'In quali eccessi' and the aria 'Mi tradì' and her shorter aria 'Ah fuggi', and the duet between Donna Anna and Don Ottavio after the Commendatore's death – all this, a good twenty minutes of music. We continued with all the solo arias for the other singers and then went on to the sextet – all of these, complete numbers. Then we started to tackle sections of numbers – these, we knew, would be risky, but we had to try, hoping that they would match when edited into their correct places. Examples of these were the end of the opera after Don Giovanni is dragged off to hell, a seven-minute stretch of difficult music for the orchestra and the other six singers, and the two trios of the three masked characters in the first act finale.

Having done this I called a meeting of all the singers at my hotel to discuss dates for the completion of *Don Giovanni* and then to dine with me. I had expected great difficulty in assembling the singers again, but had not remembered the annual relaxation of musical events between Christmas and the New Year – everyone was free from 26 December to 1 January and that period was firmly booked for *Don Giovanni*. On Christmas Day they would be scattered over two continents, Alva in New York, Sgourdas in Athens, Lagger in Berlin, Rinaldi in Milan, but that was an insignificant hurdle; we would record in London, as it would be too complicated to try and set up the whole thing again in Edinburgh. Someone asked me whether it wouldn't be difficult to match, in London, the sound we had in Edinburgh. I responded with my standard reply, 'Leave it all to me.'

I heaved a sigh of relief and said, 'So much for *Don Giovanni*,' but the Fates, or the Furies, had still not done with me over this opera. No inkling of this clouded my enjoyment, after dinner, of a séance which Rinaldi set up. He seriously believed that spirits could communicate with us and give valuable advice. I had a section of the dance floor cleared and, having placed a circular table in the centre, eight of us sat solemnly around it with our fingertips lightly touching the table top.

Rinaldi first invoked the spirit of Mozart – and when it had been clearly established that it was indeed he (by three firm, somewhat testy, taps of the table) he was asked whether he approved of the performance on the recording now under way. From the vigorous bouncing of the table it was clear that even if the composer himself had been in charge it could not have been interpreted better.

At this point the believers felt that my wife and I should withdraw from the table, as our obvious scepticism seemed to be inhibiting the spirits. I said that I had received no proof that there were spirits around and that they and not human activities were responsible for the gyrations of the table. When asked what sort of proof I wanted, I replied, my mother had died when I was ten months old, and if they could summon her spirit and get her to identify herself by her Christian name, which of the company present only my wife and I knew, I would begin to believe in table-tapping. They tried hard; at one point, someone said, 'It might be an Indian name no one here knows.' To the manifest delight of Barenboim, who saw my answer coming, I replied that it was my mother who was going to reveal her name and however complicated an Indian name it might be she would know how to spell it. I added, 'In actual fact it is a very simple English name.' When we broke up in the small hours, none of them knew that it was Jane.

I returned to London to see Rohan Kanhai and Garfield Sobers, each making his last appearance for his country in England, each score over 150 runs. I had an excited telephone call from Gerald Moore that evening. 'Suvi, did you ever see anything so exhilarating? I suppose, you lucky chap, you were there.' I admitted I was and then I rang Los Angeles to give a transatlantic summary of the day's play to another enthusiast, Zubin Mehta. I sorely missed Barbirolli, but felt sure that in whatever Elysian fields he was, he too would have followed the game.

Everything was set for the recording of the rest of *Don Giovanni*. The recording in Edinburgh had been on two tracks. For London, however, I felt it would be risky to confine myself to two tracks, for I would have a tape with no scope for alterations. If there was even a fractional difference in the positioning of a singer between the Edinburgh and the London recordings, there would be an awkward shift of the singer at the joining

150

point – and the sound would have to match. So to give myself a little more flexibility I decided on eight tracks for London. I had made plans for everything that could be foreseen.

The unforeseeable occurred in mid-morning on Christmas Eve. Helen Donath's agent telephoned to say that the singer had a severe attack of laryngitis and had been ordered not to sing till the New Year; she was heartbroken and devastated and had retired to her country residence which was not on the telephone and begged me and Barenboim to forgive her. For a brief instant I considered the possibility of cutting our losses and engaging another Zerlina, but at once rejected it. It would be totally impractical; we had three days only allotted for the remaining sections of the opera, all the singers having to leave London on the 31st to fulfil engagements elsewhere. There was no possibility of starting from scratch and recording the whole of *Don Giovanni* in three days. Besides, a new Zerlina would have had to be coached to fit into a production the other singers were familiar with and there was not time for that either.

I then took stock of all that we had so far recorded with Zerlina in it – two arias, several extended recitatives, the chorus of peasants, the sextet and the last scene with five other characters and a long recitative and duet with Leporello. This last was composed for the opera's first performance in Vienna, Mozart apparently feeling that the Vienna public needed to be wooed by an extra piece of buffoonery. All this totalled up to approximately half of the music already recorded.

I then considered the other possibilities – the simplest was to do all the sections without Zerlina and at a later time those with her. The disadvantage of this would be that we would have to assemble all the singers again, as Zerlina appears with them all in the first act finale. I thought of the costs involved and winced. Then, the solution came to me – to record everything and, later, superimpose Zerlina. I quailed as I thought of the complexity of the first act finale but encouraged myself with the phrase 'Coraggio maestro', which the leader of the Scala orchestra had reputedly addressed to Furtwängler, whose quavery down beat he had ascribed to nervousness.

I then rang Barenboim to give him the news. His first reaction was the same as mine, to find another Zerlina. I explained why I had rejected this idea, and, in any case, it would be impossible to get one in two days, and those days being Christmas and Boxing Day. We then considered cancelling this lot of sessions. It was too late for that; we simply had to go ahead. I said 'Danny, let's record *everything*, even the bits in which Zerlina sings, and when she is available we can superimpose her part.' I said I would explain, with the score, on Christmas Day, when we were to lunch together.

Superimposition, of course, is exactly what it says – the putting on of a missing voice or voices on to a tape on which all the other voices,

151

instruments, orchestra or whatever else, have been recorded. On a multi-track tape, one or as many tracks as might be required are left blank, all the other forces being distributed between the remaining tracks; later, the missing part is recorded on the blank track. Barenboim grasped the principle of the proposed operation but was not convinced of the practicability of it. He summed up his doubts with, 'You mean to say, Suvi, you are going to ask Alberto to sing "Faccia dica quel che vuole" and "Parla, forte" without Zerlina's phrases before, in between and after?' I said that was exactly what I proposed to do. His reply was 'I'll believe it when I hear it.'

When the cast assembled for the first session there was consternation when they realized that there was no Zerlina. I assembled them on the stage and explained at length what we were planning to do. To my great relief three of them said as soon as I had finished, 'Ah! superimposition' – they had done it before and imparted some of their confidence to the others. We went straight for the most difficult number – the first act finale. I wanted that out of the way before anyone else in the cast developed shingles or mumps or housemaid's knee. The most difficult sections, the opening exchanges between Zerlina and Masetto and Zerlina and the Don, proved unexpectedly easy. Rinaldi, who had done superimposition, and Soyer, who had not, both showed great imagination and artistry in the difficult task set them, for each had to build up the feeling of a scene without the intermediate arch leading from one of his phrases to the next and each had to sing a bass line with Zerlina's treble part absent. By the end of that first session we had recorded the whole of the finale to Act One – of course, without Zerlina.

I was glad that was behind me and looked around at the cast with satisfaction and pleasure, my eyes finally coming to rest, accidentally, on Soyer. The effect on him was amazing. 'No, Suvi,' he cried. Then plaintively, 'Please, no.' I looked blankly at him, for I had no idea of what he was talking about. Evans and Alva started laughing as Soyer once again said, 'Please, no, you are going now to ask me to sing "La ci darem" without Zerlina. It's not possible, absolutely no!' Turning to Barenboim he broke out into impassioned French. I managed to stop him. 'But, Roger, what on earth makes you think I am going to ask you to sing "La ci darem"?' 'It's the look in your eye – how you say, *spéculatif*,' he replied. I said that what I felt was gratitude at having such a marvellous team of singers, and if my eye had shown any other expression it was lying. 'No "La ci darem"?' 'No,' I said firmly, 'for that and for the recitatives with Zerlina you, Alberto and Geraint will have to reassemble some time next year.'

The opera was finally completed in May 1974. We first did 'La ci darem' and then got rid of all the recitatives involving Zerlina. Before we sent the other singers away and dismissed the orchestra, Barenboim asked, 'Are you sure we have recorded everything? It has been so fragmented that I have lost count of what we've been doing.' I assured him that everything had been done. 'Sure?' he asked and I said I was – absolutely. Then, on to the superimposition of Zerlina's voice in the finale of the first act. We placed two tiny loudspeakers behind Barenboim and Donath to give them the cues from the other singers and the orchestra. I impressed on her that she should follow Barenboim's beat exactly. Experienced singer though Donath was, she tended, naturally, to wait to hear her musical cues, and that made all her entries slightly late. So we switched off her loudspeaker, and she sang through that extended finale just following Barenboim's beat, not hearing a note of either orchestra or any of the other singers. It was a feat for both of them, and took a surprisingly short time once the correct method had been arrived at.

So, when the last session of *Don Giovanni* ended I had approximately one half of the opera on two-track tapes, recorded in August 1973 in Edinburgh; about three quarters of the remaining half was on eight-track tapes recorded in Kingsway Hall in December 1973 and, also on eight tracks, the remaining eighth of the opera – this lot had, on one side, long chunks of Zerlina's voice superimposed in May 1984 on two tracks of the eight. I had to put together all these bits of recording so that the seams did not show, match the different kinds of sounds and produce a master which gave the impression of a smooth, continuous performance of the opera. I suspected that this was going to be one of those fiendishly difficult jobs, and so it proved.

The recitative preceding Leporello's aria 'Madamina' illustrates the kind of problem I had to solve. The aria had been recorded in Edinburgh. Evans had to have a lead into it, and so we had recorded some of the recitative before it – not all, for the Don, who also is in it, was *hors de combat*. In London we recorded that recitative in full, up to the first bar of the aria. The most suitable point, musically and technically, for going over from the London to the Edinburgh recording was on the 's' of the word 'testimon' in the penultimate bar of the recitative. In the split second that Evans pronounced that 's' we had, simultaneously, to fade out the eight-track recording, fade in the two-track recording and make all the adjustments necessary for the two sounds to match.

It all seemed to work perfectly the first time, but when we played the resultant master the effect was irresistibly comic. Leporello's position changed at the joining point, slightly to the left and forward, exactly as if he had taken a diagonal hop like a startled rabbit. It took over an hour and a half to get this one edit to sound as if Leporello had leaned confidentially forward towards Elvira. While we were struggling with this problem one of the junior engineers said to me, 'All this effort for something not even one in ten thousand is going to hear.' He was a youngster, who had recently joined the company and showed promise and so I took time to explain why. If a thing was not right, and could be set right, it had to be done. It was dangerous to let considerations of not being found out enter into one's work, for that attitude would envelop one and infiltrate other spheres of activity. 'Besides,' I added, 'I don't make records for other people. I make them for my own pleasure and anything I notice wrong would seriously interfere with that pleasure.' When I had finished, the senior engineer said to his young colleague, 'Here endeth the first, and I hope the last, lesson. Let me not ever hear from you any talk of "Is it worth all this bother?"'

At the end of it all, I remembered wryly a remark a friend had made a few days earlier. 'You can't possibly call listening to music all day and chatting up the Barenboims and Giulinis of this world, work, can you? It must be like one long treat.' The truth of the matter is that for every day you meet with a major artist you spend twenty days negotiating with his agent or arguing with your colleagues. As for music all day, it is very hard work to listen with unremitting concentration. I have sometimes been limp with exhaustion after six hours of continuous listening.

22 A Little Scott Joplin – Baker sings Schumann – but no String Quartet

The tempo of recordings by Perlman picked up in 1974. He started the year impeccably with Bach and ended it with the first of several off-beat records. After the Bach record Perlman jumped two and a half centuries to the early twentieth and Stravinsky. It was a recital, with the Italian pianist Bruno Canino, of 'Duo Concertant', the only original work by the composer for violin and piano, and two works consisting of arrangements of other works. On the back of the record sleeve was a picture of an extremely youthful and chubby Perlman with Stravinsky, taken in 1966.

In the final stages of this recording, I was astonished by a demonstration of just how acute Perlman's hearing is. My colleagues grumble at me for the scrupulousness with which I treat any complaint from Perlman of a slightly suspect note or passage. But I am unmoved – Perlman is always justified when he asks for something to be changed. It could be a minute scratch, a tiny wavering in intensity or falling off in intonation – once he has pointed out something to me, I myself am impelled to set it right.

I had sent to New York a cassette of the final tape of the Stravinsky – two days later I got an urgent message from him, a note was missing from one bar. I heard the tape and to me the bar in question sounded perfect. I called in the senior editor; he too could hear nothing wrong. I rang Perlman and asked what exactly was missing and he said a 'thirty second note'. The editor and I played the tape again. We tried for half-an-hour and still could not hear the mistake and then played the tape at half speed; we now had to hear a note lasting one eighth of a second and even that took us some time. In the flurry of an upward run one note was missing; it is a measure of the efficiency of EMI's editing staff that putting back the note took just two minutes.

Yet again, commercial success did not follow artistic success. Perlman considers this Stravinsky to be one of his finest records, and so do I. It is repertoire not usually attempted by violinists, performed with skill and artistry. But the record-buying public was indifferent.

Next came the Dvořák Concerto with Barenboim and the London Philharmonic, for which we had to traipse all the way to Tooting. Perlman's last record of the year was unusual, and certainly out of the pattern of my normal work. Many solo instrumentalists' knowledge of

155

music and interest in it is confined almost entirely to their own instruments. Not Perlman, though; he has a wide interest in music of all kinds, and not only what we broadly call classical music. He is also familiar with musicians in those other fields. One night the car scheduled to take him back from Abbey Road to his hotel had not arrived and we stood chatting in the forecourt of the studio building. A few minutes later a Rolls-Royce, apparently with a driver in uniform and a peaked cap, turned into the gates and as Perlman and I walked up to it, stopped. I was surprised by a Rolls-Royce instead of the usual Volvo, but asked the driver, had he come to pick up Mr Perlman. Courteously, he replied he had not, drove in and parked the car. As he got out and walked up the steps his face was lit up by the studio lights. Perlman caught my arm and said, 'That, Suvi, is Elton John.'

Perlman is also interested in folk music, American country music, traditional dance music, rock and roll and avant-garde jazz. He has a wonderful capacity to listen to a new kind of music, assimilate its special qualities and absorb its style. For about a year he had talked about wanting to do a record of Scott Joplin rags; this was a name even I knew, though I hadn't heard a note of the music, and so, whenever Perlman brought up the subject, I made vaguely encouraging noises but did not take any serious note of his suggestion. Perlman, however, *was* serious, and he had also spoken to André Previn about playing the piano for a record of Joplin. Previn too had made suitable noises, without really believing that anything was going to come of it.

In the middle of the year Perlman produced dates for the recording, which he had already cleared with Previn, and I suddenly realized that a Scott Joplin record was about to happen. The recording was set for December and through summer and early autumn I kept putting off getting to grips with the problem; after all, it was some time off. Then suddenly it was November and in less than four weeks I was due to produce a record of music I knew nothing about and of which I had as yet no scores. Perlman, from across the Atlantic, was reassuring. 'Don't worry, there's no problem; I'm arranging the rags for violin and piano and will bring the music across.' Previn, who has a phenomenal capacity to sight-read music, accepted this with, 'So long as I can see the music the night before, it's okay.' But I was worried. I got all the records I could get of Scott Joplin and for two days steeped myself in the music. I am not sure that either my knowledge of the idiom or my appreciation of this kind of music was advanced to any great degree, but at least I knew what it should sound like.

Perlman arrived, this time *with* his luggage. (Baggage handlers have an uncanny knack of picking his suitcases for journeys to exotic places, far away from his own destination – if he rings me soon after he has checked into his hotel, I cut short his 'Suvi . . . ?' with 'Okay Itzhak, you want a pair of pyjamas, two sets of underwear, a shirt, a razor, and a toothbrush and toothpaste.') At last I had the music. One photostat set went off to Previn and I looked at the scores. My first thought was, 'Poor André . . .' for Perlman's arrangements followed a simple pattern – the melodic line was assigned to the violin and the piano had the basic accompanying chords, mostly tonic and dominant, in an 'oom, pa, oom, pa' or 'oom, pa, pa' rhythm.

When we met next morning Previn asked me 'Have you seen the music?' I said 'Yes', and he replied, 'Well, if that's what he wants, it's okay by me; but, Suvi, try and persuade him to give up the whole thing – it's a dead duck.' Privately I agreed with Previn that this record could not win. Scott Joplin fans would ask, 'Who the hell is Perlman?' and Perlman enthusiasts would ask, 'Who the hell is Scott Joplin?'

Perlman arrived in tearing high spirits. They rehearsed the first piece, we recorded it; I asked them to come and listen to the balance. Both said it was excellent. The music itself sounded banal; the tune was fine but the piano part was uninspiring. Previn turned impulsively to Perlman, 'Itzhak, let's drop the whole thing and do Brahms violin sonatas instead.' Perlman was firm. 'This record is going to be a success – I am depending on it for the refurbishing and redecoration of the kitchen in my New York flat.' Previn shrugged. As he followed Perlman back into the studio, I managed to get in a private word. 'André, for God's sake you've got to do something with the piano part – improvise – put in a few twiddles.' 'He'll probably not like it,' he replied, 'but I'll try something out and we'll see what happens.'

They started to rehearse again and Previn, at the end of a line, instead of holding the long block chord marked in the score, did a little run up and down. Perlman was galvanized. 'Hey, do that again – it's great.' Previn asked, 'You don't mind?' Perlman said, 'Mind? That's just what I would have written if I'd thought of it.' Previn cheered up. I saw demonstrated what a superb jazz pianist he was. The rest of the day was thoroughly enjoyable.

When the record was finished, we had something original and fresh that we could all be pleased with. I still did not think it would sell. Once again, the record-buying public demonstrated its unpredictability. The record took off like a rocket and within a year after release Perlman could, from the proceeds, have covered the walls of his kitchen with Chinese silk.

The following year was a lean one. In the course of the calendar year I produced no more than six records and half a side of a Previn orchestral record – a landmark, this last item. There was no special reason to account for this, such as illness or absence from work for a long period, though acute tiredness again caused me to spend a period of five days in hospital. For my two principal artists, Barenboim and Perlman, too, it was a lean year for recording.

I had been extremely busy for several years now and had had little time for introspection. This year I found myself at odd times turning over in my mind various aspects of my work. For instance, what were the recordings I had so far produced that I was proudest of – not necessarily which I considered to be the best, but which had given me the greatest satisfaction? There were, of course, the big sets: twelve records of Beethoven piano sonatas and twelve of Mozart piano concertos, five each of the Beethoven piano concertos, trios and violin sonatas, all three of the great Mozart Italian operas – these provided wonderful memories and were considerable achievements, primarily of the artists involved but in some measure also for me. But there were also many single records; the Annie Fischer piano concertos of Mozart, perfectly proportioned performances with a sympathetic accompaniment by Efrem Kurtz, Anievas's Chopin études, a glittering display of virtuosity coupled with musical feeling, the Melos Beethoven and Mozart piano and wind quintets, the King's records with Willcocks, the Pollini Chopin, the Mozart and Mendelssohn lieder with Fischer-Dieskau – and that is to name only the ones which came at random to mind.

I had had the opportunity of recording a vast range of works, from Elizabethan madrigals and unaccompanied Bach motets to Bartók and Schönberg, from unaccompanied violin and solo harpsichord to Busoni's piano concerto and from lieder to Bruckner masses. My mind, however, seemed to return again and again to the one gap – the string quartet.

If I could have a piece of music engraved on my heart, it would be the first four bars of Beethoven's Op. 131, the theme of the opening fugue. If there were room for more than one, the second would, without question, be the full score of bars nine and ten of the slow movement of Schubert's 'Death and the Maiden' quartet, in which the E flat chords of bar nine wrenchingly modulate to an 'incorrect' B flat chord with a G replacing the fifth, F.

And if you allowed me two, I would be greedy for more, not necessarily to wear in my heart's core but to furnish its outer spaces – the irresistible mixture of buffoonery, comedy and tenderness in the second movement of Haydn's Op. 77 No. 2, called 'Minuet' but in fact a scherzo; the slow movement of Mozart's K428, with those incredibly shifting chromatic harmonies so far ahead of its time that it seems to foretell Wagner's *Tristan und Isolde*; also from Mozart, the start of the reprise of the slow movement of his last quartet; the third movement of Brahms's A minor quartet, an elegiac, autumnal movement so characteristic of the composer. I could go on for pages.

And yet, in the list of over four hundred and twenty-five records I had already produced, there was not one work for two violins, viola and cello. There were piano quintets, an octet including a string quartet, clarinet with string quartet, even string quartet with orchestra and piano; but a work of the string quartet by itself was not on the list.

The nearest I had got to it was in 1966, when the Drolc Quartet, consisting of four players of the Berlin Philharmonic Orchestra led by its principal first violin, called on us in London. They had a contract with our German company, Electrola, and had made many records, including what I consider to be the finest performance of the first Rassoumovsky I have yet to hear. The Drolc Quartet wanted now to come over to the International Division. I was delighted to be detailed to discuss possibilities with them. They offered us the entire classical repertoire and, Drolc added, not entirely joking, any quartet Walton might care to write. It looked as if there would be no problems about coming to terms. They made only one condition, that if we wanted Beethoven it should be the entire set; they would not record the odd quartet or just a few of them. I had visions of at last realizing one of my great ambitions and for a few days I went around with my head in the clouds, but I had been in the business for long enough to be wary and to keep my feet firmly planted on the ground. The sales department and my own immediate management, of course, asked for the one thing on which the Drolc were not willing to compromise. The project died instantly; I was a little comforted by a personal call from Drolc thanking me for the great fight I had put up on their behalf; I had enough tact not to enquire how he'd got the information.

Even today, another eight years on, I have yet to produce a record of a string quartet, though I came tantalizingly close to it in 1978. On a cold January morning I received a telephone call. I announced myself briskly, but all I heard at first was heavy breathing, then a wheezing; just as I was about to put the telephone down I heard a croak which I made out to be 'Suvi?' I recognized the croak; it was one of my colleagues and, very concerned, I asked what was the matter with him. He said he had gone to bed with a slight sore throat and woken up with the father and mother of colds. 'In actual fact it sounds like a Grossmutter,' I interposed. He had two sessions scheduled for that morning and afternoon which he was in no condition to do and was I free to do them instead. I said I was. My heart leapt when he said, 'It's the Medici Quartet', and fell again when he added, 'They are to record the last movements of Haydn's Op. 64 No. 5, and if by luck you have time left over, you can start on the first movement of the Smetana.' I agreed, and gladly – after all, half of one quartet and a quarter of another was better than no quartet at all but, to date, this remains my only essay in the field and, alas, it looks like being the only one.

It was about this time that Barenboim had completed the Mozart piano concerto cycle; the last recorded had been K37. At the end of the session Barenboim closed the score with a flourish and said, 'Suvi Raj, that's it', a moment caught to perfection in the picture of us in the booklet included in the boxed set. The look of satisfaction on our faces is comment enough. It was a major achievement; as with the Beethoven sonatas, there is a youthful quality of freshness and spontaneity about the performances.

My next recording with him was in lieder. This record has a curious history. A lieder recital by Janet Baker and Barenboim which included Schumann's *Liederkreis* Op. 39, had been one of the highlights of the 1968 South Bank Festival. The rehearsal for this was scheduled for the day before the concert, in the hall itself. A week earlier Barenboim had the brilliant idea that the rehearsal should be in our Studio No. 1 and treated as a recording session. It would not matter if it did not work – if it did we would have one side of a record. It proved to be a miraculous session. After they had had a run through, which gave us time to get an agreeable balance, they gave a performance of the song-cycle which we recorded. Their concentration was the same as it would have been at a concert. There were half a dozen corrections in the whole cycle; many of the songs, such as the highly charged, atmospheric 'Die Stille' and 'Im Walde' and the fast-moving 'Frühlingsnacht' are in one take – there are no edits in them, and all this in a period of two hours and a half. We were all very pleased with the recording and with ourselves; we knew that there was only one coupling possible for this song cycle, the same composer's *Frauenliebe und Leben*, which could almost have been written for Baker, and we were all agreed that the recording of it should be set up as soon as possible.

For about two years I used intermittently to ring one or the other of them asking for dates; they were both keen to complete the recording but somehow we could not agree on a suitable date. And then I gave up; it looked as if it was going to be one of those marvellous recordings which was going to lie mouldering in our vaults, a prospect which was the more galling when at the end of the two years I sent for the tapes and listened to the recording. And then for another three and a half years it used to be, 'Suvi, when are we going to complete the Schumann lieder record?' and I replying 'Janet, as soon as you and Danny are agreed on a date, let me know and even if Karajan, Giulini and the Archangel are all scheduled to record in No. 1 on that day, I guarantee to get them out; but I refuse to get involved in a triangular search for a date.' Or if Barenboim asked me, 'What about that Schumann record with Janet?' I would reply reproachfully, 'Well, Danny, what about it? It's with you and Janet.'

I nearly died of surprise when early in 1975, six and a half years later, I got a message saying that Miss Janet Baker and Mr Daniel Barenboim would like to record *Frauenliebe und Leben* on 4 and 5 July. I asked, so as to be under no misapprehension, '1975?' and was reassured that it was indeed in that year. In another single session we had the second song cycle, and this time too there were very few corrections. The recording has the naturalness of a performance; it seems to reflect the spontaneity of the rich flow of songs in 1840 from Schumann.

160

When she had finished singing 'Du Ring an meinem Finger' there was a slight pause and Baker asked, 'Well, Suvi . . . ?' I hesitated, and she said, 'Is there something you are not sure about?' and I replied in mock despair, 'No, no, it's perfect. I was only trying to think of an excuse to ask you to sing it once more – to hear again, three times, that unexpected flattened note on the last syllable of "Ringelein" '. There was a whispered consultation in the studio and Barenboim's voice came over, 'Suvi, we are going to do the first verse and the last bit again. We think some bits can be better.' Actually they repeated the whole song as a treat for me. The last song of the cycle, the highly charged 'Nun hast du den ersten Schmerz gethan' provided a good illustration of the way they worked. They started the song – at the end of seven bars they both simultaneously said, 'no', and stopped. Baker cleared her throat a couple of times; Barenboim experimented twice with the sforzando in bar two and, without any words being exchanged between them, they started again and went through the song and Barenboim played the tender *adagio* postlude. There was again a slight pause. I said, 'End of session. Come in for coffee.' There was no need for us even to listen to the take. It was perfection.

161

23 Bumbry, Parsons, Montgomery

There was another record of lieder some four months later. I had first met Grace Bumbry when she was the alto in the Frühbeck de Burgos recording of Mozart's Requiem. I found it difficult to connect this immensely attractive but very sedate and composed person with the extravagantly erotic pictures I had seen of her as Venus in the Wieland Wagner production of *Tannhäuser* in Bayreuth. When she started singing, you felt that no Tannhäuser could possibly have resisted the blandishments of this Venus.

Bumbry's accompanist, Geoffrey Parsons, was a friend of very long standing. We had first met fourteen years earlier, when he accompanied Christa Ludwig in a recital of Schubert lieder – a record started off by Legge and completed by me.

Over the years Parsons and I had met frequently. We used to make forays into East Berlin, where books were unbelievably inexpensive, returning laden with volumes of music. We shared a joke, Parsons slightly ruefully, for I had been responsible, albeit unwittingly, for a hair-raising episode in his recording life. We had almost finished the second 'Elisabeth Schwarzkopf Song Book'. There was one session left. Since it was our last night in Berlin, Parsons and I celebrated expansively. We sat up late talking, consuming the while vast quantities of a glorious Burgundy we had discovered in the hotel. When we ordered our last bottle at about two in the morning, the night porter commented, 'If you are trying to finish off our stocks of this wine tonight, you stand no chance; we still have two cases of it left.'

The next morning we were both feeling distinctly fragile. I, of course, had no real work to do. Parsons did, but it was only the easy accompaniment to two lieder. 'Geoffrey,' I asked, 'aren't you glad it isn't *Feuerreiter?*' He replied, 'If it had been I would have been in bed at midnight, three hours and two bottles earlier.' The two songs took about an hour, and we were done.

Something about the record had been worrying me throughout the session, and suddenly it surfaced. I said to Schwarzkopf and Legge, 'You know, this record has got too many gentle, slow-moving items – there is not enough excitement in it – no really dramatic piece.' Legge looked at the list of items. 'You're quite right,' he said. 'But we'll soon fix that.' He picked up the nearest volume of music, which happened to be Volume I of Schubert, opened it at random, plonked it down in front of Schwarzkopf and said, 'There's your dramatic piece.' Parsons looking at the music over her shoulder turned an interesting shade of green as Schwarzkopf exclaimed, 'But, Walter, I've never sung "Erlkönig".' 'No time like the present to start.' She left the control room looking dubious; Parsons, as he passed me, growled through clenched teeth, 'One day I'll pay you back for this.'

They rehearsed for a few minutes and did a take. Parsons must have sweated blood, but the piano part was faultless. When, looking slightly the worse for wear, he came to listen, Legge's 'that's it, my lad' must have cheered him. We listened, and Schwarzkopf exclaimed, 'I don't feel comfortable in this key – what other keys do we have it in?' Legge's copy was in A minor – too high – mine, which is superscribed 'New Delhi, 24 July 1953', was in E minor, too low. I had a spare score in the original G minor, the key in which they had just performed the song. Schwarzkopf smiled winningly and said sweetly to Parsons, 'Geoffrey, you can transpose it, can't you?' He gulped, with the air of one who was resigned to anything, and said simply, 'Of course.' They rehearsed it and started again. Then repeated it again, and again; there were quite a few takes. Parsons's performance was faultless, each time. For sheer technical excellence I have seen few feats to excel this.

A few months later he arrived at the Abbey Road studios to complete the Ludwig record. I met him at the door and said, 'Geoffrey, you are looking well.' He replied, 'I am well and full of the joys of spring – after all, we have only to do two simple Schubert songs.' 'That, my boy, is where you are wrong,' I replied with some relish. 'Abandon all cheerfulness; Christa wants to repeat part of "Erlkönig".' 'Oh, no,' replied Parsons, 'I thought lightning never struck twice in the same place. What have I done to you, Suvi, that you should persecute me thus?' Actually I was having him on; all Ludwig wanted was to redo one bar so as to treat the grace note on the word 'Arm' as a leading note and not as a crushed passing note.

When he arrived for the Bumbry sessions, with one foot still in his car, Parsons said, 'Unless you give me an assurance in writing that I won't be required to play "Erlkönig" on these sessions – not in A or G or even in B flat – I am going straight back home.' I assured him, 'No "Erlkönig" – only "Gretchen".' 'Pooh, that's child's play,' he laughed.

The Bumbry record was supposed to consist of Schubert and Brahms. She was quite happy about the Schubert list, except that we both instantly threw out 'Ave Maria'. I asked, 'What about what Christa called "diese komische Nonne"?' Bumbry said, 'Wait till you hear me sing it'; about the other side, she was not happy at all. 'I am in a happy mood; these Brahms songs are all singularly gloomy.' I myself had thought that the songs must have been selected by someone in a fit of suicidal depression. I had already decided that I would replace some of them with more cheerful songs. We shelved the question of Brahms for the moment and began with the Schubert. 'Die junge Nonne' was a *tour de force*. She sang it through twice, and repeated one phrase to cover a slight frog in the throat. After the second performance, I said, 'Grace, bravo, and thank you for having insisted on retaining this song.' After those last exultant 'Allelujas' she was standing, eyes closed, face radiant, one hand on her heart, the picture of transfiguration. She now opened one eye, gave me a broad wink, and grinned hugely.

When she walked into the control room for a break, I asked her, 'How much Schumann do you sing?' She replied, a little puzzled, 'Not a great deal, but I love the Schumann songs.' Then, as light broke on her, 'That's the answer,' she said. 'But can we do Schumann when your people have asked for Brahms?' 'Yes,' I replied firmly, 'we can. Leave it all to me.' We spent a happy ten minutes selecting Schumann songs suitable for Bumbry's voice and for the ebullient mood she was in. When we started to record them she sailed through them with the assurance and aplomb acquired during her extensive experience in dramatic operatic roles. Her recording of 'Widmung' was an astonishing feat. She sang it through once, said it was in the wrong key for her voice, sang it through once in the new key – and that was it.

I was pleased with this record. It was with a sense of outrage and anger that I learnt that of all the companies which made up EMI, only Germany was going to release it. There never has been a market in the United States for lieder, or so we've been repeatedly told; I got no satisfactory reply but a lot of surly looks when I once asked innocently why, if the gentlemen facing me were such successful sales people, they had not succeeded in creating one.

Great changes had taken place in the structure of the record division in the fifteen years since I joined EMI. As we have seen, the power which had been in the hands of the producers, or artist managers as they were more correctly called, had been consciously and deliberately taken over by the administrators and was more thinly spread around, except for one person – the overall Manager, who exercised the power of a despot. This was absurd, since without producers there would be no record company. But though producers exercised absolute authority in the recording studio, they were left with less and less outside that sphere. A host of accountants, clerks, lawyers, publicity men, sales experts, repertoire specialists and some who, frankly, looked to the producers like plain hangers-on, descended on the division.

It would have been a highly desirable state of affairs if all this had led to greater efficiency and productivity. But it had not; on the contrary, by channelling spheres of activity into narrow confines it tended to keep the left hand from knowing what the right hand, or any other part of the body,

164

was doing, producing some strange results; a classic example was a record sleeve which announced on one side Mozart's 'Piano Concerto in B flat K238' and on the other 'Piano Concerto in B flat K328'. Any producer with a reasonable knowledge of Mozart (and anyone who has not should not be a producer) would, if a 'pull' of the sleeve had been shown to him, have instantly spotted the mistake. Some sleeves have become collector's items; a picture of the full Bournemouth Sinfonietta, complete with oboes, horns, bassoons, trumpets and timpani, on the sleeve of a record of purely string music, and a picture of the Pittsburgh Orchestra on a record of Previn conducting the Chicago Orchestra.

While this sort of thing was infuriating, there was another development, much more dangerous in its implications – the gradual infiltration of the administrators into the field of repertoire. A sales expert was entitled to say, 'In my opinion a record of X playing Schubert will not sell in Germany.' I would even accept him saying, 'I cannot sell X in Germany.' What he has no business to be saying, and what he is not, except in very rare cases, qualified to say, is, 'X cannot play Schubert' or 'X should be playing Chopin.' Or even, as on one unforgettable occasion, 'The Schumann Fantasia is a load of rubbish.' However, this was the new dispensation.

Barenboim's career proved the efficiency of the old system. We started primarily with the aim of making one record of Beethoven sonatas, the Mozart piano concertos, a few other piano solos and concertos and the odd conducting record in three years. He actually recorded over one hundred records in nine years, of which not more than ten, at the most, were commercially unsuccessful. The other ninety or so more than compensated for those ten, so that, on balance, we did handsomely out of the artist – and he out of us. His recording programme, like Topsy, just 'growed', and the system had not yet established the stranglehold it now has, to either choke its growth or stunt it by trying to force it in unacceptable directions.

I personally haven't suffered too badly from the system, for most of my artists have been powerful enough to say, 'Very well, since you are not interested in this repertoire, I am sure you will have no objections to me taking it elsewhere.' I have often enough remarked to colleagues, 'Some artists we have by the short hairs – others have us by the short hairs' – only, I have not used the term 'short hairs', but what could be fairly translated as 'round objects'. As in the case of the Bumbry record, I also had the wit to move 'sideways like the crab' and get round any obstacle.

I had so far made only a few records in England outside London. In 1975 I began working with the Bournemouth Sinfonietta; this resulted in a close friendship with their principal conductor, Kenneth Montgomery, and four first-class records of a kind of repertoire new to me. The first consisted of five symphonies, four by Arne and one by Wesley. I knew

Arne, of course, as the composer of 'Rule, Britannia', which Indians disliked as an expression of the British in their more exhibitionist moods; and I knew that he was not the composer of 'The lass with the delicate air', popularly ascribed to him. I did not know that he had written symphonies. I was able to get hold of the scores of only two of them in advance, No. 1 in C and No. 4 in C minor, and they were full of sparkling, vigorous music. I hoped that the Kenneth Montgomery I was shortly to meet would have a touch of the Beecham magic, which I felt these works called for. As for Wesley, every reference book I looked up mentioned that, as a young man, he had fallen on his head and suffered concussion and had never been the same since. When I looked at the score of his symphony I felt that if after such an experience Wesley could produce music of such invention and imagination, there were several composers I could think of who might have benefited greatly from being dropped on their heads.

I found Montgomery to be a cheerful, outgoing person. To my delight, I found on the first session that he possessed more than a touch of the Beecham magic – I had not heard anyone since Beecham produce such precision of playing and articulation in fast-moving music and yet have time to shape delicately written phrases with charm and wit. Montgomery also had an instinctive feeling for the important line at any moment. You can hear it in this record in his handling of the strings, notably the violas, the litmus test of a conductor's capacity to balance strings, and the horns; whether playing solo or only contributing to the texture of the music, there is always the right amount.

It was Montgomery's first essay at recording, but he did not seem unduly worried. He even accepted the peculiar acoustics of the Guildhall in Southampton; at the conductor's rostrum the woodwind are often blanketed by the strings in front of them and the horns and brass behind them. It takes nerve and exact judgment for a conductor to balance woodwind in a hall from what he has heard through loudspeakers in a listening room. Montgomery took practically anything in his stride. As with their conductor, it was a case of love at first meeting with the orchestra. Like all the best orchestras they enjoyed making music and I made many friends among them. To end on a sad note, I cannot hear the Arne symphonies without a slight prickling at the back of my eyes, for it brings vividly back to me the image of the young, vivacious oboe player, Judy Bass, who died tragically young, less than two years later.

This was one of the first records I made which was issued in a 'quadraphonic' format. Quadraphony was doomed to be a short-lived fad and die unregretted by the professionals in the business – the producers and the engineers. It was based on a fallacy so obvious that one despaired at the human race's capacity to be taken in. The argument went that, since in a concert hall sound reached a listener from the front and from the back, if you added two channels through loudspeakers behind you, you

166

would achieve an even greater degree of fidelity. This was the theory. It did not at all work like that in practice.

First, it assumed that the total sound could be comfortably parcelled into a front and a rear component. It could not, for from the rear and the sides came a confused and random mixture of the sound from in front. Then, you needed four discrete channels, and this was not possible on the conventional disc, which had only two possible carriers – a lateral cut and a vertical cut. So, right at the start there had to be a compromise. The left front and rear channels were combined into one and the two right channels combined into another; we were back at the beginning, but not quite; we were, in fact, slightly worse off, for the combination of the front and rear sounds produced unexpected side effects such as narrowing the stereo spread and making the sound lose sharpness and clarity. The only true quadraphony would have been to provide four separate channels on tape. How were we going to persuade a public, reluctant enough to buy cassettes, to invest in much more elaborate apparatus to reproduce these tapes? And as a corollary to that, how many households were capable of accommodating in their living rooms, four loudspeakers which had all to be of equal size and quality? So quadraphony was dead before birth, but took a long time to lie down. I, who saw from the beginning that this whole thing was a gigantic confidence trick, tried to persuade everyone to drop it, but when the sales departments of all companies jumped on to it as a gimmick they hoped would sell more records, I resigned myself to being forced into quadraphony. I made sure though that the normal stereo sound of my records was damaged as little as possible by 'quadraphony' – in other words, I used a mere soupçon of sound from the rear, just enough to make the records qualify for the epithet 'quadraphonic' under the Trades Description Act.

The fallacy in the argument about quadraphony was, of course, that in the home, as in a concert hall or studio, the sound from the loudspeakers in front of you bounces off the rear and side walls and bingo – there's your quadraphony.

In less than a month after that first record, I went again to Southampton, this time for a record of string music, and shortly afterwards for another two records full of fresh surprises. The first of these was a selection of music by Handel. I looked at the list of items chosen by the sales people and thought to myself, 'Oh yes, the usual stuff' – the Overture and the Pastorale from *Messiah*, the 'Arrival of the Queen of Sheba', bits from the *Water Music*, the Dead March – and then, I froze. Interspersed with these were, to my horror, movements which seemed to have been picked at random from various concerti grossi and violin and oboe concertos. There seemed no special reason for the selection except perhaps that someone had liked the tunes in each movement. However, the solid front Montgomery and I presented against this prevailed, and we

167

were able to substitute selections from the operas which at least did not bleed when torn out of context. The other record was of symphonies by the 'London Bach', J.C., whose music is so tantalizingly like Mozart's.

24   A Musical Sparrow, Four Out of Tune Serpents, and the Departure of a Genius

The next year began with an unusual record tinged in retrospect with some sadness – of the last two records of the year, one was even more unusual and the other tinged with more than a little sadness. The first record of the year was of a new piece, Introduction and Passacaglia for piano and orchestra, by Yardumian, the American composer of Armenian origin. The pianist was John Ogdon whose last record it was before his illness. The orchestra was the Bournemouth Symphony Orchestra under their principal conductor, Paavo Berglund. It is an extraordinary piece with many original touches – the difficulty with recording it was that it is heavily scored for brass, horns, timpani and percussion; periodically the strings vanished and you could hear the piano only if you poked your head under the lid. After several unsuccessful tries at balancing piano and orchestra, I asked the engineer to 'shove the bloody microphone into the piano and to hell with the quality of the instrument'. The engineer pushed the microphone into the piano, somewhere in the region of middle C; the sound emanating therefrom was that of a honky-tonk upright in a New Orleans speakeasy, but as Ogdon, with an unexpected touch of acerbity, remarked, 'At least you can now hear the damned thing.'

Berglund manfully strove to get some string sound through – there was a total of fifty players. They sawed away vigorously, but for all the good they did, they could have mimed their parts – both in the studio and in the control room we heard only the blaring of the brass and the horns and the clash of the percussion. The control room itself resembled one of the arrival platforms at Waterloo Station during the rush hour, for the composer himself was present along with an assortment of relatives. 'That's a filthy row – for heaven's sake get me some string sound,' I said to the balance engineer from one side of him. 'That's a great sound – can't we have more brass?' enthused the composer from his other side. There was an air of unreality about the proceedings. But Ogdon, Berglund, the orchestra, the engineer and I expended much time and care on the work to get the best out of it. I actually took a quarter of an hour from the third session, which was for the other side, Glazounov's Concerto, and was to be produced by a colleague, to put the final polish on our work. The recording finished, I walked out of the control room and my colleague

169

entered. In less than two seconds he shot out and asked me, 'Who are all those people in the control room?' I replied, 'My composer and his family.' 'It's frightful – there's no place to move around in there. Do I have to let them stay on?' he asked. 'Well – since it's not Glazounov and his family, I suppose you may turf them out,' I said, rapidly disappearing from the scene.

A handful of Perlman records followed. The first was Vieuxtemps's Fourth Concerto, in Paris. I walked into the Palais des Congrès in Paris in the middle of the dress rehearsal, with Barenboim and the Orchestre de Paris, to see Barenboim turn to the auditorium and ask, 'Where is Suvi?' 'Here,' I raised my hand. 'It's difficult to pick you out in the dark in a dark suit. Is the brass too loud for Itzhak?' 'No,' I replied, provoking a growl from Perlman to whom any orchestral accompaniment louder than a mezzo-piano is too loud.

Actually, Vieuxtemps seems not to have been quite sure whether he was writing a violin concerto or a symphony – whenever the solo part stops he launches into enormous orchestral tuttis. When Perlman enters, you are glad it is a violin concerto. His effortless brilliance in the scherzo is dazzling. I was fascinated by the way his fingers skimmed over the finger-board. Equally revealing was his playing of the slow movement. There was no soulful swaying, no swooning or dreamy looks on his face – it was so impassive he might have been reading the morning's stock market report – but from the violin there poured forth an impassioned stream of melody.

We returned to London for a record of Bruch; the two works were completely new to me, the second violin concerto and the 'Scottish Fantasia'. When Perlman started to play the concerto I saw the point of his reply whenever I asked him what sort of piece No. 2 was. 'Wait till you hear me play it.' This is one of my favourite Perlman records.

There followed Vivaldi's *The Four Seasons*. There are, to my knowledge – and I am not a specialist in the music of the composer – at least two dozen concertos which are as fine as these four, but the nickname has elevated them to a position of being the best known works of the period. Not that *The Four Seasons* are undeserving of their popularity; they display a mastery of programme music well ahead of the early eighteenth century. Perlman directed the orchestra as well as playing the fiddle; it was his first venture into the realms of conducting and he revealed an unsuspected gift for it. He had, of course, the unstinted support of the strings of the London Philharmonic Orchestra, and Rodney Friend, their leader. This is one of the Perlman records which has sold most; to date, the closest challenge to it has come from the Beethoven Violin Concerto. It is a measure of the quality of the Perlman records that two of the works most often recorded (there are currently on the market forty records of the Vivaldi and twenty of the Beethoven) are top best-sellers. The last record was a second compilation of pieces by Kreisler. The high spot for me was the arrangement of Tartini's 'Devil's Trill' sonata. The trill is indeed devilish; Perlman demonstrates how one pair of hands can produce perfectly placed double trills and chords. When we listened to the edited tape some time later we turned round to find Giulini in the listening room. He shook his head and said, 'That is almost unbelievable.' Perlman was touched. 'You know', he said, 'that's not entirely me. I play only the upper line; Pinky Zukerman plays the lower part.' It was only for a brief instant that Giulini seemed to entertain this preposterous idea, and then he chuckled. 'Even then, Itzhak, it's beautiful.'

I am still the first to be considered when a new pianist turns up. I worked with four pianists during the year – with three for the first time, while the fourth was Agustin Anievas. He recorded the two sets of Impromptus by Schubert. They were composed in the last year of his life. For me (and not only for me) one of them is as moving and disturbing as any music ever written.

There is music which seems to deeply move everyone. The slow movement of Schubert's C major Quintet is an example; and also by Schubert, the slow movement of the B flat sonata – its unusual key of C sharp minor; the disjointed, almost distracted accompaniment to the main theme; the irresolute hovering between the home key and various others, in particular E major – the whole movement inhabits a mysterious, insubstantial world; and then, that magical moment in the recapitulation, one of the great moments in music, when instead of the E major the ear expects there arrives a totally unexpected and unprepared C major chord. Why does that C major chord so profoundly move one?

Almost anyone who loves music will agree on a short list of a dozen or so pieces with a similar power to move them. But each person can also produce another list special to him or her. If I were to compile such a list it would be a somewhat mixed one. First, the madrigal 'When David heard that Absalom was slain' by Tomkins, which I cannot bear to listen to often, for the desolation of David's cry 'O my son, Absalom, would God I had died for thee' tears my guts every time I hear it. Then, from an altogether different world, Tarrega's 'Recuerdos de la Alhambra' ('Recollections of Alhambra'), which stirs in me an inexplicable, aching nostalgia – for what? I cannot tell. The slow movement of Beethoven's third 'Rassoumovsky' quartet and the minuet of Schubert's A minor – these invoke, in the former, an unrelenting despair which the jaunty C major theme does little to relieve, and in the latter sheer, hopeless melancholy. But when these pieces come to an end, I am not left desolate. The music draws those feelings out of me, and comforts me with the thought, 'I am not alone. Someone else – Beethoven, Schubert, Mozart or whoever – has traversed this stretch of human experience, and therein for me lies the power of music, as of all art – the sharing of an experience with someone else. It is as if the artist stretches out his hand and says, 'Peace, do not be troubled; I am with you. I too have been here.' Every man is an island, locked in the total isolation of his own mind. It is a solitude from which there can be no escape. Great art, but above all music, reaches that deeply recessed core in every man, which only it can penetrate.

The F minor Impromptu of Schubert is a piece which figures prominently on my list. I can analyse the piece in terms of musical structure, key relationship and so on, but I cannot explain why the middle section, in which, to the accompaniment of a quicksand of shifting harmonies in the right hand, the left hand picks out a dialogue between two fragments of a theme, above and below the right hand, is so heartrending. My wife shares this feeling, and the last time Barenboim played it in concert, Perlman said to me, 'That F minor piece . . . ,' he broke off, not quite sure how to continue, and then said prosaically enough, 'It's quite something, isn't it?' – more eloquent than any peroration. I am sure it is the touching of the core of our hearts that unites a Sindhi Hindu from the north-west corner of India, a South Indian Christian from the diagonally opposite corner of the country, fifteen hundred miles away, and a Jew who lives in the United States seven thousand miles away – and Anievas, normally undemonstrative, was so overcome, after recording the F minor, that he slumped in his chair almost oblivious of the playback.

I acquired the first of my new pianists by accident. I was working in our garden one evening when an urgent message arrived from next door – the producer of a recording was already ten minutes late and the artist was getting impatient. I took just long enough to scrape the mud off my fingernails and change into a less disreputable pair of trousers and arrived in No. 1 to greet Garrick Ohlsson, who was to record the Brahms Handel Variations. He is a pianist I had always admired and to have the opportunity of working with him was gratifying.

Later he made four more notable records with me: two of the Chopin Nocturnes, Schubert's D major Sonata D850 and two scherzi, and the Brahms D minor Concerto.

The Brahms concerto was with the London Philharmonic orchestra conducted by Klaus Tennstedt and it was a stupendous performance. As they rehearsed, I realized that this was truly going to be the performance of a concerto for piano against orchestra. Tennstedt would make no concessions to the pianist – he would have to fight to get through. They played the first movement in full, in one take. Tennstedt walked into the control room with an open bottle of beer in one hand to replenish the liquid which was pouring off him in torrents of sweat and which he was mopping up with a towel in the other hand. He saw the look on my face and putting an arm round my shoulder he said excitedly, 'We make good music, eh?' Ohlsson, looking as if he had just climbed Everest without benefit of oxygen, collapsed into his chair. During the playback I noted

Ohlsson looking anxious – even his heroic efforts were not enough to cut through the huge swell of orchestral sound. When we were alone, I said, 'Garrick, we've got you on two tracks of your own. Don't worry, I'll make sure that you don't get lost.' He left for the studio looking relieved.

Everything went normally and we had a whole session in which to do the last movement. It was going to be an easy job and I expected the session to end in two hours. Actually, it was nearly wrecked by something not much bigger than a tennis ball! While they were rehearsing I could hear, off and on, odd squeaks and chirps. I thought it must be a chair with loose joints or the conductor's rostrum, and made a note that it should be attended to before the take. They finished, and I asked, 'Ready for a take?' Tennstedt asked 'Can you hear the bird in the studio?' 'Damn,' I said under my breath, and aloud to the studio, 'I'm coming in.'

A little sparrow had somehow got into the studio just below the ceiling of No. 1 and, as I walked in, said welcomingly, 'Cheep! Cheep!' I clapped my hands and the bird moved to another strut and as if asking, 'How did you like that?' said 'Cheep! Cheep!' again. I tried to work out what options we had. There really seemed to be none. There was no way anyone could capture that bird; the ceiling of No. 1 is over forty feet high and the metal struts under it can only be reached through the roof. By the time anyone had got to within six feet of it the bird would have flown off to its next resting place, and this could go on for the rest of the session. I would also have to get everyone to vacate the studio, for I did not fancy someone walking on slender struts thirty-seven feet above a seated orchestra. The bird seemed to approve of my summing-up of the situation, for it said, companionably, 'Cheep! Cheep!' The orchestra giggled.

I tried one last ploy, not really believing it would work. Looking up at the ceiling I yelled at the top of my voice, 'Hoy!' The bird uttered a startled 'Cheep! Cheep!' and, affronted, flew off to a remote corner to sulk. We all waited, holding our breath for about a minute. Silence, and to the accompaniment of 'Bravos' from orchestra and conductor I returned to the control room. The red light went on, the orchestral buzz died down, Ohlsson started the opening theme; on the last bar, as if to applaud him, loud and clear came, 'Cheep! Cheep!' It was exactly in tempo and perfectly timed – everyone, in the studio and in the control room, laughed. The take, naturally, broke down. We started again. This time the bird felt obliged to contribute its own bit to the proceedings; on the fourth bar it said 'Cheep! Cheep!' Again everyone laughed; again the take stopped. Three times more they started and three times did not get beyond the soloist's entry. I was beginning to get concerned; the first time, and perhaps the second, it was comic to see Tennstedt with arms raised to bring the orchestra in only to drop them as he dissolved into laughter; by the fifth attempt it was not so much comic as ridiculous and then what I feared happened. He blew up. He threw down his baton and walked off the rostrum. 'This is not possible. How can we make a performance like this? It's impossible'. I was already inside the studio. I silenced the babble of voices and said 'I've sent for someone with an airgun. He will be here soon – the bird will be dead in ten minutes'.

There was a stunned silence, as my words sank in, followed by outraged cries from the orchestra. 'You can't do that!', 'No, please'. 'There must be some other way.' Tennstedt, looking slightly guilty, came up to me, 'You cannot kill a poor little bird like that,' he waved at the ceiling and the sparrow, having taken no part in the happenings of the last few minutes, uttered what the orchestra felt to be a heartrending 'Cheep! Cheep!' for they replied 'Ah!' in unison on the down beat following the second 'Cheep'. I let them all carry on for a few minutes. Then I said, 'There are only two solutions; for me to have the bird killed or for you to ignore it. We'll run through the movement twice and hope that the cheeps are in different places. We'll redo passages where there are interruptions at the same point in both takes. It's up to you to decide.' Everyone promised to ignore the bird and as I walked out the bird also agreed. 'Cheep! Cheep!' I muttered under my breath, 'Cheep! Cheep! yourself, with knobs on, you little bugger. You've lost me twenty minutes of recording time, costing £400.'

Back in the control room, the balance engineer looked puzzled – he asked how I had managed to raise an air gun, and a person to use it at such short notice? 'What air gun?' I innocently asked. 'You mean it was all a bluff?' I replied, 'Surely you didn't believe that I was going to arrange for an inoffensive little sparrow to be killed?'

Heroically, conductor, orchestra and soloist all managed to get through the bird's frequent interruptions and we did two full takes. My score, in addition to the markings I normally put in it, acquired a new one, 'Ch'. The bird was distinctly musical; it liked the movement's second theme, and punctually on the fourth bar, both in the first statement and in the recapitulation, in both takes, and in rhythm, it said 'Cheep! Cheep!' After several repetitions of these two spots I had one take of each free of the bird's comments – or so I thought. When the tape was remixed, on the fourth beat of the second theme's first appearance there was a faint but unmistakeable 'Cheep! Cheep!' which nothing I tried could get rid of. So the 'Little bugger' did have the last word.

A fortnight after Ohlsson, Daniel Adni followed – with music I had not heard before, not by an obscure composer, but by Mendelssohn. I had come across a lot of his piano music, but not the Six Preludes and Fugues Op. 35. As I flipped through the score I was grateful that the reservoir of music is so vast that even if I devoted the rest of my life entirely to listening to new music it would be as if I had scooped up a handful of water from the vastness of the Pacific.

One day during a recording session I was talking about this to Previn. I told him how I had recently heard for the first time a major work by a composer whose music I prided myself I knew without any serious gaps. I had switched on my car radio, which is tuned permanently to Radio Three, and heard the last bars of a piece which obviously was part of a string quartet. The very last bar had the cello doing an octave leap on the first two beats and the violin, playing alone, doing the same thing on the third and fourth beats. 'How very comical, and' – I was about to say 'characteristically Beethovenian', but I know intimately every movement of every one of the seventeen Beethoven quartets, and this was not one of them. What little I had heard of the piece hadn't sounded Haydnesque but I thought it probably was an early work of the older master. Haydn too I knew from Op. 20 on, though not as thoroughly as I did Beethoven. Previn interrupted, 'You really know all Haydn's quartets? How many are there – after Op. 20?' I said I did. 'Suvi, you'll never stop surprising me,' he remarked.

From the silence on Radio Three I deduced that another movement was about to follow – and in a few seconds what was obviously the slow movement began. My attention focussed sharply on the music, and I was completely puzzled; this was nobody's early work; it was a great movement with the stamp of a mature master. But who? It sounded like Schubert, modulating uneasily in the opening bars from C major to D minor, and the florid counter theme on the cello and the first violin, a few bars later, was also characteristic of him; but again I knew all the Schubert quartets. I had to know who the composer of this work was and having reached the studios sat through the rest of it – much of it sounding like early Beethoven – with my car parked in the forecourt. I was quite unprepared for the announcement that followed: 'the String Quartet in F major K590 by Mozart'. K590? I did not even know that Köchel number. If Legge, on that night sixteen years earlier, had asked me to sing the opening theme of Mozart's last quartet I would confidently have sung the jaunty B flat theme of K589! What a wonderful experience it was to discover a major work by Mozart in one's fifty-ninth year. What surprises might yet be in store for me?

The Previn record was the 'Music Night No. 2', and we had a rollicking time making it. Previn set the scene with the first item. He was determined that the overture to Glinka's *Russlan and Ludmilla* should go as fast as the London Symphony Orchestra could play it – which, I calculated, would mean as fast as it could be played. He rehearsed it at what I thought was breakneck speed. When we started to record he took it even faster. In addition, there were the Debussy *Faun*, Butterworth's lovely, evocative 'The Banks of Green Willow' and, conjuring up the smells and sounds of Spain, three dances from Falla's *Three-cornered Hat* and, what proved unexpectedly to be the most difficult to play of all the pieces, Strauss's familiar 'Emperor Waltz'.

The time the Strauss took produced a problem; at the end of it we had enough time, with just a little extra, to play once through the last item, without which the record would have been poor value for money – the famous Barber Adagio. We toyed briefly with the idea of overtime and rejected it. Previn said, 'Look, we trust each other. I'll play it through once – there'll be no time for a playback – you tell me if anything needs correction and we'll do those bits again. Let's go.' In the next twelve minutes, I doubt if my concentration would have been broken even if a houri from Paradise had performed a belly dance a foot in front of me. As soon as the take was over Previn called me, 'Keep the light on,' he said – and repeated the one passage I would have asked him to do again. At the end of this, my first extended experience of Previn's powers as a conductor, I was even more envious of his producer.

The last pianist of the year was Christoph Eschenbach, and he played three of the nicknamed Beethoven sonatas – 'Pathétique', 'Moonlight', 'Hammerklavier', and, slightly stretching the definition, the 'Funeral March', the Sonata Op. 26. He was an excellent person to work with, very experienced and thoroughly professional. He was a little difficult to get to know, being seemingly withdrawn. Only at the end of his last session did he let his guard down, when I asked in fun why he didn't include Op. 90, which had the benefit of Beethoven's own precise description of its two movements. When the sonata's dedicatee, Count Lichnowsky, asked him what the piece meant, Beethoven with a horse laugh replied, 'First movement, struggle between head and heart: second movement, conversation with the beloved.' Eschenbach, with the first smile I had seen on his face, held an imaginary telephone in his hand and said, 'Hello, heart. Head here. Time for our next struggle?'

The uncommon record which came towards the end of the year was of music by a familiar composer – Handel. Charles Mackerras conducted the London Symphony Orchestra playing two of his concertos for double orchestra and one of the most often performed works of the composer, the Music for the Royal Fireworks. But this performance was not like any of the usual ones, it was purely for wind and timpani. Mackerras had specially edited the score for the recording. The forces consisted of twenty-six oboes, fourteen bassoons, four contra-bassoons, two serpents, nine horns, nine trumpets, three timpanists each with three drums, and six side-drums. I don't know why this job was given to me; I welcomed it, for it was going to be a challenge and could be fun. I looked at the score and tried to imagine what the forces deployed would sound like. For instance, what kind of sound would twenty-six oboes produce? Or fourteen bassoons? I had never ever heard fourteen bassoons play together – I had never even seen fourteen bassoons at one time. And as for these forty instruments playing all at once, the mind boggled. And what would four contra-bassoons and two serpents sound like. Serpents?

Surely they were obsolete – there could not possibly be any players around of serpents – and what did they, the serpents not the players, look like. I pictured a Hoffnungesque instrument which coiled and writhed while the player kept changing his hold on it to prevent it slithering out of his grasp and disappearing into the woodwork of No. 1.

I then turned to practical matters. How were we going to raise twenty-six oboes? The London Symphony Orchestra probably had four to six regular players – if the other four main London orchestras contributed all their oboes, we might perhaps just make it, but I noticed that the London Philharmonic Orchestra had a concert on the night of the recording. I knew the conductor and rang him and asked, 'Danny, what are you conducting on 19 December? *Eine Kleine Nachtmusik* four times over?' 'No,' he said 'Berlioz's *Romeo and Juliet*.'

It is a measure of the enormous musical resources of London that we could muster an orchestra of the peculiar make-up we required, without interfering with the normal musical life of the city. Mackerras said that on his previous recording of the work, in 1959, the session had to start after 11 p.m. to allow players to finish playing at concerts before going on to the recording. This time the session began at 7 p.m.

We had in our studios that evening some of the most distinguished wind players in London; it was a reunion of old friends.

When Mackerras started to rehearse I heard, at last, the sound I had tried unsuccessfully to imagine; it took a little time, but the ear adjusted readily enough to twenty-six oboes instead of twenty-six violins. My immediate reaction was, 'This sound would of course have carried across the river to the assembled banks on either side.' Mackerras listened to a test recording and expressed great satisfaction with the sound. I voiced something that had been worying me throughout the rehearsal. 'Charlie, there's something out of tune in the lower reaches.' He laughed, 'Have you ever heard an in-tune serpent?' I said, 'I've never heard a serpent – period.' When the nine horns and nine trumpets and the timpani opened out, full throttle, it was exhilarating but deafening. Charles Mackerras knew how to get exactly what he wanted. Altogether, these were two memorable sessions and we all thoroughly enjoyed ourselves.

The last record of the year was made appropriately on 30 and 31 December and was filled with sadness for me and for the artist. We neither of us were sure of it then, but Barenboim and I both suspected that that record could well be the last one he would make for us in this country – eight years on, it still is. It is also one of the best records Barenboim has ever made, and that means it is one of the best records ever made. It is of Mozart's Serenade for thirteen wind instruments K361, one of the composer's consummate masterpieces.

I often wonder what made Mozart put in so much of his genius into works such as the serenades, the divertimenti and so on, which he knew would be played as background to a social occasion. Perhaps he just could not help it. Or perhaps he foresaw a Klemperer in the gathering. When I took test lacquers of Klemperer's own recording of the C minor Serenade to him in Zürich he asked for it to be played while, with a group of his friends, we were having a buffet dinner. His daughter, somewhat scandalized, asked, 'What – now, while we are eating and people are talking?' Klemperer replied, 'Mozart wrote it to be played during dinner.' I put on the record and noticed that periodically Klemperer was abstracted, obviously listening to the music and not the conversation, as indeed I was. Suddenly there was a stentorian bellow from him. 'Silence!' Klemperer's voice at full volume would have stopped a charging rhinoceros in its tracks. 'Listen,' he commanded in the hush that followed, and in silence we heard the reprise of the second movement's principal theme. 'You can now talk,' said Klemperer when it was over. A few minutes later came another of those very special moments for me. As the plaintive, bittersweet tones of the second oboe announced the theme of the trio in the minuet, a canon *al rovescio*, in reverse, in Mozart's direction, Klemperer's and my eyes met in that instantaneous recognition of a shared special moment in music. This time he did not call for silence, he just smiled at me.

The satisfaction of making this record was overlaid with regret, for me and for Barenboim, that we would not make any records together at least for some time to come. He and I are both forward-looking people, but on that night, as we saw the New Year in in my flat, we indulged in a fit of nostalgia. We did not talk about significant experiences or even about the music we had shared over the years; the conversation consisted of, 'Do you remember that little Italian restaurant off the Kurfürstendamm?' – a three-way rhapsodizing with my wife over the unique taste of mangoes or kulfi, an Indian ice-cream, and so on. I kept remembering inconsequential fragments.

Once, on a June morning, Barenboim had rung me to enquire if I was free to go out shopping with him. I told him I too had to do some shopping; I also had to go to the AA to get an International Driving Licence for a forthcoming holiday in Spain. When we met, Barenboim said, 'I suppose an International Driving Licence runs for six months?' I said no, for a year. He replied, 'Your last licence will expire on 23 November this year.' I looked at him in total astonishment. Barenboim said, 'On 24 November last year we went out together for a birthday present for Jacquie – and on that day we went to the AA in Leicester Square and you got an International Driving Licence – which should be valid for another five months. Now, what do you want to shop for?' I said, 'Sandals.' 'Suvi Raj, you are nuts. You are going to Spain and you want to buy sandals in London! Forget it. I've got to get some music. Let's go to the nearest music shop and have fun. Where shall we eat after that?'

I have had many experiences of Barenboim's legendary memory. The story of Zubin Mehta ringing Barenboim across the globe and asking him, 'What am I doing on such-and-such a date next year? I seem to have mislaid my diary' is well known to most people in musical circles. That happens to be apocryphal, but it is true in spirit.

I could see the break in Barenboim's association with EMI coming some time before it actually took place. No one in our company, or any other, had had any previous experience of so abundant a musical talent as Barenboim has and so there was a considerable puzzlement as to how to cope with it. Opinion in our company was divided between two extremes – those who felt he was a genius and should be allowed, within reason, free rein, and those who said his records, except in some specified categories, did not sell in some territories and therefore he should be asked to confine his recordings to that kind of repertoire only. There was naturally no agreement as to what this kind of repertoire should be; the Americans would take choral works, which were the best selling of his records in their country, but 'no goddam piano records'; the Germans would prefer piano music only, having sold over 100,000 copies of Mozart piano concertos, but, if it helped the Americans, would support a limited number of masses and the like; the Japanese said 'no orchestral record', but when asked whether they would support the Bizet symphony with the Orchestre de Paris shook their heads vigorously from side to side (which indicates 'yes' in Japan!) and estimated sales higher than those of everyone else put together.

I was the only person in EMI with personal knowledge of the complete range of Barenboim's activities. I was constantly aware, wherever I went with Barenboim, of the representatives of another company. They were a dangerous rival, not because they were any more successful in the making of records, but because they had more money, being a subsidiary of a huge industrial giant which was indifferent as to whether the records division made a profit or not. This, of course, gave the company an advantage in the market place when bargaining with artists.

When the question of a new contract with Barenboim came up serious differences developed as to what sort of works he should record. Understandably, Barenboim wanted to enlarge the scope of his recordings – for example, with his French orchestra (he was Director of the Orchestre de Paris) he wanted to do French opera, Debussy, Ravel, Berlioz and so on – and he wanted to record with other great orchestras of the world. EMI wanted to limit the scope to the field in which he had won acceptance in the record world – Beethoven, Schubert, Mozart and Schumann, as a pianist principally, but with the odd orchestral record thrown in. As the negotiations continued there was an unfortunate period in which no one was sure what the next few recordings were to be. Things came to a head when the Berlioz *Roméo et Juliette* with the Paris orchestra was on, off, on, off and then firmly on and finally off. This did not improve anyone's temper. Enter the new company with an offer that Barenboim would have been foolish to refuse. For them, here was a wonderful chance not only to acquire a great musical artist but, as an incidental bonus, to black a rival's eye. And so, exit Barenboim, for an unknown period of time, from EMI.

I was left with a general feeling of dissatisfaction. I had seen Klemperer through his last years and Barenboim through his early years in the recording studio. What did I have left now? And then I perked up – there was still Perlman, and something had always turned up to keep my enthusiasm for my job at a high pitch; there was no reason why that should not happen again. Several exciting things were in fact just round the corner.

25 *Perlman and Previn in Pittsburgh*

In the middle of the year just ending, a second opportunity had presented itself for me to make a record in the States. This time the recording was of the Brahms Violin Concerto by Perlman and Giulini with the Chicago Symphony Orchestra, and obviously I should have done it. A couple of months before the recording I was invited to a meeting with my chief and a colleague. I took a slightly malicious pleasure in the atmosphere of tension which I sensed in the room, for I knew in advance what the meeting was about. After various diversions he came to the point. 'About the Brahms Violin Concerto in Chicago, looking at everything I – we – feel that –' I interrupted, 'You want him to go.' I pointed to my colleague. 'I agree.' I don't think he took in what I said and continued with, 'By and large'. Again I interrupted, 'I've already said "I agree" – and if that's all, I'll be going', and I left two thoroughly flabbergasted gentlemen – in fact, they were distinctly 'discombobulated'.

Time has a habit of dealing out a kind of rough justice. In January 1977 Perlman was due to make a record in Pittsburgh with Previn, who had been newly appointed musical director of that city's Symphony Orchestra. I had not thought seriously about how it was to be achieved, but had decided that I was going to do this recording. There was no need for me to do anything. Towards the end of November the colleague who had gone to Chicago came up to me one morning and launched forth at me. He did not see why he should be required to go to the States in mid-winter to record Perlman, who was my artist anyway. I did not raise an eyebrow. I didn't even ask 'Did I ask you to go to Chicago?'

And so, after having nervously watched the temperature drop in a week to 10°F, on Monday 10 January 1977 I arrived in New York to find the streets awash with an unseasonable thaw. I took to New York at once, with only a minor panic on that first day when, after dinner, walking back to my hotel, I looked at my watch, saw it was 11 p.m. and asked myself aghast, 'What on earth am I doing strolling around the streets of New York at 4 a.m. GMT?'

The next day I had lunch with Perlman in his home. I had produced fourteen – all but two – of the records he had made for us in the six years since he joined us. In that time a warm friendship had developed between

181

us; I was now on the threshold of an even closer relationship with him and his family.

Perlman is a family man. He is restless and unsettled when he is away from home and so on most of his extended foreign trips he takes all, or some, of them with him. On one trip to Europe he came alone. I tried to persuade him to prolong that stay by four days so as to fit in a recording with Haitink and the Concertgebouw. He was reluctant, being anxious to get back to New York and when I pressed him, said, 'Suvi, do you really want to produce two violin concertos with me when I've been away from home for nearly three weeks?' I did not hesitate. 'No, Itzhak, not really.' On his next trip, when we did record those two concertos, he had his wife and three younger children with him.

He is an exhilarating companion and great fun to be with. He loves good food and is very knowledgeable about it. He also has the capacity to laugh at himself about it. 'I am on a seafood diet,' he will say. 'I see food and I eat it.' He is an excellent cook. On one occasion I watched him prepare a lunch of spaghetti with a sauce Bolognese. I was scared as he stirred the mince in smoking hot olive oil – if one blob of it had landed on a finger, it would have meant goodbye to Perlman's violin playing for a fortnight. When I voiced my fears he merely said, 'Relax, there's nothing to worry about.'

His sense of humour is Rabelaisian. He makes jokes about Jews, and also about what are self-consciously called 'ethnic groups' meaning negroes, Mexicans, Indians, Arabs and what-have-you. He tells dirty jokes, jokes with outrageous puns and jokes with the most subtle word play and conceits. He is an excellent mimic and can reproduce the speech of a Brooklyn cabdriver, an English 'pukka sahib', a Jewish grandmother and, oh yes, an Indian producer of gramophone records. Anything that lies to hand is a prop for his humour. One of his more outrageous tricks is to grab one of his crutches, apply his lips to one of the several holes cut along its length, finger the other holes and play a tune on it as if it were a gigantic flute.

Perlman's personality radiates outwardly from the music which is the inner core of the man. To illustrate the qualities of his musicianship, let us look at his playing of the first movement of the Beethoven Violin Concerto – the Everest of music for violin and orchestra. It is an incredibly difficult work for the soloist to bring off. The ritornello, the opening passage for the orchestra, extends to over three minutes, and in it all the material of the first movement is stated and developed at length. When the violin enters there is nothing new left for it to say – it enters with formal octaves. The temptation, which few avoid, is for the violin to announce in bold resolute tones, 'Here I am, the principal guest. All that's gone before is simply to herald my arrival. Let's get down to business.' Perlman's way, and very few follow it, is that of a well-bred guest, who has no need to proclaim that he is the chief guest. He enters, and stays, *piano*, as asked for by Beethoven, for the first two bars, gently leans on the *sforzando* top notes following and then goes back to *piano* for the descending triplets, and the *crescendo* over the next three bars is evenly shaped. Then, all the formal greetings attendant on arrival being over, the first theme of the movement is stated with simplicity – Beethoven's direction is *dolce*. To savour Perlman's artistry more fully and marvel at it, listen to the *dolce* trill on E, extending for nearly five bars before the second half of the theme, and the scales and arpeggios that follow. The work abounds in felicities and Perlman's playing of it is one of the great interpretations of our time. On this visit to New York the first of his two recordings of the work was still over four months away; the immediate job was the Goldmark.

I looked forward to the Pittsburgh recordings with the liveliest anticipation. But first I mentally ran through the rules under which I would be working in America – they were quite different from those to which I had been accustomed. In a three-hour session in the UK you have to give the players one fifteen-minute break; in America you have to have a twenty-minute break *every hour*. This means, in effect, that in the UK you can work for two hours and three quarters, and in America, for only two hours per session. Another rule, rigidly enforced, negates any advantage the UK might have had; you can only record, as against rehearse and make trial recordings, of twenty minutes of music in a three-hour session, while in America, if you are clever, you can record two hours of music over the actual two-hour duration of the session. (Long after that first visit, I did record the full 1910 score of Stravinsky's *Firebird* ballet in one session with the Boston Symphony Orchestra under Seiji Ozawa. Tom Morris, the manager, was so confident of his orchestra and its conductor that he said to me, 'If you don't get the work in one session, Suvi, we'll give you an extra session free!')

The twenty-minute rule in the UK is not negotiable. If the total of the music recorded averages over twenty minutes per session, you have to pay for an extra session, even if the overrun is only of half a minute. This is precisely what happened when I recorded the Shostakovich Thirteenth with Previn and the London Symphony Orchestra. Towards the end of the third and last session I suddenly became aware that the duration of the symphony in our recording was going to be sixty-one and a half minutes. I did my sums a second time and then, in a rapidly-changing kaleidoscope of ideas, considered asking Previn to redo the last movement clipping one minute thirty-five seconds off it – Previn's reaction would probably have been a horrified 'S-o-o-o-v-i!' – running the tape just fast enough to make the symphony one hour long, simply certifying that the symphony ran to sixty minutes, and one or two other possibilities which I shall not go into lest it give people ideas – and I rejected them all. The orchestra was paid for a full fourth sesson to cover the extra ninety seconds.

In America the twenty-minute break in each hour can be given at any time within the hour, but you cannot work continuously for more than one hour; a sensible arrangement, for the concentration with which an American orchestra works would be difficult to maintain for longer. On that first lot of sessions in the States, just as we began the second session of the Sibelius Second Symphony, an alarming 'hum' developed. Previn rang to ask were we ready to record and I said there was a hum which we would first have to locate and get rid of. He replied that it was present in the hall too. I was relieved, for it meant that the hum was acoustical in origin, easier to eliminate than an electrical hum. But it would still take time, and to save recording time I decided to convert the time involved with the hum as part of the first hour's break. I asked Previn to announce a ten-minute break. 'But, Suvi, it's only three minutes past ten, and we've not done anything yet.' 'André, please,' I asked, 'ten-minute break.' Previn's eminently sensible view is that if you trust your producer you have no business to start arguing with him when there is an emergency; if you do not trust him you have no business to be recording with him. 'Ten-minute break,' he said to the orchestra, and in the control room asked, 'Now tell me what it's all about.' I explained. 'Clever,' was Previn's comment. 'I suppose it's a result of the higher mathematics you studied in your youth!'

On a later visit to the States a hum developed again – this time with the Philadelphia Orchestra, on the stage in strength for the 'Alpine Symphony'. Again Previn was the conductor. I asked the engineers how long they might require to be able to tackle it. One said ten minutes, another fifteen. I told Previn twelve and a half minutes. Previn, who whatever his feelings might be always appears totally unruffled, gulped and announced, 'Break – twelve and a half minutes.' There was a howl of laughter from the orchestra, and with one incredulous voice repeating, 'twelve and a *half* minutes' they broke up. Previn came in. 'Twelve and a *half* minutes?' he asked, to which I replied, 'Sorry, André, but that was an instinctive response to two suggestions that we have a break of ten and fifteen minutes.' One of the orchestra came up to me and said, 'Boy, I have now really lived. Never before in my twenty years with the orchestra have I ever had a twelve and a half minute break!'

The rules governing conduct by orchestral players on a session are ferociously strict in America. One of the first things I saw backstage in the Heinz Hall, the home of the Pittsburgh Orchestra, (yes, named after the '57 varieties' chap) was a list of the dos and don'ts for the guidance of the orchestra. It required players always to apply their minds to the business in hand – the making of music to the best of their ability. It forbade, among other things, the taking on to the stage of reading matter or anything to eat or drink, gossiping with another player or distracting another player's attention away from the making of music, smoking, being late or generally being lax or undisciplined. The last paragraph took my breath away. It said, in effect, that any infringement of these rules was liable to lead to summary dismissal from the orchestra. I asked Seymour ('Sy') Rosen, the then manager of the orchestra, how it was possible to induce players to accept such a draconian set of rules. Rosen pointed to a pretty girl in the viola section. 'You see her? We have a waiting list of three approved viola players to fill that place. Those three, breathing hard down her neck, sure have a powerful effect on her attitude to the orchestra. Besides, Suvi, these are commonsense rules which apply in all affairs. You must be on time 'for work; during working hours you must concentrate on it. You can't eat something, drink something and still pay the attention due to your work. There is nothing strange in all this, and I have not come across anyone who has had to be reprimanded for breaking any of the rules.'

When I saw the system in action it did appear easy-going and casual; there was no forcing people to do anything unacceptable to them. Fifteen minutes before a session there was a preliminary announcement to that effect, followed by further announcements ten and five minutes before; two minutes before, a cheerful buzz of conversation outside the green room had stopped. I could see from the television screen that the players were all on the stage and over the loudspeaker came the familiar oboe's A.

The Union representative came up to me saying, 'We'd better synchronize our watches.' At one minute to, there was complete silence from the hall; the orchestra, instruments tuned, was ready to start. They were waiting for the Union man to signal the start of the session at the time agreed by him with me. (On one occasion Previn turned to the orchestra a few seconds earlier and was about to pick up his baton when the Union man, sensing this, laid his hand on the conductor's arm and said, 'Twenty seconds to go'.) During the session, concentration was total – every time the conductor stopped them there was silence as he explained a particular point. Their discipline was not regimented; their conduct was a result of a consensus of feeling that this was the best, most profitable way in which to conduct their business.

I thought briefly of London and smiled to myself. The system there on the whole works very well, but there are times when I have wished that the Musicians' Union would be as jealous about their members meeting their obligations as they are about their rights. Take for example punctuality; a session seldom starts on the dot. The fifteen-minute break always extends itself, and at the end of any playback it is a hard job to reassemble the orchestra. At the end of one session I felt I had to do something to tighten up on punctuality, not because the work we were then recording was going to pose problems, but because the next recording was going to be a tight squeeze. I asked our office to ring the orchestra's management to say that 'Mr Grubb was not pleased by the timekeeping of the orchestra'. I was greatly amused, on the next few sessions, to hear the personnel manager saying as he marshalled the players in, 'Come, come, it's getting time. EMI have complained about us, and we don't want to displease Mr Grubb, do we?' But they kept very correct time and the recording I had been concerned about was easily accommodated in a little under three sessions.

I have wandered a long way from my first visit to the States to record Sibelius's Second Symphony and Perlman playing the Goldmark Violin Concerto and Sarasate's 'Zigeunerweisen'. The only hazard I encountered was the weather, the temperature fluctuating between −10°F, a degree of cold forty degrees lower than I had previously experienced, and 15°F on one blessed day which felt to me like a heatwave!

For the concerto we had arranged for Perlman to sit slightly sideways to the orchestra, a little in front of the line of the firsts, so as to minimize the amount of orchestral sound picked up by his solo mike. When I went into the hall I found him standing disconsolately looking at his chair looking profoundly distrustful. 'This won't work. Why are you doing this to me, Suvi?' he asked in tragic tones. I said, 'Itzhak, I promise you, if it doesn't work we'll change it at once. Trust me.' 'It won't work – I know it won't work,' he insisted. I asked why he thought it wouldn't work. 'I won't be able to see André – and he can't see me. There'll be no contact between us; we'll be all over the place.' Previn stepped in. 'Sit down for a moment, Itzhak,' and when he had reluctantly done so, 'Take out your fiddle and put it under your chin.' He then got on the rostrum, picked up his baton, held his arms out, turned his head sideways and said, 'What's the problem? I can see you and you can see me perfectly.' Perlman was unconvinced. 'I still think I ought to turn around to face the orchestra,' to which Previn replied gently, 'Itzhak, Suvi doesn't try to tell you how to play the violin. Why don't you leave it to him to decide the best way to record you?' I again promised that if it appeared that it wouldn't work, we would change his seating. They rehearsed for about ten minutes and then, over the mike, Perlman asked, 'Suvi – Noo . . .?' A private term between us embracing 'What about it?', 'How are you?' and anything else you might care to make it mean. I replied, 'We're ready to do a test. From the top, please.'

They played through the exposition and came into the control room. During the orchestral introduction Previn looked briefly at me, and from that glance I knew he was satisfied with the orchestral sound. The orchestra hushed down to *piano* and clear and pure, with a heavenly sweetness overlying its steely strength, Perlman's Stradivarius announced the opening theme of the concerto. All Perlman's artistry is superbly demonstrated in his playing of this beginning of the Goldmark concerto. It is a charming, unaffected piece; Perlman wheedles you into believing that it is a great work.

186

Perlman's head had been sunk on his breast as he heard the introduction. At the violin entry it jerked up, and for ten seconds he was motionless. Sitting immediately behind him, I had the absurd notion that his ears, like those of a suddenly alerted Alsatian, were swivelling around to get the full benefit of the sound. Then he looked down at the score with an agonized 'A-a-a-o-w' at a note less than 'absolutely perfect' – this another private joke between us. He gave no indication as to whether he thought the sound 'terrible', 'awful' or – this being high praise from him – 'not bad'. All three of us got down to the music and its interpretation. 'André, horns too loud at C. Is that you or us?' 'It is us, but, Suvi, could you fix it, please? I've had a tough job getting the horns to shed their inhibitions and would hate to cramp them again.' 'Right,' I interjected, and to the balance engineer, 'You heard! Horn mike a little closer, for a tighter sound – or what?' 'André, can you give me a little more time at F? I pull back a bit' – Perlman to Previn. 'He wants to wallow in his G string' – from me – and 'Oooh, Itzie!' again from me at a particularly luscious phrase and Perlman agitating his eyebrows up and down rapidly à la Groucho Marx, but with a seraphic grin on his face. At one point Previn, reprovingly, 'Itzhak,' and Perlman's reply, 'Sorry' – and so it went on, with the normal mixture of serious comment and badinage.

While all this was going on I was tense. I had no doubts about the sound of Perlman's violin but I was not sure of his reaction to it. As I have already said I have long since given up trying to work out how violinists relate to the sound of their fiddles. The recording ran out and Perlman turned round in his chair and said, 'Hey, that's a good sound.' I replied, 'Don't sound so surprised, Itzhak.' The relief among the recording team was palpable to me. Perlman liked the sound of his violin and the first, and in many ways most important, hurdle on his sessions had been negotiated. I said, 'I think, Itzhak, there's a little too much of you. I think we should take you down a teeny bit.' 'No don't,' he replied quickly. 'I shall adjust my dynamics – I can now afford to play piani-ssi-ssi-ssi-ssi-mo' (I do not recollect how many 'ssi's he put in) 'without any fear of getting lost.'

These, my first sessions in America, were among the smoothest and happiest. Previn was pleased that we had gone over to the States to record the orchestra to which he had been newly appointed – the orchestra was overjoyed to be once again facing a battery of recording microphones and were on their mettle. And Perlman – well – Perlman was at his most ebullient; it shows in the recording.

Previn shapes the orchestral part with affection and conviction. He is one of the most skilled of accompanists; there are fewer on his level than can be counted on the fingers of one hand. To be sympathetic to a soloist but not servile, to modulate his own style to match that of the soloist and yet retain enough individuality to influence the soloist's style, to be firm when required but not overbearing, and all the time to watch ensemble

187

and balance, making changes at lightning speed for no soloist worth anything plays a passage more than once in a particular way – these require skills additional to those which make a good conductor. An easy, informal manner cloaks the formidable qualities Previn possesses. I would recommend anyone who values a first-class performance informed by good taste and fine musicianship combined with virtuosity and sensibility, to listen to this record.

I enjoyed working the American system. As for the calculations required to keep track of the passage of time, for me they were elementary. On that first session the Union was represented by one of the orchestra's viola players. He realized within the first hour that I was scrupulous about recording time but even more so about time off, and that I had no intention of trying to wangle a few extra seconds of recording time. At the end of the session he said to me, 'We shall have no problems whatsoever with you', a sentiment subsequently echoed by the Philadelphia and Boston Symphony men.

Perlman departed after the Goldmark and, freed of the restraints imposed by a soloist on the recording of an orchestra, I said to the balance engineer, 'Now for the Sibelius, and don't spare the 'osses.' In less than two sessions we finished, and as the equipment was being dismantled I smiled grimly as I recollected how I had so far been 'protected' from the 'stresses and strains' of recording in America.

Walking through the corridor outside the control room I saw the attractive viola player squatting on the floor leaning against the wall. I said 'Hello' and she replied 'Hello' and asked, 'You are one of the recording team, aren't you? What exactly do you do?' I said I was the producer. 'You must be Suvi, then. Hi, Suvi.' I replied, 'Hi! Did you enjoy playing for a recording?' She nodded vigorously. 'The last recording made by the orchestra was over six years ago, and I've been with them for less than that, so I have never before experienced a recording. Everyone who had kept frightening us newcomers with stories of what fraught occasions recordings were, with tempers running high and people stomping around yelling at each other. But it hasn't been like that at all – it's been fun and if it's going to be like this, please come again soon.' I left Pittsburgh with a warm glow which might have been somewhat instrumental in causing the second thaw which greeted me in New York.

26 Marshall Minor in Cambridge – Ernesto Halffter in Madrid

Those records in Pittsburgh were the first of a satisfyingly wide range of music: Palestrina, Handel, J. C. Bach, Mozart, Haydn, Brahms, Liszt, Chopin, Arnold, Roderigo and Prokofiev. The Roderigo was the ubiquitous 'Concierto de Aranjuez' and the less well known, but for me much more interesting, 'Fantasia para un gentilhombre'. The soloist was Angel Romero, one of the family of guitar virtuosos, and the conductor André Previn, with his London Symphony Orchestra. There was no concert performance of either work, so that we all came to the recording studio in a state of primal innocence; I much more so than Previn or Romero, who had both performed these works, though not with each other. I was probably one of the few in Europe who had never heard the Aranjuez.

In addition I had never recorded a guitar, though I had recorded Vilayat Khan's sitar both on a solo record and with the shanai of Bismillah Khan. In parenthesis, these and a solo record of Bismillah are the only three Indian records I have ever produced. The two Indian musicians were in London for a concert and we decided to cash in by making one record of duets. The balance engineer was fascinated by the sound of these two exotic instruments, and the result was a wonderfully realistic reproduction of the disparate sounds of the sitar and the shanai. The two musicians were enchanted by the recording and each asked me whether he could also record a solo recital. We had one day of the allotted two still left and so I agreed. The three records were released in the UK and in India. Three months later a plaintive letter arrived from our Indian office. Would we please not do it again. Word had got round that with the most up-to-date equipment, a very 'kind' engineer and an Indian producer to boot, records made in London were terrific – and several other Indian musicians wanted to know why they too should not make records in London!

Balancing a guitar against a full-sized symphony orchestra was quite tough. The problem was to retain the gentle character of the instrument and yet ensure that it was not swamped by an orchestra in full cry. It would have been easier if we had settled for blowing up the sound of the guitar to the size of a piano, or had aimed at the distorted sound of electrically

189

amplified guitars on pop records. At one point during a test playback Romero said in an aggrieved tone, 'But they are louder than me.' I replied rather tersely, 'When you are next in the studio, Angel, take a good look around you to see how many of them there are.' With a great deal of juggling of his positioning and trial and error and, of course, the skilled cooperation of Previn, we finally achieved a balance we felt was musical and practical.

When we settled down to the business, Romero astonished us all by his virtuosity and musical sensibility. It took some time to get used to his exuberance. He asked the balance engineer whether he was quite sure his choice of microphones was the best possible, pointed out to me the self-evident fact that when he didn't appear to strike a note clearly it was because in guitar-playing you slide up or down to a note, when he wanted to tune his instrument called loudly for silence to the orchestra without the courtesy of asking the conductor to silence them, suggested to the photographer the camera angles he felt he should use and, but that he seemed to hold Previn in some awe, might even have given him advice on conducting. You could not really take offence at anything Romero did, for it all sprang from an enthusiastic desire to be in on everything that was going on around him.

Haydn was represented by *The seven last words of our Saviour from the Cross* – the original version for orchestra. It consists of an introduction and seven beautiful, grave, slow movements, the last of which, 'Father, into thy hands I commend my spirit', goes straight into a convulsive epilogue representing '. . . and the earth did quake and the rocks were rent'. The essence of each of the sayings is beautifully captured – the rapture of Paradise, the compassion of 'Mother, behold thy son', the despair of 'Why hast thou forsaken me?', the physical pain of 'I thirst', and in the finale, death itself. My pleasure at being asked to take on this job was enhanced by the orchestra's being the Academy of St Martin-in-the-Fields under its founder and chief conductor, Neville Marriner. I had waited patiently for the opportunity of working with this unique group knowing that, one day, sooner or later, their regular producer would not be around. Well, now it had come. Marriner and I were old friends, as were many of the orchestra. I was touched when, introducing me to the orchestra, he said that for them too it was a great pleasure to be working with me. This record will always hold a special place in my memory.

In the middle of the year, also due to the non-availability of another producer, I went to Cambridge for my second set of records at King's College. That producer telephoned me one morning asking, was I free and would I be willing to go to Cambridge on Sunday to do one record of Palestrina and one of Easter music. I was free, and as for would I be willing – I said, 'Don't ask silly questions.'

The director of King's was now Philip Ledger – I had worked with him playing the harpsichord but not as a conductor. The works were Palestrina's Christmas mass 'Hodie Christus natus est' and six of his motets, and hymns such as 'When I survey the wondrous cross', anthems, among them 'Drop, drop, slow tears' by Orlando Gibbons and motets by Lassus, Taverner, Morley and Morales.

Cambridge, as ever, was lovely and the sessions so enjoyable that I felt slightly guilty about being supposed to be working. Ledger had imprinted his own style on King's and exercised his authority with an easy informality. The boys contributed greatly to the fun, when they shed the prim, demure, slightly cherubic air they put on for services and reverted to being the imps all youngsters basically are. They were tightly disciplined and concentrated intensely on the matter in hand in rehearsals and during recordings. The moment there was a lull in the musical activity they swarmed all over the place, but within seconds of the warning call 'Choir reassemble' they were in their exact places. They were engaging and totally irreverent. When I complained to Ledger about some of the soprano line seeming to drop their aspirate in one hymn, he said to them, 'Mr Grubb says he can hear some of you singing "Praise 'im, praise 'im" ' – a shrill, outraged treble voice could be heard in reply, 'Rubbish!' 'Watch it,' Ledger warned him.

The boys loved to come into the control room; they were fascinated by the gadgetry and liked to hear the tapes running back and forward at speed making a gabble of the music. Ledger allowed a selected few to come in at each playback. At every session there was one treble extra to the normal strength as a possible replacement for any voice which flagged. Marshall Minor was this supernumerary at one session, and as the choir reassembled in the chapel after a break, he sidled into the control room and said to me, 'Please sir, can I stay for a bit, sir? Mr Ledger says, sir, he doesn't mind if it's all right with you.' Of course I invited him in. He was fascinated by the machines and first crept up to the tape machine. The second engineer asked him if he would like to operate it. 'Yes, please.' Marshall Minor glowed, and for the next two takes, under guidance, he pressed the 'start' and the 'record' buttons which set the tapes rolling.

He then wandered over to the mixer and watched the balance engineer, who asked after a while would he like to operate that. Marshall Minor was in the seventh heaven. So for the next five minutes, with the balance engineer directing him, he announced the take numbers, switched on the red light in the chapel and faded the microphones in and out. When Ledger and some of the others came in for a playback Marshall Minor retreated into a corner, by a large margin the happiest youngster in the kingdom at that moment. The playback proceeded and the balance engineer's voice said 'Take forty-two'. That ended, and a high voice announced 'Take forty-three'. The look on Philip Ledger's face was indescribable; he wasn't quite sure whether someone was pulling a hoax or if the announcement had actually come off the tape. He looked round and asked in tones that forbode no good to any perpetrator of a joke, 'Who said that?' 'I, sir,' piped up Marshal Minor. In awful tones, Ledger asked, 'Marshall, have you been making a nuisance of yourself?' At which we all chipped in, on the contrary Marshall Minor had been most helpful, had relieved the engineers of some of their work, and inspired us all. Ledger looked dubious and when the choir reassembled got Marshall Minor back into the chapel; but *he* did not any more mind being just the stand-by on the session.

A most unusual stage work turned up next. The venue of this recording was Madrid. On my first visit to that city in 1965, for an aborted recording of a vocal recital by a new Spanish soprano, I had fallen in love with Spain and had since visited it several times.

The work was *Atlantida*, a huge, sprawling, hybrid piece, part cantata, part opera, left incomplete by Manuel de Falla. It was being completed by the modern Spanish composer Ernesto Halffter, with the close collaboration of Frühbeck de Burgos, and the fact that the latter was to be in charge of the forces of the Spanish National Orchestra and Opera for the recording added considerably to my pleasure; he and I, whenever we had done things together, had had the happiest of working relationships. I flew over to Madrid on a preliminary trip to discuss details of the project with the conductor and went through my usual routine in that city – a visit, however brief, to the Prado to stand in silent wonder before the works of one master per trip; this time it was Murillo.

I collected the score of *Atlantida*, or what was ready of it, and no warning bells rang when I heard that Halffter was still working on the finales to the two parts. I promised Frühbeck de Burgos to send him shortly a preliminary schedule of the recording and flew back to London with a plump, dressed, Spanish chicken in a carrier bag, as my wife had said on the telephone that there was no meat in the house; it was promptly confiscated by the Customs at Heathrow.

The recording was to start in the Teatro Real on a Monday morning – a bonus, this, for since no work can take place in Spain on a Sunday our equipment had to be set up on Saturday, leaving Sunday free for a bit of sightseeing. The Spanish branch of the company lent us a splendiferous car and we all piled into it and went to Toledo.

Atlantida was completely new to the orchestra, the chorus and the soloists; it was to the conductor and the producer also, but we had done our homework. Despite our best efforts, progress was slow and the inevitable setbacks occurred. The tenor lost his voice on his last session and we decided to have him superimposed on the orchestral accompaniment recorded in Madrid. At one time the chorus threatened to strike, but that too was sorted out.

A lighter diversion was provided when the Spanish police, having allowed us to park the EMI van on the very wide pavement outside the Teatro Real, suddenly asked for it to be removed. The local citizenry were outraged that a vehicle with British number plates should be allowed so flagrantly to flout the rules which they had strictly to obey. I complained bitterly about this to Frühbeck de Burgos but got no sympathy from him. 'They are quite right,' he said. 'Give us back Gibraltar and you can park your van on the stage of the Teatro Real if you so wish.'

What with all these alarms and excursions, it was only on the penulti-mate day that I suddenly realized that my score of the finale to part two broke off midway on an unresolved discord. I asked the conductor if he had the last bit of the score. He said no, but Halffter was working on it. I said, 'Rafael, we are due to start recording that section tomorrow afternoon and we have no idea how long it's going to be, or how difficult.' He promised to get hold of Halffter, who finally turned up late in the afternoon. 'How much more is there of the finale?' I asked him. 'A leetle bit,' was the airy reply. 'In pages – how many?' 'Oh, about ten.' 'What, ten pages more?' 'Have no care,' he said. 'Rafael and you will each have a score, complete tomorrow morning.' 'Fine,' I said. 'The orchestra will of course divine their parts by clairvoyance.' 'Please?' said Halffter. 'My God,' said Frühbeck de Burgos, and then a rapid exchange of Spanish engulfed me. Frühbeck de Burgos won. He set in train arrangements for a team of copyists to work in relays and copy the orchestral parts. Punctu-ally, one hour before the session was due to start, my score was delivered to me. An amusing sequel to all this took place the next year when Perlman made a record of Spanish music. At one point he announced, 'Suvi, my next piece is by a modern composer of whom I am positive you've never heard.' When I asked his name, Perlman replied, 'Ernesto Halffter – H-a-l . . .' '. . . f-f-t-e-r,' I concluded. 'I not only have heard of him but have worked with him.' 'How about that?' exclaimed Perlman. 'Come into the studio and let me shake the hand that has shaken the hand of Ernesto Halffter. You are sure you haven't met and worked with Brahms – B-r-a-h-m-s?'

When Horaccio Gutierrez was handed over to me I was told he was a fabulous pianist with great musical feeling, but of uncertain temperament: he was to record the Liszt sonata. There was an immediate sympathy between us when we met. By this time I was far and away the most senior of anybody regularly engaged in the production of gramophone records, and any artist allotted to me had heard of me, so I started off with an initial built-in advantage.

In the studio, Gutierrez took nearly two hours of the first session to warm up. He played bits of all sorts of works – Bach, Mozart, the Brahms D minor Concerto, Chopin and Prokofiev – interspersed with fragments of the sonata. His huge bulk hunched over the keyboard, eyes more often than not closed, he played lightning runs and arpeggios, hammered massive chords or caressed the most subtle lines of pianissimo melody. He then played the sonata in one take. It was one of the most stunning performances I have ever witnessed.

We relaxed for a few moments and then listened to the tape. There were no mistakes at all, in the sense of wrong notes or smudges. Three or four sections were perhaps less than ideally clean. I would have accepted them in most pianists, but I knew that this one could play them even better. During the recording I had been listening on one level for wrong notes (and in this sonata there are thousands and thousands of notes, some like the opening theme moving at three seconds per chord, others cascading past at about twenty to the second), stumbles, awkward phrasing, unclear passage work and the like. On a deeper level I was listening to the really important element of the performance – the shaping of the music. Did it have meaning, did it have a logical progression, and, above all, did it engage the emotions?

In just over a year Gutierrez, along with Ohlsson and Adni, had been shed by the company, two of them, even as Pollini had been, paid not to do records we were contracted for. To compound the indignity, two Schubert records made by the last two were never issued in the UK. I went through my routine of outrage and expressed my conviction that sales departments merely sat around waiting for records to sell and if they did not sell said 'get rid of that artist'. My chief remonstrated with me; I really must not disparage a splendid body of men who were doing great things for the company in general and in particular for my artists. My reply was a loud raspberry, which I amplified by adding, 'You can't be seriously suggesting that sales people go around selling Perlman's records. When I rang one of them with the news that Perlman and Zukerman had offered us Bartók's 48 Duos for two violins, his reply was a horrified, "Oh God! Bartók!" Two of the great violinists of our time offer us a work by one of the leading composers of the century, a work not in the current catalogues, and all your sales person can do is to invoke the deity. How can you expect me to take them seriously?' None of this served to save my three pianists, but at least it made me feel better. I was by now beginning to have the uncomfortable feeling that being assigned to me was, for a pianist, like the kiss of death.

There were two jobs in the last month of the year. On the face of it neither seemed especially significant. They were a record of two symphonies and one of two cello concertos, and of the three artists concerned two were old friends and one was new. Each of the jobs was to have a far-reaching effect on me, for each marked the beginning of a close association with an artist which was to quicken my spirits and enrich my working life in the years following.

The symphonies were Prokofiev's First, the 'Classical', and Seventh, with the London Symphony Orchestra conducted by Previn. I had already

194

produced eight Previn records, in which he had figured variously as a symphonic conductor, as an accompanist in four violin concertos and as a pianist, in lieder, in rags and in one of the great works of chamber music. In November I switched on the radio in my car and heard an electrifying account by Previn of Berlioz's overture *Le Corsaire*. So when the Prokofievs came along I was doubly pleased.

On the sessions themselves, I again saw evidence of how well he knew his scores. And, as usual, he wore his talents casually, with a slightly self-deprecatory air. There was also between the two of us that element which has been the most rewarding aspect of my work – a common enthusiasm for, and delight in, music. I said to myself, 'Even if I have to resort to hitting his current producer on the back of the neck with a sock stuffed with wet sand, Previn will one day be my artist.' It turned out that I did not have to resort to such extreme steps.

27 *Rostropovich and* Lady Macbeth of Mtsensk

The other artist, as befitted *his* temperament, erupted into my life like an exploding fire cracker. If that sounds extravagant, there are no measured words that would describe Rostropovich adequately. He is large physically and several sizes larger than life in temperament. He makes friends with abandon – and enemies too. I had not met him, but from colleagues and fellow musicians I learnt that those who knew him well liked him enormously, while some whose contact with him was superficial were hostile or suspicious; no one was indifferent to him.

I had heard him in the concert hall as a cellist – but what a cellist! – and was, to tell the truth, a little suspicious of his excursions into the field of conducting. When a boxed set of him conducting Tchaikovsky symphonies was released, a public reception was held to launch the records. I had then had the opporunity of meeting him, but held back as the occasion belonged properly to the colleague who had produced the records. I was curious enough to sample the set. One might have had different ideas from his about the music, but there was no doubt that Rostropovich was an accomplished conductor.

A few months later, the producer who looked after Rostropovich left the company. A new producer had not yet been assigned to him when a project came up – a film of him playing the Dvořák and Saint-Saëns Cello Concertos with Giulini and the London Philharmonic Orchestra, and only because I was the producer least employed at that moment was I asked to take over the musical production. I had never before worked in the location of the film and so I asked the producer for a quarter of an hour to get the sound right; he grumbled at what he called the 'wasted time'. When the artists arrived Giulini greeted me warmly and introduced me to Rostropovich. I outlined the procedure I thought was the best and Rostropovich said, 'Good – good – good.' When the session began, a few minutes short of the fifteen we asked for, we were ready to record and with a great flurry, the banging together of clapboards and cries of 'Stand by studio – Saint-Saëns take 1' the cameras and the tape machines started running.

We did the first section in one complete take. When the call 'cut' came, I was very pleased; there were two corrections to be made, but as for the rest, it was perfection from Rostropovich and from Giulini and the

196

orchestra. As the playback began I told them that there were only two sections to be repeated; Rostropovich said that he was not happy about two passages. When the first one arrived I stopped the tape and told them what I thought was wrong. Rostropovich replied that that was one of his two passages and, pointing to me, said to Giulini, 'He's very good.' Exactly the same thing happened at the next passage and this time Rostropovich said to Giulini, 'He's marvellous. Have you known him long?' Giulini smiled at an embarrassed me and said, 'Slava, I've known him for over twenty years.'

At that moment it was announced that none of that take could be used because of 'faulty camera angles'. I could cheerfully have strangled the whole lot of them. Giulini sighed. Rostropovich exploded. He raved at the film crew, telling them at great length what he thought of film makers in general and them in particular and then, turning to me, he said, 'From now on, you take charge of the whole thing' – which I did, unobtrusively, having had considerable experience of actually running sessions though appearing not to be in charge.

I observed Rostropovich at work with interest. His playing of the cello was phenomenal; we hardly ever had to repeat anything because of a mistake on the cello. His stamina was colossal. Halfway through the last session, having already played through the last movement of the Dvořák twice, and the earlier movements in a morning session, he still had enough energy to jump up and down half a dozen times, to, as he put it, 'get the circulation going'.

Soon after one of the takes had started, I stopped the proceedings and went into the hall to investigate, as the sound of Rostropovich's cello had gone out of focus. I explained the problem to him, and he pointed to his microphone. I noticed that it had been moved two feet away from the cello and its business end was pointing towards the double-basses on the other side of the conductor; a camera now stood where it had originally been sited. I curtly asked the operator to move the camera instantly or I would kick it into the middle of next week, and had the microphone replaced. While this was being done, Rostropovich whispered, 'There must be a girl sitting somewhere there with a short skirt, and open legs!' – but not softly enough for the remark not to carry to Giulini, who suddenly turned away, covered his face with a handkerchief but could not disguise the rich pink which suffused the back of his neck and ears. I felt that someone who in the middle of the wonderful slow movement of the Dvořák Cello Concerto could find time for a girl in a short skirt was a man after my own heart.

It was with genuine regret at the ending of so pleasant an association that I went to his dressing room to bid him farewell after the last session. His agent was with him. I said, 'Goodbye, maestro, it's been a great . . .' Rostropovich cut in. 'I want to talk to you. You know my producer has left your company. No one knows who is to take his place. I think I would like

197

you to do my records from now on. What you think?' My heart leapt. In the short time we had known each other an understanding had already begun to develop between us. It would be wonderful to work with him. I replied that I would be delighted, but the decision would really have to be taken by the head of the department. Rostropovich turned to his agent. 'We put it in the contract that I work with him,' and to me he said he would speak to my chief as soon as possible.

'As soon as possible' to most people would have meant a week or two, but not to Rostropovich. At nine the next morning I received a message at the studios; would I please go as soon as possible to the office as my chief wanted to talk to me urgently. He said Rostropovich had rung him at first light that morning. He warned me that he was extraordinarily extrovert and dealing with him would take a lot out of me. I replied that I was no shrinking violet myself, that all artists made demands. It was decided that I should do Rostropovich's next recording, due in the April following, and then, if I still felt equal to it, would continue to work with him. As I went back to my room I wondered which of the cello concertos he was due to record; it turned out to be an opera.

It was *Katerina Ismailova* by Shostakovich, or at least that was what I was told. It had been cast, and as I went down the list I was happy to come across two familiar names. Galina Vishnevskaya, Rostropovich's wife, was to sing the title role of Katerina; I eagerly looked forward to working with this galvanic, thrilling singer. An old friend, Nicolai Gedda, was her lover Sergei, and her father-in-law, Dimiter Petkov, the Bulgarian bass. Her two rivals were Taru Valjakka and Birgit Finnila, the other old friend. There were exotic sounding names: Leonard Mroz, Aage Haugland and Alexander Malta, cheek by jowl with John Noble, Leslie Fyson and Edgar Fleet. The orchestra was the London Philharmonic. When I had absorbed the fact that the cast was from about half a dozen different countries, I turned with some misgivings to the recording schedule already drawn up by my predecessor. My fears were all too justified, but there was an unusual twist to the usual circumstances; this time, two of the principal singers, Vishnevskaya and Gedda, and the third, Petkov, with only a brief absence, would be in London throughout the period of the recording. Most of the singers taking the smaller roles were going to be shuttling into and out of London like so many yo-yos; in passing, I saw that 'the old convict', who appears only in the last scene of the opera, was available for the first session only!

I was greatly intrigued by the list of dramatis personae. A merchant, his son, the son's wife and Sergei seemed fairly straightforward, as did workmen, a sergeant, a janitor and a priest, but then it took off into the territory of the thriller with an anarchist, NCOs, convicts, both male and female, and policemen. To get some idea of what it was all about, over Christmas I listened to a Russian recording of the opera. It was an exciting piece with a wonderfully controlled dramatic sweep; there were moments of fierce tension and action and passages of great lyrical beauty. The music itself was compelling and was sustained at a high level. I wondered what could have so disturbed Stalin in the original version that a ferocious attack in *Pravda* prompted by him forced the opera off the stage and into oblivion for over a quarter of a century. When it reappeared, it was modified and given a new title.

Towards the end of February I rang Rostropovich in Washington to tell him that the video film was ready and required to be approved in a hurry; Where should I send him a cassette of the music? He said he did not think that was going to be practicable, and asked whether I was satisfied with the musical soundtrack. I told him that I was not only satisfied but very pleased indeed; I had spent three agonizing days laboriously fitting the best soundtrack passages to pictures which were quite often not from the same takes, for the film had been edited without too much regard for the music. Rostropovich authorized me to approve the film and we turned to our next job. I started, 'Now about *Katerina Ismailova*. . . .' He stopped me. 'We are not going to record *Katerina Ismailova*, the work we are going to record is *Lady Macbeth of Mtsensk*.' I was delighted. This meant that we were going to make the first ever recording of the original version of the opera; it is always a special thrill to tackle a first recording. Rostropovich's reply, when I asked where I could get hold of the score, brought me back down to earth with a solid bump. He himself had not been able to get one, but he soon would and would let me know. So, it was going to be one of those; but it could not be as bad as *Atlantida*, for no disciple of Shostakovich would be putting finishing touches to it even as we were recording it.

Two of the roles with extended parts, both tenor, had still not been filled and I asked Rostropovich if he had any singers in view. He had not, but he had clear ideas on the kind of voices required. For Katerina's husband, a sweet and attractive voice, not very powerful. 'No *Heldentenor*?' I asked. 'NO' he replied in capitals, loud enough to be heard in London without the benefit of the transatlantic telephone system. The other must be capable of acting with his voice. I said, 'I know just the right singer for each role. Leave it all to me, maestro.' He didn't even ask me whom I had in mind. 'All right. We speak again soon.' I asked my secretary to get Werner Krenn for the first and Robert Tear for the second role, making quite sure that each of them could sing in Russian.

As February led to March I began to get a little concerned; the recording was less than a month away and still no score. By now I knew a great deal more about the history of the opera. When it had been, in fact, proscribed in Russia, all copies of the score with opera houses and publishers in the outside world had apparently been called back to Russia. I felt that there must be a copy of it somewhere in the West. Surely the original publishers of it must have retained at least one copy, but a three-pronged approach through me, one of our European companies and Rostropovich yielded nothing. Neither did enquiries of opera houses, radio networks or concert hall managements produce any results. It looked as if, perforce, we would have to record the opera in its later guise. I had reckoned without Rostropovich's determination. In the latter half of March, two weeks before the first session was due, I received a triumphant call from Washington. 'I've got it,' said Rostropovich. From a perform-ance of the opera by Mitropoulos he had traced a score deposited in the Library of Congress in Washington, less than a couple of miles from his hotel. 'Imagine, it was always so close. If I had stretched out my hand, I could have picked it up!'

We went into practical details. He had collated this score with material from another source (which he has never identified) and had produced what he felt was the score of *Lady Macbeth of Mtsensk*. I asked, what about the orchestral and the choral parts and a vocal score for the singers. He replied that it was all in hand and he would bring everything over with him, together with a full score for me. The prospect of seeing the score for the first time on the eve of the recording did not perturb me; I already had some idea of the music.

A week before the recording Rostropovich arrived in London with his wife and at ten in the morning I went to the flat they were staying in to discuss the project. It was freezing in the flat, but blasts of hot air seemed to be coming into the sitting room from somewhere. There were no heaters visible; I investigated, and in the kitchen the source of the heating was revealed – the cooker. Every ring, the oven and the grill had been turned on full, the rings were glowing red hot and it was a surprise to me that the fuse had not blown. When I explained the danger of a fire Rostropovich turned off two of the rings. Back in the living room, I began, 'Maestro . . .' He stopped me. 'My name is Slava – and this is Galina,' pointing to a tousle-haired, sleepy and extremely lovely Vishnevskaya, who had wandered into the room. 'I'm Suvi,' I said. We all shook hands and then got down to business.

Rostropovich has the admirable quality of not struggling against the inevitable. He did not like the disjointed sequence of the schedule of recording but accepted it as unavoidable. Then, the great moment. 'The scores,' he proclaimed and held up duty-free carrier bags in each hand. He presented them to me one after another. 'Act I, Act II, Act III and Act IV. Act II is very big; I think some of Act II papers are with Act IV.' Stuffed inside each bag were wads of pages of the score in manuscript, photocopied in blue ink, and obviously not in serial order. I caught a glimpse of one of them and thought to myself, 'Golly' – in the week remaining I had to get to know the score reasonably well, for there was no possibility of sight-reading this lot during sessions.

200

I tried to stuff in one sheet which was protruding; the string holding the bundle broke, the carrier bag burst and the pages of Act III cascaded to the floor. Rostropovich and I spent the next ten minutes on all fours collecting them and making them up into a tidy pile. Act III was now even less in correct sequence. Vishnevskaya expressed satisfaction at the spacing of her big scenes. I gave Rostropovich a schedule of the rehearsals and told him that I had engaged the Russian coach at Covent Garden to attend all rehearsals and sessions. I staggered out of the flat with three bags festooned from my hands and the burst bag clutched under my arm.

I went back to my office and dumped the lot on my secretary's table. 'Duty free champagne?' she asked. 'No,' I replied, 'the score.' She took a brief look inside and said, 'I resign. I'm not going to sort that out.' A few minutes later, as I left, I saw her squatting on the floor with four growing piles of music fanned around her; and two days later, I had five neat volumes of the score; Act II, being extra long, was in two parts.

I now set to work to study the score. I knew the story and the kind of music it was; what I was studying now was the orchestral clothing of the music. It was a large force – thirteen woodwind, four horns, nine brass, timpani, bass drum and percussion with the strings – over ninety players, on top of which I was intrigued to see a brass band of four cornets, two trumpets, six horns and two tubas, which was occasionally added on. I noted with approval that Shostakovich used the full orchestra only sparingly; most of the orchestration was of small groups of chamber music proportions. The opening scene in which Katerina bemoans the emptiness of her life in the Ismailov household is typical, with oboes, cor anglais, clarinets, bassoons and strings and occasional, soft horn chords. The passages in which the composer let all his forces loose, orchestra, chorus and solo singers, would require skilful balancing, both by conductor and the recording team.

Meanwhile, Rostropovich worked like a man possessed. He and Vishnevskaya had both, a few weeks earlier, been dispossessed of their Russian citizenship and were deeply distressed by that act. When they explained to me what it meant to them, their tears spilt over. They both knew the composer and what he had had to suffer over this opera, and were determined to show just how great a work it is, and I was resolved to do everything in my power to help them achieve that end.

The week was punctuated by a stream of telephone calls between Rostropovich and me while he rehearsed with the singers and the chorus. He had accepted my casting of the role of the seedy lout but was quite anxious as to how 'this Englishman' would cope, not only with the very difficult part Shostakovich had written for him but also with the Russian language, but as soon as Tear had left the flat he was on to me, 'Suvinka, he's fanta-a-a-stic!' The choir was John McCarthy's Ambrosian Singers and I had no anxieties about them. An hour and a half later a joyous

Rostropovich was on the telephone. 'They are marvellous, Suvinka.' 'And their Russian?' I asked. 'Very good – very good. Now for Nicolai and Galina.'

The first session was on the morning of 1 April; there was an air of expectancy in No. 1 studio. Rostropovich arrived an hour early. We discussed various points about the recording. He and Vishnevskaya were a little doubtful about the usual operatic recording set-up; they thought the singers too far away from the conductor. I promised to alter the arrangement if they felt the same after the first session.

We went on to the sound and were agreed that it should not be a warm, romantic sound but sharp, astringent and clear-textured. 'Not Rachmaninov,' I said and he echoed, 'Exactly – not Rachmaninov.' I then asked about the extra brass – should they merge with the main orchestra or be recognizable as a separate body? Rostropovich's response completely baffled me. 'Do you know focking?' he asked. I was accustomed to the unpredictability of artists; this, however, seemed to be the *non sequitur* of all time. The incident of the disgruntled *Times* compositor who inserted into a boring speech by the Home Secretary the remark that 'he felt inclined for a bit of fucking' came instantly to my mind, and I felt like giggling. Curbing the impulse, I said, 'Yes, I do.' He opened the score of Act I, riffled through it and having found the place said, 'Here Sergei focks Katerina. Here, the brass band comes in. Look' – and he pointed to one of the lines. It was an extremely energetic part for the first trombone with semitone glissandi of increasing urgency and rising pitch culminating in a high A, held for four bars – general silence for one bar – the trombone, unaccompanied, rather uncertainly descends by semitones and then abruptly collapses with a downward thump. I suddenly realized what this would sound like in performance – a most realistic representation of 'focking'. I could imagine too what Stalin must have heard, seated in a box just above the brass. I said, 'Shades of *Rosenkavalier!*' He waved that opera contemptuously aside: 'That's for children; this is the real, Roosian thing.'

On that first day we recorded the two sections of Act IV in which the old convict appears. They went extremely well. On the next session we moved the singers from the stage to behind the conductor's back for closer contact with the conductor. The orchestral part was of great complexity, but Rostropovich always knew exactly what he wanted. He rehearsed the strings alone, then the wind with the percussion – and after that everyone together. The singers joined in for the final run through before recording. We discussed problems of balance and what to do about them. Quite often when they went back into the studio he would play a section and ask, 'Suvinka, can you now hear the bass clarinet?' My usual reply was, 'Slava, please ask the trombones to give just a little less; they are swamping not only the bass clarinet but everybody else.' 'Impossible, Suvinka, it will sound like girls' school band.' (I do not know where he acquired his experience of girls' schools, but that was the ultimate insult.) So we had to accommodate trombones and tuba at full throttle and somehow get the clarinets through the din and the singers through everything else. On the whole, I think, we succeeded pretty well.

If during rehearsals Rostropovich was possessed, during the recording he was thrice possessed. Every spare moment was taken up by the opera. He rehearsed before sessions, during the breaks and in the interval between sessions. And all this on boiled fish and vegetables – it was the Russian Lent and he and his wife observed it strictly – no meat, no milk or milk products. Orchestra, cast, chorus and recording staff too were caught up in the enthusiasm of taking part in a special project; we knew this would be *the* recording of this work for years to come and we would make it something to remember. They were unforgettable sessions. I took especial pride in the fact that they ran unbelievably smoothly; there were no ructions, no failings on anyone's part. It was a producer's dream – everything planned and spaced and all my arrangements working like clockwork.

Memories of the recording are many: the dramatic intensity that Vishnevskaya could inject into any situation; bored resignation, passionate surrender to a lover, single-minded brutality and bleak despair, everything conveyed through controlled singing. Then, the miracle of Gedda – it was sixteen years since I had first met him in the recording studio. I said to him, 'Nicolai, it's incredible how your voice gets better and better all the time!' As with the two principals, there were no weak links in the cast.

Out of these wonderful sessions, one stands out – the memory of it still sends cold shivers down my spine. It was on the afternoon of 20 April. At the beginning of Act IV we see Katerina Ismailova and her lover, Sergei, along with a party of other convicts, on the long trek to their imprisonment. Sergei, for whom Katerina has murdered her father-in-law and assisted in the killing of her husband, takes up with a new girl, Sonyetka. Broken-hearted and goaded by the derision of the other convicts, Katerina pushes Sonyetka into a river and throws herself into the water. The horrified convicts are unable to help them and they are swept away. The last, despairing, sounds assigned to Sonyetka are three marks placed by Shostakovich on the top line of the treble staff. Rostropovich and I had talked about this and he had said that he certainly did not want three beautifully enunciated Fs at this point. 'They are screams, Suvinka, as she dies,' he said.

We were due to record this section after the break. Rostropovich came down to the studio from the green room where he had been rehearsing, looking very worried. He said he did not think Birgit Finnila could produce the sort of screams he envisaged coming from Sonyetka. 'What shall we do?' I said, 'Slava, leave it to me,' and went in search of McCarthy. McCarthy, in turn, said to me, 'Leave it to me, Suvi.' Five minutes later he said Linda Richardson, one of his chorus, had agreed to have a go; I asked him to take her to rehearse the part with Rostropovich in the green room. Rostropovich explained to her about the three Fs and she said she understood perfectly and would produce exactly what he wanted. She came up to me and, rubbing the tips of her thumb and her first two fingers together said, 'Extra money?' I said, 'Yes, of course.' 'Lots of extra money?' 'It's only three screams,' I said. 'The way he wants me to scream, I won't be able to sing for over a week after this session. Lots of extra money?' she asked. I agreed. 'Lots of extra money.'

Rostropovich meanwhile had told Finnila that the Fs would be sung by Richardson and not by her. Finnila came up to me in the control room in a great state and indignantly wanted to know why someone else should be asked to sing three bars of her part – F was easily within her range and it was a slur on her to allot these three notes to another singer. I waited till she had finished and said, 'Brigitte, he doesn't want three Fs at that point – he wants three full-throated screams. If you produce the sort of screams he wants you won't be able to sing for the next fortnight.' Finnila flung her arms round my neck, kissed me on both cheeks and said, 'Thank you, Suvi, for being so considerate.'

The section to be recorded consisted of exactly twenty bars; the preceding scene had been recorded earlier in the session and the final scene, with the old convict, had been done on the first session. The singers involved were Vishnevskaya, of whom we wanted a sound effect, Linda Richardson, the Sergeant and the chorus. I pointed out to Richardson the three spots from which she was to scream: the first one, marked *ffff*, dead in front of the microphone but about eight feet away from it; the second, marked *f* with the direction 'Very loud scream from Sonyetka but from far away', further away and to one side of the microphone, but facing it; the last, *p*, another two feet away and looking away from the microphone. The screams were of a drowning woman being swept away by a swift current and so it was logical that they should recede, but the third scream should still chill the blood. Linda Richardson, with supreme confidence, and a twinkle in her eye, said, 'Leave it to me.' I said to Rostropovich that I did not want the screams rehearsed; we would go for broke on the first take. I asked the orchestra for the utmost concentration as there would be only one take of these twenty bars; if Richardson produced the sort of screams I wanted she would have no voice left for another go.

All was set, and I went back into the control room. The balance engineer said, 'I suppose you said there would be only one take of this section to keep the orchestra on their toes?' I said, no, I really meant it. I do not think he believed me, but he tensed with extra concentration. 'Stand by,' I called out to the studio, and as the chatter subsided the tape machines began to run and the red light went on. There were six bars of single notes on the harp and timpani against a roll on the bass drum, all pianissimo; a gasp of effort as Katerina pushes Sonyetka into the river, and then, on the fourth beat of the sixth bar, the first scream hit us. Even I, who had been hoping for and expecting something spectacular, froze at the blood-curdling yell of terror that issued from the loudspeaker. The full orchestra thundered in, almost drowning the exclamation, 'Oh God, what has happened?' from the other convicts. A peremptory 'Do not stir' from the Sergeant, and then the second scream – combining desperate appeal and the knowledge that no help could come. Two bars later the final scream – distant but unmistakeably the gurgling final stages of drowning. The Sergeant brusquely announced, 'They are both gone – back to your places,' and the closing scene began. Rostropovich stopped everyone; that section had already been recorded.

Everyone in the control room had been shattered by the scene we had just recorded; rarely can a seasoned recording team have been so affected. My telephone rang. 'What you think?' asked Rostropovich. 'That's it, Slava.' He replied, 'I think so too.' They all trooped in, led by Rostropovich. He took one look at me, flung his arms around me in a great bear's hug, and literally did a jig around the room. We settled down to hear the take. When the first scream arrived Finnila, sitting beside me, recoiled; she looked gratefully at me for saving her from those horrible cries. I went to the rear of the control room, hugged Linda Richardson and said, 'Bless you, poppet.' 'What now?' asked Rostropovich. I said, 'Act I, figure 39.' It is an indication of Rostropovich's mastery as a conductor that when this scene was joined to the last scene recorded nearly three weeks earlier, the two sections fitted perfectly; there was no hint of a change of tempo or intensity or balance.

At the end of the last session Rostropovich had crates of champagne, whisky, gin and beer brought in and invited those of the cast still around, the entire London Philharmonic Orchestra with the brass band, the Ambrosian Chorus and all the recording team to a celebration of the successful recording of *Lady Macbeth of Mtsensk*. Fairly early in the proceedings Vishnevskaya acquired a blissful, if slightly glassy, look of supreme happiness and thereafter seemed to float rather than walk around. Rostropovich bussed everybody who came within arm's length with loud, wet smacks. And then he drank toasts – to Shostakovich, to the Library of Congress in Washington, to EMI for having given him the opportunity to record the version of the work which represented the composer's real intentions, to the singers, the orchestra and chorus and to the recording staff. We were all getting very merry. He then said, 'This is the last toast I shall drink standing up. To my dear friend Suvinka, and . . .' He looked around. 'Where is Chandrushka?' (his affectionate version of my wife's name), and, having found her, with one arm round each of our shoulders, 'To Suvinka and Chandrushka.' Everybody got gloriously sozzled. We all knew that we had taken part in a historic recording.

28 Legendary Orchestras

The first trip to the States seemed to have removed a log jam as regards trips across the Atlantic. Recordings in the first three months of 1978 took me to three great cities. In January I went to New York for Bartók's Duos for two violins with Perlman and Zukerman. It was my first recording in a city to which I was to return for many more. It also marked a less alluring first; it was my first experience of an aircraft I was travelling in developing a disinclination to go to my planned destination – Kennedy Airport being closed by a heavy fall of snow, my plane was diverted to Washington and I passed out of the ken of my American colleagues who spent a frantic night trying to locate me.

Next, an idyllic week in Berlin making a three-record set of all the Mahler songs for men with the incomparable Fischer-Dieskau and the equally incomparable Barenboim. The range of these songs is vast – from the innocence and simple pleasures of the *Aus der Jugendzeit* and the more extended songs of *Des Knaben Wunderhorn* to the last Rückert songs. The quality of this set can be sampled in the mysterious 'Wo die schönen Trompeten blasen', the shaping of the long melodic line and the wonderfully varied control of tone and colour by Barenboim who convinces you that you do not need real trumpets to make you hear them playing softly in the distance.

The recording itself was made in far from ideal conditions. Periodically we had to suspend recording – to bribe a local gardener to mow his lawn at some other time, to wait for a dust cart to empty all the bins in the immediate vicinity, and to investigate a hum which came out of nowhere and disappeared abruptly, just as mysteriously – this last nearly did for me. When I returned to London I discovered that the hum, when it went, had taken with it the two voice channels, so that for the rest of the day's recording – one whole side – I had only the two piano tracks, with Fischer-Dieskau's voice distantly recorded on them. I consider the salvaging of this side as one of my major technical feats; in the course of doing so I ran through six balance engineers.

The sessions occupied only part of each day; for the rest, it was a holiday for Barenboim and for me and my wife. Barenboim was in an apartment-hotel, and he persuaded us to move into a suite immediately below his. We had a great time shopping, cooking, playing records and listening to Barenboim playing the piano. It was an extremely agreeable and civilized week.

When Barenboim played the piano, which he did often, just for sheer love of playing, my wife and I would listen to what actually was a private recital given for just us by a great pianist. It was enlivened, as he played, by comments – sometimes drawing attention to some special aspect of the music, sometimes of exasperation when his fingers did not readily accommodate themselves to a difficult phrase. At other times he played in rapt silence, forgetting his audience of two.

I returned from Berlin to learn that I was to go back there in less than three weeks en route to work with one of the great orchestras of the world. I would not like to be pushed, but if I were, I would place the Dresden Staatskapelle as the finest for its overall excellence – the unique quality of its strings, the purity of intonation and sense of chording of its woodwind, the special timbre of its horns and brass and the players' instinctive feeling for internal balance. I already knew something of this orchestra's quality from 78s such as the Brahms Fourth under Karl Böhm. We were due to make two records with the orchestra in collaboration with the East German record company. The conductor was Paavo Berglund, my artist, but I had been told that the East Germans would provide their own producer as well as their balance engineer. Berglund, however, had other ideas; he stated flatly that unless his own producer was in charge of the recording the whole thing was off. I rejoiced at this; and the repertoire was of music I loved – the complete cycle of the six tone-poems of Smetana's *Ma Vlast* and Dvořák's Scherzo Capriccioso and third Slavonic Rhapsody.

My visa for entry into East Germany was processed in record time and my passage through Checkpoint Charlie was ridiculously easy, for I was the guest of the government and therefore a VIP. In East Berlin the driver and my escort were both charming and on the way to Dresden we picked up Berglund and his wife.

The next morning the recording engineer, an engaging person, arrived in his car to take us to St Lukaskirche, the home of the orchestra for recording. I sat next to the driver. Before he switched on the engine he explained to me in broken English the part I had to play in getting us to our destination. 'I say "hilf",' he said, 'you' – he pointed to me and showed me in pantomime what I had to do. 'Pull?' I asked. 'Ja, ja, pull' – and he indicated what I had to pull. It was the clutch pedal, and he demonstrated what the problem was. When he declutched abruptly the pedal got stuck and stayed in the depressed position so that the engine and the wheels were uncoupled. 'Pedal kaput,' he explained and laughed uproariously.

The car, a Wartburg, proceeded in a series of sharp explosions, and I mentally christened it 'fartbug'. After I had dived under the dashboard to free the pedal for the fourth time in response to an agonized 'Hilf!', Berglund asked from the rear seat, 'Are you all right, Suvi?' I said, 'Yes, sir! I am all right. I'm merely making sure that we all arrive in one piece.' When the car drew up at the church the engineer looked triumphantly at me and said, 'Is simple.' I, nursing a bump on the top of my head, replied, 'Ja, ja – is simple.' Happily, before the next trip, the car had been repaired.

The Dresden Staatskapelle seemed touched when I told them how proud I was to be working with them. I stayed in the church for the first twenty minutes of the rehearsal, revelling in the glorious sound the orchestra produced. They began with the first Smetana piece, 'Vyšehrad', which starts with a long, free passage for the two harps, goes on with the woodwind taking up the theme, horns, trumpets and timpani joining in and then, at last, the strings. The way the Dresden strings make their entry in this passage is pure magic. On the first run through the phrasing was perfection – for four bars, *mezzo-forte, crescendo, decrescendo* in each bar, with a *sforzando* in the middle of the third bar. Just from listening to the orchestra I could have inserted the correct dynamic marks into a blank score. I went into the control room with my heart singing.

The rules under which the orchestra worked were different from those of the UK, Europe or the States, as I learnt just before the second session began. The session in the morning had mostly consisted of rehearsing the first piece, after which we had done a test run-through of it. As we assembled in the evening a deputation from the orchestra called on me. 'We have a problem,' they said.

It was obviously a serious one, for they looked very glum. Their spokesman cleared his throat and asked, 'Did you record anything this morning?' I said we had but would have to do it all again. 'In that case – we shall not be paid for this morning,' he said, with the melancholy satisfaction of one whose worst fears have come true. 'What?' I was startled. 'But you did a whole session.' He gently explained; they were paid for what they actually recorded at each session, not for just playing in a session. There was nothing satisfactorily recorded that morning – therefore, no pay. It took me only two seconds to arrive at a decision. 'Leave it all to me,' I said and went in search of Berglund. 'Paavo,' I said, 'we start this session with a complete take of "Vyšehrad" – then corrections – a break and playback and when we reassemble, "Vltava".' I explained why. Berglund was equally horrified and agreed to my plans. After the playback I announced on the loudspeaker, 'No. 2 – "Vltava".' There was a buzz of satisfaction round the orchestra and I was rewarded by a thankful squeeze of my shoulder by the leader of the delegation.

On the day before I left Dresden the committee of the orchestra called on me and asked me earnestly to try and persuade some of my other artists – they mentioned Previn and Barenboim – to visit Dresden and to make records with them. I promised to do my best. I did arrange for Previn to record the Brahms Requiem in Dresden, but to everyone's chagrin circumstances beyond our control prevented it from actually taking place.

Chronologically, *Lady Macbeth* was sandwiched between Dresden and my next visit to the States, and during the opera itself I made an 'Encores' record and an album of Spanish music with Perlman and his accompanist, Samuel Sanders. Sanders is of the exclusive breed of top pianists who devote their energies almost entirely to playing in concert with other players.

Under an unassuming, somewhat lugubrious exterior Sanders conceals a keen musical mind backed up by superb technical ability – and he is an extremely entertaining person. He is an experienced recording artist, but seeing him at work you would not think so. Any slight smudge and he would stop, to the accompaniment of a simultaneous fusillade from Perlman and me. 'Sam, that bar is okay; don't worry about it.' 'Just go on; it's the fifteen bars following that we are trying to cover.' They would resume playing and Sanders would again stop. Turning vaguely in the direction in which, behind two walls and a corridor, he knew I was, he would say something which would be totally unintelligible to me. 'Sam, talk into your microphone – the one next to the keyboard.' Sanders would peer around. 'Sam,' from Perlman, pointing with his bow to the microphone less than three feet from Sanders, 'that one.' 'Suvi, bar 38, just after the first . . . chord . . .' And the voice would tail off as Sanders gradually turned to where he knew I was, though out of sight, which was in the opposite direction to which he was being asked to speak.

I have recorded Sanders with Perlman and with Perlman and Zukerman and like all the great accompanists he is the perfect foil to the artist he is playing with. There might not be a great deal to the accompaniment of most of the Kreisler pieces, but the piano parts of pieces such as Debussy's 'En Bateau', Falla's 'Suite populaire espagnole', and any of the Sarasate pieces which make up the second side of the Spanish album, are vital to set, sustain and accentuate the mood of the music. Sanders's response to the atmosphere of a piece is always right.

On the next transatlantic trip there were, among other items, two records with Previn and the Pittsburgh. The first was of Haydn's No. 94, the 'Surprise', and No. 104, the 'London'. Previn is a Haydn enthusiast and he interprets him very well indeed, steering a perfect course between the Scylla and Charybdis of pomposity and prissiness, which are the twin dangers of conducting Haydn. As on my first visit to them, I marvelled at the burnished sound of their strings. This had, so far, been a wonderful beginning to the year – the Dresden, the London Philharmonic, the Pittsburgh – and still to come, another of the world's great orchestras.

The other work in Pittsburgh was for me the realization of a long held ambition. When in 1962 I had assisted Legge in the recording of Klemperer's performance of Mahler's Fourth Symphony with Schwarzkopf, I had wistfully hoped that I would be in a position to produce a record of this, my favourite of the Mahler symphonies – and sixteen years

210

later, here it was. The soprano was Elly Ameling, whose clear, pure voice was ideally suited to the simple text of the last movement. She was so accomplished a singer that the entire movement was recorded in less than half a session. As I watched Previn I wondered once again by what magical process does a conductor get an orchestra to play exactly as he wants it to. There were no flamboyant gestures, no histrionic attitudes, not very many words even, and effortlessly the symphony unfolded in a stream of warm, rich sound. There was no need for many words between Previn and me either; every time we worked together the understanding between the two of us grew. Once, when I looked up, he said, 'Yes, I know. I'll ask the horns to play down a bit.' Another time, when he looked at me I answered the question I saw in his face. 'That is lovely.' 'Is it a little over-indulgent?' and I cut in 'Oh, no – for me, it's just right.' At the end of the recording we adjourned to my hotel to join my wife. 'Three ice-cold beers,' I ordered. 'Sorry, sir,' was the reply. 'It's election day – no liquor till polling ends.' I have always considered the licensing laws in Britain absurd – it seemed as if there were pockets of the ridiculous in other countries too.

We flew that evening (and as soon as the plane took off, we could begin to drink ourselves silly had we been so inclined) to Los Angeles, where we were royally entertained by my colleagues in our American head office.

On the way back to New York we took three days off in Phoenix, Arizona, using it as a base for seeing the Grand Canyon. As I checked in, the bell-boy, a youngster in his middle teens, looked over my shoulder and drew a sharp breath, 'Is that Abbey Road, London, England?' he asked. I said it was. 'The Beatles' Abbey Road?' I said, 'Yes – and when you next look at the sleeve of the record, notice the gate next to the studios – that's the entrance to where I live.' The youngster could not contain his excitement – he called out to a fellow bell-boy in the other corner of the lobby, 'Hey – here's a guy who lives in Abbey Road – next to the Beatles,' and to the reception clerk, 'Isn't that something?'. He pumped my hand, shook my wife by the hand, and generally cavorted around like an excited puppy chasing its tail. We were almost royalty during our stay in Phoenix.

In New York, two more records. One with Perlman and Samuel Sanders – a third Kreisler album for which Perlman suggested the title 'Scrapings from the bottom of the barrel' (as of the date of the writing of this he has come up with a list of items for 'Kreisler – Volume IV!'). For the other record Zukerman joined them for pieces by Moszkowski and Shostakovich.

There was a third trip to the States in the year – another special occasion for me – to record the Philadelphia Orchestra, that almost legendary body which had first introduced me to Bach, Weber, Beethoven and Schubert. I was very proud to tell them how well I remembered their black label recordings of 'Invitation to the Dance' and Toccata and Fugue in D minor and the red label little G minor fugue – and that my first

211

introduction to their present conductor had been through a record with the Minneapolis Symphony Orchestra of Dvořák's Scherzo Capriccioso. 'Heavily cut,' muttered Ormandy under his breath.

We were in Philadelphia to record the Tchaikovsky Violin Concerto with Perlman. But before I could get down to the main business I had to get out of the way one of those small but extremely time-consuming jobs. Perlman had earlier in the year appeared on a popular television show and played Bazzini's 'Ronde des lutins'. The American company had been inundated with enquiries as to whether Perlman had recorded this item. He had actually not. It seemed a sensible idea to record the Bazzini as quickly as possible and add it to the 'Encores' record he had done in London. Someone said, 'Why not in Philadelphia?' We were landed with the job of matching the sound from Philadelphia to that of Kingsway Hall, half the size of the Philadelphia venue. We also had a different piano – at least the pianist was the same! Sanders was flown in to Philadelphia, driven straight to the hall and back to the airport as soon as the recording was over. The rondo lasts for about four minutes. The recording took two hours and a half; the first three movements of the Mahler Fourth had taken exactly the same amount of time to record! Long before the end of the session I had named the piece 'Rondo for cretins'. At the end of it all I said, 'Itzhak, the things you make me do; but I forgive you everything for the way you play that cretinous piece!'

The hall in which we were to record was grandiloquently called 'The Old Met'. Its days of grandeur, when Caruso sang in it and premieres were presented there of some of the great works of the current repertoire, were long past. It was now in a sorry state and the entire area around it too smelt of decay and of violence. Its reputation was such that the orchestra would not risk driving there and leaving their cars outside the building; they were bused there.

I had been warned in London that Ormandy was a difficult man. I found him wholly charming and very easy to work with; his experience of recording was vast and, unlike some of the older school of musicians, he liked making records. I had written to him before leaving for the States and had received a warm, friendly reply, inviting me to share Mrs Ormandy's box for the concert. He was outraged that we should have booked three sessions for the Tchaikovsky concerto and the leader of the orchestra, Norman Carol, explained why. 'In three sessions we would aim to record with the maestro the Fourth, Fifth and Sixth Symphonies of Tchaikovsky and have a little time left over for the *Nutcracker Suite*.' But Perlman is a perfectionist who seeks something beyond the right notes; he too is capable of recording the Tchaikovsky concerto in one session, but the special Perlman imprint is not at all that easy to obtain. He sometimes drives his accompanist, be it pianist or conductor, his engineers, the editors and even his producer to distraction by repeating a passage apparently out of self-indulgence; somewhere, along the way, he gets just what he had been aiming for. I, who invariably recognize it, at that point say to him, 'That's it, Itzhak,' to which his usual reply is, 'All right; one more time for luck and then we'll go on.'

29   Previn, Ashkenazy

I saw 1979 in, feeling very sorry for myself, running a temperature of over 103° in a hill station in the neighbourhood of Bombay. On New Year's Day I looked at my commitments for the year. I had just under four years to go to retirement. If I had been asked what recordings I would still like to make, my list would have included working with Ashkenazy, Mehta, Haitink; to record just three more of the world's great orchestras, the Concertgebouw, the Vienna and the Berlin Philharmonic; and, of course, to produce a string quartet. Three of my wishes were to be realized in 1979; the others – except the Berlin Philharmonic and the quartet – were granted in the years following and are, therefore, outside the limit I have set for this book.

Early in the year I started a set of Dvořák symphonies and orchestral works with Rostropovich. I was asked to persuade him to undertake this project, but I was highly dubious about the commercial viability of the scheme. Even the Tchaikovskys, despite their tremendous artistic success, had not been commercially profitable. In any case, the fashion of recording complete sets of works has no basis of sound sense. It is the artificial brainchild of those whose 'knowledge of the repertoire has been gathered principally from the pages of a record catalogue' – in one of Walter Legge's more splenetic utterances. Why should not a pianist record, say, five of the Beethoven sonatas, or three of his concertos – or a conductor two of the Brahms or Schubert symphonies? If a violinist suggested that he wanted to record three Beethoven sonatas, the 'Spring', the 'Kreutzer' and Op. 96, the instant reaction of a record company would be, 'Oh no, he must do the lot'; in other words, instead of two records he must make another three to accommodate the rest of the canon. It could be useful, and artistically rewarding, to have on records all the works of a composer. But no one who wants to record just a few of these complete oeuvres should have a pistol pointed at his head and told, 'You shall record all, or none.'

With Rostropovich we started off in fine style with Nos. 9 and 7 – or to be unequivocal, the 'New World' and the D minor. Rostropovich's 'New World' is not the comfortable, familiar piece it is in most performances; it is dark, brooding, with violent changes of mood. No. 7 is more obviously a dark, tragic work. Artistically, the records received acclaim – commercially they failed, but before that was accepted and the series ground to a halt, we did another two symphonies, Nos. 8 and 6, and a staggeringly virtuoso Scherzo Capriccioso. To anyone who might wonder whether this great cellist is also a great conductor, I would recommend the performance of this last work and draw special attention to just two sections – the clarity and the wit of the chattering downward runs for the two clarinets in bars 202 to 220 and the atmospheric, evocative shaping of the *poco tranquillo*. The balance, the transparency of texture, despite the composer's habit of tripling and quadrupling most of the lines of his melody, and the rhythmic buoyancy and lift all betoken a master of the conductor's art.

In the months between *Lady Macbeth* and the Dvořák series I had a brief experience of another unexpected facet of Rostropovich's genius; he accompanied his wife on the piano in a recital of songs by Rimsky-Korsakov and Prokofiev. Had he chosen the piano as his instrument, he would be one of the top pianists today. I said, during the session, that it was unfair. He asked, 'What? What?' 'You play the cello, you conduct, you play the piano and – as if all this were not enough – you are married to Galina. It's not fair that one person should have all these things!' Rostropovich beamed at me and Vishnevskaya gave me a roguish look.

A few months later, on 5 June, I stood at the top of the stairs leading to the raised ground floor of 3, Abbey Road. A car drew up in the forecourt and a slim, compact figure emerged from it. I went down the stairs and greeted him. 'Hello, Vova.' It was a long awaited moment. I had known Ashkenazy for many years. We had met at concerts and at receptions and we had had dinner together, with Previn, in a restaurant perched high above the twinkling lights of Pittsburgh. I had always admired him as a person and as an artist. Today we were going to work together. He had already appeared on the EMI label as a conductor; this time he was going to play the piano. It was not going to be a single record – a 'one off' as it is sometimes slightingly referred to – but the first of a five record set of the Beethoven trios, the other two artists being Perlman and Lynn Harrell. They had played together, as a trio, over a period of time and were now ready to make records. Perlman and Harrell were under contract to us. Thanks to the efforts of the artist himself, Ashkenazy, still under a general contract with another company, was free to make this set of records for EMI. As I escorted him to No. 1, I had a brief and bitter recollection of the Mozart double and triple concertos, but it was swept away by the excitement of the immediate occasion.

Ashkenazy is very particular about the instrument he plays on; his favourite London piano had been installed in the studio. The other two arrived, and to the accompaniment of a good deal of badinage and serious discussion of the works to be recorded, they settled down to play themselves in, and I got down to the business of balancing them. Though they had played extensively together as a trio, each was a strongly individual soloist, accustomed to dominate any performance he took part in, and it was their first time together in a recording studio. I had expected it to be difficult, and so it was. I knew the piano would not present any serious problem, and so at first concentrated on the two strings. When Ashkenazy heard the first test he said, 'I know I'm the only non-house artist, but must you rub it in by making me sound as if I was a mile up the road?' He pretended to burst into tears; there was subtle point to this remark, for his parent company had a studio about a mile from us. Perlman consoled him: 'There, there; even I think there's not enough piano.'

We tried all the usual positions; the normal concert seating – they could not really see each other properly; with the strings facing the piano – the result was a swirling welter of uncontrolled sound; with them turned sideways, endways, full frontal and every other possible combination – nothing produced a natural, well-balanced sound. During all this time I discovered how reasonable and practical Ashkenazy's attitude to record-ing was – and what reserves of patience he had. At one point I said, 'Sorry it's taking so much time, Vova,' and he replied, 'Take all the time you want – and, considering you have no previous experience of balancing me, you are not doing too badly.' Perlman asked, 'Aren't there any other positions we could try?' I could not resist saying, 'No, unless we try some of those listed in the *Kama Sutra*.' Studio 1 was at its most difficult that afternoon. Finally, though it went strongly against the grain because it was unnatural, I had Perlman and Harrell placed on the wrong side of the piano – on Ashkenazy's left. This solved one set of problems and created others – balance between the piano and the strings, for neither Ashkenazy nor Perlman and Harrell could accurately judge the weight of tone of the piano or the violin and cello. I was glad on this occasion to have the flexibility of a multi-track recording, and we never again adopted this seating.

On this first lot of sessions we recorded Op. 1 No. 2, the early G major trio of 1793 to 1795 and the mature, highly organized and unusual 'Geister' (Ghost) trio in D Op. 70 No. 1 of 1808. Only fifteen years separated the two, but they are worlds apart, one belonging to the eighteenth century and the other, equally indisputably, to the nineteenth. The 'Ghost' movement is unique in Beethoven's music; there is no parallel to its mysterious, eerie atmosphere. When the recording was finished, we all took out our diaries to pencil in the dates for the continuation of the series. I was slightly taken aback to find that they stretched out to 1984. 'I hope you chaps realize that it will be my grandson who'll produce that last recording,' I said. 'And I'll be about ninety,' retorted Perlman, and started to play one of the long-held chords of the 'Geister's' slow movement with a quavery tone and intonation.

The recordings did extend to 1984, and the last sessions were as relaxed as the first ones had been; but not so carefree, for it was to be my last working assignment with each of them. Characteristically, none of us made any grandiloquent gesture – just a slightly warmer than usual embrace when we said goodbye. In the intervening years, the series was continued in London and in two different studios in New York, and was briefly interrupted to record the Tchaikovsky piano trio. Every time we met it was like four old friends getting together again. We enjoyed each other's company. We worked hard and in between fooled around a great deal. While we were recording the first movement of the C minor, someone's finger slipped and instead of Beethoven's major third we heard what sounded like an extract from the prelude to Wagner's *Tristan und Isolde*. Instantly, the others joined in, and for the next minute we had grinding chromatic harmonies deliberately played slightly out of tune by the two strings. Then, from Perlman, a peremptory 'sh'. Complete silence for a few seconds, and there followed the cool, refreshing C major of Beethoven's reprise, sounding the more orderly for the heated preceding minute.

The periodical incursions into light-heartedness were very necessary to dissipate the tension engendered by spells of intense concentration. If Perlman produced the odd scratch or whistle he would draw his bow roughly across the strings to produce grating noises that set one's teeth on edge. 'Stradivari must be revolving in his grave, Itzhak,' I once said. 'How about this then,' he replied and broke out into a country dance. Harrell joined in with a pizzicato boogie-woogie accompaniment; or, the two of them would put on a joint act, with Harrell producing the sound effects and Perlman the commentary on a racing circuit, complete with the crunch and noises of a crash – Perlman's commentary accelerating with the action. All the while, oblivious to the raucous din produced by the other two, Ashkenazy would play the serene slow movement of Brahms's D minor Concerto; he was performing the work a great deal of this time, and at any interruption he would instantly switch over to it. We also had marvellous meals: Peking style Chinese in London, Japanese raw fish and Italian pasta of a melting softness in New York, and unexpectedly excellent tandoori and other Indian dishes brought to us from a Manhattan restaurant.

We shared wonderful musical moments, as when Ashkenazy, quite absorbed, was quietly playing to himself one of the Chopin preludes and, suddenly realizing there was absolute stillness in the studio and control room, somewhat self-consciously stopped. There was a concerted groan from everyone. On an impulse, I asked over the microphone, 'Vova, can I please make a request?' 'Surely, Suvi,' he replied – and I asked for Rachmaninov's G minor Prelude. So that there should be no misunderstanding, Perlman sketched the first two bars on his fiddle; then Vladimir

217

Ashkenazy played the piece to a private audience of two fellow artists and a group of five admirers in the control room.

The constant change of venue meant that for every set of sessions we had to go through the agonizing business of balancing the three artists afresh. Despite this, the Beethoven trio sessions are among the happiest and the smoothest I have produced; and my memories of the recording world would be that much poorer if I had not worked with Ashkenazy.

Later in the same month another long-awaited moment arrived; I took over as Previn's producer. The previous incumbent left us for other fields – I asked, could I please have Previn as my artist, Previn asked could he please have me as his producer – and it was done.

I could not have asked for a more fitting culmination to my career than the records Previn made in the following years. Every one of them is musically and technically worthy to stand beside the three superb records with which I was introduced to the recording studios – and about Previn too I feel exactly as about Ashkenazy.

The programme for the months immediately following was full of treats – Vaughan Williams's *Tallis Fantasia*, Debussy's *Images*, Shostakovich's Thirteenth, the 'Babi Yar' symphony, Strauss tone poems with (my reaction to this was a delirious 'Oh frabjous day!') the Vienna Philharmonic, and the Berlioz *Grande Messe des Morts* (like *Romeo and Juliet* with Barenboim, this work was on, off, on, off and, blessedly, finally on). There were to follow Strauss's 'Alpine', Debussy's *Nocturnes* and *La Mer*, the Prokofiev ballet *Cinderella* and, by Ravel, the enchanting fantasy *L'Enfant et les Sortilèges* and *Daphnis and Chloe*. (Everything after 'Images' is outside the boundary of this book.) The first work I recorded under the new arrangement was, however, none of these but the dream child of all record sales departments, but uninteresting stuff for recording teams, Ravel's Bolero. Just around the corner, though, lay an exciting innovation.

The coining of a word to describe a new thing and the subsequent development of that word affords a fascinating subject. Take the word 'gramophone'; it was originally a patented trade name describing the product of one company. Others with a similar product had to exercise some ingenuity to make up words such as 'graphophone' and 'phonograph', which were near enough to the original word for the product to be identified but not so close as to infringe copyright. Now, of course, the word has passed into common usage and is no longer the property of one company.

The word 'digital' has undergone an even swifter transformation of meaning. It used to mean 'relating to a finger or a number'. Gradually it was widened to embrace a process based on digits (or numbers), their collation and organization into a system of storing information. The process was used to make certain apparatuses work. You had calculators which gave even the dullest arithmetical duffer the capacity to do complex sums at the touch of a few buttons. There were watches operating on the same system, in which instead of hands indicating the time, winking numbers displayed the passage of the seconds and hours, and even days of the week and dates. The development of computers and digital machines took off in a big way from the 60s.

In the recording world there were whispers of a new system of recording being developed which would be digital. EMI had been one of the firms experimenting on computers. The research engineers engaged in this work were very proud of their achievements and they had every cause to be, for the body scanner, an electronic aid for looking at and studying what was happening inside a body was an EMI invention.

By 1979 EMI, and every other record company, was working reverishly to be first in the race towards digital recording. Early in that year one company proudly announced the release of the first ever digital record. There were mixed reactions among the others. Some preferred to wait for the new system to be rigorously tested before taking it up. Some stepped up their efforts to try not to be left too far behind. We plunged headlong into the digital whirlpool, though not really fully equipped then to do so. At a meeting of the producers we were told that the top management was not overjoyed at our being, yet again, pipped at the post and wanted to know what we proposed doing about it. Various suggestions were made. I asked what I knew was the really pertinent question. 'When will our digital recorder be ready?' I was told, about the middle of June. I looked at the recording schedule and one item leapt to my eye – the Debussy *Images* with Previn and the London Symphony Orchestra. Taking a deep breath, I said, 'If the machine is really ready by then, let me have a shot at *Images*.' Everyone thought it was an excellent idea.

I knew that it was the ideal sort of work, with its pellucid, colourful scoring, for high fidelity recording. I could not ask for a more cooperative artist than Previn. We would of course have as a stand-by a normal or 'analogue' recorder (this was another word which had undergone a weird transformation from the original 'that which is analogous to something else').

I told Previn on the telephone that *Images* was going to be a digital recording. 'Explain it to me before the session,' he said. I put the telephone down and scratched my head. To quote one of the funniest writers in the English language, if my understanding of digital recording had been transformed into silk there would not have been enough to make a pair of cami-knickers for a sparrow. Nothing in my university studies had equipped me with even the basis of what might have helped me to understand this process. I knew, of course, that there was only one new factor in this set-up – the digital recorder which, instead of registering a magnetic pattern, would convert the information fed into it into a bank of

219

numbers and store it for reconversion into sound. Numbers? It seemed ridiculous that the 'Unfinished' could be converted into numbers; and when it was said that the machine sampled the signals sent into it 50,000 times a second, the whole thing appeared to become as unreal as science fiction.

When this last fact was imparted to Previn his reaction was, 'Really? How would you know if the machine decided to cheat and did the sampling only 45,000 times?' We saw a squat, black cabinet with calibrated scales illuminated by dancing beams of light; but like an ordinary tape machine it too had threaded through it a one-inch tape. Standing near by was an unassuming, bespectacled young man, and Previn, when he could get no clear understanding of the object from me, turned to him and said, 'I suppose you understand it as little as we do.' The young man shyly replied, 'As a matter of fact I helped to design and build this machine.' We looked at him with new eyes, and Previn said, 'Excuse me – my mistake.'

I had asked Previn to be allowed to say a few words to the orchestra before the session began, and when the time came I stood next to the rostrum and said, 'Good morning, everyone. You must all have heard of a new process called digital recording; *Images* is going to be EMI's first venture into this field. I could not have asked for a finer group of people to do it with.' I had their complete attention now, some looking interested, others wary, not quite knowing what was going to be asked of them. 'There are a few specific points to remember on this lot of sessions. Digital recording is of a high degree of fidelity – any noise, however slight, a creaking chair or corset, heavy breathing, will be picked up and reproduced faithfully. Please be careful, and wait till the red light goes off before slumping down in your chairs. Next, editing is extremely complicated, expensive and time consuming. I want to keep it down to the minimum, so please – a little extra concentration.' Previn cut in, 'What Suvi really means is that these are seven and eight minute pieces, so if anyone makes a boob at six minutes he'll ask us to go back to the beginning and start again!' 'Good luck,' I said. 'And to you,' responded the orchestra.

I had not heard the digital recorder demonstrated; I took on trust the claims made for it by its creators since I had faith in them. First we had to go through the usual routine of balancing. As for any recording, while Previn rehearsed, the engineer moved microphones, adjusted the controls on his panel and had a running conversation with me about the sound. Our digital recorder had the facility to use only two tracks. The engineer and I had talked this over and decided that our back-up machine also should be a two-track analogue recorder. Dr Johnson said that the prospect of being hanged would concentrate the mind wonderfully; the knowledge that what we were going to record on the sessions would be the final form of the tape would certainly concentrate our hearing wonderfully.

We were ready. We warned the studio. The engineer called, 'Take one.' The red light went on, and the recording began. The sound coming through was of a clarity and luminosity which was quite beautiful; it had bloom, breadth and depth. All this was no more than I had expected. I had one small reservation but decided to let it wait till the playback. What was new and breathtaking was that when you went from the sound going into the recorder to that coming from it, there was no audible difference to two pairs of very acute ears – the engineer's and mine.

The orchestra played the whole of the first piece, 'Gigues', and Previn, accompanied by the principals, and it looked like quite a large proportion of the others, came in to hear the take. The muted second violins and the trumpet at the beginning had an instant impact: the sound did not have to fight its way through a mush of background noise; it came from utter and complete silence. Other instruments entered: first violins, the flute, harp, celesta, horn, limpidly beautiful and clean. When the oboe solo began, Anthony Camden, principal oboe of the London Symphony Orchestra, said, 'Christ! Listen to the sound of that oboe.' Previn looked at me and then his eyes swept towards the recording machine, with a look which clearly said, Is *that* responsible for what we are hearing? And then, 'Perhaps a little more definition, and precision on the woodwind?' he asked the engineer and me. That had been the little niggle for me. 'I've asked for the same, André,' I said. The engineer, who hadn't agreed with me earlier, looked at us. 'All right, I bow to a majority.'

Then something unexpected and splendid happened. The orchestra and Previn had been pleased by EMI picking them for its first classical digital recording. Having heard what that digital recording sounded like, it was almost as if they collectively said to us, You have shown us what you can do. Now we'll show you what we can do. They played at top form – and at that level there is no orchestra in the world which can surpass them. Except for a minor accident in one take necessitating a restart, every take was of a complete movement, and the final master has fewer than ten edits – about fifty to sixty being par for an LP. At the end of the sessions, we all knew that we had entered an important new era in recording. I rather ruefully calculated that I had no more than a little over three years left to use this new system.

We knew we had a special record; just how special it was hit us about four months later when test pressings went out to reviewers and the trade. Everyone who heard the record was as startled as we had been on the first playback; journalists, engineering correspondents of record magazines, the BBC and commercial radio and just about everyone else descended on me. The record went on to win various prestigious awards; but not everyone was impressed. The French, the most chauvinistic of musical nations, sneered, not at what was on the record, but at the mere idea (*'quelle horreur!*) of a non-French orchestra and conductor playing Debussy; a reviewer in America held forth at length that the record showed every fault of self-indulgent multi-track remixing by an egocentric producer; the Germans, believing as they do that music was a purely Teutonic invention, ignored the record. The final verdict, however, belonged to the ordinary record buyers, who bought the record in vast numbers. I still consider this and the other recording on our own EMI machine which I produced, the Berlioz Requiem, to be two of the dozen or so best digital recordings I have ever heard. And, without comment – in less than a year EMI had abandoned that recorder and decided not to develop it. There is no other machine I have heard comparable to it.

And so to the Brahms Double Concerto, for violin and cello, with Perlman, Rostropovich and the Concertgebouw Orchestra conducted by Haitink, which chronologically took place just before *Images*. The recording had taken over two years to set up and for me it brought about the realization of two wishes – to work with the Amsterdam orchestra and with its conductor. I had heard the orchestra several times in London but only once in its native habitat. I was told that for recordings they did not occupy their normal place on the stage, but sat in the auditorium, cleared of its seating. I was intrigued by this, and when the orchestra asked if I was free, a month before our recording, to attend a set of sessions for their usual company, I jumped at the chance of hearing what the sound would be like. But that recording company were horrified at the thought. 'If Mr Grubb attends one of our sessions, he will be able to study our microphone set-up and that won't do at all!' I was so incensed by this that I said, 'Tell them that Mr Grubb was making records while they were still climbing trees!' I do not know whether this message was conveyed to them; it has been now!

I had met Haitink for the first time some months earlier and I found him all that I had expected him to be from his musical personality. After a concert at the Royal Festival Hall I had taken backstage a friend who wanted Haitink's autograph. As I approached the conductor I said, 'Mr Haitink, you don't know me, my name is . . .' Haitink took my hand and said, 'Mr Grubb, I have heard a great deal about you from Danny and many other of your artists, and I've admired your work with Klemperer. I'm pleased to meet you.' It takes a lot to render me speechless – but now I was. I was quite overcome with pleasure, pride and embarrassment. We did manage briefly to talk about the possibility of Haitink recording for EMI. And here was EMI's first ever recording with the Concertgebouw.

When I looked out of the window at my hotel at seven in the morning it was dull and foggy and my heart sank. Perlman, Haitink, who had been rehearsing at Glyndebourne, the recording staff and I were all safely settled in Amsterdam, but Rostropovich was arriving that morning, by a private plane chartered by EMI, the only way he could get to Amsterdam in time. Due to a confusion of dates he had booked himself to conduct *Eugène Onegin* at Aldeburgh on the night before the recording. The fog looked as if it would prevent any plane from landing in Amsterdam for the next two days. I rapidly ran through all the works Perlman and Haitink might record, but we seemed to be running out of violin concertos. Just as I began to run through orchestral possibilities the hotel reception office downstairs announced that my secretary had arrived, which meant that Rostropovich had arrived too, for the plane hire company had insisted that an EMI representative be on the plane with him.

The orchestra were intrigued by an Indian who seemed to be wandering about with the recording team, and occasionally some players smiled amiably at me; they realized that I was the person in charge of the whole thing only when Haitink introduced me to them. After the initial exchanges of courtesies everyone got down to work. The Brahms 'Double' is devilishly difficult to balance, whether for a concert or for a recording; one soloist plays in the middle reaches of the orchestra's heaviest instruments, while the other can soar up, clear of 'middle moo'. There had been no concert or rehearsals for the participants to sort out problems and we had never before recorded in the Concertgebouw. There was one additional factor to compound our difficulties; the plane in which Rostropovich had flown in had not been pressurized and his ears had been affected; on the first session he had difficulty with his hearing. But there was ample goodwill all round and we got over all the difficulties; the only casualty was that it was impossible to achieve a uniformly even balance and so we had reluctantly to revert to the analogue multi-track recorder.

30 'Good morning Mr Beethoven'

I have gone a little beyond the event with which I had planned to end this book. Even so, it has taken me only to 1979 and at the time of writing, six years on, I am still actively engaged in the making of gramophone records. There are many stories untold: of Klemperer and the acoustic expert; of a colleague walking into a listening room in Abbey Road and finding Rostropovich and me both kneeling, facing each other with palms pressed together as if we were about to embark on a joint commination service; of the shortest orchestral session I ever did, dismissing the Vienna Philharmonic Orchestra after two minutes in which not a note was played; of my two easiest recordings, in which I had no music to follow or wrong notes to pick up – all I had to do was to lean back and enjoy music from four expert jazz players and a fifth who progressed from being a raw recruit to an expert in the course of three hours; of how, after missing each other, mostly by a few hours, in Los Angeles, London, Berlin and New York a countryman of mine and I managed to be in the same place at the same time for long enough to make records together. I could go on, but I have to stop somewhere, and I have arbitrarily chosen this point at which to do so. Perhaps some other time?

A few years ago, when two books of memoirs by two practitioners of my profession were in the news, a columnist in *The Times* commented, somewhat sourly, that the business of making classical gramophone records seemed to have an embittering effect on those engaged in it. But I have not found it to be so. On the contrary, it has been an enriching experience. To meet musicians of all kinds, of all degrees of proficiency, of various levels of fame – to work closely with them, observe the different styles of their music making – to help them to achieve what they set out to do – often, to give them advice – and then to imprison the rapture of their performance in the permanent form of gramophone records, which in turn would enable countless others to enjoy that music – this cannot but be one of the most rewarding of the activities touching music. If you are blessed with the gift for it, you make music, but if you are not able to do so, I cannot imagine any other business in which you come closer to music and musicians. If after a lifetime of associating with some of the greatest of the world's music-makers, all you can remember of them is that X was penny-pinching, Y had a whining accent or Z caused you grey hairs, it is not a reflection on the musicians concerned. As Klemperer once remarked, dryly, 'If you hit your head with a book and the result is a hollow sound, it does not necessarily mean that the book is empty.'

This does not mean that in the recording studio I have had nothing but success – that it has always been a bed of roses. I have had my share of the failures and the disappointments inevitable in any sphere of human endeavour. I have also made mistakes – how could I not have in a career spanning a quarter of a century? The first one was brought to my notice in swift retribution following a boast. Late on a Thursday afternoon, some four years ago, I said rather smugly to a colleague, 'Well, anyway, I have never left out two bars on a recording, and that's something in over twenty years!' My come-uppance could not have arrived more rapidly. It was just after half past five on the Friday when my secretary rang to ask, 'A reviewer wants to know in which edition bars x and y are repeated in piece A.' Not knowing the piece by heart, I replied, 'Tell him I'll get in touch early on Monday morning.' I replaced the receiver, practically jumped over the wall between my flat and the studios, collected a score and a test pressing and listened to the disc at home. The unthinkable had happened. There were two bars in twice on the disc. There was nothing I could do immediately; the weekend seemed unending. The Monday morning brought comfort; the record had not yet been pressed. I was able to have production of it stopped and get the tape corrected.

Two years later, the incident had faded to only an uncomfortable memory, and I did it again – that is, boasted again – that, after all, one mistake in twenty-two years was pardonable. It was a wanton tempting of fate; I had also forgotten the fact that boobs come in pairs. This time, nemesis caught up with me even more swiftly. A few hours later I received a message that one timpani note was missing in one of my recordings. When I heard the tape I wondered how I could have missed so blatant a mistake. That too was corrected at once.

There have sometimes been differences of opinion with artists, but none have been serious. There has never, ever, been any acrimony or bitterness between any artist and me. Everyone, without exception, I have ever worked with has been, and is, a friend. I have a wonderful storehouse of memories of musicians; I also have heart-warming and affectionate memories of colleagues – secretaries, engineers, fellow producers, administrators and critics (and sales people too!). I hope one day I am able to write about all these people.

Looking back on my twenty-five years in the business, I hope I have not lost the humility with which I started. A few years ago, I was invited to Amsterdam to receive an award for the Perlman–Giulini–Philharmonia Orchestra recording of Beethoven's Violin Concerto. As I walked up the steps on to the stage of the hall in the Concertgebouw where the presentations were made, I had no idea what I was going to say. Then

I saw, high up in the centre of the rear wall of the stage, a bust of Beethoven. That sparked my speech.

'There are at least seventy-eight other persons who have a greater claim than I to receive this trophy. One of them is of course up there' – and I pointed with my thumb over my shoulder to the representation of Beethoven. 'Another of them is somewhere out there' – I pointed vaguely in the direction of New York. 'A third is, I believe, in that direction' – this time I was even more vague, for I had no idea in which direction Italy might be. 'As for the Philharmonia Orchestra, even EMI cannot afford to fly seventy-five of them out here to take part in this event. I shall convey to these seventy-seven what an honour it was for me to represent them on this occasion. As for him . . .' I turned round and looked up briefly at Beethoven. 'When the time comes for me to say "Good morning, Mr Beethoven," I hope he will reply, "Good morning, Mr Grubb; that was a good recording of the violin concerto." '

Discography

Complete list of recordings mentioned in the text

Abbreviations:
ASM	Academy of St. Martin-in-the-Fields
BBCSO	BBC Symphony Orchestra
BPO	Berlin Philharmonic Orchestra
BS	Bournemouth Sinfonietta
BSO	Boston Symphony Orchestra
CSO	Chicago Symphony Orchestra
DS	Dresden Staatskapelle
ECO	English Chamber Orchestra
KCC	King's College Chapel Choir
LPO	London Philharmonic Orchestra
LSO	London Symphony Orchestra
NBCO	NBC Symphony Orchestra
NPO	New Philharmonia Orchestra
NYPSO	New York Philharmonic – Symphony Orchestra
OdeP	Orchestre de Paris
Phil O	Philadelphia Orchestra
PO	Philharmonia Orchestra
PSO	Pittsburgh Symphony Orchestra
RPO	Royal Philharmonic Orchestra
VPO	Vienna Philharmonic Orchestra

The numbers given of the records are those they carried when they were last available.

André Previn's Music Night 2: Russlan and Ludmilla (*Glinka*): Overture,
    Adagio for Strings (Quartet op. 11) (*Barber*), The Three-Cornered
    Hat (*Falla*): Suite No 2, Prelude à l'après midi d'un faune (*Debussy*),
    The Banks of Green Willow-Idyll (*Butterworth*), Emperor Waltz
    (J. Strauss 2nd) – LSO, Previn .... ASD 3338

Arne: Symphonies Nos 1 in C, 2 in F, 3 in E flat, 4 in C minor/Wesley:
    Symphony in D-BS, Montgomery .... CSD 3767

Bach, J.C.: Symphonies in E flat op. 6 No. 3, in E flat op. 9 No. 2, in
    B flat op. 18 No. 2, in D op. 18 No. 4-BS, Montgomery .... ASD 3544

Bach, J. S.:
Cantata No. 147 ('Herz und Mund'); Motets: Der Geist hilft unsrer
    Schwachheit auf, Fürchte dich nicht, Lobet den Herren alle Heiden-
    Ameling, Baker, Partridge, Shirley-Quirk, KCC, ASM, Willcocks ...... HQS 1254

Flute Sonatas: No. 1 in B minor, No. 3 in A, No. 5 in E minor –
Schaffer, Malcolm, Gauntlett   ASD 633
Flute Sonatas: No. 4 in C, No. 6 in E, No. 2 in E flat, No. 1 in G minor
– Schaffer, Malcolm, Gauntlett   ASD 2268
Fugue in G minor, Choral Prelude 'Christ lag in Todesbanden' (arr.
Stokowski) – Phil O, Stokowski (78)   DB 1952
Magnificat in D/Bruckner: Te Deum-Popp, Pashley, Baker, Finnila,
Tear, Hemsley Garrard, NPO and Chorus, Barenboim   ASD 2533
Mass in B minor: Giebel, Baker, Gedda, Prey, Crass, NPO, BBC
Chorus, Klemperer   SLS 930
Motets: Jesu meine Freude, Singet dem Herren ein neues Lied,
Komm, Jesu, komm-KCC, Willcocks   HQS 1144
St Matthew Passion: Pears, Fischer-Dieskau, Schwarzkopf, Ludwig,
Gedda, Berry, etc, Boys of Hampstead Parish Church Choir, PO and
Chorus, Klemperer   SLS 827
Suites complete Nos 1 to 4 – NPO, Klemperer   SLS 808
Toccata and Fugue in D minor (arr. Stokowski) – Phil O, Stokowski (78)   DB 2572
Violin Concertos: in D Minor for 2 violins, in E major, in G minor –
Perlman, Zukerman, ECO, Barenboim   ASD 2783
Violin Concertos in D minor, in A minor, in D minor for violin and
oboe – Perlman, Black, ECO, Barenboim   ASD 3076

Ballet Music from the operas: Aida (Verdi), Khovantschina (Mussorgsky/
Rimsky-Korsakov): Dances of the Persian slaves, Prince Igor
(Borodin/Rimsky-Korsokov & Glazounov): Dances of the Polovtsian
Maidens, Polovtsian Dances, Gioconda (Ponchielli): Dance of the
Hours, Tannhäuser (Wagner): Venusberg Music – PO, Karajan   SAX 2421

Bartok:
44 Duos for 2 violins – Perlman, Zukerman   ASD 4011
Piano concertos Nos 1 and 3 – Barenboim, NPO, Boulez   ASD 2476
Piano Concerto No. 2 (see Prokofiev: Piano Concerto No. 5)

Beethoven
Fidelio – Ludwig, Vickers, Berry, Frick, Hallstein, Unger, Crass,
Wehofschitz, Wolansky, PO and Chorus, Klemperer   SLS 5006
Mass in C op. 86 – Ameling, Baker, Altmeyer, Rintzler, NPO and
Chorus, Giulini   ASD 2661
Mass in D op. 123 ('Missa Solemnis') – Söderström, Höffgen, Kmentt,
Talvela, NPO and Chorus, Klemperer   SLS 922
Piano Concertos:
Nos 1 to 5, Fantasia op. 80 – Barenboim, Alldis Choir, NPO Klemperer   SLS 5180
(No. 1 in C op. 15-ASD 2616: No. 2 in B flat op. 19/Fantasia op. 80 –
ASD 2608: No. 3 in C minor op. 37 – ASD 2579: No. 4 in G op.
58-ASD 2550: No. 5 in E flat op. 73 'Emperor' – ASD 2500)
No. 4 in G: Rondo in G op. 51 No. 2 – Richter-Haaser, PO, Kertesz   CFP 155
Piano Sonatas:
Barenboim: complete Nos 1 to 32   SLS 794
    op. 2 No. 2, op. 78, op. 109   HQS 1203
    op. 10 Nos 1, 2, 3   HQS 1152
    op. 13 ('Pathétique'), op. 27 No. 2) ('Moonlight'),
       op. 57 ('Appassionata')   HQS 1076
    op. 14 Nos 1, 2, op. 26   HQS 1206

op. 28, op. 2 No. 3	HQS 1185
op. 49 No. 1, op. 81a ('Les Adieux'), op. 111	HQS 1088
op. 101, op. 7, op. 79	HQS 1205
Eschenbach op. 13 ('Pathétique'), op. 26, op. 27 No. 2 ('Moonlight')	ASD 3695
Fischer, Annie – op. 31 No. 3, op. 111	SAX 2435
Richter – Haaser – op. 31 Nos 1 and 3	SAX 2523
op. 31 No 2, op. 109	SAX 2385
op. 106 ('Hammerklavier'), op. 90	SAX 2407
op. 110, op. 111	33CX 1666
Piano Trios:	
complete – Ashkenazy, Perlman, Harrell (not yet released)	
complete – Barenboim, Zukerman, du Pré, de Peyer	SLS 789
Quartet in F op. 59 No. 1 ('Rasoumovsky') – Drolc Quartet	Electrola: C80548
Quartet in C sharp minor op. 131 Busch Quartet (78 – transferred to LP with various numbers)	DB2810-4
Quintet for Piano and wind in E flat op. 16/Mozart: Quintet for Piano and wind in E flat K452 Melos ensemble, Crowson	ASD 2256
Symphonies:	
complete Nos 1 to 9 – PO, (in No 9) Schwartzkopf, Höffgen, Haefliger, Edelman, Chorus of the Gesellschaft der Musikfreunde, Vienna, Karajan	SLS 5053
No. 7 in A op. 92/Rameau (Klemperer) Gavotte with 6 variations, NPO, Klemperer	ASD 2537
No. 9 in D minor op. 125 ('Choral') – Davis, Cathcart, Betts, Lowenthal, Phil O and Chorus, Stokowski (78)	DB 2327–35
No. 9 in D minor op. 125 ('Choral') – Nordmo-Lovberg, Ludwig Kmentt, Hotter, PO and Chorus, Klemperer	SAX 2276–7
33 Variations on a waltz by Diabelli op. 120-Richter-Haaser	SAX 2557
Violin Concerto in D op. 61-Perlman, PO, Guilini	ASD 4059
Violin Sonatas: complete – Zukerman, Barenboim	SLS 871

Berlioz

Grande Messe des Morts-Tear, LPO and Choir, Previn	SLS 5209
Overtures – Le Corsaire, Beatrice and Benedict, Benvenuto Cellini, Les Francs-juges, Le Carnaval romain, LSO, Previn	ESD 2900301
Symphonie Fantastique op. 14-PO, Klemperer	SAX 2537

Bishop.: Lo! Here the gentle lark/Moore: Last Rose of Summer – Galli-Curci (78)	DA 1011

Bismillah Khan: Sarang, Dadra, Chandra Kauns, Kajaree	ASD 2446

Bismillah Khan/Vilayet Khan: Jugalbandi, Raga, Gujaree-Todi, Chaiti-dun, Bhairavee-Thumree (with Shantaprasad-Tabla)	ASD 2295

Bizet:

Carmen: Suite No 1, Jeux d'enfants: Suite, L'Arlesienne: Suite No. 1 – O de P, Barenboim	ASD 2915
Carmen: Suite No. 1, L'Arlesienne: Suites Nos 1 and 2 – RPO, Beecham	SXLP 30276

Symphony in C, La Jolie Fille de Perth: Suite, Patrie Overture – O de
P, Barenboim   ASD 3277

Symphony in C (RPO), Berlioz: The Trojans: Trojan March and Royal
Hunt and Storm/Delibes: Le Roi s'amuse: Ballet music – French
Nat. Radio Orchestra, Beecham   SXLP 30260

Boccherini (see under Haydn: Cello concerto in C)

Brahms

Cello sonatas: No. 1 in E minor, No. 2 in F – du Pré, Barenboim   ASD 2436

Clarinet sonatas: No. 1 in F minor, No. 2 in E flat – de Peyer,
Barenboim   ASD 2362

Deutsche Volkslieder: complete Nos 1 to 49 – Schwarzkopf, Fischer-
Dieskau, Moore   SAN 163–4

Eine Deutsches Requiem op. 45, Alto Rhapsody, Tragic Overture
– Schwarzkopf, Ludwig, Fischer-Dieskau, PO and Chorus,
Klemperer   SLS 821

Double concerto for cello and orchestra-Perlman, Rostropovich,
Concertgebouw, Haitink   ASD 3905

Lieder: various – Fischer-Dieskau, Barenboim, Moore, Sawallisch   SLS 5002

Piano concertos:

No. 1 in D minor op. 15 – Barenboim, NPO, Barbirolli   EMX 41 2085

No. 1 in D minor op. 15 – Ohlsson, LPO, Tennstedt   ASD 3762

No. 2 in B flat op. 83 – Arrau, PO, Giulini   CFP 40034

Piano Quintet in F minor op. 34 – Previn, Yale Quartet   ASD 2873

Piano Trios in C op. 87, Horn Trio in E flat op. 40 – Yehudi Menuhin,
Hephzibah Menuhin, Gendron, Civil   ASD 2354

Die schöne Magellone – Fischer-Dieskau, Richter   SAN 291

Symphony No. 4 in E minor op. 98 – DS, Böhm (78)   DB4684–9

Variations:

on a theme by Handel op. 24, on a theme by Paganini
op. 35 – Anievas   HQS 1028

on a theme by Handel op. 24, on a theme by Paganini
op. 35 – Ohlsson   HQS 1379

Violin concerto in D op. 77 – Perlman, CSO, Giulini   ASD 3385

Bruch

Violin concerto No. 1 in G minor (see Mendelssohn: Violin concerto
No. 1 in E minor)

Violin concerto No. 2 in D minor, Scottish Fantasy op. 46 – Perlman,
PO, Lopez-Cobos   ASD 3310

Bruckner:

Mass No. 3 in F minor – Harper, Reynolds, Tear, Rintzler, NPO and
Chorus, Barenboim   ASD 2836

Symphony No. 4 in E flat – PO, Klemperer   SXLP 30167

Symphony No. 7 in E/Wagner: Siegfried Idyll
(original version for 16 strings) – PO, Klemperer   SAX 2454–5

Symphony No. 9 in D minor – NPO, Klemperer   ASD 2719

Te Deum (see Bach: Magnificat)

Busoni: Piano concerto op. 39, Sarabande and Cortege op. 51 – Ogdon,
RPO, Alldis Choir, Revenaugh   SLS 776

di Capua: O Sole Mio/Verdi: La donna e mobile ('Rigoletto') – Caruso
(78)   DA1303

Charpentier: Messe de Minuit/Purcell: Te Deum – Cantelo, Gelmar,
Bowman, Partridge, Keyte, KCC, ECO, Willcocks   ASD 2340

Chopin
Cello sonata in G minor op. 65/Franck: Sonata in A – du Pré,
Barenboim   ASD 2851
Etudes: complete – Anievas   HQS 1058
Nocturnes: complete – Ohlsson (not issued in the UK) Angel   SZB 3889
Piano concerto No 1 in E minor op. 11 – Pollini, PO, Kletzki   SXLP 30160
Recitals:
Barenboim – Barcarolle op. 60, Berceuse op. 57, Fantaisie op. 49,
Polonaise – Fantaisie op. 61, Souvenir de Paganini, Variations
Brillantes op. 12   ASD 2963
Pollini – Ballade No. 1 op. 23, Nocturnes: op. 15 Nos 1 and 2, op. 27
Nos 1 and 2, Polanaises: op. 44 and op. 53   ASD 2577
Sonata No. 3 in B minor op. 58/Liszt: Sonata in B minor – Anievas   HQS 1246
Waltzes: Complete Nos 1 to 19 – Anievas   HQS 1208

Debussy
Images, Prèlude à l'après midi d'un faune – LSO, Previn   ASD 3804
La Mer, Nocturnes – LSO and Chorus, Previn   ASD 1436321

Delius: Appalachia, Brigg Fair – Jenkins, Ambrosian Singers, Hallé,
Barbirolli   EMX 412081

Duets: Lilius, Schütz, Handel etc – Baker, Fischer-Dieskau, Malcolm
(Recorded at the Royal Festival Hall)   ASD 2710

Dvořák
Cello concerto in B minor op. 104, Silent Woods op. 68 – du Pré, CSO,
Barenboim   ASD 2751
Quartet No. 12 in F op. 96 (see Smetana: Quartet No. 1)
Scherzo Capriccioso (see Dvořák: Symphony No. 8 and Smetana Ma
Vlast')
Serenade for Strings in E op. 22/Tchaikowsky: Serenade for Strings in
C op. 48 – ECO, Barenboim   ASD 3036
Symphony No. 7 in D minor op. 70–LPO, Rostropovich   ASD 3869
Symphony No. 8 in G op. 88, Scherzo Capriccioso in D flat op. 66 –
LPO, Rostropovich   ASD 4058
Symphony No. 9 in E minor op. 95 ('From the New World') – LPO,
Rostropovich   EMX 412051
Violin concerto in A minor op. 53, Romance in F minor op. 11 –
Perlman, LPO, Barenboim   ASD 3120

Elgar: Enigma Variations (see Vaughan-Williams Fantasia on a theme by
Tallis)

Elisabeth Schwarzkopf Songbook: Schubert Schumann (Widmung),
Wolf, Wolf-Ferrari-Moore   SAX 5268

231

Elisabeth Schwarzkopf Songbook Vol 2: Schubert (Erlkönig), Mozart,
  Schumann, Mahler, Wolf, Strauss, R, etc – Parsons   ASD 2404

Encores Vol 2: Wieniawski, Foster, Vieuxtemps, Traditional, Bazzini
  (Ronde des Lutins) etc – Perlman, Sanders   ASD 3810

Falla: Atlantida (realised Halffter) – Tarres, Ricci Sardiniero, etc
  Spanish National Chorus & Orchestra, Children's chorus of our
  Lady of Remembrance, Frühbeck de Burgos   SLS 5116

Foster: Poor old Joe, Old Folks at Home-Robeson (78)   B 3664

Flotow: Marta: M'appari tutt amor', Pagliacci (Leoncavallo): Vesti la
  giubba-Caruso (78)   DB 1802

A French Song Recital: Chanson de Bilitis (Debussy), Duparc, Fauré-
  Baker, Moore   ASD 2590

Gerald Moore
Farewell Concert: Haydn, Mozart, Schubert, Mendelssohn, Brahms,
  Schumann, Rossini, Wolf-de los Angeles, Schwarzkopf,
  Fischer-Dieskau   SAN 182–3
70th Birthday: Traditional, Bach, Strauss, R. Weber, Mahler, Fauré,
  Wagner, Debussy, Dvořák, Tchaikovsky – de los Angeles, Goosens,
  Fischer-Dieskau, de Peyer, Baker, du Pré, Schwarzkopf, Menuhin,
  Barenboim   SAN 255
Glazoonov: Piano concerto No. 1 (see Yardumian)

Goldmark: Violin concerto in A Minor/Sarasate: Zigeunerwiesen –
  Perlman, PSO, Previn   ASD 3408

Handel
Messiah (complete) – Schwarzkopf, Hoffman, Gedda, Hines,
  PO and Chorus – Klemperer   SAN 146–8
Messiah – For unto us a child is born, Recit: There were shepherds,
  Glory to God – Suddaby, Philharmonic Choir, Scott (78)   D 1876
Royal Fireworks Music, Concertos a due cori Nos 1 and 2, Concerto
  No. 3 in D – LSO, Mackerras   ASD 3395
A selection: Excerpts from Messiah, Berenice, Water Music, Solomon,
  etc – BS, Montgomery   ESD 7031

Haydn
Cello Concerto in C/Boccherini: Cello concerto in B flat arr:
  Grützmacher – du Pré, ECO, Barenboim   ASD 2331
Cello concerto in D/Monn: Cello concerto in G minor – LSO,
  Barbirolli   SXLP 30273
Quartets op. 64 Nos 1 to 6 – Medici String Quartet   SLS 5077
The Seven Last Words – ASM, Marriner   ASD 3451
Sinfonia Concertante in B (see Mozart Sinfonia Concertante in E flat)
Symphonies Nos 92 in G ('Oxford') and 95 in C minor – NPO,
  Klemperer   ASD 2818
Symphonies Nos 94 in G ('Surprise') and 104 in D ('London') – PSO,
  Previn   CFP 4400

Holst: Planets Suite op. 32 – NPO and Chorus, Boult   ASD 2301

John, John put your trousers on/In the land where the women wear the
   trousers (78)

Joplin: Easy Winners, etc – Perlman, Previn   ASD 3075

Kern: Old Man River, I still suits me – Robeson (78)   B 8497

Kreisler:
Recital – Vol I – Caprice Viennois etc – Perlman, Sanders   ASD 3258
Recital – Vol II – The Devil's Trill etc – Perlman, Sanders   ASD 3346
Laughing Song/The whistling coon – Sheppard   B 468

Lehár: Gold and Silver Waltz (see Strauss, J, The Blue Danube)
Die lustige Witwe – Schwarzkopf, Steffek, Gedda, Wächter etc,
   PO, Chorus, Matacic   SLS 823

Liszt: Piano concerto No. 1 in E flat (see Schumann: Piano concerto)
Recital: Grandes etudes de Paganini, No. 2 in E flat, etc – Ogdon   ASD 2416
Sonata in B minor (see Chopin: Sonata No. 3 in B minor)
Sonata in B minor, Mephisto Waltz etc – Gutierrez   HQS 1427

Ludwig: Lieder Recital: Schubert-Erlkönig, etc – Parsons   SAX 5272

Mahler: Aus der Jugenzeit, Aus des Knaben Wunderhorn, 5 Rückert
   Songs, Lieder eines fahrenden Gesellen – Fischer-Dieskau,
   Barenboim   SLS 5173
Das Lied von der Erde – Ludwig, Wünderlich NPO, Klemperer   SAN 179
Symphony No. 2 in C minor ('Resurrection') – Schwarzkopf,
   Rössl-Majdan, PO and Chorus Klemperer   SLS 806
Symphony No. 4 in G – Schwarzkopf, PO Klemperer   ASD 2799
Symphony No. 4 in G – Ameling, PSO, Previn   ASD 3783

Mendelssohn: Lieder-Fischer-Dieskau, Sawallisch   SLS 805
Nocturne (Midsummer Night's Dream) – BBCSO, Boult (78)   DA 1318
Preludes and Fugues op. 35, Etudes op. 104 – Adni   HQS 1394
Violin concerto No. 1 in E minor op. 64/Bruch Violin Concerto No. 1 in
   G minor op. 26 – Perlman, LSO, Previn   ASD 2926

Monn: Cello concerto in G minor (see Haydn: Cello concerto in D)

Monteverdi: L'incoronazione di Poppea (Ottavia's Lament and
   Farewell), Arianna (Arianna's Lament)/D. Scarlatti: Salve Regina/A.
   Scarlatti: Cantata pastorale – Baker, ECO, Leppard   ASD 2615

Moszkowski: Suite for 2 violins and piano/Shostakovich: Three violin
   duets/ Prokofiev: Sonata for 2 violins – Perlman, Zukerman, Sanders   ASD 3861

Mozart:
Cosi fan tutte:
Schwarzkopf, Ludwig, Steffek, Krauss, Tadei, Berry, PO and Chorus,
   Böhm   SLS 5028

Schwarzkopf, Merriman, Otto, Simoneau, Panerai, Bruscantini, PO
and Chorus, Karajan   RLS 7709
Price, Minton, Popp, Alva, Evans, Sotin, NPO, Alldis Choir,
Klemperer   SLS 961
Don Giovanni:
Sgourdas, Harper, Donath, Alva, Soyer, Evans, Rinaldi, Lagger, ECO,
Edinburgh Festival Chorus, Barenboim   SLS 978
Watson, Ludwig, Freni, Gedda, Ghiaurov, Berry, Montarsolo, Crass,
NPO and Chorus, Klemperer   SLS 1434623
Lieder: Fischer-Dieskau, Barenboim   ASD 2824
Mass in C minor K 427: Cotrubas, te Kanawa, Krenn, Sotin, Alldis
Choir, NPO, Leppard   ASD 2959
Le Nozze di Figaro: Söderström, Burmeister, Grist, Berganza,
Bacquier, Evans, Langdon, Alldis Choir, NPO, Klemperer   SLS 955
Piano concertos:
Barenboim – complete for solo piano, Rondo in D K382 – ECO   SLS 5031
Nos 1 in F K 37, 2 in B flat K 39, 3 in D K40, 4 in G K 41 – ASD 3218;
Nos 5 in D K 175, 9 in EbK271 – ASD 2484; Nos 11 in F K 413, 16
in D K 451 – ASD 2999; Nos 12 in A K 414, 19 in F K 459 – ASD
2956; Nos 20 in D minor K 466, 23 in A K 488 – ASD 2318; Nos 24
in C minor K 491, 18 in B flat K 456 – ASD 2887
No. 25 in C K 503, Serenade for 8 wind in C minor K 388 –
Barenboim, NPO, Klemperer   SAX 5290
Nos 24 in C minor K 491, 27 in B flat K 595 – Fischer, A, NPO, Kurtz   SAX 5287
Piano Quartets: Nos 1 in G minor K 478, 2 in E flat K493 -Fou T'song,
Menuhin, Gerhardt, Cassado   ASD 2319
Quintet for piano and wind in E flat K 452 (see Beethoven Quintet for
piano and wind)
Requiem in D minor K 626:
Armstrong, Baker, Gedda, Fischer-Dieskau, Alldis Choir, ECO,
Barenboim   ASD 2788
Mathis, Bumbry, Shirley, Rintzler, NPO and Chorus, Frühbeck de
Burgos   CFP 4399
Serenades:
No. 10 for 13 wind in B flat K 361 – members of the ECO – Barenboim   ASD 3426
No. 10 for 13 wind in B flat K 361, Nos 11 in E flat K 375 and 12 in C
minor K 388 for 8 wind-members of NPO, Klemperer   SXDW 3050
No. 13 in G ('Eine Kleine Nachtmusik') K 525, Marches in D K 335,
Divertimento in D K 205 – ECO, Barenboim   ASD 2610
Sinfonia Concertante in E flat K 364/Haydn: sinfonia concertante in B
– ECO Soloists, Barenboim   ASD 2462
Symphonies:
No. 33 in B flat, No. 29 in A – NPO, Klemperer   SAX 5256
No. 35 in D ('Haffner'), No. 36 in C ('Linz'), Seraglio Overture – PO,
Klemperer   SAX 2436
No. 39 in E flat, No. 40 in G minor – ECO, Barenboim   ASD 2424
Violin concertos: No. 3 in G K 216, No. 5 in A K 219 – ECO, Maazel   Electrola No.
(not issued in the UK)   SHZE310
Di Zauberflöte:
Lemnitz, Berger, Roswaenge, Husch, Streinz, etc, Favres Chorus,
BPO, Beecham   RLS 1434653
Jurinac, Lipp, Dermota, Kunz, Weber, etc, Singverein der Gesellschaft
der Musikfreunde, VPO, Karajan   SLS 5052

234

Janowitz, Popp, Gedda, Berry, Frick, etc, PO and chorus, Klemperer   SLS 912

Music for Holy Week: Morley, Gibbons, Victoria, di Lasso, Hymns, etc –
    KCC, Ledger   ASD 3450

Mussorgsky: Pictures at an exhibition/Debussy: Prelude à l'après-midi
    d'un faune – PO, Maazel   EMX 2008

Oh Donna Clara: tango/You have become so terribly blonde – Dol
    Dauber and his Orchestra (78)   B5905
Orf: Carmina Burana – Popp, Unger, Wolansky Noble, NPO, and
    Chorus, Frühbeck de Burgos   ESD 7177

Paganini: 24 Caprices op. 1 – Perlman   ASD 3384
    Violin Concerto No. 1/Sarasata: Carmen Fantasy – Perlman,
    RPO, Foster   ASD 2782

Palestrina: Missa Hodie Christus natus est, 5 Motets – KCC, Ledger   ASD 3559

Philharmonia Promenade Concert: Skater's Waltz (Waldteufel) Tritsch-
    Tratsch Polka (J Strauss 2nd) Espãna (Chabrier) etc – PO, Karajan   SAX 2404

Poulenc: Trio (Oboe, Bassoon, Piano), Sonata (Clarinet,
    Bassoon)/Ravel: Introduction and Allegro/Francaix: Two
    Divertimenti – Melos Ensemble   ASD 2506

Prokofiev:
Cinderella (ballet) – LSO, Previn   SLS 1435953
Piano Concerto No. 5/Bartok: Piano Concerto No. 2 – Richter, NPO
    and OdeP, Maazel   ASD 2744
Six Folksongs op. 104/Rimsky-Korsakov: Songs – Vishnevskaya,
    Rostropovich   ASD 3731
Symphonies No. 1 ('Classical') and 7 in C sharp minor op. 131 – LSO,
    Previn   ASD 3556

Rachmaninov: Piano Concertos Nos 1 to 4, Rhapsody on a theme of
    Paganini – Anievas, NPO, Frühbeck de Burgos (Nos 1 and 4),
    Atzmon (No. 2 and Rhapsody), Ceccato (No. 3)   SLS 855

Ravel:
Bolero, Daphnis and Chloe Suite No. 2, Pavane pour une infante
    défunte – LSO, Previn   ASD 3912
Daphnis and Chloe, complete – LSO and Chorus Previn   ASD 4099
L'Enfant et les sortilèges: Daveny Wyner, Taillon, Berbié, Bastin,
    Huttenlocker, Langridge, Augér, Finnie, Richardson, Ambrosian
    Singers, LSO – Previn   ASD 4167

Rimsky-Korsakov: Songs (see Prokofiev: Six Folksongs)
Rodrigo: Concierto de Aranjuez, Fantasia para un gentilhombre –
    Romero, LSO, Previn   ASD 3415

Rossini: Semiramide (Overture) – NYPSO – Toscanini (78)   DB 3079/80

Sarasate: Carmen Fantasy (see Paganini violin concerto)
Zigeunerweisen (see Goldmark)

Schönberg: Verklärte Nacht op. 4/Wagner: Siegfried Idyll/Hindemith:
Trauermusik – Aronowitz, ECO, Barenboim   ASD 2346

Schubert:
Erlkönig (see Elisabeth Schwarzkopf Songbook Vol 2)
Impromptus: complete D 899 and 946 – Anievas   HQS 1397
Moments Musicaux D 780/Schumann: 4 Nachtstücke op. 23 – Gilels   ASD 2483
Octet in F – Melos ensemble   ASD 2417
Piano Sonatas: in C minor D 958 and A minor D 784 – Richter-Haaser   SAX 5255
Recital: Schubert (Die junge Nönne etc) Schumann (Widmung etc) –   Electrola
Bumbry, Parsons (not issued in the UK)   02794
Symphonies:
No. 5 in B flat, No. 8 in B minor ('Unfinished') – NPO, Fischer-
Dieskau   ASD 2942
No. 8 in B minor ('Unfinished') – Phil O, Stokowski (78)   D 1779–81

Schumann
Frauenliebe und Leben op. 42, Liederkreis op. 39 – Baker,
Barenboim   ASD 3217
Nachtstücke op. 23 (see Schubert: Moments Musicaux)
Piano Concerto in A minor op. 54/Liszt: Piano concerto No. 1
in E flat – A Fischer, PO, Klemperer   SAX 2485
Symphonies:
No. 1 in B flat op. 38 ('Spring'), Manfred Overture – PO, Klemperer   SAX 5269
No. 2 in C op. 61, Genoveva Overture op. 18 – NPO, Klemperer   ASD 2454
No. 3 in E flat op. 97 ('Rhenish'), Faust Overture – NPO, Klemperer   ASD 2547
Widmung (see Elisabeth Schwarzkopf Songbook and Schubert: Recital
– Bumbry)

Shostakovich:
Lady Macbeth of Mtsensk: Vishnevskaya, Valjakka, Finnilä, Gedda,
Krenn, Mroz, Petkov, Haugland etc,
Ambrosian Chorus, LPO, Rostropovich   SLS 5157
Symphony No. 13 in B flat minor op. 113 ('Babi Yar') – Petkov LSO,
Previn   ASD 3911
Three pieces for Violin (see Moszkowski: Suite for two violins and
piano)

Sibelius:
Symphony No. 2 in D op. 43 – PSO, Previn   ASD 3414
Symphony No. 5 in E flat op. 82, Finlandia op. 26, PO, Karajan   SAX 2392

Smetana:
Ma Vlast: complete/Dvořák: Slavonic Rhapsody in A flat op. 45, No. 3,
Scherzo Capriccioso op. 66-DS, Berglund   SLS 5151
Quartet No. 1 in E minor ('From my life')/Dvořák: Quartet No. 12 in F
op. 96 ('American') – Medici String Quartet   ASD 3694

Song of the Volga Boatmen (Traditional)/Rimsky-Korsakov: The Prophet
– Chaliapin (78)   DB 1103

Sousa: Marches: El Capitan, The Washington Post – Black Dyke Mills
  Band (78)   BD 758

Spanish Recital: Falla, Granados, Halffter, Sarasate – Perlman, Sanders   ASD 3910

Stevenson: Passacaglia on DSCH – Ogdon   ASD 2321/22

Strauss J.: Blue Danube Waltz/Lehár: Gold and Silver Waltz – Marek
  Weber and his Orchestra (78)   B 3726
Emperor Waltz (see André Previn Music Night No. 2)
Tales from the Vienna Woods: Waltz – Marek Weber and his Orchestra
  (78)   B 2406

Strauss, R:
Alpine Symphony – Phil O, Previn   ASD 1435771
Also sprach Zarathustra, Till Eulenspiegels Ulstige Streiche op. 28 –
  PO, Maazel   SAX 2467
Der Rosenkavalier: Schwarzkopf, Ludwig Stich Randall, Meyer,
  Welitsch, Edelman, Gedda, Unger, Wächter, PO, Karajan   EX 2900453
Töd und Verklarung, Don Juan, Till Eulenspiegels Lustige Streiche –
  VPO, Previn   ASD 3936
Vier letzte Lieder, Zueignung, Muttertändelei, Die heiligen drei
  Könige, Freundliche Vision, Waldseligkeit – Schwarzkopf, Berlin
  Radio Symphony Orchestra, Szell   ASD 2888

Stravinsky:
L'Oiseau de Feu (1910 version) – BSO, Ozawa   ASD 1436341
L'Oiseau de Feu (1910 version) – OdeP, Ozawa   EMX 412094
Divertimento, Suite italienne (after Pergolesi), Duo concertant –
  Perlman, Canino   ASD 3219

Tchaikovsky:
Piano concertos Nos 1 to 3 – Gilels, NPO, Maazel   SLS 865
Piano Trio in A minor op. 50 – Ashkenazy, Perlman, Harrell   ASD 4036
Symphonies Nos 1 to 6, Manfred – LPO, Rostropovich   SLS 5099
Violin concerto in D op. 35, Sérénade Mélancolique op. 26 – Perlman,
  Phil O, Ormandy   ASD 3726

Vaughan-Williams: Fantasia on a theme by Tallis, The Wasps
  (Overture)/ Elgar: Enigma Variations – LSO, Previn   ASD 3857

Verdi: Falstaff: Schwarzkopf, Moffo, Merriman Barbieri, Alva, Gobbi,
  Panerai, PO and Chorus, Karajan   SLS 5211
Otello: Nelli, Vinay, Valdengo, NBCO and chorus Toscanini   ALP 1090–2
Quattro pezzi sacri: Baker, PO and chorus, Guilini   SXLP 30508
Requiem Mass: Schwarzkopf, Ludwig, Gedda, Ghiaurov, PO and
  chorus, Guilini   SLS 909
Rigoletto: La donna é mobile (see di Capua: O Sole Mio)

Vieuxtemps: Violin Concertos No. 4 in D minor, No. 5 in A minor –
  Perlman, OdeP, Barenboim   ASD 3555

Vilayat Khan: Jaijaiwanti, Rageshree   ASD 2460

Vivaldi: The Four Seasons – LPO, Perlman   ASD 3293

Wagner: Der Fliegende Holländer – Silja, Burmeister, Kozub, Unger,
   Adam, Talvela, BBC Chorus, NPO, Klemperer   SAN 207–9
Die Meistersinger – Grümmer, Höffgen, Schock, Unger, Kusche,
   Frick, Frantz, etc, BPO and Chorus, Kempe   RLS 740
Siegfried Idyll (see Schönberg: Verklärte Nacht and Bruckner:
   Symphony No. 7)
Tannhäuser: Venusberg Music (see Ballet Music from the operas)
Tristan and Isolde: Flagstad, Ludwig, Thebom, Suthaus,
   Fischer-Dieskau, PO, Furtwängler   RLS 684
Die Walküre: Act I, Act III – Leb'wohl-Dernesch, Cochran, Sotin,
   Bailey, NPO, Klemperer   SLS 968

Weber: Invitation to the Waltz op. 65 – Phil O, Stokowski (78)   D1285

The Whistler and his Dog:/Warbler's Serenade – Pryor's Band (78)   B2373

Wesley: (see Arne Symphonies)

Wieniawski: Violin Concertos Nos 1 and 2 – Perlman, LPO, Ozawa   ASD 2870

Wolff: Italienisches Liederbuch – Schwarzkopf, Fischer-Dieskau,
   Moore   SAN 210–1
Lieder Recital – Schwarzkopf, Moore   SAX 2589
Society editions: Gerhardt, Trianti, Rethberg, Ginster, McCormack,
   Hüsch, Janssen, Kipnis, Bos, Müller, Moore etc (78)   Vols 1 to 6

Yardumian: Passacaglia, Recitative and Fugue/Glazounov: Piano
   Concerto No. 1 in F minor op. 92 – Ogdon, Bournemouth SO,
   Berglund   ASD 3367

INDEX

The major recordings discussed in the text are listed under the composers.

239

240

Maazel, Lorin, 13, 20, 94, 98, 135–7
Mackerras, Charles, 176–7
Mahatma Gandhi Hall, 2, 4–5
Mahler, Gustav, 59, 87, 212; *Das Lied von der Erde* (Klemperer), 58; lieder (Fischer-Dieskau/Barenboim), 207; symphonies (Klemperer), 13, 90, 210, (Previn), 211
Malta, Alexander, 198
Marina, Princess, 57
Marriner, Neville, 190
Marshall Minor, 191–2
Marx brothers, 15; Chico, 36; Groucho, 187
McCarthy, John, 99, 204
McCormack, John, 14
Medici, Quartet, 159
Mehta, Zubin, 122–3, 150, 179, 214
Melos Ensemble, 33, 61, 73, 158
Mendelssohn, Felix, 35; lieder (de los Angeles/Fischer-Dieskau/Moore), 71, (Fischer-Dieskau/Sawallisch), 105–6, 158; piano (Adni), 174; violin concerto (Perlman/Previn), 134
Menuhin, Hephzibah, 54, 57
Menuhin, Yehudi, 40, 57; recordings, 53–5; and Moore, 86–7
Minneapolis Symphony Orchestra, 212
Minton, Yvonne, 110
Monn, Georg, cello concerto (du Pré/Barbirolli), 68
Morales, Christóbal, 191
Monteverdi, Claudio, 89, 143
Montgomery, Kenneth, 165–8
Moore, Enid, 86, 89
Moore, Gerald, 13, 103, 116, 150; recording, 41–2; farewell concert, 70–2; 'Tribute' to, 85–9, 125; and Baker, 90
Morley, Thomas, 40, 191
Morris, Gareth, 27
Morris, Tom, 183
Mozart, Wolfgang Amadeus, 40, 144, 168, 171, 189, 193, 215; SRG's knowledge of, 5–6; lieder (Fischer-Dieskau/Barenboim), 116–18, 158; Mass in C minor (Leppard), 139–40; Operas: *Cosí fan tutte*, 30, 56, (Karajan), 4–5, 16, (Böhm), 13, 20, (Klemperer), 98, 110–11, 158; *Don Giovanni* (Klemperer), 58–9, 91, (Barenboim), 145–54; *Entführung*, 125, 138; *Nozze di Figaro*, 40 (Klemperer), 95–7; *Zauberflöte*, 20, 30, (Beecham and Karajan), 23, (Klemperer), 25–9, 57; piano concertos, 121, 134, (Fischer/Kurtz), 52–3, 158, (Barenboim), 61–5, 67, 79, 131, 159, 165, (Barenboim/Klemperer), 76; piano quartets (Fou Ts'ong, Menuhin, Gerhardt, Cassado), 53; piano and wind quintet (Melos), 33; piano sonatas (Barenboim) 51, 67, 158;

Requiem, 67, 82, 139 (Barenboim), 118 (Frühbeck de Burgos), 73, 162; serenades (Barenboim), 177–8 and *Eine Kleine Nachtmusik*, 65, 177; (Klemperer) 124–5; and string quartets, 158, 175; symphonies, 38, 67, (Barenboim), 79, (Klemperer), 17–18, 77, 93; violin concertos (Maazel), 98
Mroz, Leonard, 198
Mussorgsky, Modest, 9, 20

Nehru, Jawaharlal, 80
Neveu, Ginette, 3
Noble, John, 198

Ogdon, John, 73–4, 169
Ohlsson, Garrick, 172–4, 194
Oistrakh, Igor, 131
Orchestre de Paris, 131, 143, 170, 179
Orff, Carl, *Carmina Burana* (New Philharmonia Frühbeck de Burgos), 59
Ormandy, Eugene, 212
Ozawa, Seiji, 130–1, 183

Paganini, Niccolò, caprices (Perlman), 121–2; violin concerto (Perlman/Foster), 120–1
Palestrina, Giovanni, Mass, 'Hodie Christus natus est' (Kings/Ledger), 189, 191
Paranjoti, Victor, 40
Parson, Geoffrey, 162–4
Pashley, Ann, 81
Perlman, Itzhak, 49, 125, 172, 180, 193–4, 225; SRG's introduction to, 119–20; his stamina, 121–2; and Previn, 134, (Joplin), 156–7, 181, 186–8; recordings, 130, 155, 170–1, 212–13, 215–18, 222–3; character of, 182; and Zukerman, 207; and Sanders, 210–11
Petkov, Dimiter, 198
Peyer, Gervase de, 66–7, and Moore, 86–7
Philadelphia Symphony Orchestra, 35–6, 184, 188, 211–12
Philharmonia Orchestra, 1, 9, 17, 20, 114, 116, 225–6; and see Legge; and Chorus, 2–4, 8; and Concert Society, 3, 6; as New Philharmonia, 24, 44, 53, 80, 131, 136, 141
Pittsburg Symphony Orchestra, 165, 181, 184–5, 187–8, 210
Pitz, Wilhelm, 2, 81, 109, 145
Pollini, Maurizio, 82–4, 158, 194
Popp, Lucia, 27, 29, 59, 81, 110, 138–40
Pré, Jacqueline du, 49, 63, 71, 104, 122–3, 129, 143, 148; SRG meets, 61–2; recordings, 65–8, 94, 143; and Klemperer, 77; visits SRG in hospital, 79; and Moore, 86, 88; her illness, 125–7
Previn, André, 165, 174, 209; as pianist, 133–4; and Perlman, 134–5, 156–7, 181, 186–8; recordings, 175–6, 194–5, 210–11, 218; and

242

orchestral rules, 183–6; and Romero, 189–90; and digital recording, 219
Price, Margaret, 96, 110
Prokofiev, Sergey, 189, 193, 218; piano concerto (Richter/Maazel), 98; songs (Vishnevskaya/Rostropovich), 215; symphonies (Previn), 194
Puccini, Giacomo, 5
Purcell, Henry, 'Te Deum' (Kings/Willcocks), 74
Rachmaninov, Sergey, 62, 203, 217; piano concertos (Anievas), 46, 73, 139; Rhapsody on a theme of Paganini (Anievas/Atzmon), 46, 73, 139
Ravel, Maurice, 87, 179, 218
recording; and SRG's apprenticeship, 8–14; and dynamics, 21; and stereo, 9, 25–6; and opera, 26–9, 151–4; and piano, 53–4; philosophy of, 56–7, 224–5; and scheduling, 58; balance, 59–60; and engineers, 62–3; and the cello, 65–6; 'live', 70–3; and accoustics, 82; and editing, 93; and rerecording, 112–16; and multi-track, 127–9, 216, 223; and quadraphony, 166–7; and American orchestras, 183; and the guitar, 189–90; digital, 218–22
Revenaugh, Daniell, 74
Richardson, Rev. E. R., 36–7
Richardson, Linda, 204–5
Richter, Sviatoslav, 94, 98–9; and Fischer-Dieskau, 103–5; and Mrs Richter, 104–5
Richter-Haaser, Hans, 8, 15–16, 22, 30–1; SRG's friendship with, 31–32
Rimsky-Korsakov, Nikolay, songs (Vishnevskayo/Rostropovich), 215
Rinaldi, Alberto, 146–50, 152
Rintzler, Marius, 109–110
Robeson, Paul, 1, 35
Roderigo, Joaquin, 189
Romero, Angel, 189–90
Rosen, Seymour, 185
Rossini, Gioacchino, 71–2, 139–40
Rostropovich, Mstislav, 224; his character, 196; recordings, 196–7, 199, 214–15, 222–3; *Lady Macbeth of Mtsensk*, 198–206
Royal Festival Hall, 2, 21, 40, 70–1, 92, 109, 134, 138, 222
Royal Free Hospital, 79, 131, 146
Royal Opera House, Covent Garden, 3, 201
Royal Philharmonic Orchestra, 74, 120
Rubinstein, Arthur, 32, 68

Saint-Saëns, Camille, 38; cello concerto (Rostropovich/Giulini), 196
Sanders, Samuel, 210–2
Sarasate, Pablo, 186, 120, 210
Sawallisch, Wolfgang, 105–6

Scarlatti, Alessandro, 89
Scarlatti, Domenico, 89, 143
Schnabel, Artur, 14, 32, 81
Schönberg, Arnold, 67, 158; *Verklärte Nacht* (Barenboim), 65
Schubert, Franz, 5, 15, 40, 47, 53, 85, 127, 144, 179, 194, 211, 214; SRG's knowledge of, 6; lieder (Fischer-Dieskau/Moore), 71–2, (Ludwig/Parsons), 162–3, (Bumbry/Parsons), 163–4; *Erlkönig* (Schwarzkopf/Parsons), 163; Octet (Melos), 73; piano: Impromptus, 171–2, (Anievas), 46; *Moments Musicaux* (Gilels), 46–7; sonatas 171, (Richter-Haaser), 31–2, (Ohlsson), 172; string quartets, 158, 171; string quintet, 53, 125, 171, symphonies, 38, (Stokowski), 36, (Fischer-Dieskau), 141–2
Schumann, Clara, 45
Schumann, Robert, 36, 77, 85, 165, 179; lieder (Fischer-Dieskau/Schwarzkopf/Moore), 71–2, (Baker/Barenboim), 160–61, (Bumbry/Parsons), 164; *Nachstücke* (Gilels), 46–7; piano concerto (Fischer/Klemperer), 17–19; symphonies (Klemperer), 90–1, 93
Schwarzkopf, Elisabeth, 3–4, 14–15, 114, 210; recordings, 13, 20, 23, 28, 41–4; and Moore, 70–2, 86–8; and Parsons, 162–3
Sgourdas, Antigone, 146, 148–9
Shaffer, Elaine, 32
Shelley, Keith, 89–90
Shostakovich, Dmitry, 198, 211, 218; *Lady Macbeth of Mtsensk* (Rostropovich), 199–206; symphonies (Previn), 183
Sibelius, Jean, 14; symphonies (Karajan), 9, (Previn), 184, 186, 188
Smart, Clive, 101–2
Smetana, Bedřich, 40, 159, 208–9
Sobers, Garfield, 100, 150
Söderström, Elisabeth, 96
Solomon, 40
Solti, Georg, 18
Sotin, Hans, 95, 110, 138–9
Sousa, John Philip, 35
Soyer, Roger, 146–9, 152–3
Spanish National Orchestra, 192
Steffek, Hanny, 20
Stern, Isaac, 40
Stokowski, Leopold, 35–7
Strauss, Johann, 35, 75
Strauss, Richard, 14, 20, 41, 43, 218; Klemperer's opinion of, 81; Alpine symphony (Philadelphia/Previn), 184; lieder (Fischer-Dieskau/Moore), 88, 163; *Rosenkavalier* (Karajan), 114–15
Stravinsky, Igor, 62; 'Duo Concertant' (Perlman/Canino), 155; *Firebird* (Ozawa), 131, 183
Studios, 1 & 2, see Abbey Road

243

Szell, Georg, 18, 41, 43–4

Taddei, Giuseppe, 20
Tarrega, Francisco, 171
Taverner, John, 191
Tchaikovsky, Pyotr, 59; piano concertos
(Gilels/Maazel), 135; songs (Gedda/Moore),
89, symphonies (Rostropovich), 196
Tear, Robert, 81, 199, 201
Teatro Real, Madrid, 192–3
Tennstedt, Klaus, 172–4
Times, The, 1, 7, 139, 202, 224
Tomkins, Thomas, 40, 171
Toscanini, Arturo, 31, 37–9, 142

Valjakka, Taru, 198
Vaughan-Williams, Ralph, 218
Verdi, Giuseppe, 5, 113; *Falstaff* (Karajan), 115;
Otello (Toscanini), 31–2; *Quattro pezzi sacri*
(Giulini), 21; Requiem (Giulini), 22–3
Vienna Philharmonic Orchestra, 23, 145, 214,
218, 224
Vieuxtemps, Henri, violin concertos
(Perlman/Barenboim), 170
Vilayat Khan, 189
Vinay, Ramon, 32
Vishnevskaya, Galina; in *Lady Macbeth of
Mtsensk*, 198, 201–6; SRG meets, 200;

recordings, 215
Vivaldi, Antonio, *The Four Seasons*
(Perlman/London Philharmonic) 170

Wagner, Richard, 67, 82, 217; *Meistersinger*
(Klemperer), 97, (Kempe), 113; 'Siegfried
Idyll' (Barenboim), 65; *Tannhäuser*, 162
(Karajan), 9; *Tristan*, 158, (Furtwängler), 112,
Walküre (Klemperer), 94–8; 'Wesendonck
Lieder' (Schwarzkopf/Moore), 88
Walter, Bruno, 38
Walton, Bernard, 19
Walton, William, 56, 159; *Belshazzar's Feast*, 14
Weber, Carl Maria von, 35, 87, 211
Webern, Anton von, 145
Wesley, Samuel, 165–6
Wieniawski, Henryk, 130
Willcocks, David, 74–5, 158
Wolf, Hugo, 3, 13, 70, 86; lieder
(Schwarzkopf/Moore), 71–2
Woolley, Frank, 100

Yale Quartet, 133–4
Yardumian, Richard, Introduction and
Passacaglia (Ogdon/Berglund), 169–70

Zukerman, Pinchas, 49, 98, 125, 171, 194, 210;
recordings, 94, 119–20, 129–32, 207, 211